Heartsound

Clare Stevens

Inspired
Quill

Published by Inspired Quill: March 2024

First Edition

Content Warning:
This title contains mentions of the following: Queerphobia, Hospitalisation, Death of Parent, Terrorist Attack (off-page), and Drug & Alcohol Use.

Heartsound © 2024 by Clare Stevens
Contact the author through their website: https://clarestevens.com/

Chief Editor: Sara-Jayne Slack
Proofreaders: David Smith & Peter Smith
Cover Design: Rebekah Parrott (www.roseandgracedesign.com)
Typeset in Minion Pro

Paperback ISBN: 978-1-913117-23-8
eBook ISBN: 978-1-913117-24-5
Print Edition

Printed in the United Kingdom
1 2 3 4 5 6 7 8 9 10

Inspired Quill Publishing, UK
Business Reg. No. 7592847
https://www.inspired-quill.com

Praise for Clare Stevens

Blue Tide Rising

A debut novel that deftly steps between gritty reality and magic realism with an agility that many more seasoned writers would envy, this is a book that has a beating heart within its fascinating central character.

– Matt Turpin,
Nottingham UNESCO City of Literature

A timely novel of mental health issues, of understanding when to cease blaming ourselves for other people's actions, and of finding a safe home [...] this novel is strongly rooted in a recognizably British reality so I think even readers who aren't magical realism fans would enjoy this accomplished debut.

– Literary Flits

In a culture where staying 'pure' is still regarded as a woman's ultimate virtue, in a system that prefers silence and secrecy to truth and justice; amidst a mindset that does not mind crushing a woman's dreams if it feeds male entitlement, it feels novel to imagine that lives like Amy's are getting redeemed somewhere out there. That voices like hers are being heard. That experiences like hers are being counted. Even if it is set in another land. Even if it is all fiction.

– *The Hindu (Newspaper)*

To JP, always my first reader.
Thank you for the music.

Prologue

S TEVIE STEALS IN by stealth. Through the back gate. Looking both ways to check for prying eyes. You can't be too careful.

There's an unseen menace out there. It's everywhere. Even in the air.

An existential threat to the human race. As we cower, fearing death, the birds outside burst forth with life, louder than ever.

Stevie enters the garage, silently. I take a while to notice he's arrived.

"How are you, darling?" Stevie blows me a kiss from a safe distance.

Just yesterday we were here, with Paul and Charlotte, drinking gin, beer and wine on our last night of freedom. Playing the juke box game, summoning Siri from his globular speaker placed in the centre of the table like a Ouija board. We played apocalyptical songs. The evening had a finality about it. The end of the world as we know it.

Stevie's brought his own mug. It has a picture of the Welsh dragon on it and permanent coffee stains. I disinfect my hands, and fill the mug with a double shot of espresso from the machine. Stevie loiters in the garage, which isn't, technically, in the house. The rules are hours old and already we're bending them.

"Can we resurrect this?" he runs his finger in the dust along the edge of the table tennis table. Folded up to make room for all the boxes. "Could be the ideal lockdown pastime."

I google the length of a standard table tennis table. 2.7 metres. Perfect for this thing called social distancing we're all supposed to be doing.

"We'll have to move the boxes."

Stevie helps me shift them. "What's in them? Why have they got dates on them?"

"It's like my filing system. It's all stuff from my life. Letters, photos, diaries You know, the emotional baggage you accumulate through the years."

He picks up the biggest box. It's made of heavy-duty cardboard, sealed in thick, black masking tape. "This one weighs a ton," he says, squinting at the faded label with a date still visible. "Nineteen eighty-one must've been a heavy year."

"I need to go through them, decide if anything's worth keeping and bin the rest. I'm waiting for a rainy day."

"Or a sunny lockdown day," he says, looking outside to the blazing March sunshine.

Then he chuckles. "Christine Carlisle's past in sealed boxes. I'll help you if you like. Who knows what secrets they'll unleash?"

I shake my head. This is something I must tackle alone.

PART ONE

The Strawberry Girl

I'm not ready to open the suitcase yet, the little pink case Nan gave me that was good for nothing else but storing letters – me being a rucksack girl. Instead, I dig out the framed photo of us all at Melcombe, taken the summer before we left. The class of '81. Here we all are, in our navy and white uniforms with the red and gold school ties. There's me and Claire in the middle, flanked by the boys. Andy, long and lean, still in his mod phase, opting for a razor-thin non-regulation black tie with his school blazer. The tie is knotted half way down his chest and slightly skewed. I think he's trying to be Paul Weller. I've got cat-eye make-up, angular eyebrows drawn on in thick black pencil, and deep red lipstick. My hair, short and still dark from the remnants of black dye, is spiked up. Claire's next to me, petite and pretty, pink streaks in her hair. And then there's Mike, standing strong, legs apart, shoulders splayed, oozing testosterone. A bunch of hopefuls on the cusp of life. Whatever happened to all that youth?

I show the photo to Stevie. "You look like a little Siouxie Sioux," he says. That's who I modelled myself on.

Chapter One

Hey Siri, play 'Christine' by Siouxie and the Banshees.

September 1981

I 'M WALKING ACROSS the courtyard to the hotch-potch of buildings that make up Stoke College. I'm sixteen years old and on the brink of a new adventure. It's the first day of term and the future's looking bright, like the weather. Crisp, sunny, September.

I'm wearing the leather biker jacket my cousin brought back from New York with my fifties strawberry-print dress and docs. I've used the belt of the dress to make a head-band. I've got my retro leather satchel slung over my shoulder and my hair's spiked up with orange mousse.

I missed the bus with the others because Mum had an urgent call-out this morning so I had to walk the dog. David, my brother, could have done it but he seems incapable of getting out of bed these days. It's a two-bus journey to college. So now I'm late, and flustered, trying to remember the way to the common room, having only been there once when we came for the open day.

I'm smoking a rollup to steady my nerves, hoping I don't get the legendary one pound fine for anyone caught smoking on college premises. I don't usually smoke in the daytime, but these are exceptional circumstances.

Students in groups of twos and threes are approaching the buildings from various directions. I look around for familiar faces but there's no-one I know. These people must all be from different schools. This day is just for us, this year's intake, so everyone is new, I guess. But I'm alone.

I'm conscious of a couple walking near me on a parallel path. Both tall, beautiful and obviously moneyed. He has a Stray Cat quiff and wears an ankle-length black coat. She has long blonde hair with just the right amount of wave. They walk with confidence. They seem older. They have an air of sophistication.

I suddenly feel small.

There's a shout from somewhere up above and everyone in the vicinity looks round. I see Andy and Mike framed in a window. They've opened it right out and they're sitting on the sill. Claire appears between them and Ian behind her. Four faces, all mine. They whoop, and wave, then Andy dives inside and reappears with a giant speaker which he wedges in the window. It blasts out 'Christine' by Siouxie and the Banshees.

My song. The one that earned me the nickname 'Strawberry Girl.'

I have a fleeting feeling that I've lived this scene before.

The tall girl with the long blonde hair looks from the faces in the window to me as the song bearing my name reverberates at volume across the courtyard. I have a sense of being noticed. Of being someone.

At this moment, I know I've arrived.

Stoke College, up on a hill just out of town, is a meeting of the schools. And in Bath there are so many schools, mostly private, each with its own distinctive uniform. It's the college of choice for those of us from Melcombe Comp thought clever enough to go on to university. From Melcombe there's me and Claire, Lisa Scott-Thomas, Andy Collins, Mike Fairfax, and the twins Ian and Sandy. (Oh, and four girls from the Knitting Brigade, but we don't really talk to them.)

Our common room is in one of the grand old houses that form part of the complex. The room is massive. Someone said it used to be a ballroom. It has big bay windows and original fireplaces at each end.

As I enter, I see our lot have already colonised one end of the room, the end with the stereo. There's vinyl spread over the tables along with copies of NME and Sounds. (We're too cool for Melody Maker.) There's a row of LPs lined up in the recess of the old fireplace. Someone's even created a listening booth in the corner.

Andy's brought in some of his avant-garde post-punk collection.

"Chrissieeeee," they shout in unison as I walk in. Claire moves her bag and pats the sofa next to her. I sit down in the seat she's saved for me.

Claire and I have stepped up together to sixth-form college. I've known her since I was nine when we bonded as best friends. Now, we sit side by side facing the room, flanked by our friends as other people, from other schools, take up the spaces in the room that will become their territory. There's an energy in the place, part nervousness, part excitement. We're at the start of something.

"What time's Assembly?" asks Lisa, clutching her Blondie bag to her chest.

"It's not called Assembly here. It's *induction*," says Claire, combing through her hair with her fingers.

"Induction – what's that when it's at home?"

"Posh name for Assembly," I say.

The college is built partly on the site of an old entertainment complex, most of which has been knocked down to make room for the new block, but they kept the art deco cinema which is referred to as 'The Theatre.' This is where we go for our induction.

On the way, we stop at the notice board to scour the timetable of classes and a list of who's doing which subjects. At Melcombe Comp, we could recite the register from memory. Claire and I were next to each other followed by Andy. It went, Christine Carlisle, Claire Cole, Andrew Collins. It's strange to see the list of unfamiliar names. But somehow exciting.

"Aye aye, who's this imposter?" says Claire. We are no longer adjacent on the list. There's someone called Tara Clinton in between.

"How dare she?" I peer closer. "Whoever she is, she's doing Psychology."

"Like you," says Claire.

We arrive early at the Theatre, sit near the back and watch everyone file in. I nudge Claire as Dr Powell, the attractive music teacher, who's also our head of year, appears on stage. We saw him at the open day and Claire said he was a good enough reason to apply.

He's well known around Bath because he heads up various jazz bands, choirs and orchestras, as well as setting up a recording studio for aspiring college bands.

He's wearing a dark suit with a black polo-neck jumper and slightly tinted glasses. Already he owns the stage.

"That guy's just so cool," says Claire.

"Ok, let's play 'Guess the School'," I say, as groups of

students arrive.

Claire stands up with her back to the seat in front of her to get a better view.

"Hayesfield," she nods towards a bunch of girls with Banamarama hairstyles and ripped jeans.

"Oldfield?" I say as another group takes the seats below.

"Hmm. My money's on Bath High."

"What about this lot – they look posh?"

"Must be the Royal."

"King Edwards," I say, as a group of boys file into the row opposite. They've got that clean-cut, assured, rugby player look you'd expect from the place.

But Claire doesn't answer. She's staring at the boy at the end of the line and he's staring back. It's like a jolt of electricity has passed between them. I watch her face flush. I can almost hear her pulse pound, can almost feel the adrenaline shoot through her as Dr Powell taps the microphone to call the room to order.

"I have to know who he is," Claire whispers as she sits down.

Already I sense I've lost her.

Powell's speech, short and pithy, is lost on her now as she strains to see past me to the boy.

I'm closer, so I can get a proper look. The boy is short, but so is Claire. Good looking, granted, but he's our year and I thought we agreed we were only interested in older boys. I thought we decided people our own age were immature.

"I *have* to meet him," she says as we all file out.

She doesn't need to wait long. The next evening, there's a welcome party in the hall. Like grab-a-fresher night at university. A party to suss out the talent and size up the competition.

Claire and the boy gravitate towards each other like nobody else exists, then slip into the shadows. I glimpse them later at the back, snogging to Adam and the Ants while the rest of us dance. They snog all night. They leave together.

And now, it's never just Claire any more. It's Claire-and-Simon. Andy calls them "the couple who share a tongue".

Chapter Two

A record sleeve from a seven-inch single. I lift the disc out, and run my fingers across its dusty grooves. It's warped, but even if it wasn't, I'd have nothing to play it on. Instead, I have the great juke box in the sky that is Siri.

Hey Siri, play 'Echo Beach' by Martha and the Muffins.

September 1981

W E'RE STACKING UP the singles on the stereo and it's my turn to choose. I've brought in a copy of Echo Beach that I picked up from the ex-chart singles section in the shop next to Reg Holden. It's playing now as the tall couple I saw on the first day enter the room. The girl clocks the music, glances at her quiffed companion and does a little understated dance move as they pass. I'm standing by the stereo and she looks directly at me. "I just *love* this song," she says. And I feel a little swell of pride, like a teacher or someone in authority has complimented me.

They haven't graced the common room until now, although we've spotted them driving up to college in his vintage open topped car, the girl wearing dark glasses and a scarf wrapped around her head like Jackie Onassis. "He drives a Triumph Stag," said Mike. "There's money there."

We all know they're from Kingswood. You can tell. There's something lofty and confident about them. Of all Bath's many private schools, Kingswood is the most exclusive. Kingswood kids are rare at college as they have their own A-list sixth form. Tara's here to study psychology, a new A-level subject this year – most schools don't offer it.

Tara wears skin-tight jeans on legs that go on forever and an expensive-looking shoulder-padded jacket. Her long blonde hair is perfectly crimped, probably done at a hairdresser's, not plaited while wet, then moussed up, which is how the rest of us do it. She has a chiselled face and a pretty, upturned nose. She looks about six foot tall. She walks with style and self-assured elegance. Like a model.

When she walks in, all the girls hate her and all the boys want her.

"Jason, look at this!" she stops by the old fireplace, but she's not looking at the records we've piled up in the recess, she's admiring the architecture as she runs her finger over the marble top. She's not from round here. She has an accent I can't quite place.

"What period is this?" she asks her friend, who's examining the frieze carved into the plaster.

"Georgian. I'd say early eighteenth century. Queen Anne design." He has a smooth, velvety voice.

Tara and Jason glide through the room like a piece of performance art, then settle at the far end, the opposite end to us.

This first week is a whirl. Boundaries give and loyalties shift, and there's a sense, particularly for me, as I watch my best friend disappearing into the sunset, that life will never be the same.

On Saturday, Claire brings Simon round to ours. They sit at either end of the sofa, for once not snogging or touching. Looking at them side by side it seems inevitable that they should be together. They look the same. Same build. Same symmetrical perfect faces. Him slightly taller than her, slightly darker hair. Like bookends, my mum says.

I feel a little lost without my best friend by my side. But it frees me up to be my own person. To hang out with the boys. To pursue my love of music. To meet new people.

I next see Tara the following week in Psychology. She sits at the front and answers intelligently in her strange accent. Is she Irish? It's different from Nan's Cork accent but has a kind of lilt. She knows about Gestalt theory and Melanie Klein and Jung's collective unconscious. I sit at the back with Lisa Scott-Thomas from Melcombe, who after two weeks drops out and transfers to Bath Tech. So the third week into term Tara and I are thrown together for a practical. Two oddballs without a partner.

"Are you Irish?" I ask, still trying to suss the accent. And because it's something to say.

She looks at me down her chiselled nose and wrinkles it slightly.

"I'm part Canadian," she says. "I was born there."

"Oh really, how long have you been over here?"

"This last time?" she asks, like I'm supposed to know she's lived here more than once. She then tells me she's spent her childhood jetting between London, Hong Kong and Vancouver, never staying more than a few years in each. Now her parents have split up and she's living with her mum in Bath.

I don't know what to say. Her life is oceans apart from

mine. We spend an hour not connecting as I wait for the session to be over so I can get back to my mates.

THE NEXT DAY I have a free period and decide to spend it in the common room. There's nobody much around. I'm heading for our end of the room when I see Tara, sitting with her back to me on one of the comfy chairs in the middle, legs draped over the armrest, body twisted, head in a book. Even like that she looks a picture of poise and elegance. I'm about to walk past when she looks up and says, "Hi Chrissie." Despite the awkwardness of yesterday, I feel a little shiver of pride. She's remembered my name.

"Hi Tara."

"How ya doin'?"

"I've got a free period. I'm supposed to be doing my French essay. How come you didn't do French? Don't you speak it over there?"

She shakes her head. "Wrong part of Canada. You're thinking Quebec."

Now I know she's Canadian, I can clearly hear it in her accent.

"Anyway, I suck at languages," she adds.

I laugh.

She nods towards the chair opposite. "Why don't you sit?"

I sit.

"So what're you reading?"

She shows me the book. Jean-Paul Sartre's *Nausea*, English translation. It has a surrealist picture of a beachscape on the front cover.

"We're doing him in French," I say. "Did you know his

eyes looked in two different directions?"

It's the most unsophisticated thing to say to someone like Tara. But, to my surprise, she laughs.

"I did *not* know that. I've learnt something today. Maybe I can learn more from you than from the tutors."

"I'll try and come up with another gem of knowledge for you tomorrow," I say, racking my brain for a way to keep the conversation going.

One of the knitting girls comes in, nods at me and scuttles off to a table in the corner.

"Did she go to the church school?" Tara asks.

"No. She went to our school, Melcombe Comp, but she didn't hang out with us. We called her and her mates the knitting brigade."

"Do they knit?" Tara's voice is loud.

I keep mine muted. "They look like they ought to."

Tara laughs out loud then. "I thought they might be convent girls."

"Nah the Catholics have their own college. They don't mix with the likes of us. And anyway, Catholic girls are all sluts – you'd be surprised."

Tara laughs again. "I'm learning a lot from you, Chrissie."

Why do I get a thrill when she says my name?

The door swings open and Andy, Mike and Ian appear. "Oi Strawbs! What's going on?" says Andy when he sees me sitting somewhere different. Then he clocks Tara and the shock is palpable. The three of them swagger over. "Who's your friend?" says Mike, jerking his head towards Tara.

"Mike – Tara, Tara – Mike," I say. Tara merely says hi, then returns to her book.

Not a prayer, I think, as I watch Mike trying to big

himself up. The three of them saunter off back to our end of the room.

"Why do they call you Strawberry Girl?" Tara asks when they've gone. "Your hair's not strawberry blonde anymore."

I've recently henna'd it a deep dark red.

"It's a line from a song by Siouxie and the Banshees called Christine."

She shrugs. "Punk kinda passed me by. You'll have to educate me."

When Claire-and-Simon show up, I leave to join the others. But a part of me feels pain at parting. And a part of me can't help looking over at the back of Tara's armchair.

"What you doing hanging out with her? Didn't think she'd associate with us," says Mike.

"Tara's cool," I say. "You're just miffed 'cos she doesn't fancy you."

"Is she going out with that poof with the quiff?"

"You mean Jason?" I say. "Dunno. Think they're just mates."

"Mike!," says Claire. "You smitten? She's obviously out of your league."

Chapter Three

A photo of us all leaning on the wall by Parade Gardens. Probably on our way to some gig. There's Andy, man in black at the back, hair glued into vertical spikes. Apart from Ben who's wearing a cap to hide his bald spot, we all have gravity-defying hair. I'm dressed in a square-shouldered man's jacket I got from Oxfam and my old red and gold school tie is in my hair. My eyes, as usual, are outlined in thick black kohl. They look huge and rounded. I wish kohl had that effect on me now.

Hey Siri, play 'The Velvet Gentleman' by Erik Satie

September 1981

I'VE KNOWN ANDY all through school, right from infants. He's another West-Melcomber, like me and Claire. But it's only since coming to college that we've had much time for each other.

He was a grubby kid with a runny nose who turned into a nerdy, spotty teenager with a lock of dark hair that fell into his eye. He developed a head jerk, almost a tic, to shake the stubborn bit of hair away from his face. He grew at an exponential rate, so he was always about a foot taller than everyone else, then started rounding his back to compensate. In 1978 when we were fourteen he turned punk overnight. He shaved his hair at the sides and glued the rest of it up into a Mohican which he dyed with red food colouring. His mum said all his pillows were pink. Then a year later he went mod. Short hair, long sideburns and a Parka. Now, in 1981, his hair's black and gelled up, goth style. As the day wears on the gel wears off and once again his hair flops into his eyes. These days, he dresses all in black. Black drainpipe jeans with a studded belt worn loosely round the hips. And a black outsize shirt – that's his signature attire. Despite his long bendy back he's somehow standing taller, like he's finally grown into his height. And I have to admit this is the best I've ever seen him look. Plus I'm developing an interest in music. And where music's concerned, Andy's your man. He's somehow made his way to the cutting edge of the music scene. His ability to play the keyboard and to string together a lyric has got him into a band, and now he's studying the subject for A-level.

As well as being a meeting of the schools, Stoke College is a meeting of the subcultures. There are goths, punks, post-punks, new romantics, plus still a few Cindy girls. Claire and I used to be very scathing about Cindy girls, with their bleached blonde hair and penchant for pink. Now, Claire's starting to resemble one herself. She's toned down her hair. Gone are the pink streaks and it's now in a neat bob. Although she's a natural blonde. Of course.

We maintain our spot by the stereo, but our circle's widened to include a few people from other schools, the common factor being music. One of these is Ben, who – at the age of seventeen – is already balding. What hair he has is wispy and ginger and gelled up in the centre of his head so he looks like TinTin. But Ben's cool. His older brother lives in London and writes for the NME and Ben got a byline on a review he wrote when The Psychedelic Furs played Bristol Locarno. I feel an instant affinity with him. There's something reassuring and uncomplicated about Ben. All he's interested in, all he ever wants to talk about, is music.

IT'S SATURDAY, AND Andy and I get off the bus at Bear Flat to pick up Ben, then walk into town for some serious record shopping. Ben knows the places to go for all the best bargains. First stop's the shop next to Reg Holden with the ex-chart singles. I pick up a copy of Ghost Town by The Specials for fifty pence. Then it's Southgate where we spend half an hour browsing the fabulous first floor of John Menzies, before heading up to Woolworths, Owen Owen and the one on the corner of the Corridor. We take in Milsoms, WH Smith and Duck, Son & Pinker – where Ben picks up an obscure punk album by a band even Andy's never heard of. Then it's up to Walcott Street market for bootlegs. On our way back we cut through the narrow street past Jaberwocky café, where there's a tiny bookshop underneath the art gallery. I've never been in before, it sells mostly art books but they have a few records in the window, so we wander in. One of Mum's social worker colleagues, Mo, is in there talking to the hippy guy who runs the place.

Mo is loud, and from London, and the only real-life lesbian I've ever met. She stands out in a crowd. Today she's wearing bright orange leggings that hug her ample thighs, and a gigantic man's jumper. Her girlfriend, whose name I don't know, is in the shop too, browsing while Mo chats.

She's like a smaller, quieter, darker-skinned version of Mo. She's wearing a khaki combat jacket with badges all over it that say things like 'Make Love Not War'. I try to fade into the background so I won't be recognised, but it's impossible in a shop this small.

"Christine!" Mo hails me in her booming voice. "Just the person! Want a Saturday job? They need someone here!" Rob, the owner, interviews me there and then while my mates hover. He tells me I can start next weekend.

So I land myself a job, and at £10 a day it pays better than Sainsbury's, which is where most of my friends end up working.

THE PLACE IS fusty, low-ceilinged, and scruffy, with wonky floorboards and floor to ceiling shelving. My induction is laid back, like my employer. He demonstrates how to use the till. It's as antiquated as the books and shuts with a satisfying ding, like the toy cash registers I played with as a child. He gives me a tour of the shelves so I can familiarise myself with the stock.

"Here we have the big fat art books," he says. "This section is mostly art history. There's society and politics along the back wall and photography books at the end. Things are mostly alphabetical. If someone comes in and asks for something you can't find, take a phone number as we might be able to get hold of it."

As well as books, there's a single rail of clothes – mostly tie-dyed skirts and beaded kaftans that smell of petunia – and a tiny record section.

After showing me the kettle – which lives behind a purple curtain at the back – Rob says "How about some music?" puts a record on the turntable then leaves me to my own devices until lunchtime.

The music is classical, and atmospheric. I look at the sleeve. It's 'The Velvet Gentleman' by Erik Satie. It's not my kind of music, but there's something haunting about it. Something dreamy.

I sit at my counter by the window, serve a couple of Japanese students and a university lecturer, and talk to a man who's made the journey from Glastonbury for a specific avant-garde art book we don't have. At one point there are four people in the shop and it feels crowded.

After a couple of hours, there's a lull, so I put the record on again and dip behind the purple curtain to make myself a coffee, when the bell on the door signals customers. I hear a familiar voice saying "Jeez, Jason, I *love* this place, It's so shabby." I emerge from the back room to see Tara and Jason. They're both studying art history, so of course they would come here.

"Wow, it's you!" says Tara. "Do you actually *work* here?"

I swell with pride.

Chapter Four

A list of names on a yellowed A4 sheet. Four names picked out in orange highlighter. Christine Carlisle: French, Maths, Psychology. Tara Clinton: Art History, English, Psychology. Claire Cole: Biology, Physics, Chemistry. Andrew Collins, Maths, Physics, Music.

September 1981

A FTER OUR CONVERSATION in the common room and our encounter in the shop, I don't mind being paired up with Tara in psychology. In fact, I relish it. She sits at the back with me now in the seat vacated by Lisa Scott-Thomas. And I'm throwing myself into the subject, learning new stuff – seminal stuff.

The teacher is a Ms not a Miss or Mrs and she prefers us to call her by her first name – Imogen. She heads up the college debating society and she sets us off on a project to debate the merits of psychoanalysis versus behaviour therapy. Tara and I have been picked to lead the debate, on opposite sides.

Tara – perhaps because she's North American – has

grown up around the idea of everyone having their own psychoanalyst. She thinks you need to delve deep into people's childhoods to get to the root of the problem.

I – perhaps because my mother is a social worker – believe that approach is a money-spinner that fosters dependency and keeps people in therapy. Behaviour therapy works, and it works fast.

We hold the debate in the Theatre at lunchtime and have invited the rest of our year. Tara and I sit on chairs at either side of the stage, with Imogen between us holding a stop-watch. It's like we're on Question Time or something.

I clock a line of my mates in the front row, rooting for me.

I kick off.

"Psychoanalysis has its roots in Freud, and we all now know him to be a fraud! Freud the fraud!" I pause for effect, liking my alliteration.

"Plus," I add. "He was obsessed with sex. Everything, according to Freud, has to be about sex."

Tara cuts in. "Everything *is* about sex."

Titters from the audience.

"Chrissie, continue," says Imogen.

"That's as may be. But, Freud's version of sex was at best naïve, at worst downright chauvinistic. Girls, do we *really* have that penis envy thing? Boys, how many of you can honestly tell me your deepest desire is to screw your mother?" More laughter. Louder this time.

I'm enjoying this. I use words that people can understand and I get kudos for saying the word "penis" on stage. I know there's a certain prejudice against Tara – with her sophistication, her use of academic words and her alien accent – and right now, I'm playing on that.

Now it's her turn.

"Freud is irrelevant to this debate," she says. "He may be the father of psychoanalysis but the work has progressed hugely since his time." She reels off a list of names, dates and academic studies.

"We now know that the causes of neurosis are complex. All behaviourism does is treat the symptoms. That's like trying to cure cancer with a common cold cure." Her turn to alliterate. "The only way is to cut the cancer out, right? It's the same with a sickness of the mind. You have to get to the root cause."

I have the final say and I use it to my advantage.

"There are cases in the States of people hooked on psychoanalysis. They've been going to see their therapist for twenty, even thirty years and they still haven't got to the root cause! All that's good for is the therapist's bank balance. You could say this approach has fostered a nation of neurotics!

"I really hope we don't go down that route in the UK. What we have in behaviour therapy is a cheap, effective, fast-working treatment that works! Which would you rather have?"

Imogen declares the result a draw.

"You won that debate hands down," says Andy afterwards.

"It was a draw!"

"You won. She hid behind big words and statistics but you spoke to the people."

I get the feeling he doesn't like Tara. I've heard he and Mike tried to chat her up at the bus stop but she wasn't interested.

ALTHOUGH OPPOSITES IN the debate, the project draws Tara

and I closer together. She won't come to our end of the common room, preferring to sit in the 'library' end, which is quieter, so I divide my time between my mates from Melcombe and the other musos at our end, and my exclusive chats with Tara. We take to staying in the classroom after psychology, finding a quiet corner of the refectory or going to the library where we work and whisper together. We also go up to the art room on the top floor of the new block to see her friend Jason. He's studying art and he practically lives up there, surrounded by large canvases.

"Why won't your posh mate sit with us?" asks Mike, when Tara heads for the other end of the common room.

"We're not good enough for her, obviously," says Andy.

"She's actually quite shy." I say, but nobody believes me. How can someone so outspoken in class and confident with adults be shy? They can't work her out. And I can't work out what it is that makes me feel uncomfortable mixing her with my old mates. I have a feeling of jumping between two worlds and sense a need to keep them separate.

Tara remains someone I see at college, though. Evenings and weekends are taken up with hanging out with the old crew, going to gigs, exploring music. For now, our home lives stay unconnected.

Chapter Five

*A cassette box. Labelled in my own writing with the words **Psychology: interviews – Chrissie and Tara.** It still has the tape inside. I turn to my local community Facebook site. Anyone still possess a cassette player? In among the laughing emojis and ironic comments there's a message from some kind person offering to drop one off. I have it within the hour.*

At first, I think there's nothing on the tape, except the white noise of the cassette player whirring. I turn the volume up in case whatever is recorded is so quiet I can't hear it. Suddenly there's a loud click then my sixteen-year-old voice, deafening and stifling laughter, reels off the questions on our psychology interview sheet.

Chrissie: So, Tara, tell me about your childhood?

Now comes Tara's voice, quieter. She must have been sitting farther from the mic. If we even had a mic.

Tara: My childhood was a mess. We were always on the move. We zig-zagged between continents. I was born in Canada. Then we lived in Hong Kong 'til I was ten. When I was seven they sent me to boarding school in England.

Chrissie: On your own?

Tara: Yeah. On a twenty-one-hour flight. We stopped at places like Bahrain, Delhi, Calcutta, Karachi, and Tehran, and then Rome or Frankfurt for refuelling. With the time difference It felt endless. I had a sign around my neck saying "unaccompanied minor".

Chrissie: Like Paddington?

Tara: What? Oh yeah.

Laughter.

Chrissie: What was boarding school like?

My accent was distinctly Somerset then. I rolled the 'r' in 'boarding school.'

Tara: Pretty grim. Bullying was institutionalised. Prefects had too much power. You had to toughen up to survive. I survived.

Chrissie: How d'you think that affected you?

I'm pretty sure I'm going off script here, but I'm glad I did – this is fascinating.

Tara: It made me build a shell around myself, to shield my emotions. It gave me the ability to be two people. On the outside, calm and in control, on the inside, a gibbering wreck.

Chrissie: So what brought you to Bath?

I pronounce it Barrff.

Tara: After my parents divorced Mum moved back to the city where she grew up.

Chrissie: What's your relationship like with your mother?

Back on script

Tara: We hate each other.

Nervous laughter on the tape.

Chrissie: You can't mean that?

Tara: Chrissie, I do.

Chrissie: Ok, final question. If you could have a magical power, what would it be?

Tara: I'd be able to fly. Like a bird. Across oceans. Across continents.

Chrissie: So you wouldn't have to sit on a plane with a label 'round your neck?

The tape stops then, abruptly. Presumably Imogen called time. Then it's my turn, with Tara asking those same scripted questions.

Tara: So, Chrissie, tell me about your childhood.

Her voice is languid, and she lingers over my name.

Chrissie: Boring compared to yours. I've always lived in Melcombe and I'd never been out of England until last year when we went on the French exchange. It's just me, my mum and my younger brother at home.

Tara: What happened to your father?

Chrissie: Oh. Sorry, I didn't say. He died when I was nine.

Tara: I'm so sorry to hear that. How did losing a parent so young affect you?

There's a pause on the tape. Maybe I'm upset. Tara says "take your time." I come back sounding slightly muffled.

Chrissie: It was still a shock even though he'd had cancer for a long time. Mum's a social worker and she works funny hours, so me and my brother got farmed out to Nan's house after school or to one of my aunties. I've got aunties all over the place as Mum's one of seven sisters. Mum's social worker friends all piled in and tried to counsel me and David. We had lots of therapy!

Laughter.

We went to this really awkward family counselling thing. Me, David, Mum and Aunty Shauna sat in a circle in a tiny room. Aunty Shauna started crying for no reason, then spent the next five minutes apologising. Then it all went quiet and the therapist said "Silence. What's happening in this silence?" and

I caught David's eye and we both started giggling. Mum told us off later and we never went again.

Tara: It didn't work then?

Chrissie: It made us laugh. So maybe it did.

Tara: Thank you Chrissie. Now tell me about your relationship with your mother.

Chrissie: It's normal I s'pose. We argue.

Tara: Ok Chrissie, now to our last question – what's your superpower?

Chrissie: Well I already fly, so it won't be that.

Tara: What d'you mean you already fly?

Chrissie: Not with wings, like a bird. I kind of levitate, looking down on everything. I fly all around Melcombe. Sometimes as far as Bath.

Tara: So you, like, detach? In your dreams?

Chrissie: It's not a dream. It's pre-dream.

Tara: Like an out of body experience?

Chrissie: Sort of, but I'm not looking down at myself. I fly to other places and look in on other people. They never know I'm there. It started when my dad was dying. I wasn't allowed to visit, but I looked down at him on his hospital bed. Mum was sat on a grey plastic chair next to him, holding his hand. There was a nurse with frizzy ginger hair and a sparkly pen in her pocket who came over and said something, then Mum knocked a glass of water all over the bed. Three days later my Dad died in those exact same circumstances.

Tara: So it was a premonition?

Chrissie: Kind of. It happened a lot around that time. I'd see something, then it would happen. Claire and I cashed in on it by writing people's horoscopes. We called ourselves the Claire Voyants and charged them ten pence a go!

Tara: You're telling me as a child you were running a fortune-telling racket? How enterprising!

Chrissie: Yeah. You could write any old rubbish and they believed it. Then one time I predicted a bus crash involving a girl at school's mum and it actually happened. After that the teachers closed down our little enterprise. But I carried on seeing things. My Aunty Nessa who's psychic says it's a special gift. Mum thought it was a delusion caused by the trauma of Dad dying. The counsellor said it was dissociation. But it's not, because when you've got that you feel like you don't exist. I know I exist.

Tara: I'm very glad you exist, Chrissie.

Chapter Six

Another cassette case. This one has "Sounds of Canada" written on the spine in precise, sloping handwriting. The writing is faded, but I can still make out most of the titles on the cover. Neil Young, Rush, Joni Mitchell, Leonard Cohen. The case is empty.

September 1981

"ANYWHERE IN TOWN we can get a decent coffee?" Tara pronounces it "carfee". So instead of going to the common room after psychology we walk down into the city centre. But coffee shops – apparently common overseas – haven't yet made it to the UK. We stick our heads into a quaint Bath tea-room where the waitresses dress as French maids, but although they do seventeen blends of leaf tea they don't, evidently, do anything that qualifies as decent coffee.

"We could have tea instead," I say. She wrinkles her nose. "I don't get this English obsession with tea. Let's go to the apartment."

She leads me through town to a street around the corner from the city's famous Pulteney Bridge, and stops outside a four-storey Georgian townhouse. She looks up, at an open first floor window, and says, "My mum's in." There's a certain resignation in her voice, a weariness that I find hard to fathom. Inside, we climb a wide staircase covered in plush plum carpet. She pushes open the door to a first floor flat. A whiff of cigarette smoke meets our nostrils, mixed with the smell of wood-polish and the sort of incense aroma you get in hippy shops.

We enter a hallway where there's an antique mahogany sideboard with a pile of glossy magazines on top. In the corner, hanging on a wooden coat stand, there's a fur coat that looks real and a patchwork suede seventies-style jacket. We walk through into a dining room where a woman sits, smoking a cigarette and reading a magazine. The woman looks up. She has thick, straight, ash-blonde hair in a long bob. Her face, expertly made up, has a bronze glow and no visible wrinkles. It's hard to guess her age. She has full lips glossed in a dark rose, her eyelids blended in shades of brown. Her eyes themselves are grey, not brown like Tara's. Something about them seems dead.

She balances her cigarette on the ashtray then rises to her feet. She's tall, like her daughter. She wears a long white house coat with square shoulders, and cropped, black trousers. Her clothes look tailored and expensive.

She looks nothing at all like a mum.

"Mum, this is Chrissie."

I sense Tara's mother sizing me up, assessing my thrown together outfit and finding me lacking. She stretches out her hand. "I'm Grace, Tara's mother." Her voice is posh, English – unlike Tara's – and husky. Her handshake is brief, barely pinching my palm with cool fingers. She doesn't smile.

She strides over to a sideboard against the wall and picks up an airmail letter resting on the top. She carries it over to us, holding it by one corner as though it's on fire, then hands it to Tara.

"This arrived," she says.

"Thanks," Tara takes the envelope. Her mother stands in front of her, waiting.

"I'll open it later."

Grace sniffs, then resumes her seat at the table, picking up her cigarette and drawing on it. She blows the smoke vaguely in the direction of the open window. Most of it trails back into the room.

Tara looks at me. "Let's go to my room."

Tara's room is spacious. The full-sized double bed is huge compared to my single at home. There are no posters on the wall, just a framed painting of a girl. It looks familiar. I wonder if it's by a famous artist. Possibly even an original. Her desk is antique mahogany with a green leather top, like something you'd see in a country house. There's even a two-seater settee in the room.

She has a decent stereo, of course. Silver turntable, separate tape deck and amp, which sits on a sideboard like the one in the hall. I thumb through her records.

"Put something on if you like, but my taste's a bit old school."

Dylan, Leonard Cohen, Neil Young, Beatles, Stones, some early Led Zep. It's like a cross between my mum's and my brother's collection.

I scrutinise her row of cassettes, and pull out a compilation tape which has 'sounds of Canada' written on it in neat italics.

"How about some music from your country? I don't know many Canadian bands."

"You must know Neil Young? He's Canadian. So's

Leonard Cohen. And Rush. Oh, and 'Echo Beach' by Martha and the Muffins, You've got the single in the common room. They're from Canada."

I put the tape on. The deck responds to the lightest of touches, opening slowly. Everything is smooth. Not like my clunky music system at home.

"Come and sit down," she pats the sofa next to her. I sit. She peels off the edge of the airmail letter and starts to read.

"It's from my dad," she says, lowering her voice. "Mum's very bitter."

She's told me before, that her dad "ran off with a Chinese woman," when they were in Hong Kong. I look over her shoulder and notice the letter is signed "Roger" not "Dad" and in a different hand "Aisee".

"He always had women on the side," she says. "He had this thing about oriental women. Mum calls it yellow fever. But this time he acted on it, left mum and married her."

"And don't you mind?"

She shakes her head. "It's his life. I'd rather he was happy living apart from us than unhappy living with us. Aisee's cool."

"Is it true your mum's a model?" So says the word on the street at college.

"Not like a career catwalk model, although she was once featured on the cover of Vogue. There's a print of it in the hall. She was more like a, what do you call it, an It Girl? A Debutante? Do they still have those?" She looks at me as if for confirmation. I can't help her as I know nothing about such things.

"Before she met my dad she hung out with London's elite artists and photographers. She knew people like Lord Snowdon – you know, Princess Margaret's ex? Dad took her away from all that. That's another reason for her to resent him." Tara makes it all sound so matter of fact.

The tape plays at low volume, which seems strange given the capacity of the machine and the size of the speakers.

"Can I turn it up?" I ask.

"A bit, but if it's much louder, she'll be in," Tara nods towards the living room.

Sure enough, after a couple of tracks, there's a tap on the door and her mother appears in the doorway, eyebrows raised, visibly disapproving.

"Hi Mum," Tara sounds bright, but defiant.

"Would your friend like to stay for dinner?" Grace looks from one to the other of us as we sit on Tara's sofa.

"I don't know. Would you, Chrissie?"

"I'd love to, but only if it's convenient," I feel gauche and unsophisticated in the presence of the two of them.

"It'll be my pleasure to cook for my daughter's guest," she says, still not smiling. "It'll be ready in about an hour. We don't normally eat this early but I'm going out."

I'm not sure whether she really wants me there or not.

"She's a good cook," says Tara after Grace has gone.

The aroma of cooking soon mingles with the cigarette smoke and fragrance of essential oils.

We have red wine with dinner, brought over from Bordeaux. The first course is chicken cooked in wine, with perfect new potatoes and green veg, served on plain white plates, bigger than the ones we have at home. It's like a meal you'd get in a restaurant, not something your mum cooked.

Beyond asking me what subjects I'm doing and what school I went to before – she curls her lip slightly when I mention Melcombe Comp – Grace seems uninterested in me. I detect a hint of boredom when I answer. She becomes more animated over the wine, however, and starts to tell me things about herself.

"I used to live on Sloane Street."

I've heard of Sloane rangers. This must be what they're like.

Tara picks up the plates and takes them into the kitchen. Grace lights a cigarette which she holds in the hand not clutching the wine glass.

"I had so many men before I met Tara's father," she says. "I was in demand."

"Really?"

This doesn't surprise me. What *does* surprise me is that she sees fit to impart this information to me – someone she's only just met.

"*So* many men," she says, sighing a little. I wonder if she used to smile back in the days when men were abundant.

She turns to Tara, who's reappeared with the pudding – three individually served chocolate mousses, in glasses with stems and frosted sides.

"What did your father have to say?"

"Not a lot. They've been back to Hong Kong. Aisee's mother's ill."

Grace winces slightly, like she has toothache, then turns back to me.

"Are there any good-looking young men at college?"

"Um, dunno really. Maybe a few. What d'you reckon Tara?"

It occurs to me I've never talked to Tara about boys.

Tara laughs. "They're boys, mother, not men."

"Tara's friend Jason's probably about the best looking," I say.

"But he's queer," says Grace.

This is news to me.

Tara bristles. "You say 'gay' mum, not 'queer'."

Tara's mother frowns. "He's no good to us, whatever he is."

"Simon's good looking," I say, to brighten the mood. "But short. And taken, of course. Snapped up on day one of college by my friend Claire."

Tara laughs. "If I didn't know better, I'd say they were brother and sister, separated at birth."

After the meal, Tara says she'll walk me to the bus stop. I wait in the hallway while she gets ready. In a frame on the wall is the infamous cover of Vogue, featuring a much younger Grace, hair done up in bouffant style, eyelashes coated with heavy mascara, a fur coat resting on her shoulders. She's looking into the camera in a way that's almost insolent, hands on hips, full lips pouting. She looks like a 1960s film star.

Chapter Seven

Diary Entry October 1981

Crush list – top five:

1. *The Simon-Le-Bon lookalike in the year above, name of Alistair. He brushed past me in the corridor yesterday and I caught his eye.*

2. *Drew, Simon's mate from King Edwards*

3. *Dr Karl Powell – yes for the third week running there's a teacher in the top 5*

4. *Tara's mate, Jason, you gotta admit he's gorgeous (shame he's gay)*

5. *Robert Smith from the Cure*

Claire and I used to do this every week. Now it's just me. One thing is clear, I need to get myself a boyfriend.

DR POWELL STOPS us on our way out of class. "Tara, how's it going?"

He's suave and sophisticated in his dark suit.

"Hi Karl."

Trust her to be on familiar terms with a teacher. And not just any teacher. The one everyone lusts over.

"How's Grace?"

Tara shrugs and a veil comes over her face, the same expression she used when she took me to the flat.

"She's fine. Usual stuff."

"Give her my best," he says, pressing her shoulder as we move on.

"What's with the first name terms?" I say.

"Oh. I've known Karl years. He had a thing going with my mum. She's in one of his choirs."

Karl Powell, as far as I know, is married. He brings his pretty Yugoslavian wife to college concerts. She's petite, dark and gorgeous.

"You kept that one quiet," I say.

She shrugs again. "It's not a big deal. It's like an on-off thing and it's currently off."

We're heading for the college gate when she asks if I want to come back to hers again.

"I've got to go home and walk Arnold – that's our dog. Mum's working late and you can't rely on David."

He's bunked off school for a week with some mystery illness which doesn't prevent him eating and watching TV but he's apparently too ill to take the dog out.

To my surprise she says, "Can I come?" so we get the bus to West Melcombe together.

My brother's playing Def Leppard in his bedroom. The bass booms out around the house. I yell up to him. Of course he can't hear, so I go up and hammer on his door. Tara follows. I hear "*What*?" above the din. I push the door open. David's quilt is mostly on the floor and he's lying on his bed in his Motorhead t-shirt and boxers, staring at the ceiling. I march over to the stereo.

"What?" he says again.

"If you won't turn it down, I will. You can hear it all over the house. I wouldn't mind if it was decent music."

He scowls.

"We've got guests," I say. Tara leans round the door. "Tara, this is my brother."

"Hi brother," she says, and gives him a little wave.

His face turns from pale and creased up to a deep puce. It's comical to watch. He sits up, pulls the duvet up over him and hugs it to his torso.

The Tara effect.

David grunts something.

"My brother hasn't learnt to speak properly yet," I say. He blushes once more and gives me the look. The one that says "I hate you".

As we leave the room the music goes up again but to an acceptable volume.

We walk Arnold over on the rec. Tara won't throw the ball because it's covered in his slobber. If he gets near her, sniffing her groin, she pushes him away.

"I'm more of a cat person," she says. "We had one in Hong Kong called Lady Fuchsia."

Even her pets are exotic.

We walk back through the old part of the village, so Tara can see the houses. She's into historic buildings. I point out Aunty Nessa's cottage, with its long garden path overgrown with giant chamomile daisies, ivy and brambles.

"She's my psychic aunt. The one I was banned from visiting."

"Why?"

"We got farmed out to different aunties after Dad died.

When we went to Nessa's she told us stories that kept us awake. She was always seeing ghosts. She speaks to spirits. She thinks Arnold is an angel."

Tara laughs. "An angel that likes to sniff people's crotches."

"Mum says Nessa's crazy. Nan says she's in league with the devil."

Tara laughs. "Does she practise dark arts?"

"She does this thing with keys. She can tell things about people from their house keys. Just by holding them. Mum says it's all mumbo jumbo. She's been proved right though."

I tell Tara about Corrie. The youngest of my mum's sisters. My cool aunty who went to live in London with an attractive, rich, older man when she was seventeen. Aunty Nessa somehow got hold of this guy's keys and predicted he had a wife and kids in some foreign location. And it turned out to be true. He had a whole other family in Thailand.

"Can we go see her?" Tara stops by the gate to Nessa's cottage. "I want to meet this woman. See what she knows about me from my keys. Or give her my mum's keys. See what she makes of Grace."

"Yes but not right now, she doesn't like surprises. You never know quite how she'll react."

Last time I saw Nessa in the street, she screamed.

I invite Tara to tea, but she declines because we're having leftover roast pork. She hasn't been able to eat pork since boarding school where, apparently, they were served a vile pork dish every Monday, and one girl got a tape-worm because it wasn't cooked properly.

I see her to the bus stop.

"YOUR NEW MATE'S a bit classy," David says later. "She

American?"

"Tara's Canadian."

My classy Canadian friend. My blonde bombshell. Men drool at the sight of her, but she either doesn't notice or doesn't care. Such power.

Chapter Eight

A yellowed piece of A4 card headed **Stoke College Film Club Autumn Term Screenings**, *with a list of films from 1981.* Airplane. Grease. Pop Eye. The Empire Strikes Back. *Wonder why I kept this? I hardly ever went to film club. I turn it over, and on the back I've drawn a glass with a cocktail umbrella and the words 'Happy 18th Tara – have a G&T on me! xxx'*

October 1981

I T'S THURSDAY. WE have psychology straight after lunch, then the rest of the afternoon free.

"What are you doing now?" Tara asks after class.

"No plans. Why?"

"Come with me," she says, waving a set of keys.

She leads me around the back of the new block and up the back stairs of the theatre and unlocks the door of the projection room.

"I got the keys from Jase," she explains. Jason's the film club projectionist.

The room is lit by a single low-wattage lightbulb. As my

eyes adjust, Tara moves around in the gloom. The space is small and full of wires, extension leads, the odd spotlight, and boxes of bulbs.

"This is the lighting desk," she says, pointing out a board containing rows of switches. "Shall we light the stage?"

Evidently Jason showed her how it works.

"What if someone sees?"

"They won't. The only windows are in the roof. And if they do see a light on, they'll just think it's someone in here rehearsing."

We fumble around, trying out switches until we have power. We twiddle the dials on the rig, fading colours in and out, giggling. At one point she presses something that makes the lights flash.

"Oops, someone might notice if we go for a full strobe effect."

She asks me to choose colours. I go for red and green. The red bulb is out of action, so we settle for green. It casts an eerie light over the stage, which has a four-poster bed in the middle of it. The drama society have been rehearsing for Hamlet.

"I've brought refreshments." Tara opens her bag to reveal a half bottle of London gin and some tonic. "Wonder if there's any glasses back here."

She roots around in the shadows and fishes out a couple of aged, yellowed tumblers from somewhere.

She inspects them for cleanliness, discards them and delves in her bag again, producing two plastic beakers.

"These'll have to do." She pours two gin and tonics, heavy on the gin.

We perch on tall stools overlooking the rows of seats, which are in darkness, and the stage beyond, lit green.

"Cheers!" she says. "Sorry there's no ice."

This is a new side to Tara. Drinking alcohol in the afternoon on school premises feels deliciously forbidden.

"Glad you were free. I can't think of anyone better to celebrate with."

"Celebrate what?"

"My birthday!"

Tara's older than the rest of us. Somewhere in transit between Canada, Hong Kong, and the UK, she lost a year of education. She was already seventeen when we started college.

"So this is your eighteenth? You never said."

She raises her mug again, her eyes dancing in the dim light, "So now I can legally drink!"

I laugh. Most of us have been drinking for years. Although still only sixteen, I have no trouble getting served in pubs. Claire often gets refused because she looks younger. That's what comes of being little.

"You can vote, too!" I say. "Are you allowed to vote in England?"

"I'll have to check that out."

She's sitting on the edge of the stool, swinging her long legs. She swills the contents of her beaker.

"Funny how the legal age for sex here is two years younger than when you can legally drink," she says. "How do they figure this stuff out? There's states in America where you can't drink till twenty-one, but you can be a child bride, forced to have sex with your forty-year-old husband from the age of twelve!" she scowls.

"Gross," I say, taking a long draught from the tumbler. "Talking of sex…"

Claire and I know each other's history intimately. With

Tara I've never had the confidence to ask. The gin gives me courage.

"You want to know how many times I've had it?" she says, draining her drink and topping us both up.

I notice she says "how many times", not "if".

"If you mean intercourse. Once, when I was fifteen. On a beach in Vancouver, known locally as Wreck Beach. It was with this guy called Dwane who I'd just dropped acid with."

I already feel out of my depth.

"It was awful!"

"The sex or the acid?"

She laughs. "Both. It was the first and last time I took acid and it was what you'd call a *bad* trip. Have you ever taken LSD, Chrissie?"

"Nope. I smoked dope a couple of times up on the rec with the Melcombe crowd but that's about my limit."

"Will you indulge me while I describe the experience? It was both terrifying and magical."

As she speaks, I feel like a child drawn into a fairy tale. Tara's blonde hair is lit by the dim bulb. Like a halo.

"I was in Vancouver on half term. My dad had just moved with his girlfriend to near the university. A girl from school was staying, and we started hanging out with some guys who were students there.

"Someone scored some acid and dared us to take it. Izzy – my friend – was older than me and I thought if *she* did it, it would be ok. We both chewed on half a piece of blotting paper that contained the hits. The guys picked up a couple of six packs of beer then we walked down this heavily wooded, steep path that leads down to Wreck Beach. It's a nudist hangout colonised by hippies in the sixties, a place where students could hang out and smoke dope without being hassled.

"The sand down there is scattered with cedar driftwood from the forests. It was close to nightfall and we gathered some wood and built a fire, had a couple of beers and lay back, watching the stars come out, waiting for the acid to take effect. We were starting to wonder if we'd been sold a dud, so we popped the other half of the blotting paper into our mouths."

She stops to drain her cup and refills us both.

"Izzy and I went for a walk. We came across this seesaw made of a log and I sat on one end and Izzy the other. That's when I started to trip. As my side went up I shot up into the stars like a rocket. It was truly cosmic. I threw myself off the log and laughed, picking up grains of sand and feeling it trickle through my tingling fingers – it was the most beautiful sensation."

Her description is so vivid I feel as though I'm there, in that weird scene on that far-off beach. I look out towards the stage. There are dust particles dancing in the beam of green light, which makes it all the more surreal.

"We were both lying on the sand, laughing. I looked at Izzy and felt this intense, almost uncontrollable desire for her body. I knew that acid has this effect and I didn't want to make a fool of myself so I managed to suppress it.

"The guys found us there. And now I desired them too, all of them. I felt this sublime connection to everyone and they all looked irresistible. Somehow me and Dwane got separated from the rest and the next thing I know I'm under him. I want to shoot up into the stars again but his weight is pinning me down. I can't remember the sex, actually. I just remember he had green hair then the stars began to web with light and the whole sky fell in on us. I was gripped by this awful terror.

"Next thing I know, I'm scrabbling up the path again. I can hear the others, they're around somewhere, shouting, but I'm on my own, clutching at the trees like they'll save me. But the branches reach out like they're trying to trap me – like a scene from Tolkien. Some people we vaguely knew were on their way down to the beach and I said, 'You have to help me,' but they just told me to stay cool."

WHEN TARA TALKS, I digest information in sizeable chunks that sometimes stick in the throat. In the space of a few minutes I leap across oceans and continents of experience. I'm left reeling. I don't know what to say. How can I ever match this? But she continues.

"By then I'd lost Izzy but somehow by some miracle found my way back to my dad's. Dad went ballistic at the sight of me but Aisee, his girlfriend, persuaded him to go out and look for Izzy while she stayed with me. I just collapsed on the floor in my room and told her I was tripping bad on acid. And she was brilliant! Like some guardian angel. She just sat on the floor with me and told me nothing lasts forever. Even this.

"Next day I was still coming down and Izzy and I were piecing together what we remembered, and it occurred to me I'd lost my virginity. I bled like a pig. I hurt for days."

"So did you meet the guy again?" I ask.

"Nope. I'd have been mortified if I'd seen him. In hindsight I'm not sure I was even capable of consent. What kind of a name is Dwayne anyway?"

Tara looks up, and shakes out her hair like she's shaking off the memory and resurfacing into the present.

"So that was my one experience. Then there was an

almost-encounter with Jason last year."

"Really?"

"Yeah but we didn't exactly consummate it."

"Because he's gay?"

"Something like that. But, you know, the best experiences I've ever had in bed haven't involved penetration. Now tell me yours!"

I tell her about Neil Marchand from Melcombe on my sixteenth birthday last May. How we'd dated for six weeks but waited for the big day. How we'd got our alibis sorted for the occasion, got on the bus to Glastonbury with a tent, walked for miles and pitched up in a disused quarry.

"Despite being a boy scout for years he couldn't get the tent up."

"Is that a euphemism?"

"Maybe it was a sign!" I tell her how it rained all night and we warmed up on vodka, which helped me relax but it didn't help him. He couldn't get a hard on, so we gave it up as a bad job.

"He loved me though. He was devastated when I got off with his brother."

Neil's brother was nineteen and had no such problems. "We did it in his parents' bedroom when they were out and Neil was at Rangers."

"Rangers, what's that?"

"Like boy scouts for older boys." Tara looks as amazed as I felt when she told me about the acid.

"And was it better with his brother?"

"Well, he succeeded in breaking my duck. But that was about it. I remember him coming at me with his erection like a weapon. He'd never heard of foreplay."

"Course he hadn't. He's a man."

"And if I hadn't stopped him and said, "Hey, how about precautions?" I could've ended up pregnant. He humped away for ages and I couldn't wait for him to finish. Afterwards I had a massive bruise on my pelvis."

"So that was the end of him, was it?"

"Nope. Like a fool I went back for more."

She laughs. "Did it get better?"

"Hmm, no! I just liked the kudos of being with an older guy. After a few weeks he dumped me for a Cindy girl." I have to explain to Tara what that means.

The gin bottle's almost empty and she pours the last drops out. I'm feeling quite woozy. Tara's face looks huge and for a minute the projection room spins into orbit.

"There's something else I want to tell you, Chrissie, but not yet," she says. "We'd better get out of here before they lock us in the building."

We link arms as we walk across the site, Tara steadying me. We bump into Karl Powell en route. I bite my lip to stop myself giggling.

Chapter Nine

A bunch of receipts from Bath stores. Yellowed and faded. I can just about make out the names of the shops. Chelsea Girl, Top Shop and Jean Jeanie. I squint at the price tag for a pair of jeans. £13.99.

October 1981

"C'MON, LET'S HIT the High Street," I don't often do mainstream stores, preferring second hand places or charity shops, but Tara has birthday money to spend and I've saved up a bit from my Saturday job, so we head into town. When Claire and I used to mooch round the shops we'd spend hours trying things on, parading in front of each other and rarely buying. With Tara it's like a military exercise. We do them all, one after another. Top Shop, Chelsea Girl, Jean Jeanie, up to the top of Milsom Street and back down the other side. She makes a beeline for the stuff she likes, tries on without ceremony, peeling off her clothes in the communal changing rooms, oblivious to the envious looks of women and girls around her. Tara stands head and shoulders above the rest, stripped down to her peach-coloured bra and matching bikini-briefs. It's now I notice the tattoo, a striking, colourful design of a bear on her left shoulder-blade, just to the right of the bra strap. Inexplicably, this shocks me. It should be me with a tattoo, I'm supposed to be the bohemian one. Tara's more clean-cut and conventional in her dress. Each outfit she tries on looks fantastic. Most, she discards with short shrift, barely even asking for an opinion.

In Top Shop, she buys a pair of tapered tartan trousers. Tara finds it hard to get trousers long enough. These, though, are just the right length. She also buys a couple of lacy new romantic tops. Occasionally, she picks things out for me to try. "This'll look great on you Chrissie," she hands me a red dress. I try it on, conscious of her watching me strip to my non-matching underwear. It does look good, but the price-tag puts me off.

"It looks stunning Chrissie, why don't you buy it?"

"Hmm, not sure. I might come back for it," too embarrassed to give the real reason.

No such qualms for Tara, she evidently has a bottomless purse. She also has a credit card. I don't know anyone else who's got one. Not all the shops will take it. She buys pink jeans in Jean Jeanie, ankle boots from Dolcis and a jacket in a posh shop I never normally set foot in.

"Don't you ever shop in High Street stores?" she asks. It's handy to pretend the reason I don't is because I prefer vintage. I take her to GladRags up on Walcott Street. But I see her nose wrinkling as we enter and we're met with that musty second-hand smell. She can hardly bear to touch the stock.

Perhaps she is a snob after all, like people at college say. But when we squeeze into the tiny cubicle for me to try on a 1940s fitted frock, a pair of Italian army trousers which she says look great – so I get them – and a vintage silk blouse, which I also get, she raves about my sense of style.

"I wish I had your vision," she says as we come out of the shop. "I just can't imagine going into a place like that and finding stuff I like. But all those clothes look amazing on you." Maybe not a snob after all.

Although when we get back to her flat and review our purchases she asks me if I have to wash everything before I wear it.

"I'm pretty sure they clean them in the shop," I say. It's never occurred to me I might catch something from wearing clothes off the rail in GladRags.

"So what's with the tattoo?" I ask as we once more strip off to try on our outfits.

"I got it on holiday last year. Have you got any?"

"I'd love one, but you have to be eighteen here."

"Same in Canada. But we found a man who did it. No questions asked."

"We?"

"Me and this girl who I met out there. We both got the same. It's the spirit bear. One of the symbols of Vancouver."

Grace comes home as we are trying on our new clothes.

"This is what I bought with my birthday money, Mum." Tara sashays across the room, catwalk style, modelling the tartan trousers, white lacy shirt and ankle boots.

Grace looks her up and down, touches the lace trim on the shirt and says: "You all look like you're in period costume these days with all these frills." She then examines the trousers. "I'm not sure women are made for tartan. Those chequered lines accentuate your hips."

I'm amazed. How can she be so critical, when Tara clearly looks fabulous? Such a contrast from my own mum, who tells me I look great whatever I wear.

Back in Tara's room, she says, "Grace hates me."

I'm about to protest then she adds, "It's because she's jealous. She sees her own body ageing and she sees me like she used to be, and she hates it. That's how Dad explained it and he's right. I used to get upset but now I understand it. She's jealous of our youth, Chrissie."

I'm not sure what to say. These are new concepts to me. What I do say comes out bland, and I'm not sure I believe it. "I'm sure she loves you really."

Tara shakes her head. "She's a sociopath, my mum. She doesn't know the meaning of the word love. You don't know her yet. You'll see."

Chapter Ten

Hey Siri, play 'Happy Birthday' by Altered Images.

October 1981

"STAY STILL AND don't blink."

I'm sitting at Tara's antique dressing table in her bedroom, looking at myself in an out-of-focus mirror as Tara does my make-up. I'm wearing eye shadow and mascara tonight as well as my usual black eyeliner. We have a swift G&T as we get ready. Grace is out, so we turn the volume up on the stereo. 'School's Out' by Alice Cooper.

Appropriate as it's Friday night and we've just broken up for half term. We're hitting the town for Tara's belated birthday bash.

I wear a short black and white striped cotton rah-rah dress, new from Chelsea Girl, with opaque black tights, chunky boots and my biker jacket. Tara's in her tartan trousers and one of her white shirts with the lacy neck. She's got her hair straight today and flicked to one side. I'm staying the night at Tara's, to spare my mother the hassle of having to pick me up in the early hours.

We meet Tara's friends at the Alehouse – there's a crowd of around ten occupying two of the cellar booths. Apart from

Tara and Jason, the others are all people from Kingswood who I don't know.

I'm chatted up by a guy with a plum in his mouth who tells me his name's Tarquin.

I down two pints of cider in quick succession to drown my awkwardness.

The club is a huge, sunken mosh pit with a line of sofas at the back. We make our way as a critical mass into the middle of the floor and start to dance. The booze has worked its magic and I move to the music, conscious of a guy on the periphery who looks and dresses like Robert Smith from The Cure – my absolute idol. He seems to know some of Tara's mates. We clock each other and I sense possibility. He moves in closer.

The DJ puts on "Happy Birthday" by Altered Images. Maybe someone requested it for Tara. I turn to her, mouthing the words.

She looks elegant as ever, but I can tell she's not enjoying herself. She seems restricted in the high-necked top and keeps pulling at the collar in a futile attempt to let some air in. She must be hot too, in those trousers. Jason is nowhere to be seen and the boys we arrived with are now dripping with sweat, lurching across the floor, clumsy with drink. The only one who keeps his cool is the Robert Smith lookalike.

Mid-track, Tara turns, yelling in my ear as she passes, "I need some air." For a second, I feel torn. Should I stay and dance, or join Tara? Loyalty wins and I follow as she pushes through the crowd. We sit on one of the sofas at the back.

"You ok?" I ask, as a couple, unsteady on their feet and entwined, tumble into the sofa next to us. As they snog each other's faces off, the guy sticks his hand up the girl's skirt. They're close enough to smell.

"This place is a meat market," Tara says. "I'm leaving."

"I'll come with you."

"Don't feel you have to. You seem to be having a good time."

We leave anyway, Tara taking great gulps as the cool air hits us.

It's not even midnight, and we have permission to stay out till one.

"Let's take a slow stroll back," says Tara.

We walk over North Parade, pausing in the middle of the bridge to look down at the river. It's a clear night and moonlight glints off the water. We look out towards the weir and Pulteney Bridge opposite with its Georgian arches and the quaint little shops across its span.

"Sorry to drag you away," she says, taking deep breaths of the outdoors air as though trying to cleanse her lungs of the nightclub fug.

"Don't be."

"Did you like that guy you were dancing with?"

"Kind of. He looked interesting."

"He's the brother of someone I knew at Kingswood," she says. "He's a stoner. Bit of an oddball. Used to slit his wrists at regular intervals."

"Oh well. I'm probably better off out of it."

We stand in silence for a moment, watching the lights play on the water.

"What about you? Was there anyone there you liked?"

"To be honest, it wasn't really my scene."

Strange. I thought it was. They're her friends, after all.

"Too much of a meat market?"

"Yeah, kind of."

I sense something's wrong tonight. I pick up on her pain.

A pain that has no apparent reason, no logic.

She seems lost in thought, mesmerised by the water, reluctant to move on.

"Don't you just wanna dive in?" she says. "The water draws you to it."

To me, the river Avon looks anything but inviting. Cold, dark and murky. And talk of jumping in scares me.

My dad used to work for the Water Board. I remember him coming home one day and telling mum they'd found a body in the river.

"You wouldn't last long in that water."

"We used to swim in lakes in Canada."

"Bet that was cold."

"It was freezing. But *so* exhilarating. Are there any lakes around here?"

"There's Chew Valley reservoir. They drowned a village to make it, and in the drought in seventy-six you could see the church spire above the water level."

"Maybe one day we could go there and dive down to find the long-lost village," she says.

We stand a moment more, watching the ripples, then eventually she says, "Shall we walk back by the river?"

Normally I wouldn't go down there after dark. Beautiful by day, the river path can be murky at night, and you have to access it via the urine-stenched spiral staircase on North Parade. But tonight the moon casts its thin light over everything and it feels like some weird dawn.

As we emerge onto the path we hear the Abbey clock chime midnight.

"Don't the boats look cosy," I say as we walk past a barge, woodsmoke wafting from its chimneys, an orange glow in the windows.

"Can you hire them?"

"Some of them, yeah. People go on holiday in them."

"Maybe you and I should sail away in one," she says, linking arms with me. "And leave all this behind."

There's a note of melancholy in her voice.

When we get to the Pulteney Bridge steps she hangs back, eyes on the weir, watching the way the moonlight plays on the cascading water.

Now the heat of the club has worn off, I'm shivering in my thin cotton dress. Even the leather jacket doesn't give much warmth. Although it's mild for late October there's a bite in the air. But Tara seems in no hurry to move from this spot. When she speaks, she doesn't look at me. Instead, she keeps her eyes on the water as though transfixed.

"Chrissie, you know on my birthday I said I had something to tell you?"

"In the projection room?" I vaguely remember after an afternoon of intimacies through a haze of gin there being more revelations to come.

"You know I said tonight wasn't my scene?"

"Yeah."

"Thing is, Chrissie, I'm not really into guys."

"You mean?"

"I like girls, Chrissie. I'm a lesbian. Gay. Whatever you want to call it. I'm sexually attracted to women. Not men. There I've said it."

And as she says it, I have a feeling of having been in this exact same spot before, with the moonlight playing on the ripples, a taxi going past on Grand Parade, and a police siren somewhere in the city, listening to those words. As though I've lived this moment many times.

It's like, on some level, I already knew.

"Say something." She looks at me now, and her expression is anxious, almost in pain.

I don't actually know what to say.

"Thank you for telling me."

"You're the first."

"First what?"

"First person I've told. On my birthday, I decided. You were the one I'd confide in."

"Well, that's an honour," I say. "Thank you for trusting me."

"You've no idea what a relief it is to finally tell someone," she says as we head up the steps. "I wanted to get it out of the way before we face my mum."

"She doesn't know then?"

"God, no!"

Outside the flat we look up to see a light in the living room.

"Why does she insist on waiting up?" says Tara.

Grace is lounging on the sofa in cerise-coloured silk pyjamas watching a late-night movie with the lights down low. She switches the TV off as we come in.

"I thought you'd be *much* later," she says, looking at the clock. She sounds disappointed.

"We left early," says Tara.

"Not really our scene," I chip in, and steal a look at Tara. For a second, she looks defenceless, as I've never seen her before. Like the veneer of sophistication has fallen from her face. And that look says so much. It says we share a secret.

"I'd better get the camp bed out for Chrissie," says Grace, heaving herself up from the sofa.

"She can sleep on the couch in my room. It's more comfortable than that old thing," says Tara, but Grace is already rummaging in a cupboard, huffing as she disturbs stacked paraphernalia to unearth a fold-out metal-framed camp bed.

She sets it up in the living room with a sleeping bag and quilt on top, then takes herself off to bed.

Tara stays in the room as I get undressed and climb into the sleeping bag. It smells of fabric conditioner.

"If you lean back on that thing it shoots into the air," she says. I lean back on the camp bed, and it does. We laugh as I lie there with my feet reaching up to the sky like my legs are in traction.

Tara grabs the other end of the bed and pulls me down, giving my foot a squeeze through the sleeping bag.

"You know what I told you earlier," she says, lowering her voice. "I can trust you not to tell anyone?"

"Of course."

"I want to come out in my own time."

She lowers herself to the floor and sits next to the bed, legs pulled up to her chest.

"So nobody knows? Except me?"

She shakes her head. "You're the only person who knows. Although Jason may suspect. I've never explicitly told him. Just like he's never explicitly told me about him. I think I will tell him now, actually."

"How long have you known yourself?"

"Probably forever. But I didn't admit it to myself. I had a massive crush on a girl at school when I was thirteen. Nothing happened. She was three years older than me. I was her fag."

"Her what?"

"Oh. It's a boarding school thing. You're like a servant for a sixth former. You have to do tasks for them. Like carry their books. And make them coffee. She got me to run the shower for her till it ran hot. And sit on the toilet seat to warm it up. In return you got to hang out in their room and escape the dorm. Six-formers had their own rooms. They also pay you. And your status depends on how popular the girl you fag for is."

"Bizarre," I say. "Sounds like something out of *Tom Brown's Schooldays*."

"It was exactly that. It's a centuries-old English public-school tradition. Mostly in boys' schools. We were told it was a privilege that we had fagging, as a lot of girl's schools didn't. But if you ask me, it was a licence to abuse power. Some fags got bullied terribly. But this girl was ok. I got over my crush and we're still friends even now."

She falls silent for a while, and I sense she's reaching into the past. Reliving the longing.

"Anything else you want to ask me, Chrissie?"

There's one thing I'm curious to know.

"So have you ever…?"

"Only once. When I was on holiday with my Dad last summer." She looks distant now, no longer focusing on me. Lost in the memory.

"We were staying on a houseboat in a marina complex in the Great Lakes. This girl was there with her family on another boat. We were just kind of drawn to each other. Then one night we got together. After that I was with her every night till she went home. That's how I knew for sure."

"Was this the girl with the tattoo?"

She nods. "We got mirror images of the same thing."

"And did you keep in touch?"

"No. It wasn't like it was ever gonna be a relationship. We both knew it was just a holiday fling. It was just sex."

As she says that her face changes again. The vulnerable expression replaced by something hard-faced. Almost callous.

Again I feel that gulf of separation that I so often feel in her company, and I don't know what to say.

"Did your dad know?"

"He was in the bar on the complex each night till late. She slept in my cabin and crept out in the morning. Her parents thought it was all very sweet. Like a teenage sleepover. I'm pretty sure Dad never noticed a thing."

She stands up then and yawns, like she's now bored of the topic.

"I'd better hit the sack. We're off to London in the morning."

She's going away with Grace for half term. She says she'll miss me. Wishes I was coming too.

"Why don't you come up for the day? It'd be so much fun hanging out in London with you. I could show you my old haunts."

"I'd love to, but I'm working at the shop, then we're going up to Whitby later in the week."

Plus there's the small matter of the train fare to London.

"Well I might phone you in the week. Would that be ok? And thanks for tonight, Chrissie. You're a true friend. Sweet dreams." She blows me a kiss and leaves the room.

I lie on the camp bed, waiting for sleep, listening to the sounds of the city. The flat is lighter, and noisier, than at home and the old sash windows rattle. I hear the abbey clock strike the hour. I count the chimes. One o'clock, two o'clock, three... Each chime reminds me I've still not slept. Every time a car goes by, headlight beams reach into the room and slant across the ceiling, like a searchlight.

Scenes from the evening play over in my brain. Altered Images' 'Happy Birthday' on repeat, the oddball self-harming Robert Smith look-alike dancing into my orbit, just out of reach, and Tara in the moonlight, trusting me with her secret.

The clock on the sideboard ticks all night as I lie, zipped into the sleeping bag on the narrow bed, too constrained to move. Eventually I drift off, but my sleep is infused with dreams of water. We're on the river bank, Tara and I, and she strips to her underwear and dives in. She disappears beneath the surface, leaving only ripples. I watch the spot where she entered. She emerges, her long limbs covered in water weed. "Come in Chrissie," she reaches out an elegant arm to beckon me in.

There are several of these dreams, each morphing into the next. Some feature the river Avon, others are unknown, foreign, waterside locations. Always with Tara in the water, waving. In the last one, I'm looking down from the bridge, at a figure beneath the water, and as I wait for her to surface, she extends one arm. The arm with the bear tattoo.

I wake to the smell of proper coffee and the sound of Grace coughing.

Chapter Eleven

Diary Entry
Half term 1981
Crush list.

The name at the top is eradicated in thick black marker pen.

October 1981

I'M HOME, AND my mind keeps returning to Tara and what she'd told me. It must have taken a lot for her to confide in me. "You're the first," she'd said. I feel special. Chosen.

I bought two albums in town on my way home and now I'm taping them for Tara.

Tired from last night, I lie on my bed, listening to the music and drifting in and out of sleep.

I keep going over the things she said, especially the bit about the mysterious girl at the holiday marina complex. Sex with a girl. I catch myself going there in my head. What would that be like? I slip into a kind of half dream, imagining myself being around at the time, watching the two of them.

"Chris!" David's voice interrupts my reverie. "Someone here to see you."

Andy's downstairs.

"What you up to later?" he asks.

"Not a lot. Why?"

"There's this band on at Moles," he shows me a clip from the student newspaper. "Wanna come?"

So I find myself out on the town again, this time in an entirely different setting. The band are little known, but – according to Andy – going places. I've not been to Moles before. It's members only, but Ben, who's recently turned eighteen, has managed to get himself a much-coveted membership card and he's got us in. It's a small, dark, basement space. And although it's packed, it feels intimate and not at all threatening. It's full of cool people. The band, on a tiny raised stage, are close enough to touch.

It's such a contrast to the meat-market we were in last night. Tara might actually like it here. I make a mental note to suggest it when she's back from London.

It's just me, Andy and Ben. Everyone else is busy or away for half term. Andy's attentive, buying me drinks. It strikes me how much he's changed, even in the weeks since we started at college. No longer the nerdy, greasy kid I grew up with. I sense girls eyeing him up, looking at the three of us, trying to figure out the dynamic. Wondering if Andy's with me. Is that envy in their eyes?

Ben knows the band's sound man, so at the end of the night we go backstage, to a subterranean cave-like cellar. It's strange to see the people we've just been watching on stage dripping with sweat, makeup running. They're having a sort of after party, downing small glasses of spirits. They give one each to me, Andy, and Ben. We neck them fast. Ben whips out a notebook and starts to interview the lead singer, but Andy puts his arm around me and we leave.

It's just companionship, of course, and drink, that makes me lean into him as we walk to the taxi rank to catch a cab back to West Melcombe. Andy feels safe, and oddly substantial. And even I have to admit, he really is looking good. So in the back of the taxi we snog. All the way home.

"I feel like I've come home," he says as we stand outside my house, wrapped in each other, me pressing myself into the wall in case anyone in the house is watching. "Chrissie I've *always* fancied you. Even when we were six."

Those words break the moment. This is Andy Collins who used to eat slugs from the garden and piss all over the toilet seat.

Even though I'm drunk I know this is a mistake. It's already over before it's begun. As I push him slowly away I feel a great weight of responsibility. I know I have to let him down. I resolve to leave it till tomorrow to phone him. I'll blame the drink.

I don't need to. He phones me the next day. "Can I come round? I can't wait to see you. I've written you a song."

"Andy what happened last night. It... wasn't meant to happen."

There's silence on the other end of the phone.

"I thought..."

"I'm sorry, Andy."

"Is there someone else, Chris?"

"No. Nobody. I just... I don't want to ruin our friendship. You and me. We're just not meant to be."

There's a pause on the line then he says quietly, "Okay. I'll see you around." And the relief I expected to feel doesn't come. Instead, I just feel mean.

DAY THREE OF half term and I'm restless, mooching around the house. I should be studying, but I can't settle.

The phone rings. Hoping it's Tara, fearing it might be Andy, I pick up.

"Fancy coming over this evening?"

"Claire?" She hardly ever calls these days. "Be great. Yeah."

"Simon's away."

Of course. But the prospect of getting my old friend back to myself for a few hours is appealing. Plus, Tara's in London.

Claire's got a bottle of Cinzano in and her mum is out for the evening, so we have the place to ourselves. We put Duran Duran on the stereo and bop around the living room. It's like having the old Claire back.

"So what've you been up to?" she flops on the sofa, reaching for her drink.

I tell her about Andy.

"It was a mistake."

"Poor Andy. He's always had a thing about you."

"So he said."

"You sure you've made the right decision? He's looking really good these days. You're well matched with the music and everything. Couldn't you go on a few dates, just to see how it goes?"

"No Claire. That'd only prolong the agony."

"You heart-breaker!" she says, then reaches out to hug me. "It's great to have you round. We should do this more often."

"Maybe Simon should go away more often then." As soon as I say it I wish I hadn't.

"I'm sorry Chris," she sticks out her lower lip in a mock pout. "I'll make an effort to be more available."

"Okay, I'll hold you to that."

"And Maybe *Tara* could go away more often too."

"What d'you mean?"

"Well she does monopolise you. Mike was saying just the other day how they hardly ever see you now because you're always with Tara."

This is rich coming from Claire, but I bite my lip.

"Honestly Chris, what d'you see in her?"

"She's good company. She's funny. She's intelligent. She's interesting."

"Really?" says Claire. "Can't say I've noticed. I'd say she's a snob. That's how she comes across to everyone else. Like none of us are good enough, except you for some reason."

"She's not like that. Not when you get to know her," I say.

A big part of me wants to tell Claire about Tara. To explain why she's aloof. Maybe telling Claire, in confidence, of course, might help her to understand? But I promised not to breathe a word. I feel isolated and burdened by the knowledge.

Claire swings off the sofa and goes back into the kitchen for the bottle. I take a top-up to keep her company, but I worry when Claire drinks. She has a low tolerance. She can suddenly turn.

I leaf through her records. All New Romantic of course. Depeche Mode, Spandau Ballet, Human League.

"Got anything new?" I say, in an effort to move the conversation away from Tara. But Claire won't let it go.

She takes a deep swig of her drink then says, "Admit it Chrissie, Tara's someone with money and privilege who went to posh private school. She's got a rich model mum and a swanky flat in Bath and she's looking down her nose at the rest of us. Why can't you see that?"

"Oh come on, Claire. Living in that flat with just her mum isn't great, you know. Her mum's very bitter about the divorce and Tara's stuck in the middle. She got shunted off round the world to boarding school from the age of seven. She hasn't exactly had it easy."

"None of us have," says Claire. "Your dad died. My parents split up too, remember. But of course *my* dad lives in Bristol not Vancouver – not quite so glamorous."

The fact neither of us had fathers was one of the things that drew Claire and I together when we were at primary school.

"Claire, let's not argue. Let's just agree to disagree or we'll ruin this rare evening together."

The phone rings. Claire jumps up to answer it, then shuts the door on me as she talks to Simon in the hallway. As I sit there listening to her mock kisses through the door as she tells him how much she's missing him, I feel a sudden gulf of separation from my old friend and a longing for the old days, when neither of us kept secrets from one another.

She's on the phone for what seems an eternity. For the couple that share a tongue, even a separation of a few days must be unbearable.

"He's at his cousin's in Wales," she says when she returns. "Back Thursday."

"Bet you're counting the days."

She splits open a packet of Twiglets and we have more Cinzano to wash them down. Then when that runs out we raid her mother's drinks cabinet and find some vodka.

We're drunk now and I can sense my judgement going. The conversation from earlier niggles. So I go back to it, like an itch that must be scratched.

"D'you just dislike Tara because she's rich? Half the people at college are rich. Your own boyfriend even – Simon went to private school and his dad's a lawyer and they live in a big house, don't they?"

Claire stares at me.

"Yeah… but…"

"But what?"

"Simon's home life lately hasn't been the best."

"Like how?"

"I can't say."

"Why not?"

Emboldened by the vodka, I keep at it.

"What's going on?"

"Promise not to tell anyone?"

"I won't say a word. You know I can keep a secret. We used to tell each other everything."

"It's his Dad. He's…. had some sort of breakdown and he's lost his job."

"Really?"

"Yeah. And he didn't tell them for months, just kept putting on his suit and going out at the normal time like he was going to work. But he came back reeking of booze and falling over furniture. Then he said he was off sick but they wouldn't give him any sick pay. Simon's mum went to his office and they said he no longer worked there."

"Blimey!"

She tells me Simon didn't invite her round for ages when they first got together. He was too embarrassed by his dad's behaviour.

"His dad's off the booze now and on tablets. I do go there, but It's not a very nice atmosphere. Everyone walks on eggshells around him. I dread going round there, Chrissie. I only do it for Simon."

"Oh Claire," I say. "I didn't know any of this."

"But you must absolutely promise never to say anything to anyone. Simon would be mortified. His mum would be. She's totally ashamed of the whole thing."

I promise.

"It's been so hard not being able to talk about it. I don't like having secrets. Especially from you."

I reach out to hug her, and we nestle up next to each other on the sofa like we used to when we were kids.

It's that feeling of homecoming, and the vodka, that makes me say it.

"As it happens, I know something I'm not supposed to tell anyone too. About Tara. There's something that makes her life more difficult. It explains why she finds it hard to open up to people."

Claire's eyes widen. "What's that then?"

I make her swear not to tell a soul. She duly promises. Then, at the end of that alcohol-fuelled evening, I divulge Tara's secret.

As is Carlisle family tradition, we head up to Whitby on the north Yorkshire coast later in the week to stay in Aunty Annie's static caravan. I pass the time reading and playing crazy golf with David, and running with the dog on the beach. These are the things we've always done, but something in me has changed. Something in me is dissatisfied, itching for the week to be over. Something in me is now an observer, looking on at my every move with a discerning, Canadian eye.

I store up things to tell her. Hold hypothetical conversations with her in my head. Rehearse my lines.

And something else in me says *Hang on a minute, what's this all about?*

We don't arrive back till late Sunday. Traffic's murderous, and what should be a six-hour drive stretches to eight. When we finally get home everyone's tired, and I'm not in the right frame of mind to phone Tara although she should be back from London. I'll see her the next day at college anyway as we have double psychology in the afternoon.

Chapter Twelve

Hey Siri, play 'Glad to be Gay' by Tom Robinson

October 1981

I'M EXHAUSTED BUT I struggle to sleep. I wake up early with a strange, slightly giddy sensation running through my body. I go downstairs in my pyjamas. It's back to college for me and school for David. I have to hammer on his door twice to rouse him. He emerges grumpy and dishevelled.

"How come you're so awake this early on a Monday morning?" he asks.

"She's excited about going back to college and seeing all her friends," says Mum, bustling around with bags full of folders.

"You're weird," says David.

Excited about seeing my friends. That must be it. One friend in particular.

After David's been bundled out the door and Mum's left for work, I linger. I have no classes until psychology after lunch, so I can afford to take my time. I'll arrive at college during the lunch break. Before half term, Tara invited me round after college today to have dinner with her. I wonder if she'll remember.

Tara. Is it her I'm dressing for? Is she the reason I try on different outfits, a heap of discarded choices on my bed? I pile on extra makeup to hide the dark bags under my sleepless eyes.

Eventually I'm ready, and make the bus with seconds to spare. It's a two-bus journey to college, the number ten from Melcombe, then a short hop up the hill from town.

On the journey I have time to think. To examine my feelings. Why the nerves? What is this feeling? I realise it's been building all week. Is it just the excitement of forging a new friendship? It's been a long time since I've had that, me and Claire being together since childhood, only letting others in by mutual agreement.

Except for our rare evening together last week, I hardly see Claire now Simon's on the scene. So is Tara my best friend now? Is it immature to even talk about best friends at our age? Can you have a best friend you know so little about? Her week in London is a mystery to me. Then I remember, she told me something she hadn't told anyone else. My best friend has a secret. My best friend is gay. But I also remember it's a secret that I – to my shame and in a moment of weakness – have divulged. But Claire promised not to tell anyone. Claire will keep to her word, won't she?

THERE ARE TWO staircases that lead to the common room, one wide and carpeted, the other poky – presumably designed for the servants when this place was a grand old house. I take the back stairs that lead to our end of the room. Now called 'Electric Avenue' after Ben picked up a street sign from some junkyard and fixed it above the fireplace. Andy and Mike are there. Andy's by the stereo. He has a record poised, ready to play. Mike's sitting on the window sill, looking out. It's like they're waiting for someone.

It's the first time I've seen Andy since our little encounter. Since I dumped him. I hope this isn't going to be awkward.

He spots me as I walk in, and looks away. Maybe it *will* be awkward for a while.

The door at the other end swings open and in walks Tara, Jason by her side. I catch her eye as she scans the crowd, and smile as she starts to walk towards me.

"Now," says Mike, and Andy lowers the stylus. I catch a look between the two of them. There's something ugly in that look.

It takes a second to register what the song is, then I realise. It's 'Glad to be Gay' by Tom Robinson, blasting out of the giant speakers at full volume.

Tara stops in her tracks, shoots me a look that is pure hatred, turns around and walks out. Jason follows.

Mike creases with laughter, Andy smirks.

I try to get to Tara. I push my way through groups of students, bumping into one of the knitting brigade who spills a pile of books all over the common room floor. I apologise and help her clear them up, then continue to look for Tara. I scour the corridors, but there's no sign. I see Jason on his way back into the common room.

"Where's Tara?"

He doesn't answer. He marches across to our end and kills the stereo. The record stops mid-track with an abrupt, distorted sound. Jason approaches Andy.

"Wanker," he says and walks out.

I scuttle after him. "Jason, where's Tara?"

"She's gone home. She's very upset."

"I didn't know they were going to play that."

He looks at me now, scrutinises my face, and says: "She said you were the only one who knew."

"I only told Claire," I say. "Where the fucking hell is Claire?"

Neither Claire nor Simon are anywhere in sight.

Jason shrugs. "It only takes one person." He turns away. I watch him stride down the corridor. Elegant. Composed. I feel like an immature kid compared to him.

I vow to make amends. Right now.

"Can you tell Imogen I have to skip psychology?" I say to a classmate in the corridor.

"You as well? Tara's bunked off too."

Chapter Thirteen

I used to have one of my waking dreams around that time. I was flying above the common room and along the corridors at college. Looking for Tara. I tried to find her but there were always people and obstacles in the way. And in this dream – or whatever it was – I always ended up on the bridge, watching.

I STAND ON the kerb outside Tara's flat, looking up. Both windows that front onto the street are open at the bottom. Tara's curtain's half shut, billowing out a little in the breeze. So she's in. I press the buzzer. No answer. I press it again. Still no response. Hmm, what to do? I perch on the wall. I contemplate shouting or throwing something up at her window. I doubt I can aim that high. I stand poised by the buzzer, about to try again, when I hear a slam. I look up. Tara's window's now shut.

Her mother, obviously, is out. Actually, I remember Tara saying Grace would be out, and inviting me round today after college. So I have a right to be here. I'm invited. I ring the buzzer repeatedly in short, sharp bursts.

I hear the click of the intercom receiver and I lean towards the speaker. "Tara, it's me." All I get is the white noise of disconnection. But she doesn't hang up. She's still there. "Tara, can you let me in? Please let me in."

Silence, but the connection is still open.

"I saw what happened at college. Are you ok?"

I have to raise my voice to be heard, but I feel self-conscious, aware of the glances of passersby.

Tara's voice, coming through the intercom, sounds strangled. "You bitch," she says. "How could you?"

"I know what you're thinking but it wasn't how it seemed. I knew nothing about it. Please let me in and I can explain."

She says nothing. There's a pause, then the click of the catch being released.

I walk up the stairs. She isn't waiting for me on the landing as she usually is, but the flat door is on the latch. I knock lightly. Call "hello" and, when there's no answer, push the door open and walk in.

Tara sits on the sofa, pushed up against the arm rest, hugging her knees, eyes fixed on the TV which is showing some old black and white film. She's wearing a faded pair of jeans and a baggy washed-out pale pink sweatshirt with a picture of a bear and 'I ♥ Vancouver' on it.

She doesn't look round or acknowledge my presence, she just stares at the screen.

"*Please* speak to me." I stand in front of her, blocking her view of the TV. She jerks her head, reaches for the remote and turns the volume up, placing the remote back on the sofa arm.

I grab it and mute the sound.

She looks at me then, her eyes narrow and, I notice, red. "Give that back!"

"I will in a minute, but I want to talk to you first."

"Why are you here?"

"You invited me. Don't you remember?"

"Jeez," she says. "That was before."

"Before what?"

She stands up now, towering over me.

"Before you and your *mates* humiliated me in front of the whole fucking common room."

I open my mouth to protest. "It was nothing to do with me. I wasn't in on it!"

"*You* were the only person who knew, Chrissie. It could only have come from you."

"I…"

"Don't deny it."

"I'm not denying it. I really am sorry."

"I trusted you."

"I know."

"And you betrayed that by telling the whole world I'm gay. I'd never told *anyone*, Chrissie."

"I only told Claire."

"Christ!" she says, flopping down on the sofa again, spreading one leg out, the other one bent up towards her chest.

"You tell Claire. That's equivalent to telling the whole fucking universe. That's like putting a big fat poster on the college noticeboard."

I sit down on the other end of the sofa, leaning forward.

"Please listen."

"I'm listening, but this better be good."

"Claire and I used to be best mates, back at Melcombe. Before we came here. Before she met Simon."

"So?" she shrugs.

"I thought we'd drifted apart. I hardly ever get to see her.

Anyway. I went round there at half term when you were away. We had some vodka. And it was like old times, sort of. And she said she was jealous. Of me and you – of our friendship. She said she thought I'd outgrown her. She thinks you're perfect. Privileged. I was *defending* you."

Tara arches her eyebrows.

"She said you'd never had to struggle for anything with your rich model mum and your posh flat in Bath and your private education and your expensive clothes. And I got angry. Told her your mum isn't exactly a model mum and you had stuff to deal with too.

"She obviously didn't believe me, and *that's* when I told her."

I watch Tara's face as this information sinks in.

"I made her promise. I trusted her. Now I know I shouldn't have. She must have told Simon. Then Simon would've told someone else and that's how it got out."

She looks at me then and I sense I'm finally getting through to her.

"It was as much a shock to me as it was to you when they played that record. I tried to find you. I came straight round here." I said. "I'm really, really sorry."

The phone rings. Tara gets up to answer it. She turns her back to me and stretches the receiver as far away from me as possible.

"Just about. Chrissie's here. Yeah." She looks round at me then. "She's apologised. I haven't decided… Thanks for phoning. Bye, sweetie."

"Jason?" I say.

She nods.

"When did you tell Jason – about you being gay?"

"I met up with him last night, after we got back from

London. I said I'd already told you and that you two were the only ones who knew. He said he already suspected. And we talked about him being gay too. We had a nice long chat."

"He's a good friend."

"At times like this, a girl needs friends." She looks at me, eyes narrowed again.

"I've said I'm sorry." I say again. "And I want to still be your friend, if you'll have me. We can get through this together."

I look at the silent screen. The movie's now cut to credits.

"I've made you miss your film. What was it anyway?"

"I wasn't really watching. Couldn't concentrate. Fancy a drink?"

"Yes please."

I follow Tara into the kitchen. She surveys the cupboards. "Thank God, we have gin."

I watch as she mixes us both a gin and tonic, using tongs to put the ice in, giving each drink a brief stir, then placing the glass in my hand. Even in her distress, and in her scruffs, she's a picture of composure and elegance.

I lift my glass. She hesitates a moment then clinks glasses. "To friendship?" I say.

"Maybe."

"To second chances?"

She smiles despite herself. "Maybe," she says and sashays back into the living room.

"Wanna hear some music?" I reach into my bag and pull out the cassette I recorded for her. I move over to the stereo and start the tape.

"Who's this?"

"Joy Division. Their new album. D'you like it?"

"So far."

"So what did Jason say?"

"He just phoned to check I was ok. He told Andy what he thought of him, apparently. Called him a wanker."

I laugh. "He did! I saw him do it. Andy didn't know what to say!"

"He fronted up to him even though all the others were in there. Now *that's* what true friendship is."

I bristle. Wishing I'd had the guts to do the same.

"At least. At least it's out there now Tara. It might actually be a good thing."

She rounds on me. "Bullshit, Chrissie. You really have no fucking idea. I wanted to come out when I chose to, on my own terms, not have it forced on me."

We sit listening to the music. We drink our gin. She tops us up.

I sense we're on the edge of something pivotal. As the gin takes hold, I feel a sweet feeling of something give within me. And underneath, a warning voice. *You're making a choice here.* It tells me. *Are you sure you want to go this way?* I ignore the voice. Friendship is paramount.

Tara likes the music. The sparse sound and style seems fitting. Misery music to match her mood. I've got something right, at least.

"What are you going to do tomorrow?" I ask.

"What d'you mean?"

"I mean the sooner you go back to college the easier it'll be."

"I'm never setting foot in that place again."

"Tara you have to. If you don't – they've won."

"You mean your mates?"

"Andy can be a twat. Granted. But he didn't really mean it. You need to walk in there, with your head held high, and show everyone that you're not gonna let idiots like him affect you. And I'll be right by your side," I say, adding to myself, *and this time I won't let you down.*

"I SHOULD GO," I say, after my third gin and tonic.

"You're supposed to be here for dinner, remember. I invited you."

Grace has left a lasagna in the fridge. So we eat, and sober up a bit. And the evening becomes almost normal. But all the while I have a nagging feeling that I ought to get away. That the longer I stay, the deeper I'll get sucked in. But still, I stay.

We move back into the living room and listen to the other side of the tape. It's 10 pm. Definitely time to go. The last bus back to West Melcombe's in fifteen minutes.

"Chrissie, don't go," she says, suddenly looking vulnerable again, her eyes glistening. "Stay here. Mum's away. I just…"

"What is it?"

"I just don't wanna be on my own tonight. You can sleep in Mum's bed."

"Ok then. I'll just phone home and let them know."

David answers the phone so the conversation is over in three grunts. I'm relieved I don't have to speak to Mum. Mum has rules about staying out on a school night. Although I've stayed at Tara's before, it's always been at weekends, and I have a nagging feeling that the rumours about Tara now doubtless floating around Stoke College might have already reached further afield.

"We're all out of gin," says Tara. "Want to go to the pub?"

We make it to the one round the corner in time to catch

last orders. I'm conscious of two men at the bar eyeing us up as we walk in. I'm now used to the Tara effect. Even now, in washed-out jeans and shapeless sweatshirt, she turns heads.

"All right girls?" They look like they've been in here all evening.

"Wanna have a drink with me and my mate?"

Tara looks them up and down, then, quick as a flash, says, "Sorry not interested. I'm a lesbian." She picks up our drinks and walks away.

We sit at a table in the corner, convulsed with laughter.

"Wow!" I say. "You should've seen his face."

She beams. "Might as well tell the world! Actually, you've no idea how liberating this is!" We clink glasses, giggling. The men at the bar keep glancing over at us. Getting closer to hear each other above the din, I get that feeling I only get with Tara. Bewitched. Like we're in a bubble with no outside world. I want nothing better than to go back to hers and talk all through the night. We sink our drinks quickly.

When we get back to the flat we're still giggling.

"That bloke's face."

"I'm gonna use that line to get rid of people from now on!" she says. "Shame about the gin, I've got a drinking head on now. Let's see what Ma Grace has got squirrelled away."

We find vermouth. We drain what's left in the bottle. We sit closer now on the sofa.

"Can I tell you something, Chrissie?"

Draw me in, Tara. Into your world.

"Guess what I thought the first time I saw you?"

"No idea."

"I spotted you that first day walking across the courtyard. Your friends were hanging out the window waving at you. Then I saw you again at the induction in the theatre, sitting with Claire and the others. I thought you were incredibly good looking. I could hardly take my eyes off you."

"Most people notice Claire, not me."

"She's just conventionally pretty. Like any magazine cover girl. You were different. Interesting looking. You wore quirky clothes. And I noticed how popular you were – always surrounded by people. Then you had your hair cut and looked even better. I used to watch how you'd got your hair. What you were wearing. Your style. I just knew I wanted to know you."

I tell her I saw her and Jason approaching the building on that first day, elegant and poised. I had no idea she even noticed I existed.

Now it happens. We look at each other and move in closer, the warning voice in my head now silenced. I'm doing this. This is what I want. We kiss. And it's … *exquisite*. We come up for air.

"Wow," I say.

"Are you okay?"

"Yes. I've never kissed a girl before. I like it." So we kiss some more.

We fall into Tara's bed, curl up together, then move apart. The night has a dream-like quality. I watch her sleep. Even in sleep, she's beautiful. She wears a nightshirt. I sleep in the shirt I've worn all day.

Sometime in the night we find each other. This time, it moves on from kissing. She touches my breasts. Gently, expertly. My whole body tingles. We connect without words. She kisses my stomach, and moves lower, hands stroking my thighs, parting my legs. She kisses me till I come.

All that time, we haven't said a word. She joins me on the pillow, turns my face to hers. "Are you ok with that?" she asks.

"No-one has ever made me feel like that."

I ask her if she wants anything. I feel nervous now, out of my depth. I don't know what to do. But she says no, just hold me, and we fall asleep again.

Chapter Fourteen

I WAKE TO sobriety and the sound of the dustbin men emptying the bins behind the flats. They're loud and jarring. The orange dial on the clock radio by Tara's bed says seven am and the chime of the abbey bell eats into my brain. It's only just light. I look at Tara, still sleeping. Was last night a dream?

My stomach lurches as vermouth-tinged acid rises in my throat. I sit up and swallow it down.

I have to get home, to get changed before college. I swing my legs onto the edge of the bed.

"Don't go," she says, eyes now open. "Stay with me, Chrissie. The moment you go, you'll break the spell."

She makes me coffee and brings it to me in bed. We talk. We laugh. And everything feels unreal.

"I want to walk into college today with you by my side," she says. Then she kisses me again, and I know I'm lost.

My shirt's crumpled, so Tara picks out a top from her collection for me to wear. The arms are too long. I roll them up. It smells of her.

She heats up croissants in the microwave oven, and we have them with jam, and more coffee.

I'm in Grace's chair, going through my bag, looking for my kohl eyeliner; my essential make-up. I can't leave the house without it. Tara looks on as I unpack the contents. She laughs as I pull out my Walkman, wires all tangled up with a comb.

"You have an afro comb, but you don't have afro hair," she observes.

"True."

"You have an inhaler."

"I have mild asthma."

"You have cigarette-making materials," as I unearth rolling papers and tobacco.

It occurs to me I've never smoked around Tara.

"I smoke occasionally, usually when I'm drinking."

"Aren't those two things incompatible?"

"Smoking and drinking?"

"Your mild asthma and your occasional smoking habit."

"I normally only smoke at gigs."

Not like Grace and her twenty-a-day habit.

"Roll one."

"You want me to have a cigarette now?"

"Roll it for later"

She watches as I flatten out the rolling paper, pinch the tobacco with my fingers, distribute it evenly in a line along the centre of the paper, then roll a perfect, thin, cylinder. It's a skill I'm proud of.

"Put it in your mouth."

She holds Grace's lighter to the end, I draw on the cigarette. I blow a mouthful of smoke out in her face. She coughs and recoils.

"That's supposed to be sexy," I say.

"It isn't."

She takes the cigarette out of my hand. I think she's going to try it, but she extinguishes it in Grace's ashtray, then leans in to kiss my smoke-filled mouth.

"Now that *is* sexy."

I smoke the rest of it on the way to the bus stop.

"You shouldn't smoke though, Chrissie," she says.

"Even though it's sexy?"

"It isn't really. Look at Grace."

"Ok, boss," I smile up at her. The look she gives me sends a tingling sensation up and down my spine.

At the bus stop, there are people waiting. As the bus approaches, Tara briefly brushes the inside of my palm with her fingers. My skin tingles. We sit upstairs, at the back. We hold hands under the seat where nobody can see. I feel the thrill of secrecy.

Chapter Fifteen

"**Y**OU READY FOR this?" Tara says, as we approach Stoke College. *Ready for what?* I'm not even sure what she means. My stomach twists as – for a second – I imagine her grabbing my hand in front of everyone and declaring us lovers. I'll *never* be ready for that.

In the event, walking into the common room is an anti-climax. We are, of course, a respectable distance apart, and hardly anyone's here. The knitting brigade are in their corner, oblivious. Ben sits alone at our end, headphones on, equally oblivious. He looks up and nods as I approach, makes as if to say something, then clocks Tara. Tara heads for the other end of the room, but I call her back.

"Sit here," I say, indicating "our" seats. I feel strong now. Bring it on.

The others arrive all at once, in a rush. I look up as Andy, Ian and Mike walk in, closely followed by Claire-and-Simon. The shock on their faces is palpable. Claire looks from me to Tara, then down at the floor, her face reddening.

Andy lumbers over to the record player. It's been left with the lid up and a LP on the turntable. I wonder if it's the Tom Robinson one from yesterday. He glances at the record, starts to lift the arm across to play it, then thinks better of it. Instead, he slumps in one of the sofas and stares out of the window. The others sit down near him, not speaking.

And it occurs to me, they feel more awkward than we do.

They don't know, of course, about me and Tara. They only know about Tara. As far as they're concerned, I'm just standing by my mate.

Claire and Simon sit together at the table, talking in a huddle. At one point, Claire looks over and catches my eye. I fix her with a glare. She blushes again and looks away.

Ben comes over to me then, to show me an article in the NME, and everything becomes almost normal.

Almost.

The bell sounds. We all disperse to our classes. I walk out alongside Tara and say, "Well done."

In Maths, Andy and I pointedly ignore each other, and afterwards, as I walk past the labs, I see Claire perched at her bench, lab-coat and protective goggles on. I glare at her through the glass.

She sees me, jumps down from the bench, and runs after me.

"Chrissie, please, can we talk?"

"Nothing to say to you."

She notices the shirt I'm wearing. "New top?"

"It's Tara's."

She nods.

"Please. I only told Simon."

"*Only!* You promised not to tell a soul. You broke that promise and exposed my friend to humiliation in front of everyone. You proud of that?"

"Chris, please!"

"Aren't you in the middle of a chemistry lesson? You'd

better get back or your experiment might blow up," I say, putting my Walkman headphones on and walking off.

I feel a weird kind of high all morning. Spacey from the booze and giddy from the night. Every so often, remembering. No-one has ever touched me like she did. Ever.

No psychology today, so we're apart, but I see her and Jason walking across the courtyard on their way to their art history lesson. I watch with wonder. This beautiful creature – desired wherever she goes – is somehow mine. The day has an unreal feel. She said she would see me at lunchtime.

I wait in the common room for her to arrive, butterflies doing somersaults in my stomach. She walks in with Jason and catches my eye. I feel a rush of something. Some chemical sensation shooting up through my spine as our eyes lock. She and Jason exchange glances, he looks at me and nods. It's a look of knowing. Jason peels off and Tara approaches.

"Hi."

"Hi Tara." Even saying her name has a different quality to it now.

"You coming to lunch?"

I know we're not acting normally, but I can't remember what normal is. I gather my books and join her. We get to the canteen early and find a table on our own in a corner.

I see Claire come in, she stands with her tray scanning the tables and I sense her looking at me, but I blank her and she goes to sit somewhere else.

Karl Powell strides over with Imogen. "Girls, mind if we join you?"

I'm with the grownups now.

Karl eats his pie and meagre serving of chips, then leaves,

but Imogen tries to engage us in conversation. When she eventually goes, Tara says: "How long before the news about me reaches the tutors? If Grace gets even a whiff of it, I'm in deep shit. And if Karl knows, it won't be long before it reaches her."

Evidently Karl and Grace have recently rekindled their liaison.

"Would Grace mind, seriously?"

"For sure she would. She may make out she's a modern woman but she actually hates gays."

"Why?"

"Prejudice runs deep. Plus half those boho artists she dated in London before she met Dad turned out to be gay. Surprise, surprise."

"Well we have to make sure it doesn't reach the teachers," I say. "But how?"

"Create a counter story? Something about your little friend Claire that will discredit her? She's jealous of our friendship and she made it up?"

I catch Claire's eye as she leaves the dining room.

"I can try and persuade her to say she got it wrong." I say. "Make it a condition of our friendship. We've been friends since we were eight."

As we leave, Tara looks at me and says "Wish there was somewhere we could go."

"What about the projection room?"

"We'll have to get the key off Jason."

We spend the rest of break trying to find him, only to be told he's gone home.

"How about we go home too?" says Tara.

"Can't. I've got double French."

"Damn," she tosses her hair behind her head. "Come

back for a coffee after?"

"I really should get back to mine," I say. "I haven't been home since yesterday."

She pauses. "Okay. But I'll walk you to the bus stop."

She's waiting for me when I come out of French. I feel that same mix of nerves and excitement when I see her in the corridor.

We can't kiss, there are too many people around, but she hugs me as the bus approaches and whispers in my ear, "God, I want you."

She phones that evening and I sit on the stairs trying not to be heard.

"You don't regret last night?" she says.

"No. No way. I never felt like that with anyone."

Chapter Sixteen

A flyer for Moles club with a list of fixtures. Underlined and highlighted is a band called The Yin Yang Twins

Hey Siri, play Yin Yang Twins – but Siri says "I couldn't find that in your library or in Apple Music."

October 1981

A ND SO IT begins. Clandestine meetings. Sneaking away to the projection room. Stealing a kiss behind the library stairs. Discovering deserted alleyways in Bath I'd walked past so many times but never ventured down. Seeking out places where we can be alone.

We go back to the pub around the corner from Tara's flat, the place where she declared her sexuality to the two men at the bar. It has a cosy snug at the far end which we often have to ourselves. A small, intimate space where we can get close in the shadows and nobody notices. We make this place our own. It becomes our refuge.

There's a Canadian rock band with an all-female lineup coming to Moles. I tell Tara and she's interested. Ben gets us tickets and brings us in as guests.

The music is ethereal and slightly psychedelic. It's got a dreamy sort of energy which is unlike anything I've heard before. I'm transfixed by the bassist. While the singer and lead guitarist strut around on stage, she remains cool and expressionless, hiding behind her thick dark fringe. At times she even plays with her back to the audience.

After the gig, Ben asks to interview the band and Tara and I tag along. We go to an upper room, not the dank backstage cellar where we went before. As Ben and Tara talk to the singer and other band members, I pluck up courage to speak to the bass player. I tell her I like their music. I ask how long they've been together. She says three of her bandmates are sisters. They all grew up in the same town in northern Canada. This is their first overseas tour. She has an accent like Tara's, except her speech is faster and less languid. She doesn't smile, and there's an intensity about her that I find magnetic. It's the first time – other than Tara – that I've fancied a girl.

On the way back to the flat, Tara raves about Moles. She loves the place, so she applies for membership. To become a member, you have to be interviewed by the club owner and he's apparently very discerning. Ben and I brief her on what to say. She mentions world music, forks out the five pound membership fee, and she's in.

After this, Tara and I head there sometimes of an evening after the pub shuts. We mostly hang out in the upstairs room, where it's quieter but you can still hear the music. Apart from Ben – who practically lives in Moles these days – we're unlikely to meet anyone from college. We like the vibe. It's a place where we can relax and – almost – be ourselves.

We keep our relationship secret. To go public would be

social suicide at college. We don't want any rumours reaching either of our mums.

We work on our counter-story. I go to see Claire. "There's one thing you can do to save our friendship."

"What's that then?"

"Kill the story about Tara being gay."

"How? It's out now?"

"Say you made it up. You were jealous of my friendship with Tara. Or just say you got it wrong. Say Tara's with Jason – everyone thinks so anyway."

Claire plays along. Tells everyone she was misled.

Jason plays his part with aplomb. Turning up to collect Tara from the common room, holding her hand as they walk out together.

The cover works both ways, as a lot of people suspect – rightly – that Jason is gay. In fact, some of those not in the know thought the record stunt was aimed at him, not Tara.

"Look at this," says Mike.

We watch from the window as Jason kisses Tara in full view. It's a proper, full-blown kiss, and they both look like they mean it. I feel more than a twinge of jealousy. Even though I know it's all for show.

"Thought she was meant to be batting for the other side?"

I laugh.

"Have you ever seen a lesbian who looks like Tara?"

I watch doubt creep into their faces. I'm playing to their own prejudices, of course. In their minds lesbians are big butch women who look like Mum's friend, Mo, not fuckable blonde beauties like Tara.

Andy frowns. "How come she walked out when we played Glad to be Gay?"

I glare at him. "Did you put that on to embarrass her because you thought she was gay?" I laugh. "Pathetic. Her walking out probably had nothing whatsoever to do with you."

"And why did the poof with the quiff call me a wanker?"

I shrug. "Because you are?"

Andy blushes and the others laugh.

"The lesbian thing's just a line she uses to get rid of men. She gets blokes coming onto her constantly."

I watch their faces compute, then I walk off, chuckling.

Our strategy works, up to a point. Andy and Mike may not be convinced, but we've spread sufficient doubt to dilute or at least confuse the story, or push it back underground, for the moment. Although we both know that once the seed of a rumour is planted, it's lodged forever in the collective unconscious, dormant, to resurface later.

Chapter Seventeen

A photo of the two of us taken on a decent camera. Tara stunning in a long black coat and flame-red scarf. I'm in my leather jacket and a little green polka-dot dress and a pair of chunky boots I don't remember owning. We look bright, and mischievous. We have our arms wrapped around each other and we're smiling for the camera.

November 1981

S ATURDAY. TIRED AND dusty after a day at the bookshop, I head to Tara's.

"I've run you a bath," she says.

The bath at the flat is deep and old fashioned, the enamel sides cold to the touch. She's put candles on the window sill and round the bath. The bathroom is spacious, like a proper room. There's even a chair beside the bath. A chair with arms and a wicker back. She sits in it as I undress, dropping my clothes to the floor. She picks them up and folds them. I have a change of clothes in my bag for going out later.

I suddenly feel self-conscious, lying naked in the bath with Tara looking on.

"You're not shy about your body are you, Chrissie?"

I tell her I'm not used to anyone in the bathroom with me.

She laughs. "I forget you never went to boarding school. When I was at prep school you'd be having a bath while everyone else milled around the bathroom, brushing their teeth, pissing, pooing. Hard for me as an only child but you just got used to it."

She turns off the light. I feel less awkward now in candlelight.

I lie, stretched out, strains of Neil Young coming in from the living room.

"That looks so inviting," she says.

"Why not get in too? There's loads of room."

"I already had one earlier," she says, but she kneels by the bath, leans in and washes me, soap smooth on my skin, rough flannel tingly.

"I can't get over how good it feels when you touch me," I say.

"Think about it, Chrissie," she says. "It takes a woman to know what a woman wants."

She splashes me then, playfully.

"Ever had a jacuzzi?"

I don't know what one is.

"They have them in hotels in the States. There are jets of water bubbling up all over the place, it's the most sensual feeling."

As she says this the music stops abruptly.

"Shit my mum's here." She leaps up. "Stay there. I'll say I just brought you a drink."

So I lie in the now cooling water, as Tara goes to greet her mother.

"You're all flushed." Everything Grace says sounds accusing. "Have you got a man here?"

"No mum, sorry to disappoint. Chrissie's here though. She's in the bath. We're going out later."

Afterwards, in Tara's bedroom, we giggle.

I SLEEP AT hers again. This time, her mother is in, so we have to be discreet, going to our separate sleeping spaces until we hear Grace snore, then creeping around in the night to be together. The irony is, Tara says, if I was a guy we wouldn't have to sneak around like this. Grace prides herself on being an open-minded, modern woman. She'd have let Tara sleep with a boyfriend.

We wake to a crisp, bright morning and a landscape white with frost.

"Let's go for a walk to the park," says Tara, unhooking an expensive looking camera from the coat hooks in the hall.

The leaves on the ground are frozen rigid and brittle beneath our feet. I love days like this. Everything looks magnificent in the autumn light as we head up through the city.

"Look, Chrissie," she points at a street sign up above that says "Gay Street."

"We could get someone to take a photo of the two of us under the sign."

We ask a passing couple. They oblige.

"Can you take a wide angle one that shows the whole building?" Tara asks them. Little do they know, it's the sign we want in the shot.

"Fall in England is so beautiful," Tara says, as we make our way up through the Circus. "I envy you growing up in this city."

I feel a swell of pride, looking up at the grand buildings, the ring of majestic horse chestnuts. The outline of the trees intricate and skeletal, the autumn reds vivid against the clear blue. The ground crisp with freshly fallen leaves.

"I envy you with your jet-set childhood," I say.

"It wasn't glamorous, believe me," she says. "A couple years here, a couple there. Different climates. Different countries. Different schools. Having to adjust each time to fit in. That's why I'm so mixed up."

She's joking of course. Tara's the most together person I know.

"You're not mixed up. You know who you are."

"It's all a front, Chrissie."

We head up towards the Royal Crescent, that sweep of elegant regency houses which features on all the postcards.

"Doesn't Karl Powell live in one of these?"

She nods. "It's one of those at the end. It's the one with a door-knocker shaped like a treble clef."

"I've never been inside one."

"I'll blag you an invite to one of his soirees."

We walk in silence for a bit. Then she says, apropos of nothing, "They used to call me the Ice Queen."

"Who?"

"Boys, back in Canada. They said I was frigid."

"Because you didn't fancy them. Pathetic!"

I can see it though. That's how she first appeared to me. Cold and aloof. It's why people say she's a snob.

We arrive at Victoria Park. It's too cold to sit on a bench. There are a few people around, mostly older people walking dogs or families out for a stroll. But it's a big park. Easy to lose people. We turn off down a narrow, tree-lined walkway, secluded from the main paths. She reaches for my hand. We stop. She turns to face me, wraps her long scarf round both of us and pulls me towards her. We kiss on the lips. Outside, in broad daylight.

Too late, we hear the whirr of wheels, as three youths on bikes speed past. I try to pull away, but Tara holds me close, her lips locked on mine.

The boys stop just past us. I feel them staring. Then the insults start to fly. "Lezzies!"

"'Look at this pair of dykes."

We pull apart. One of the boys lets his bike slide to the ground. "What's up, can't get any cock?" He clutches his crotch and thrusts as the others laugh.

"Fuck off, squirt," Tara calls after them. They ride off, laughing.

But the moment is broken.

"Want to carry on walking?" I look at her but she shakes her head, her face stony. The beautiful morning turned ugly.

"I have a dream," she says as we walk back, no longer touching, "That one day people like us can be open about who we are. That in some enlightened future it will all be okay."

People like us?

"Chrissie, I want you to know, whenever you're ready to come out, I'm right by your side."

And I say nothing. Come out as what? What am I?

Chapter Eighteen

From my half-century vantage point, I ask myself, are we now in that enlightened age? My daughter is attending a same-sex marriage via Zoom. Hard for her generation to appreciate the strength of taboo that once existed.

B ONFIRE NIGHT SEES the annual gathering at West Melcombe. Gone is the clear weather. Now it's damp, and the fog of fire hangs in the air. We head up to the fireworks up on the rec. Tara, David, and me. Aunty Meg's here, with Nan in her wheelchair. Mum will join us later. It's a regular old family gathering.

"Ooh look, a beer tent," says Tara. "Do you guys fancy a drink?"

"David's not old enough," I say.

David scowls. "Neither are you!"

"But *I* look eighteen. I'll get served."

"Not with old Hoppo on the bar." He means Bertie Hopkinson, the village butcher, who's a special constable in his spare time and – for the purposes of this event – a temporary barman. The trouble with West Melcombe is that everyone knows who everyone else is, *and* how old you are.

"I'll get us drinks," says Tara. "I'm eighteen and I can prove it."

She returns with three pints of very rough cider. It tastes like vinegar.

"Let's have a drinking race!" says Tara. "C'mon David, down in one!"

Tara gets my little brother drunk. And I have to admit it's hilarious to watch. By the time the fireworks start he can barely stand up. Somerset farm cider should carry a health warning.

We see Claire-and-Simon briefly, faces glowing in the light cast by the bonfire, carrying sparklers, but they don't hang around with us. There's no sign of Andy or any of the other West Melcombers from college.

Tara and I stand back a little from the rest, obscured in shadows, and she wraps her scarf around both of us again and tickles the inside of my palm. We link arms and whoop as the rockets soar into the sky. She's at her playful best tonight.

After the fireworks we leave David with two of his friends, and head back to the bar, which has a late licence till midnight. The bar is in a marquee with hay bales for seats. We're three deep into the queue when I hear a voice from the corner.

"Christine Carlisle, well I never."

I turn to see Aunty Nessa in the corner swigging Guinness with a very old man from the village. I nudge Tara. "That's my psychic aunty I told you about."

Tara turns to look at Nessa. "Wow. She looks like something out of a Thomas Hardy novel."

Nessa is wearing ankle-length voluminous skirts with calf-length lace-up boots, a fitted bodice jacket and her long once-red hair done up in a bun.

"I'm gonna get her to do the keys thing."

We go to join Nessa. We present her with Tara's keys and pretend we've found them on the rec.

"Can you do your thing with the keys?"

Nessa shakes her head. "I haven't done that for years. I don't know if I still have the gift."

"Go on, Aunty Nessa, I've been telling Tara about your special powers."

"You might help us reunite these keys with their owner," says Tara.

"Better to get an announcement made on the loud hailer," she says, but she reaches for the keys, shuts her eyes, cups them in her hand, and runs her fingers over them, testing their weight.

She passes the keys quickly from hand to hand.

"They're heavy," she says. "And hot. Almost too hot to handle. Too heavy to hold."

I look at Tara.

"Can you tell us anything about the owner, Nessa?"

"I can't see them properly. There's something in the way. Smoke maybe. Or mist rising from water. The shape is shadowy. That happens sometimes. This person is an enigma. But I sense some kind of danger."

She opens her eyes then and hands the keys back to Tara.

The ancient next to her is rising, unsteadily, to his feet. Nessa helps him up and lets him lean on her as they start to walk towards the exit of the tent. As they leave, she turns and calls to us.

"Those keys lie."

"That's astute,' says Tara as we watch Nessa leave. "She *knows* they're mine. She knows we tricked her."

Chapter Nineteen

Hey Siri, play 'Walk on the Wild Side' by Lou Reid

November 1981

TARA PERSUADES ME to miss maths so we can take the afternoon off and head back to West Melcombe. She says she wants to spend more time with me in my natural environment.

"Sounds like a nature programme on TV." I say. "Like I'm a wild animal."

Tara laughs. "We're here to observe the mating habits of the lesser spotted Christine Carlise." She tickles me on the back seat of the bus.

"I also wanna sleep with you in your own bed in the room you grew up in," she whispers.

I feel a surge of excitement, mixed with fear.

When we get home she mooches around the house, getting a look in all the rooms, commenting on the décor, the seventies style furniture, the books on the shelves, even the architecture. Things I'd never given a second thought to living in a 1930s semi all my life.

"This house has a shower!" she says. "Let's take a shower together."

The shower is over the bath, the jet is uneven and it only has two settings. "It's an English excuse for a shower," she says. Compared to the sort of showers she's used to, it lacks power. But it'll do.

It feels daring, showering together in our bathroom at West Melcombe. Even though Mum's at work all day and David's at school.

Our shower is confined within an oblong ring of metal at one end of the bath, shielded by a flimsy, plastic shower curtain. There's barely room for the two of us, and the wet plastic clings to our bodies. Tara rubs soap on me, lathering it over my skin. Her every touch is sensual. She unhooks the shower head, adjusts it to a single jet, and directs it at my body, aiming the flow between my legs, using it to massage me as I moan. Expertly, she makes me come, right there in the shower.

We've trailed a speaker in from my stereo and placed it on the bathroom floor where it's playing Lou Reid, loud. It's only when we turn the shower off and step out of the bath that I hear a door shut somewhere in the house.

"Someone's home."

This wasn't supposed to happen.

Tara giggles as she dries me. I pull my clothes on and emerge first, checking the coast is clear. I see David's door is slightly open.

"That you, David?"

"You finally out the bathroom? I'm bursting."

"Tara's in there now," I hold out my hand to stop him entering. He reddens at the mention of her name.

"How come you're home from school anyway?"

"Could say the same about you."

"I'm in sixth form college, David. We have free periods,

study periods, y'know."

"Mrs Freeman's ill again."

"You're still supposed to stay at school."

He shrugs. "How long's Tara gonna be? Don't they have showers in her place in Bath?"

"No. Only a bath in Bath."

The joke is lost on him, or he chooses to ignore it.

Tara emerges then, wearing my towelling robe, clutching her clothes, pink bra and panties clearly visible.

"Sorry, David, it's all yours now!" she says. David turns puce.

The bathroom is steamed up. I wonder how much he's noticed. Better David than Mum though.

I say as much to Tara later, but to my surprise she rounds on me.

"You're ashamed of me," she says.

"No way!"

"Then why the ultra-caution every place we go?"

Strange, I thought we were *both* being cautious. I thought the last thing we wanted was for anyone to find out. Especially Grace.

"You have to admit it's difficult. It's not like it's a normal relationship."

Immediately I regret my choice of words.

She rolls her eyes. "So only straight is normal?"

"I didn't mean it. That came out wrong. This is nineteen eighty-one. It's ok to be gay."

"Yeah, right," she says. "Tell that to your neanderthal small-town mates."

I compare it to when I started seeing Matt Harris back at Melcombe Comp in the fourth year, when I *wanted* us to be seen. I want her, Tara, what we have, how it makes me feel, but I don't want anyone to know. I'm fiercely protective of our secret. And the secrecy adds spice to our relationship. Or so I thought.

"HAS SHE BEEN taking bad acid?"

We're downstairs at mine, and I'm introducing Tara to music she missed out on when she was "living under a stone" in Canada. We're watching a video of Siouxsie and the Banshees on the brand-new VHS recorder Aunty Corrie got Mum for her birthday. Siouxsie struts around on stage like some psychedelic peacock.

"Probably," I say, as we come to the song that bears my name.

"This is my song."

"D'you know what this song's about, Chrissie? I was reading about it."

How can Tara know more about *my* music than I do?

"It's about Christine Costner-Sizemore. She was an American woman diagnosed with multiple personality disorder. She had twenty-two distinct personalities."

"And here was me thinking it was about a teenager trying on different identities."

"Haha. Wonder how many identities you've got, Chrissie? I'd say at least two."

"What d'you mean?"

"There's gay you when you're with me and straight you when you're with your real friends."

She strokes my hair as she says it, and I force a laugh, but she's touched a nerve.

Chapter Twenty

Hey Siri, play 'Don't you want me?' by Human League

December 1981

"WHAT DO YOU and Grace do at Christmas?"

It's only just December, but Christmas items have been in the shops in Bath for weeks and the lights are in place, ready for the big switch on. I swear it gets earlier each year.

"Last year we went away. Mum wants to go somewhere again, but I don't think I'll go. I'd rather stay here."

"Would she leave you here on your own?"

Tara shrugs. "Don't see why not. I'd have a solo Christmas in the apartment. You could join me."

I wonder how my family would react if I spent Christmas with Tara.

"We always have a Christmas dinner with family round, but I could come over later. Or you could come to ours?"

I picture our typical family Christmas. Mum, David, Aunty Meg, Uncle Richard and Aunty Shauna, Norman and Nan, and assorted cousins all crammed into our dining room which is no bigger than Tara's bedroom in Bath. I try to stretch my imagination to a scene where Tara joins us around the dinner table.

"Hmm. An English traditional Christmas could be quite appealing," she says. But I swear I detect a hint of condescension in the way she says it.

"You'd have to put up with my Uncle Richard chatting you up. He fancies his chances once he's had a few."

"Your Uncle Richard would get a slap if he tried anything with me," she says. I laugh. But I'm not entirely sure she's joking.

Eventually, we arrive at a loose plan which involves me going to Tara's flat after dinner to spend the evening with her. There are no buses on Christmas Day so I'll have to cycle the four miles over to Bath – weather permitting. I doubt whether any of the adults will be sober enough to drive me. Tara can drive, but her licence is Canadian and she can't drive a manual – which seems a waste as Grace's TR7 sits in a garage somewhere in Bath, mostly unused.

The arrangement stays vague, and even when we break up from college Tara still isn't sure what she's doing. It seems to change daily. The arrival of snow and the availability of transport casts further uncertainty over the ability to plan.

"I don't get why this country can't cope with snow," says Tara. "In Vancouver we sometimes get snow on the ground up to three foot deep. People just put on their winter tyres and get on with it. Here it brings everything to a standstill. Looks like this little bit of weather could ground flights, so my mum might stay here. And now she's saying she doesn't want me to be here on my own over Christmas. It doesn't bother me, but suddenly it bothers her."

"Well, you are her only daughter," I say. Tara shrugs. As if the whole concept of family eludes her.

It isn't till the 22nd, when I phone her, that she tells me.

"We're packing. We're off to the Bahamas."

"When?"

"Tomorrow."

"But I thought you didn't want to go? I thought you were staying here if your mum went away."

"She's gone and booked tickets. So we're going," is all Tara will say. "I can't very well say no now."

Yes you can. You said you would.

"What time are you going?"

"Our flight's at seven. We have to be at the airport for five am. So we're leaving in the middle of the night."

"So I won't see you?"

"Not till I get back. I'll try to phone," her voice sounds muffled then, and I can hear Grace in the background.

"Promise you won't forget me."

"I'm only going for ten days."

To me it might as well be a lifetime.

"Look, I've got to go now. Love you." She whispers the last two words. I take some comfort from them.

She loves me, but she's leaving me at Christmas. And if I hadn't phoned, was she even going to tell me?

"Tara's going to the Bahamas for Christmas," I tell Mum.

"Really?" The concept of going away at Christmas, let alone to a foreign country, is a new one on Mum. I watch her face as she tries to process this information, finds no frame of reference, and dismisses it.

"So I won't be going there on Christmas Day. She's away for ten days."

"Ah well. Saves you cycling over there in the snow. We can all have a proper Christmas here instead." She couldn't look more relieved if she tried.

I used to love Christmas. Even after Dad died, we did our

116

best. Family and friends rallied to help us celebrate. We kept the old traditions alive. Home-made Baileys. Mince pies. Sherry on Christmas Eve at the Perkins' next door. Party games and Christmas hats. Aunty Meg and Uncle Richard coming round on Christmas morning. Uncle Norman bringing Nan, and Grandpa when he was still with us. We had to wait till Mum got the turkey in the oven before we were allowed to open our presents. Christmas songs on the stereo. When Noddy Holder bellows out "It's Christmaaas" Uncle Richard says. "I'm amazed he's got any voice left." He says it every single year.

I loved the run-up, too. Decorating the house with home-made paper chains. The hunt for the lights. Dressing the tree. I always liked dressing the tree.

This year is different. I see everything through Tara's jaded eyes. "Christmas is just a consumer-fest," she said. To her it's something to be got through. A time of inconvenience when services stop running.

It was Christmas, she told me, when Grace discovered the first affair with the Filipina maid in Hong Kong. Tara was too young to truly understand, but Grace dismissed the young woman summarily.

"So Christmas doesn't have a great track record in my book," she said. "I can't wait for it to all go back to normal. I prefer New Year."

Bath is tasteful, of course, and so is Melcombe, with its miniature Christmas trees nestled in the gables above the High Street shops and its Dickensian craft fair where they serve mulled cider in porcelain goblets.

A WEEK BEFORE she went away Tara invited me to carols at the Circus. It's an annual event that happens within the historic circle of grand Georgian townhouses near the Royal Crescent. "Grace is performing in her choir," she said. Tara looked traditional that day. Long winter coat, flame-red bobble hat to go with the long red scarf. We stood with a group of posh Bath people. My biker jacket wasn't warm enough for the sub-zero temperatures. "Can I have some of your scarf?" I asked Tara, hoping she'd wrap it round us both like she did at the bonfire in West Melcombe.

"You should have borrowed one of my coats," she said, unwrapping her scarf and handing me the whole thing, then turning the collar of her coat up to block out the cold. Evidently, there was going to be no mischief here tonight. She stood apart and didn't sing. Even though she has perfect pitch. I stood next to her, eventually joining in, but conscious of my reedy, tuneless tone. Afterwards we went back to Karl Powell's place in the Royal Crescent with some of the choir. We all trooped into a front room off the hallway with a grand piano in the corner and various musical instruments on stands around the walls. Karl played the piano while Eva, his Yugoslavian wife, served mulled wine and little snacks. Canapés, they called them. Karl invited Grace to stand next to him and sing. It was like a scene from a Jane Austen novel.

CHRISTMAS IN WEST Melcombe isn't like that. Nobody plays the piano, because we haven't got one. Instead, Mum puts on a compilation tape of Christmas songs and we get merry on sherry before sitting down to eat.

But this Christmas I can't relax. I look at everything through a critical lens. I cringe when Uncle Richard tries to tickle me.

Nan arrives, her wheelchair festooned with tinsel, bags bursting with presents hanging on the arms. Uncle Norman curses and he tries to push her in through the front door. We've told him before, it's easier round the back. As he wheels her into the living room, she scrutinises me through the upper section of her bi-focal glasses and says: "Why've you cut your hair so short? You're not women's lib, are you?"

She hands me her present, unwrapped. A pink, heart-shaped suitcase. Like something you'd give to a Cindy-girl, or a twelve-year-old.

"Lovely," I say, knowing I'll never use it.

Mum, vying for space with Aunty Shauna in the kitchen, is flushed and flustered. We have a last-minute guest coming for dinner. Mo, mum's lesbian social-worker colleague, is apparently facing Christmas alone because her girlfriend's upped sticks to join the women's camp at Greenham Common.

"I couldn't let Mo be on her own on Christmas Day." I sense resentment coming off her like steam.

Mo makes even more of an entrance than Nan, stamping the snow off her boots, spreading out her arms and announcing herself in her booming voice.

"I'm here! Let the festivities begin." She then gives a blast on a party trumpet before flopping down on the sofa where she stays until we eat two hours later.

Mum's jigging away to "Wombling Merry Christmas" as she stresses in the kitchen.

"You okay, Mum?" I ask as I pour everyone a sherry.

"There's so much to do. And nobody's helping."

I offer, but she dismisses me with a flap of her hand. Best left alone when she's stressed.

The phone rings. I answer it, but it's only Uncle Bob phoning from Wales. I hurry him off the phone to keep the line free. Tara *has* to phone today, surely?

I'm used to slipping away to the hallway to phone Tara, but now I can't. We can't afford an international call and I don't even know where she is. When I asked where she was staying, she just said, "Some hotel."

I've never stayed in a hotel.

I waited for a phone call the day they arrived. Then when no call came, I decided she'd phone the next day – Christmas Eve – to wish me a happy Christmas. She didn't. Surely she'll call me on Christmas Day?

I've worked out the time difference between here and the Bahamas and made sure I'm in for when she might call. When I've been out, the first thing I say when I get back is "Any phone calls?"

It's three pm here, It'll be ten in the morning there. Even if she's had a lie-in she should be waking up by now on Christmas Day, thinking of me…

I settle down on the sofa next to Mo, squashed up against the armrest.

I steal a sideways glance at her in her bright red leggings and outsize Christmas jumper and try to feel a sense of solidarity with her – as the only 'out' lesbian I know – but try as I might, I feel nothing.

The house feels even more crowded than usual for a Christmas Day and I find myself questioning – for the first time – why it's always us that hosts. True, we *are* the only ones with a downstairs loo that Nan can access, but it's always been us, even in Nan's pre-arthritic days.

I listen out above the din for the sound of the phone. It rings twice more throughout the day. Each time I get to it first. But it's only Aunty Mary phoning from Bexhill, then David's mate's mum telling us he's left his Walkman round at theirs.

"You look like you're in love." says Nan, observant as ever. "Got a young man, have you? Or aren't you letting on?"

"I don't need a young man."

She frowns.

"Not women's lib are you?"

"Who needs a man?" says Mo, picking up on the conversation.

She and Nan glare at each other across the room, like two indomitable, opposing spirits.

The day is lost in drink. In the evening, up in my room, I start writing another letter to Tara. I ripped up the one I wrote yesterday. Why is it so hard to find the words when I have so much to say?

HUMAN LEAGUE'S 'DON'T you want me?' is Christmas number one and it's on everywhere, all the time. It's cruelly poignant. *Don't you want me, Tara?*

On Boxing Day I run into Claire – we're now back on speaking terms after she went along with our counter story. She also apologised to Tara for the 'outing' incident. She found us in the art room one lunchtime. She actually ventured up there on her own, no Simon in sight, and said "I have something to say to you Tara. I want to apologise for what happened the other week." As she stood there, pretty, petite, uncomfortable, blushing, she shot up in my estimation. Tara forgave her graciously. Even gave her an awkward hug. I felt a huge sense of relief.

Shame I can't say the same about Andy, who never apologised and now mostly ignores me.

"What you up to today, Claire? Fancy coming over?" She

has Simon visiting, of course, but says we can meet up the following day. We can even go to town. Still no buses but Simon, fresh from passing his test first time, drives us there in a clapped-out Mini that belongs to his brother. It slides around on frozen slush.

The Jabberwocky café's open. We lounge on a sofa making one mug of tea last an hour.

"It's like the old days," she says.

Except it isn't. Claire's now second best.

Chapter Twenty-One

I bite the bullet and dig out the letters from the pink case. Letters from Claire (why did we write to each other when our houses were just two streets apart?), in her neat, rounded hand-writing, envelopes decorated with drawings of animals.

Letters in red pen, green pen, on pale blue A5 Basildon Bond paper. Envelopes with fourteen-pence stamps and Radstock, Bath postmarks.

Letters in my own handwriting. The ones Grace returned to me, still in their envelopes, bundled together in an elastic band.

And here, a pile without envelopes. Letters I'd written, never sent.

I pull one out at random.

1 January 1982
Tara Tara Tara

You're all I think about from the second I wake up to the moment I fall asleep. You're constantly in my head. You won't leave.

Except you did leave. You left me for a WHOLE TEN DAYS.

You say you love me, but you jet off half way across the world when we'd planned to spend Christmas together.

You say you'll phone. But day after day I wait by the phone and there's no call. They have phones in the Bahamas, don't they?

You say I'm special. But you swan off without a second glance. And I wonder who you're with.... Is it out of sight, out of mind? Do you think of me at all out there?

You say you've never felt like this. But I wonder if you're even capable of feeling. Are you a sociopath like your mum? Maybe it runs in the family?

Right now, I'm missing my old life. Missing my mates. You've driven a wedge between me and them, and it's not the same any more. It'll never be the same.

Right now, I'm missing men. I'm straight at heart, you see. But I could never tell you that.

Right now, part of me wishes you'll never come back. Wishes I'd never met you. Never picked psychology. Chosen a different path, so my life could be uncomplicated and happy.

But a bigger part of me is counting every second till I see you again.

This has become almost a poem. Or a lyric. Andy could write it into a song. He could if he was still speaking to me.

I probably won't send this, because it's not good

enough.

I'll never be good enough. Sophisticated enough. Cultured enough. Travelled enough. Well-read enough.

For you.

I love you. I love you. I love you.

AND I HATE MYSELF FOR LOVING YOU

January 1982

THIS WHITE-OUT IS driving me insane. They say it's the coldest winter on record. It takes an absolute age to get anywhere and I'm desperate to see green through the snow. As the days go by with no word from Tara I sink deeper into despair. I drive myself mad wondering where she is and who she's with, my mind keeps returning to the girl at the holiday marina. Has she met someone in the Bahamas, even if it is "just sex"? Is that how she sees *me*? I don't know the rules of the game I'm now in. Are we supposed to be faithful? We've been together for eight short weeks. Eight weeks that have turned my life upside down.

Mostly, I stay in and drift around the house. I have essays to write, due in on the first day of term, and mountains of reading material, but it all stays stubbornly undone. I get up late, slob around in leggings and a baggy jumper, and can't be bothered to go out. Not that there's anywhere to go unless you want to trudge miles through the snow.

"Are you *ok*, Chrissie?"

I hate it when Mum notices stuff. Usually, she doesn't. I can be having a mini-breakdown and she wouldn't realise because she's too tied up in her social worker world and her committees and all the other causes she carries on her shoulders to pay attention to what's going on in her own house. But now she's noticed, so my mood must be obvious. I make an extra effort to look alert.

"Just sick of the snow," I say.

She wears her concerned look. Slightly raised eyebrows, leaning forward, chin in her hands as she sits at the kitchen table.

"David's gone sledging," she says. "Why don't you go too, like we all did that year we had the big snow."

"That was when I was a kid."

We all went up to the hill behind the rec, sledging on anything we could lay our hands on. Sledges, trays, even plastic bin liners did the job. But that was then.

David comes home at lunchtime, hungry. "Chris your mates are up there. Everyone's asking where you are," he says.

"Who?"

"Claire, Andy, a whole load of them."

Mum looks at me, eyes wide, smile fixed. "It might do you good, Chrissie, to get out, get some fresh air. It's sunny now. Might take your mind off it."

"Mind off what?" says David.

Mum scowls at him.

In the end, I wander over to the rec. Half the village are there. Andy has some young punkette with him. She has spiked purple hair and multiple piercings and she's about half his height. She sits in front of Andy on the sledge, his arms and legs wrapped around her. She squeals as they slide down the slope.

"Who's that with Andy?" I ask Claire.

"Oh didn't you know? He's pulled. He met her at the Underground club. They're totally into each other." She looks at me. "Missed your chance there Chris!"

Simon's there of course, looking rugged and ridiculously handsome in a donkey jacket, black woolly hat and scarf. How can someone always, consistently, manage to look good?

Claire and Simon make an effort to include me, so I sledge down with Simon, then Claire, then both. And as the cold air whips around my face and the sunlight penetrates my fog, my mood starts to shift, until I'm squealing with the rest of them. We stay about an hour, then walk home together, throwing snowballs all the way. And it occurs to me, I've actually had fun. Without Tara. And if Tara had been around, I probably wouldn't have gone.

"That's better," says Mum as I walk in the door. "You've got some colour in your cheeks now." She makes me a cup of tea, pulls a chair out for me at the table, shuts the kitchen door, then proceeds to give me a pep talk.

"I've been meaning to talk to you Chrissie."

Oh no.

"Oh yeah?"

"About your friend Tara."

Uh oh – here we go.

"What about her?"

"I've been hearing things."

"Like what?"

"I've heard that she's…"

Say it Mum.

"What Mum?"

"I've heard she thinks she's a lesbian."

"So?"

My social worker mother ought to be able to deal with this, surely?

"I can't help noticing you've been getting very close to

her."

"And?"

She says nothing. Her brow is furrowed, and she's wiping at a crumb on the work surface.

"I'm just saying be careful."

I glare at her.

"What are you saying, Mum? You think I'm one too?"

"Well, are you?"

I laugh. "Of course not."

She scrutinises my face.

"You can always talk to me, Chrissie, if anything's bothering you, you know that."

I squirm.

"You're very young to be putting a label on yourself. I don't want you to go down a route you might later regret."

Funny, I'm sure she wouldn't give me the "labelling yourself" line if it was a boy I was seeing.

"Ok, Mum, is the lecture over? Can I go now?"

"D'you understand what I'm saying?"

"Not really. Tara and I are mates, ok? I'm not going to drop her just because she may or may not be gay. I'm sure you'd agree that wouldn't be fair. There's enough prejudice around as it is. Like if I told you not to go near Mo at work? You'd be the first to call out discrimination!"

Mum bristles, then, takes a deep, sharp breath.

"That's different. Mo's clear about who she is and she's a mature woman."

"So's Tara."

Mum sighs.

"I'm just saying. Don't be too exclusive."

"You didn't lecture me like this when I was hanging out with Claire. We were best mates for years. Can't get more exclusive than that."

Mum sniffs. "It *is* different. I've watched you and Tara together. Your whole dynamic is different. You and Claire used to sit next to each other and face the world. You and Tara sit opposite each other and shut out the world."

I stare at her.

"What are you on about, Mum?"

"You need to get out and about and meet new people, not spend time with just this one girl."

"Mum! Where've I just been? I've been up at the rec all afternoon with all the Melcombe Comp lot. You happy? Now can I go and get changed out of these wet clothes?"

I stand up and walk towards the door.

"Did you mean what you said earlier?" she says. "When you said you're not a lesbian?"

"Yes Mum. I'll say it again. I. Am. Not. A. Lesbian. Okay?"

I go upstairs, pretty sure that what I've just said is an accurate representation of the truth. I still fancy guys. I must be bisexual, I suppose. To be honest, though, I don't know what I am.

And in my head I'm already walking away from Tara. They have phones in hotels, don't they, even in the Bahamas, but it's now more than a week since she went and there's been nothing. She can't even be bothered to call. Out of sight, out of mind.

I proved today that I don't need her. The sooner she's out of my life, the better. Then I can get on with the things I enjoy, like going out with my mates.

Chapter Twenty-Two

1982 DIARY

Name: Christine Carlisle

Height: Five foot four

Weight: Don't know. The scales are broke

Age: 16 and a half

Favourite colour: Purple

Favourite bands: Siouxsie and the Banshees, Joy Division, The Cure

Favourite food: Pizza

Favourite poem: Catullus Odi et Amo – I LOVE AND I HATE

About me.

I'm Christine Carlisle. I'm 16 going on 17 and I'm into punk, post punk, new wave and electronic/synth pop. I love music and gigs and getting drunk with my mates. I'm like any other sixteen-year-old girl really. There's just one difference. I can fly. I don't do it all the time. Often I go months, years without flying, but

I never lose the ability. Aunty Nessa says it's a gift. The shrink I saw after Dad died says it was a psychological condition but I know it's a super power.

I'm also in love. And it hurts.

Tonight I flew over oceans and continents to the Bahamas, looking for Tara. I couldn't find her. I flew over beaches and tropical sand dunes and bars with thatched parasols and waiters serving cocktails with rum in them and little paper umbrellas. I swooped down close enough to hear the reggae beat. But I still couldn't find her. Then I flew over an azure sea, and I saw a hand stretching out. An arm with a bear tattoo. I knew it was her.

Hey Siri, Play 'Wish you were Here' by Pink Floyd

January 1982

IT'S THE SATURDAY after new year and Rob's opened the shop despite the snow. Get here if you can, he says. I can. I need the money. Uncle Richard drives me there in his Land Rover, which is about the only vehicle that can cope with the weather. He drops me at the top of the hill on the edge of the city to avoid the abandoned cars. I slip twice on the trudge into town. I thought Doc Martens were supposed to have good grip. There's hardly any customers so Rob lets me go early, but it still takes till five pm to get home on account of the bus getting stuck on the hill, so we have to wait for another one to turn up.

This evening, two of my aunts – Meg and Shauna – are here, but I don't feel sociable. They stay till ten and I'm just about to turn in for the night when the phone rings.

"Chrissie, it's me!"

Finally.

"Tara?"

"Don't sound so surprised. Did you forget me already?"

"No, of course not, it's just, I didn't think you'd call."

Actually I thought you'd call earlier.

"We just landed half an hour ago. We're in London. We're staying the night here because the trains aren't running due to this bastard weather."

She's phoning from a call box. A series of beeps indicates she's run out of coinage. I wait while she feeds the machine.

"Chrissie It's so good to hear your voice. I've missed you *so* much."

"Why didn't you call?"

"I tried but I couldn't work the bastard pay phones over there. I bought a phone card but it just ate credit and then cut me off. And I had to share a suite with Mum, so I couldn't even use the phone in the hotel room."

I feel flat now, my resolve weakened.

The pips go again and she puts more money in.

"So how've you been? Did you get my postcard?"

"No?"

"I *knew* it'd arrive after I did, if at all. Hey Chrissie, I'm heading back on the first train to Bath in the morning. Wanna meet me in town?"

I'm powerless to say no.

NEXT MORNING THE postman delivers a card. David picks it up in the hall and brings it to the breakfast table. "Freeport?" he says, reading the postmark. "Where's that when it's at home?"

"Give it here," I say, but David's reading the message on

the back aloud.

"'Two lost souls swimming in a fish bowl ...' That's a line from a Pink Floyd song."

"I know."

"Wish you were here – I get it. Clever!" He hands me the card. The picture is of a clear blue sea with two yellow and black striped fish swimming around in it. It's signed off simply *Txxxx*

I meet Tara off the train. We go straight to hers. She's bought me gifts. She watches me unwrap them. A batik dress, a small bottle of rum, and a conch shell bracelet. She produces another bottle of rum from her suitcase and mixes us both a cocktail.

"Try on the dress."

I do. She tells me I look amazing, and kisses me.

"Keep it on. I want to take my girlfriend out for lunch."

I wear it with my leggings and docs and my new bracelet and Grace's fur coat – which is much too big – as it's freezing. We go to a little bijou French restaurant down a cobbled side street and have a carafe of wine with lunch. Tara pays with her credit card and won't let me see the bill.

"I missed you so much," she says again. "Jeez, I'm jet lagged."

We go back to the flat and fall into bed together. We're still there five hours later when we hear Grace return. We pull on our clothes, giggling.

Something happens when I'm with Tara. A kind of magic. It pulls me in and holds me in a space that shuts out the world. Something that makes being with her the best place on earth.

Now I'm back in my bubble with Tara. My exquisite, beautiful bubble. Nothing compares. How could I have contemplated ending it?

Chapter Twenty-Three

A yellowed, gilt-edged A5 programme:
An evening of choral, orchestral and jazz music with
the Crescent Choir, Slaughterhouse Six, and Bath
Symphonic, plus solo performers. Conducted by Dr
Karl Powell. Saturday February 6th 7.30pm.

February 1982

E VA POWELL HAS a sweet soprano voice and perfect pitch.
She also plays a full-sized cello which dwarfs her.

We're at a classical music performance at the Bath
Assembly Rooms and I sit fidgeting at the front next to Tara,
who seems enraptured by the music. Later, Grace performs a
solo. Her stately presence and deep contralto in marked
contrast to Eva.

At the interval Karl stands, majestic in black tailcoat,
white shirt and dickie bow, engaging with his public, with
Grace on one side, Eva on the other.

I wonder what the deal is with the three of them.

"Do Grace and Karl's wife get on?" I ask Tara.

She says she thinks they have some kind of an
arrangement.

"Mum says he rescued Eva from behind the Iron Curtain so she puts up with playing second fiddle," Tara then realises what she's said, and we both laugh.

We go to join them, lifting flutes of champagne from a silver tray brought by a passing waitress. Tara wears a long satin dress that hugs every perfect contour of her body. I'm wearing the cotton floral frock I wore for Aunty Alice's wedding. The poshest thing I own. It feels too summery for the occasion. I loiter awkwardly on the edge as they talk. They use words like aria, libretto and sonata. Words I can't even spell let alone know the meaning of.

I've finished my champagne, I hang onto my glass and want another. Drinking gives me something to do with my hands. I crave nicotine, but nobody's smoking, not even Grace. A man – one of the musicians – is talking to Tara about places I've never heard of. I search around for someone to rescue me, anyone to pretend to make conversation with so I don't stand out as the only person in the room with a non-speaking part. Help comes from an unexpected direction. Eva's at my elbow with another glass of champagne. She spirits the empty glass away somewhere, then returns.

I look at her closely now, marvelling at her beauty. She has long, straight, dark brown hair which hangs half-way down her back; pretty, wide-open, light brown eyes that glisten and dance, and a flawless oval face, lightly tanned.

It's hard to tell her age. She may not even be much older than me and Tara. She doesn't smile, but there's something in her look that says connection. As though we both know we are the ones who don't fit in. I'm grateful for her company.

"The choir are visiting Ljubljana in my home country at Easter," she says, nodding towards Tara and the musician.

"Tara and Grace are coming. That's what they are talking about."

Tara turns round then. "Why don't you come too, Chrissie? Would you come to Ljubljana with us?"

"Love to!" I say. Wondering instantly how Mum would afford it. I've never even heard of the place before today.

Chapter Twenty-Four

March 1982

"SOME OLD FRIENDS of mine are in town. Wanna come up with me and meet them? I'm going up Friday on the train."

I realise by "town" Tara means London.

"Can't. I'm working Saturday."

"Can you take the day off?"

"Not really, it's too short notice."

Plus the train fare to London costs money.

In the event, Tara takes Friday off college and travels up Thursday night.

"I'll phone you when I get there," she says.

She doesn't. I have that gut-wrenching feeling of not knowing where she is, what she's doing or who she's with. Of having lost her to that other world she inhabited before I knew her. Like Christmas all over again.

This time though, I'm not waiting in. Rob, my boss at the book shop, has asked me to help him set up an exhibition after college on Friday. He'll pay me extra for my time. And he says I can come back later as a guest at an exclusive "meet the artist" event. "Bring a friend," he says. I can't think of anyone. Then, by chance, I bump into Jason in town. I tell him what I'm doing.

"D'you need an escort?" he says.

When he picks me up from my house in the Triumph Stag I realise he's the perfect person to take to an exhibition. For a start, he looks divine. Dressed in dungarees and black suede boots. His hair, no longer quiffed, is now a more textured, floppy style and he's wearing it with a headband. He's a natural among the arty people, knows what to say without a hint of pretension. And I feel unexpectedly comfortable in his presence.

He steers me away from the crowd, takes me round the paintings, comments on them in terms I can understand. He puts his arm around me to pose for a photographer from the Bath Evening Chronicle. I swell with pride.

We have a glass of wine with cubes of cheese and pineapple on a stick. We giggle together.

"D'you think Tara will mind? Us being at this without her?" I ask. Coming here with Jason feels ever so slightly disloyal.

"Why should she?" he says. "She's gone off and left us!"

It's tongue in cheek, and he nudges me as he says it. But I sense he understands.

"When she went away at Christmas, she said she'd phone, but she didn't." I say.

He looks thoughtful then, his head slightly to one side as he surveys a painting.

"She never does. But if you're lucky you might get a postcard."

Sure enough, next day at breakfast, there's a postcard for me. It's a waxwork of Bob Dylan from Madame Tussauds.

And on the other side, in Tara's sloping handwriting, is

written the first few lines of "Forever Young".

David grabs it from me. In our family we read each other's post-cards because Mum says "postcards are fair game". He reads the lines aloud. "May God's blessing keep you always…"

"It's from Tara. She's in London," I say.

"Is Tara a poet?" says Nan, here to stay for the weekend.

David laughs. "Tara didn't write that. It's by Bob Dylan, Nan."

Mum tuts. "Even *I* know that."

THAT AFTERNOON, AT the shop, we have a visitation. Tara bursts in with a strange woman who wears a long suede coat, flares and platform boots, looking like she's stepped straight out of the seventies.

"Chrissie, let me introduce Izzy."

"I thought you were in London."

"We were," says the strange woman. She has implausibly arched eyebrows. "It's the spring equinox and we're heading over to Glastonbury." She has a harsher accent to Tara's and is more obviously North American.

"Want to come?" says Tara. "We're gonna camp out there up at the tower."

"You mean the Tor?"

"Yeah. Can we borrow your tent?"

"I haven't got one."

"I thought you camped there with your boyfriend last year. You know, the one who couldn't get it up, the tent I mean," Tara gives Izzy a sideways glance and they both laugh.

"It was his tent, not mine. He was a boy-scout,

remember?"

"Jeez, of course. We'll just have to sleep under the stars. Or in the van. Izzy's hired one."

Rob, coming in and out carrying gear from the exhibition, stops to offer us his tent. He also gives us the name of a camp-site nearby in case we can't pitch up at the Tor. "Not sure they allow it. And the ground may not be suitable," he says. "It's on a bit of a slope, you see," he winks at me.

He then shows me a photo in the Bath paper of me and Jason at the exhibition last night. It's captioned *"Art fans Christine Carlisle and Jason Flint browse the exhibit."* The photographer's made us look like the coolest, most beautiful people in town.

"Oh wow!" says Tara. "Did you and Jase go there together? Wish I'd been there."

I feel a little surge of pride, mixed with something else. Something almost vengeful.

TARA'S FRIENDS PICK us up in their hire van. There are two other women as well as Izzy, and a man.

There's Valerie, long Pre-Raphaelite curls and an ankle-length tie-dyed dress; Maxine, a woman at least six feet tall with huge scary eyes, and Gez, who wears a cheesecloth shirt, flares and a headband, continuing the seventies theme.

I'm by far the youngest there.

"Where is everyone?" says Izzy as we park up on a country lane near the Tor. "I thought they'd all be heading here for the equinox?"

"I think you're thinking solstice," I say quietly. She stares at me like I'm something from outer space.

"We're druids, in search of the Isle of Avalon," says the giantess, as we trudge through the field leading up to the hill. She has an upper-class English accent. She's the only one dressed for the occasion in fleece and walking boots, and the one who looks least like a druid.

Some lambs, almost fully grown, stray across the path and Valerie coos at their cuteness. They're very tame, apparently unfazed by human proximity. They start to follow.

Maxine, Tara and Gez stride ahead, Valerie mingles with the sheep and Izzy and I bring up the rear. I struggle to keep up. I eye a bench near the top longingly, but nobody stops.

In an effort to make conversation, I ask Izzy if she grew up in the same part of Canada as Tara.

"I'm from the States. I knew Tara at school."

Of course. Boarding school.

"She was my protégé. The only fag I didn't fire. We've stayed in touch ever since."

The penny drops. So *this* was the woman Tara told me about. Her teenage crush. The girl she shared the acid experience with on the beach in Vancouver.

Tara reaches the summit first and stretches out her arms, in salute to a non-visible sun.

"She was a gawky teenager but she's turned into an absolute stunner," says Izzy, eyeing Tara like she's a thing of her own creation.

I say nothing. I'm breathless and I sense my asthma kicking in.

The only other person on the Tor is a middle-aged man walking a dog, who takes one look at us and heads off down the slope.

At the top, we sit leaning against the tower, looking out

across the Somerset countryside. It's grey and uninspiring under a leaden sky. The idea is to watch the sun go down, but it's obscured by cloud, and nobody can work out which way is west.

It's also very windy up here, on all sides of the tower.

We move inside the portal and sit on the stone benches, leaning on the walls, but it's no warmer. I'm still in the clothes I wore to work. The cold seeps through my jacket, right through to my bones. I sit hunched, my shoulders tense.

Gez rolls a joint and passes it round. It's strong. I feel it go to my head after just one drag and I begin to get a sense of unease. Maxine produces a ukulele and starts to strum and sing in a low, warbling contralto. I vaguely recognise it as a Joan Baez song. Tara joins in, introducing some harmony, rocking slightly.

"Are you guys a couple or just friends?" Gez asks. I sense he fancies Tara. Doesn't everyone?

"We're *good* friends," Tara says, putting her arm around me and pulling me close.

"You're a cute kid," he says to me, and rolls another joint.

Tara stands, stretches, exits the tower and walks a few paces away, where we can still see her. She does a handstand on the grass. She holds the pose for a few moments, her long, elegant limps framed by the archway and silhouetted against the sky.

"Take my advice, kid," Izzy says to me. "Enjoy her while it lasts, because knowing that one, she'll get bored. Right now, she's enjoying playing with the children. But as soon as she gets restless, she'll be off."

There's a hint of menace in her voice. I say nothing. I can't speak. It's as though I've been turned to stone by her words or the place's ancient magic.

Izzy looks at me. "Wonder what she sees in you, little mouse. Must be your youth and English novelty."

Tara returns, and Izzy brings out a package wrapped in tin foil. I hope it's edible. I'm starving. I only had a sandwich at lunch.

"I got home-made shortbread," she says, offering it round. I take a piece.

"Is this..?" asks Tara, breaking off a tiny chunk.

"Gez's special recipe. Yeah."

It's strange seeing Tara with her old friends. It's like she's a different person. Different again from all the other Taras.

As they talk, I feel rooted to the spot, still unable to speak, like some mute kid dragged along with the grown-ups.

I'm also feeling decidedly strange. My pulse starts to race for no reason.

"I need to wee," says Valerie, skipping off behind the tower and squealing as she urinates.

"There she goes," the others laugh. And I realise I too need to wee, but I'm incapable of speech or movement. The people around me are talking, but there's no logical thread, just a series of randomly formed sentences. I wonder if I'm invisible, if I am in fact no longer here.

"Hey," says Valerie, back from her ablutions. "Let's get naked."

I think she's joking, but the four of them start to shed their clothes and dance around in the fading light.

"C'mon Tara," calls Izzy.

"You've got to be kidding me, it's freezing."

Gez dances up to us, his body white, his little penis swinging. He sits down near us and the three women join him, forming a circle around him.

"Three vaginas, one penis," Valerie announces.

"It's small because I'm cold," says Gez, standing up again "But I own it."

He does a circular gyrating motion, face upturned to the patch of darkening sky visible through the roofless tower.

"Man, can't you just *feel* those ley-lines?"

"This is getting weird," says Tara to me. "Shall we go?"

I'm grateful. I've been wanting to get the hell out since we arrived. There are rain clouds rolling in. And I'm cold to the bone, and weak with hunger.

"Guys, we're gonna go find somewhere to pitch our tent," Tara calls to the others. They barely notice. The women are closing in on Gez. As we leave, they seem to be entering into some sort of four-way kiss.

"Will they sleep up there?" I say, as we reach the bottom and see the van.

"Who knows what those crazy guys will do. I guess they'll head back down and crash in the van."

We retrieve our tent and trudge through the lanes until we find the place my boss told us about. It's a proper campsite, but there's hardly anyone around and nowhere obvious to pay, so we pitch up without paying. I'm too wasted to work out how the tent goes up. A man from a nearby campervan – who appears to be the only other camper – helps us out, explaining each stage like he's talking to children. I sense Tara's irritation that some man sees fit to step in, but all I can feel is grateful.

"You ok?" asks Tara. It's the first time all day she's expressed any interest in or concern for me.

"I feel weird. I'm hungry."

"The munchies?"

"I only had a couple of drags of that spliff."

"But you had Gez's flapjack. What you need to know about Gez is everything he cooks has dope in it."

Nice of them to tell me.

The only thing we have to eat is a four-finger Kit-Kat, which we share without speaking. Then we go to sleep, together but not together.

I wake up tired, to a fine drizzle. We walk to the bus stop in Glastonbury and wait forty minutes for a bus back to Bath.

Chapter Twenty-Five

Hey Siri, play 'Solsbury Hill' by Peter Gabriel.

March 1982

I T'S A WEEK on from that ill-fated trip to Glastonbury and the weather has taken a turn for the better. It's bright and mild and there's actual warmth in the sun. At last it feels like spring. Tara's invited me and Jason on a picnic up at Little Solsbury Hill.

Jason collects us from the flat in his Triumph Stag. Tara sits in front, looking cool and elegant in dark glasses. I'm crammed on the tiny child's seat, wrapped in a tartan picnic blanket.

We drive through the narrow, tree-lined lanes to get to the start of the walk, park up, then begin the hike up the hill. Jason carries the picnic basket with a guitar slung over his shoulder, me with the blanket draped over my arm, Tara carrying a bag of clinking bottles.

"Climbing up on Solsbury Hill," Jason starts to sing.

Tara chimes in with the next line of the song.

They both have beautiful voices. Hers like an American folk artist, his a cool, lazy jazz singer. They stride effortlessly up the slope and I feel dull and dumpy next to them. Once again, like last weekend at Glastonbury, I'm wondering if this was a good idea. If I can ever really enter Tara's world. If I can ever compete with her older, sophisticated friends. Although after the exhibition I know I feel comfortable with Jason.

It's windy at the top, and we huddle together for warmth, leaning up against the triangulation point. Grace has made us light, fluffy quiche and a salad with tiny tomatoes and proper dressing made of oil, vinegar and herbs, instead of Heinz Salad cream like we have at home. I brought some flapjack. "But it's not like Gez's flapjack," I say. Tara laughs.

I'm not sure about the dynamic between us. How much Tara's told Jason about the two of us. But Jason's cool, more like a father figure or an older brother than a love rival. Tara opens a bottle of sparkling wine and pours it into plastic flutes.

After we've eaten, Tara stands up to her full height, and challenges us to a race. Jason declines. Tara and I run on the bumpy ground, but she outpaces me. "Not fair, longer legs," I say, breathless. Tara laughs.

I sit back down on the rug with Jason as Tara does handstands on the grass.

"It's like she's a kid again," I say.

"You bring that out," says Jason. "It's great to see the two of you together."

He knows then.

"You don't mind?" I ask, "I know you and her were close."

"We're even closer now we've got the sex stuff out of the way," he says. "It was never going to work between us, for obvious reasons."

We sit in companionable silence, watching Tara leap

around. She's like an athlete.

"When she first came to Kingswood there were only a few girls at the school. Tara turns up, and she's an absolute stunner, and I mistook my feelings for something else. Aesthetically, I can look at a beautiful woman and feel kinda dreamy. But sexually, I'm attracted to men. Always have been. That's the difference. It just took a while to work that out."

He says it all in a matter-of-fact way, like a person totally at peace with himself.

"Tara wants me to come out. To tell people about us," I say.

Jason shrugs. "It's not an easy thing to do. You have to do it in your own time, Chrissie, if that's what you want."

He sighs.

"I know *I'm* not ready yet," he says. "To tell people, I mean. I've only just come to accept it myself. I used to agonise about my sexuality. Now I look at it all philosophically. I reckon, in two thousand years' time me being gay won't matter."

"By then, attitudes will have changed."

He laughs. "I bloody hope so. Hope I don't have to wait two thousand years to be open about who I am."

Jason has a sexy voice. I've always thought so. His accent is more estuary than South West. Not posh like Grace and her elite, more like a rock star. A David Bowie voice.

Tara rejoins us, face flushed, and flops down on the rug, close to me. She pours another glass of bubbly for us both. Jason declines as he's driving. He takes out the guitar and starts to pluck the strings, producing a half-familiar riff that develops into 'Stray Cat Strut'. He's a good guitarist.

"You gotta play Peter Gabriel now," says Tara, so he

does, and this time we all sing.

"How come this place got its name – can you see Salisbury from here?" Tara asks. For once I feel more knowledgeable than her.

"It's Solsbury spelt with an 'o'."

Walking back down, Tara drapes her arm around me, and Jason walks apart. As we get to the car, Tara says. "You ride in the front, Chrissie, I'll be the kids in the back." So she climbs onto the back seat, folding up her long legs while I sit up front, hair billowing in the wind.

Chapter Twenty-Six

A yellowed front page cutting from the Sun, dated April 3 1982.

IT'S WAR

40 Warships ready.

Paras are called up.

Prince Andy to go.

Full story pages 2,3,4,5 & 6.

April 1982

"WE'RE AT WAR."

David's in his dressing gown eating Frosties and watching the news, which is on all day – all other programmes cancelled. He has the curtains drawn, even though it's light. I watch with him as hundreds of troops board a massive vessel. Thatcher appears, severe-faced on the screen, standing next to some senior naval bloke festooned in medals.

"Where exactly are the Falkland Islands.?" I ask.

"South Atlantic. Near Antarctica."

"How come *we* own them?"

He shrugs. "It's empire, Chris."

David has suddenly become grown up. He knows things I don't. Unlike me, he seems to actually be interested in history.

There are women on the shore, seeing off their sweethearts, waving flags.

"It's like something from the war," I say.

"It *is* the war. *A* war, anyway."

"Who will win?"

David weighs up the merits of the military capability on each side. "They have more manpower and they're near home territory so easier to refuel. We have better troop morale and better strategy. Oh, and we have Thatcher. For her, losing isn't an option. So we'll probably win. Eventually."

"What if they start calling people up. Would you go?"

"Too young," says David. "Unless I lie about my age and run away to sea like people used to in the old days."

"Will it be over by Easter? I'm supposed to be going away with Tara. I don't want to get caught up in some stupid war."

Easter Monday is the day our flights are booked for Ljubljana, and I've only just learnt how to pronounce it.

David laughs.

"The Falklands are about eight thousand miles in the other direction, Chris. I don't think it'll affect your trip."

IT'S THE START of the Easter holidays, and we're at Heathrow. In the end, Grace paid for my flight. Mum tried to protest, but Grace brushed her aside, saying, "It's only money. Anyway, I got a deal with the airline."

I can't decide if Grace was being gracious or

condescending. But it doesn't matter, because Tara and I will be together for four whole nights, and Tara is already planning how we can break away from the others and have fun.

"There's an underground punk movement over there," she says. "You'll love it!" There is also an emerging gay scene, and Tara is determined to seek it out.

I've only flown once, on the school trip to Bordeaux with Claire and a bunch of kids from Melcombe, a teacher shepherding us every step of the way. We went from Bristol airport which was tiny in comparison to Heathrow, where we are now, boarding a British Airways flight to Ljubljana.

Grace, Karl and Eva sit together in a three-seater row, Karl in the middle. Tara and I are across the aisle from them. I remember the feeling of flight, that giddy, leave-your-stomach-behind feeling as the plane gains height. Like being on a Ferris wheel at the fairground. I feel that same bubbling up of excitement I experienced when we'd set off for France, me giddy, Claire scared.

I look at Tara, her face expressionless. To her, flying is a common occurrence.

"They should bring us a G and T in a minute, that'll steady your nerves," she says, mistaking my giddiness for fear.

"I'm not nervous, I'm excited!" I say. "I love flying. Don't you?"

"Not really. I don't like being confined in a metal tube thirty-five thousand feet in the air. For me it's a means to an end. At least this is only two hours."

She asks why I love flying. I try to put it into words.

"It's like a different world up here," I say.

Back on the ground in the UK, it was overcast, but here,

above the clouds, it's blue sky and sunshine.

"Plus I like that giddy feeling in your stomach when the plane takes off."

"This is what I love about you, Chrissie," she says. "You've got a child-like enthusiasm for things. When everything's new. But you wouldn't feel like that if you hit turbulence!"

Grace hates flying, apparently. She's got what Tara calls frequent flyer syndrome, where you believe each time you board a plane the odds of you crashing get higher.

I'm not sure how that stacks up statistically.

"She particularly hates landing. She had a bad experience once when the wheels didn't lower."

Perhaps that explains why Karl grips her hand as we come in to land.

WE'RE MET AT the airport by a man in uniform who leads us to a waiting car then drives us to the hotel, a big concrete structure on the edge of the old town where another man in uniform presses a button for the lift and watches us go in.

Tara and I have a room to ourselves, with twin beds.

Tara wrinkles her nose. "This place smells of cabbage and disinfectant," she says.

I can't say I've noticed.

"What d'you think of the room?" I say. It seems modern to me, and clean.

"It's a bit stark," she says. "But you have to remember this is a communist country."

She sounds like Grace.

We freshen up and meet the others for dinner in the dining room, before heading out to the first of the performances.

In the city there are shops open, even though it's evening, and cafés and bars with people sitting outside. The whole place has a friendly buzz.

"I'm surprised it's this lively," says Grace in a too-loud voice. "I thought communist countries were supposed to be drab? It feels almost western."

"Ah, we are not communist here. We are socialist," says Eva. "The people have plenty of freedoms. We can travel anywhere."

Grace sniffs, swooping through the streets like she's royalty.

LJUBLJANA IS BEAUTIFUL, particularly the old town where the music events take place. We wander alongside the river, across little bridges, weaving our way along cobbled streets between buildings painted pink and cream and yellow. Tara admires the architecture, which she says is renaissance or art deco. To me, it's a bit like Bath, but not as big, and less busy.

For the first two days Tara and I dutifully troop round with the others, sitting through lunchtime, afternoon and evening concerts, but on day three we have other plans.

"We're not coming to the concert tonight," Tara says over dinner. "We're off to a gig. There's this band Chrissie's interested in."

To get to the club where the gig is we pick our way through a maze of backstreets. Here the streets are less pretty. Some of the buildings have seen better days, and there's graffiti everywhere. There are very few people about. The sound of our shoes echo as we walk. We have to keep stopping to look at the map. At one point we feel completely lost, but some kind local asks us where we want to go and, despite the language barrier, sets us off on the right road.

The place we are going to is literally underground. We descend two flights of basement steps to get there. There's no sign, no bouncer on the door, no sound audible from the street. Nothing to indicate what lies within except an arrow chalked on the wall and something scrawled in Slovenian. I'm beginning to wonder if we're in the right place, or even whether we've been duped into walking into some trap. We tap lightly at the door. An unseen arm opens it to admit us. Inside, it's dark. Too dark to see people's faces. I'm dimly aware of a corridor with another chalked arrow. We follow the direction the arrow points in. There's an edginess, a slight air of danger which adds to the excitement.

"They're playing Bauhaus," I say as we emerge into the club. And it is a club, with graffiti-art on the walls and low mauve lighting. As my eyes adjust to the gloom and I make out figures around me I conclude this is honestly the coolest place I've ever been in.

The band play a mixture of post-punk, goth, and new wave. Modern and edgy. All around are men dressed like Andy and ten times more attractive. Mostly dark, tall, with lean, long faces. My sort of guy.

Two of them approach us, drawn, no doubt, by Tara's stunning looks and my alternative outfit. I'm wearing my bright orange dress with the tartan bits, with fishnets, leather jacket and docs.

"Are you English?" the one nearest says. He makes just those three words sound indescribably sexy.

His name is Luka, and I want to die in his arms.

We talk, as far as the language barrier and sound levels allow. We talk of bands, and music, and what it's like growing up in Ljubljana.

"Ljubljana is changing," he says. "And all this," he waves

his hand to indicate the venue "is part of it."

I look over at Tara, talking to Luka's mate. Worried this isn't her scene, and she'll want to leave, but she seems engrossed in conversation. I see the guy she's with write something on a cigarette packet for her. She puts it in her pocket.

Later we dance, the four of us, shuffling around the floor in the darkness. The two guys go off to the bar, they look round at us and I wonder what they're saying. Luka looks at me, eyebrows slightly raised. His look is questioning.

"Are you okay?" I ask Tara.

"Yeah. I love this country."

Funny. Earlier in the day she described it as "backward".

"What about your new friend?"

"That's Jakob," she says. "He's cool. He's given me the name of somewhere we can go tomorrow."

She shows me the torn off bit of cardboard.

They come back then, with drinks. This time, Luka hangs back, avoiding eye-contact. I wondered what's been said.

The band has finished and it's getting late. We need to get back to the hotel, although the club shows no signs of closing. So we say our goodbyes. Luka smiles, from a safe distance, once more questioning. His friend then scribbles something on another bit of cardboard for me and hands it to me.

"For you, to go tomorrow," his English isn't as good as Luka's. "It is on the university park. You can walk there. This place. I don't know how to say. My English is not as we wish. It's ok. For gay."

So that's it. Tara has told him about us.

During the long trudge back to the hotel, I silently fume, and think of Luka.

THE NEXT NIGHT, we head for the place Jakob's given us the name of. Walking in, you wouldn't obviously know it's a gay club. "Is this the right place?"

"Gay friendly, I think, more than openly gay," Tara says.

In Bath we avoid such places. There's too much chance of being recognised. We once looked in on a gay club in Bristol. A place with a glitter ball and strobe lighting and a disco beat that made me feel like I was back in the seventies. We had an argument because I said the music was crap. She said, "it's better than that deathly wrist-splitting stuff you like," and we left.

Here is different. It doesn't seem dissimilar from the place we were in last night. And they're playing decent music.

I don't know what I expected. Men snogging in corners, or disappearing off to the toilet together. There's none of that. Apart from the fact that the clientele is predominantly male, I wouldn't have known. Some are wearing eyeliner – but so do a lot of straight men in these New Romantic times.

Tara nudges me as a big group of women comes in. Now these are more obvious. Butch, even. Women with short hair, shaved at the sides, and sensible shoes. They move en-masse towards us. They're talking German. And I feel an uncomfortable sensation as they look me up and down. Something I've only ever felt in the presence of men. There's something predatory about them.

Tara and I sit down at the side. The night's getting going and the music's getting louder.

We hit the dance floor. And Tara moves like I've never seen her before. Wild and uninhibited. She grabs my hand, we gyrate round the floor. She draws me in towards her and we kiss, right there on the dance floor, and nobody bats an eyelid.

"This is so free!" she screams above the sound system and waves her hands in the air, but as she does so the sound cuts, the lights come on, stark and blinding, and the place is filled with police.

"Shit it's a raid."

The uniformed officers move with efficiency across the floor, stopping people, questioning them. Some of the club-goers attempt to flee, only to be blocked by batons. This is scary.

In the melee, I catch sight of our friends from last night. They move towards us at speed, "Best to go out," Jakob says. "Come with us." But the officers intercept us.

They round on Tara, firing questions in Slovenian. Luka, wonderful Luka, translates.

"He wants to know why you two are in this club. We told them you're with us."

All is pandemonium, my only consolation being that Luka keeps his arm around me as the police back us into a corner. They stand, not letting anyone leave, while one who seems to be the chief interrogates the barman.

"What's going on? What the hell is all this about, Luka?" I ask.

"Don't worry. They're not here for you. They'll let you go."

Another officer approaches. This one speaks English. He wants our names, passports and the address where we are staying. He then disappears for a while and comes back.

"Come," he says, and marches me and Tara outside and bundles us into a police car. I catch a last glimpse of Luka and Jakob standing by the road as the car speeds off.

"Shit, where are they taking us? I will not be locked in a Yugoslav cell all night. I demand to see a lawyer," Tara says loudly. The officers in the car say something in Slovenian. Then the car draws up outside the hotel.

Grace is standing outside with Karl and Eva.

There's a quick exchange between Eva and the officer, and we are released.

Inside the hotel, Grace bundles us into the lift.

"Just what do you think you were doing in a gay bar? Don't you know it's *illegal* to be homosexual in this country?"

"Actually, in Slovenia the law is changed since last year," Eva says quietly. Grace brushes her aside and marches Tara and me along the corridor to the suite. The anger in her eyes is clearly visible.

"We were with two guys. They told us to go there," I say weakly.

"Really?" says Grace. "So where are these two guys?"

"They went when the police put us in the car."

'How convenient," says Grace, her eyes narrowing. "They are not here, because they don't exist."

"They do, don't they, Tara? They were called Luka and – what was your one called again?"

"Jakob," says Tara. But then she fronts up to her mother.

"But we weren't with them. They kindly provided cover for us. We'd never be with them. Why? Because Chrissie and I are gay, mum. That's why we were in a gay club. We have a lesbian relationship. So deal with it."

"No!" Grace's face is immediately stormy. "No child of mine is a lesbian."

She turns to me. "What have you done to my daughter?"

"I was gay long before I met Chrissie," says Tara. "I've had girlfriends before her. Just what is your problem with this?"

Grace stands, hands on hips, looks from me to Tara and

snarls, "It's depraved. I did not bring you up to be a deviant."

Tara shouts back at her.

"You're such a fucking hypocrite. You have the gall to criticise my behaviour. You object to me having a loving monogamous relationship with Chrissie when you're fucking Karl Powell, right under his wife's nose."

Grace steps forward and slaps her in the face.

Tara springs back.

"What the fuck, mother?"

Karl announces his presence with a tap on the door and an "everything okay?"

Grace glares at him, lets out a noise that's half wail, half scream, then leaves the room.

"Reckon they grassed the place up?" says Tara later.

"Who?"

"Luka and Jakob. Reckon they tipped off the authorities?"

"Of course not. Why would they? They were helping us."

Tara sniffs.

"I'm not so sure. That guy, Luka. He fancied you. It was obvious. He didn't like the fact that we're gay. Some people don't like it, you know. Especially in a *backward* country like this."

So we're back to backward.

Something about what she says makes me see red. Now it's my turn to raise my voice.

"Well, you know what? I fancied Luka too," I say, enjoying the look on her face. "And you know something else? I'd have shagged him if it wasn't for you."

I say things I know I'll regret. I tell her I had no inclination towards women until I met her. "And whatever you've manipulated me into thinking, I'm actually *not* a fucking lesbian. Okay?"

We stay in our separate twin beds that night. Not sleeping.

The next day is the day we fly back.

"I'm sorry," I say in the morning, hung over with regret.

"I can't deal with this right now," says Tara. "I've got enough to handle with Grace. But once we get back to the UK we really need to talk about last night."

Chapter Twenty-Seven

"FLIGHT DELAYED, ALL we need," says Tara as we check into the airport. It's the first thing she's said since we left the hotel. Today is such a contrast to when we set off, just five days earlier.

Grace barely speaks either. She sits, surrounded by bags, in the smoking area at one end of the airport lounge, while Tara sits, head in a magazine, at the other end. Karl and Eva browse the airport's shopping offerings and I – not knowing where to put myself – loiter somewhere in the region of Tara.

I've got the mother of all hangovers. Bile is rising in my throat and my pulse pounds. I feel like I'm running a fever. I wonder what was in the drinks I had last night. Right now, I want to die.

It's still morning, too early for alcohol, but I eye the small bar longingly. Anything to get us through the awkwardness and calm my raging angst. Once again, help comes from an unlikely source. Eva approaches, gentle as a bird, and perches near me.

"How have you liked Ljubljana?" she asks, quietly.

"I think it's a cool place," I try to capture how I felt before last night. She then tells me some of the history of the city. I'm only half listening, but something about her voice lulls me as she talks about baroque architecture, the Julian Alps, Lake Bled, and how Slovenia has a separate, independent spirit. Then she says those magic words, almost whispers them. "The bar is open, would you like something?"

Hair of the dog. Not a good habit to get into, but today it's a lifesaver. I go to the bar with her. She orders us both a schnapps, and one for Tara too. Tara says nothing when I hand it to her, but downs it.

On the flight back, we sit separately. Tara and I have aisle seats opposite each other. Grace sits alone. Karl and Eva are on a two-seater further up. I take advantage of the free G&T.

In the car, driving down the M4 from Heathrow, nobody speaks. Eva sits in the back between me and Tara. Karl puts music on the car stereo to mask the heavy silence. They drop me off first at West Melcombe.

"I'll call you," Tara says from inside the car. I thank Karl as he retrieves my case from the boot. Grace sits in the front seat, staring forward, as if made of stone.

Mum, who's obviously been looking out for us, comes out to greet us, but the car speeds off before she's had a chance to say anything.

"Welcome back!" says Mum, giving me a hug. "How was your trip?"

I burst into tears.

Chapter Twenty-Eight

I SIT ON the upper deck of the bus to Bath, watching the familiar countryside roll by, my stomach knotted. I've done this journey so many times, with so many emotions. It's Saturday, the day after that agonising journey back from Ljubljana, and Tara has summoned me.

"Can you come over tonight? Mum's out. I want to clear the air before we go back to college."

I have a feeling this visit is a game changer. It could go either way. I don't know what will happen, or even what I *want* to happen.

It's the slow bus, the one that goes round the villages and takes forty-five minutes to get into town. I usually avoid it, but today it buys me time.

To carry on in a relationship with Tara seems impossible, to be without her doubly so. Until the trip to Ljubljana, I was on a track I couldn't get off. But that final night derailed it. And now, alongside a feeling of apprehension, I feel a flutter of freedom.

This heavy yoke I've carried could lift off me tonight. It's up to me.

The bus fills up as we get closer to the city. Young people

from outlying villages are heading into town, dressed for a night out. Another Saturday night with Tara. Saturday night used to be when we'd all congregate in the Alehouse or the Huntsman, then go on to a club. There was always a big gang of us. But Tara changed all that. I can't remember the last time I had an uncomplicated night out with my mates, and part of me longs for the pre-Tara days.

Luka's face keeps flashing through my mind; a flashback to a lost opportunity. And with it comes confusion. Luka was all male, and I'd wanted him.

Our meeting isn't the two-way discussion I hoped for. Tara sits me down and gives me an ultimatum.

"We're either together or we're not. And if we're together I want you to go public."

I sit on the edge of the sofa. She hasn't even offered me a drink. She stands and paces while I sit, staring at my shoes, wishing I was anywhere but here.

"How d'you think it feels, knowing you're too ashamed to tell people about us? How d'you think I felt the other night when we got picked up from the gay club and you were still pretending?"

I was trying to protect you actually, Tara.

"It's time you grew up, Chrissie. Stop fretting about what your silly little friends and family think and come out. I had to, thanks to your immature mates. Now it's your turn."

I hoped we'd have a conversation, tell each other how we felt. Instead, I feel like an admonished schoolgirl while Tara continues to rant.

"We've been seeing each other for months now. We've been having a full, sexual relationship, haven't we, Chrissie? And you've enjoyed it. Told me you'd never felt like this with anyone else. But you want the best of both worlds, to enjoy being with me, but to pretend you're not. What do you actually *want*?"

I look at her and shrug. "I don't know. I'm confused."

She's standing in front of me, hands on hips. "That thing you said in the apartment, about that Slav guy. You'd have fucked him. How *I* stopped you. Have you any idea how much that hurt?"

"I was drunk. I said it in the heat of the moment. I *said* I was sorry. How many times d'you want me to apologise?"

"Sorry's not good enough, Chrissie. You have to make up your mind. You can't sit on the fence any more. Either we're in a relationship or we're not. What's it to be?"

I walk over to the window, look out over the Georgian architecture and the hills beyond, and sigh.

My voice, when I find it, comes out shaky.

"I'm telling you the truth, Tara. I *am* confused. I don't want to come out because I don't know what I am. I don't want to be labelled as one thing when I might not be that thing. I never fancied girls before you, and it's all been a whirlwind that's carried me along with no time to think. And seeing Luka made me realise I still like men. Possibly more."

I say all this looking out of the window, but now turn to face her. It might not have been much of a speech, but at last I feel able to be honest.

"When I'm with you I get kind of carried along with it all, but when I'm away I worry whether you've just manipulated me into it."

Tara's face is granite, for a second she looks like Grace.

"Fine," she says. "Blame me. It takes two to tango."

"Sorry," I say. "That didn't sound right. I just need a bit of time to…"

"To what?"

"I just think we should press the pause button for a while, to give us both time to think."

She doesn't say anything. She turns her back on me and walks into the kitchen. I don't know if I'm supposed to follow. Eventually, I do. She's sitting at the table where Grace sat smoking that first time. She has a glass of clear liquid. Vodka or gin. She hasn't offered me one.

"You've made it clear you don't want me," she says. "So go."

"But Tara…"

"I can't do this 'we're on a break' crap. We're finished Chrissie. Just go."

She lets me see myself out.

I step out into the city, to a crowd of people, already lairy as they head out for their Saturday night.

I need a drink. I need company.

I know where they'll all be, probably, unless they've changed their habits. I open the door of the Alehouse, get myself a cider, and go downstairs. Sure enough they're there, crammed into of one of the cellar booths. Andy, Mike, Ian, Ben, Andy's little punkette girlfriend with the pink hair and the multiple piercings. And others I don't recognise.

I move over to them. "Room for a little 'un?"

Is it my paranoia or is there something grudging about the way they shift up to make room? The only person who seems pleased to see me is Ben.

Wedged between Mike, who's chatting up some girl, and Andy's girlfriend who – beyond telling me her name is Jet – seems incapable of coherent speech, I nurse my half of cider. And it dawns on me, I'm now an outsider.

Ben, sitting opposite, leans over, and I'm grateful. At least I can still talk to him about music.

"How come you're here tonight?" he says.

I so want to tell him, to tell *anyone*. I've been seeing someone and it's all over. We just broke up tonight. But I can't. My clandestine love must stay that way, even when it's over. I'll have to grieve alone.

Someone I don't know buys me a pint of cider when mine runs dry, and I continue to sup, now in my own little world, surrounded by voices. They sound oddly distant. They might as well be talking in a foreign language.

At closing time, everyone gets up to go. They're moving on somewhere and nobody's asked me.

I nudge Ben. "Where you off to?"

"The Underground. It's where we go now," he says. "You coming?"

But it's an afterthought, and I'm not wearing the right gear for the Undergound's alternative dress-code. I'm dressed for a cosy night in with Tara.

I decline.

"Well it's nice to see you out," says Ben.

Chapter Twenty-Nine

S UNDAY, THE DAY after the break-up with Tara, I wake with a banging headache. And it can't be booze-related – I only had a pint and a half of cider. I pop a painkiller and go back to sleep, waking several hours later drenched in sweat. Mum takes my temperature, says I have a fever, and sends me back to bed. For the next couple of days, my body aches and I spend a lot of time shivering or sweating. Mum declares it flu and phones college to tell them I won't be in.

Whether it's full-blown flu or not, it gives me a kind of delirium. Everything that happened since Ljubljana, since Tara even, now seems unreal. But as the week goes on, and I start to return to normality, I wait for the phone to ring.

By now, Tara will have heard how ill I am. Despite what happened between us on Saturday, surely she can find it in her to phone?

I've spent so long when I'm with her sharing my soul, and when I'm not, I store up things to tell her. But now I'm in a vacuum. My voice has nowhere to go. Whether we're together as a couple or not. I just want, need, to *talk* to her.

By Thursday, I'm well enough to get up. I hang around in the living room all day in my pyjamas, wondering whether to phone. I know Tara has a free morning on a Thursday. She might just be at home. But although I hover near the phone, and even pick up the receiver to dial the number, I think better of it. Let *her* ring *me*. I'm the one who's ill, after all.

That afternoon, Claire calls round on her way back from college, bearing chocolate.

"You okay, skiver?" she says.

"Not skiving, Claire, I've been really ill."

"You look a bit peaky." She sounds just like her mum.

She asks about the trip to Ljubljana. She glazes over when I talk about the city, but looks interested when I tell her about the two blokes and the way we'd been apprehended by the Police.

"Why? What'd you done?"

"They raided this club we were in." I omit to tell her it was a gay club. "It was probably operating without a licence or something. Karl's wife talked us out of trouble."

I ask her about college, if I've missed anything. She says no. I want to talk about Tara, but can't find a way that won't lead to an argument.

"Andy says he saw you down the Alehouse," she says. "He said you left early."

"Yeah. I just popped in. They were all going on to the Undergound. I wasn't really dressed for it. I'd been to see Tara."

"Uh huh."

"We had a bit of an argument."

"You and Andy?"

"Me and Tara."

"Oh."

"She hasn't phoned me since."

"Oh," she says again.

"D'you know if she's okay?", I ask. Fishing for information. Any information about Tara, even from Claire.

"No idea," says Claire. "I haven't seen her around college."

After she's gone, it occurs to me that Tara might also have the flu. We did share a room together for a week. Again, I hover by the phone. Again, I fail to call.

Each time the phone rings, I hope it's her, and when it isn't, I sink further into despondency.

ON FRIDAY I manage a short walk with the dog. The sunlight lifts my spirits, and when I get back, David, who's bunked off school claiming he's caught my lurgy, says: "Some bloke rang for you."

"Who was it?"

"Dunno."

"Great. So you didn't get a name or number or anything?"

"Nope."

Later, the mystery man phones back. It's Jason.

"I got your number from Claire," he says.

It's good to hear that velvet voice, but also slightly alarming.

"Is Tara with you?"

"Tara? No. Why, should she be?"

"Oh. I forgot you'd been off. She hasn't been in college all week. And Karl Powell says she's left."

"What d'you mean, left?"

"Packed in college. She sent a letter to the college secretary. I can't get hold of her. I thought she might be with you."

His words hit me like a fist in my solar plexus. With the

news that Tara might not return to college, the fragile edifice of my world begins to crumble.

"I've had flu all week and I haven't heard from her," I say. "Not since we got back from Ljubljana. Maybe she's ill too. Can't you ask Grace?"

"That's the weird thing, Chris. I keep phoning the flat but there's no answer. I've been trying all week. Different times of day. But nobody's there. That's why I thought she might be with you."

It's hard to read Jason at the best of times, especially over the phone, but I think I detect a note of anxiety in his voice.

"Maybe they've gone somewhere together, London or somewhere?" I say. But it doesn't seem likely, given their frosty relations just last week.

"Maybe," he says, but he doesn't sound convinced. "She went missing once before you know."

"What d'you mean, missing? When?"

He tells me Tara ran away once when she lived in Canada. "She'd had a row with her parents and she just took off. Drove somewhere. Stayed with friends. Sparked a massive search and didn't tell anyone where she was."

"Blimey, so d'you think that's what she's done?"

"I don't know. I can't get hold of Grace."

I promise to phone the flat myself and let him know how I get on.

Grace picks up straight away.

"Can I speak to Tara please, it's Chrissie."

The line goes quiet.

"Grace, please can I speak to her?"

"She's not here."

"When will she be back?"

"I've no idea." The voice is cold and perfunctory. "She's

gone."

Tara's mother has a habit of putting the phone down on people before the conversation is ended. She does it now. And when I phone back, there's no answer. I call Jason who's spoken to Karl Powell, and we finally have some of the details.

The night Tara and I broke up, the Saturday I went to the Alehouse, Grace returned late. Tara was already in bed. They saw each other briefly on Sunday morning before Grace went out to sing in her choir at the Abbey.

When Grace got back that afternoon, Tara wasn't there. Some time later Grace discovered a suitcase was missing and with it half her daughter's clothes. So by the time I got to hear about it, Tara had been gone nearly a week.

And Grace, apparently, has done precious little about it. I phone and phone, and eventually get through. "Have you reported her missing?" There's a pause on the line. A Grace silence. "I've spoken to everyone who needs to know," she says.

"So you've told the Police?"

Grace sniffs. "I'm dealing with this through the proper channels. Now if you don't mind. You're not helping Chrissie. *Please* don't call here again. This is getting tiresome."

Chapter Thirty

Diary Entry, scrawled in thick black marker pen.
    Right now, I hate the world. I hate the police. I hate Grace. I hate the press. I hate everyone – the only exception being JASON FLINT

"I'VE COME TO report a missing person."

The policeman at the desk is called P.C. Stephen Walker. It says so on a nameplate on the counter.

"Name please."

"Tara Clinton."

"Name of missing person?"

"Tara Clinton."

P.C. Walker looks at me like I'm mad or stupid or both.

"You're reporting yourself missing?"

"No. My name's Christine Carlisle."

He sighs. Stretches slightly in his chair, then winces, clutching his side.

"Let's start again, shall we? What's your name?"

So we go through the rigmarole again. P.C. Walker is not a fast mover, all his actions are methodical. I wonder what he'd do if he had to chase a criminal.

"Are you the next of kin?"

"No."

"Are you a relative?"

"No. She's my friend."

"You're reporting your friend missing?"

"Yes."

He moves his hand through his oily grey hair, combing it with his fingers, squinting at the paperwork in front of him.

"Name of next of kin of the missing person," he said.

"Grace," I say. Then I hesitate. Is Grace's surname the same as Tara's?

"Grace Clinton. That's her mum."

"Date of birth?"

"I don't know."

"Is there a photograph of the missing person?"

I hand over one of just three prints I have of Tara. It's the one Jason took the day of the picnic on Solsbury Hill.

P.C. Walker scrutinises it. He has bulbous eyes. Like my mum's friend Marjorie's. Only she has glandular problems that cause it. I wonder if P.C. Walker has those too.

"So when was Miss Clinton last seen?"

"Er. Sunday morning."

"Time?"

"Erm. I'm not sure. I know when I last saw her it was Saturday evening around nine pm."

"What was she wearing?"

"On Saturday she was wearing jeans and a green top."

"When she was last seen."

"Oh. I don't know. I wasn't there."

"So who was the last person to see her?"

"Her mum. Grace."

"I see," he says, chewing the end of his pen. "Now really it's her mother we should be talking to. Do you have her phone number?"

I leave frustrated. And when I phone later that day P.C. Walker is off shift. The woman I speak to says she can't discuss the case with me.

I phone Grace.

"I've spoken to the police," she says. "They have all the details. Now we must leave it to them."

"But what are they doing about it?"

"We must leave it to them," she says again, and puts the phone down.

I cry for about an hour.

David is the only one that notices, as he's the only one who's in.

"Why are you crying?"

"Because my friend's gone missing and I don't know if she's alive or dead and no-one seems to care."

David looks blank for a moment, then a lightbulb goes on.

"Tara?"

I nod.

"You don't know if she's alive or dead?"

"No-one knows where she is. She could be in some swanky hotel in London. She could be shacked up with one of her old mates, or she could be lying at the bottom of the river." I sniff.

He computes for a moment, unaffected by my emotion, then says, "Well, if you don't know, it's both. Like Schrödinger's cat."

"What?"

"Is the cat in the box dead or alive? You don't know until you open the box. So until you open the box, it's both dead *and* alive. It's quantum physics, see."

I EXPECT TO see MISSING posters appear across town. It doesn't happen. I phone Grace. No response.

"D'you think she's been abducted?" David seems to be relishing it. "Maybe the police are in on it and it's a cover-up."

"You watch too many cop-shows," says Mum.

"Why don't you try the paper?" I stare at David in astonishment. For once my brother might have actually suggested something useful.

So I take another one of my precious photos into the Bath Evening Chronicle. I stand at the reception desk while a man in front of me kicks off about an error in last Saturday's sports pages. He's clutching a torn off cutting and getting very heated. I try to tune out from the commotion and focus on a display of black and white photos in the window.

They send a junior reporter to see me. We sit side by side on a low green bench.

"So a girl's gone missing?"

"Yes."

"How old?"

"Eighteen."

"Oh." He looks disappointed. Like he'd have preferred a fifteen-year-old. That would make a better story.

I show him the photo. "We can use this," he says, now animated. The papers love beautiful blondes.

He fires questions at me. Is Tara volatile? Did she have a row with her parents? Her boyfriend? Has she gone missing before? Anything suspicious happen in the run-up? Any strange assignations?

He'd make a better investigator than P.C. Walker.

I tell him Tara and I had a bit of a falling out. I don't tell him about our relationship, of course.

"I'll need to speak to the mother."

I give him Grace's phone number and address.

I leave feeling that at last I could be getting somewhere.

I phone Jason from a call box to tell him what I've done. "Well done," he says. "At least you're doing something. Now that's enough for one day. You need to go home and get some rest."

I do that, and as soon as I walk in the phone rings and it's Grace.

"I had a reporter ringing the doorbell," she says. "I told them to go away"

"Why, Grace? They can help. Someone might have seen her."

There's a pause on the line, then she says. "I do not want my family business plastered all over the papers." Then she hangs up.

"Tough!" I say, although no-one's listening. Later David brings me a copy of the paper. There's a small photo of Tara on the front page, with the headline "Fears for missing teenager," then the full story inside. "College girl vanishes after row with best friend."

Tara's mother declined to comment. Mr. Collins, our headteacher, is quoted as saying what a bright student she is, and he hopes she'll soon be found.

I have Jason on side. He cuts out the article and makes it into a poster with some clever artwork. *Have you seen missing Tara Clinton?* We make copies and post them all around town. In shop windows where they let us, on billboards, we even pin them to trees.

"Grace will not like this," I say.

"So what?" says Jason. "She's not exactly doing much to help."

We go to all our old haunts, the Alehouse, the Huntsman, the Salamander, Moles, and the pub round the corner which became our sanctuary. Two men are at the bar. I recognise them as the ones who tried to chat us up. As I walk away, I hear the murmurings. "She that lesbian girl?"

"Wonder where she is?"

"They tried the river?"

NEXT DAY, WALKING through town on my way to college, I pass a lamppost where we'd stuck the poster. It's been ripped down, only the drawing pin with a strip of one corner remains. I sigh. That happens, it's illegal to fly-post. But the next one I pass makes my blood run cold. Someone has defaced the poster. In thick, black marker-pen, they've daubed the word 'QUEER' across Tara's face. I tear that one down myself.

Later, at home, I get a call from Scott, the reporter at the Chronicle. "Is it true you and Tara had a... very close relationship?" he says. "A lesbian relationship?"

"No it's not true and even if it was it's hardly relevant," I say, and end the call. When a call comes later from a producer from Points West News, I get my brother to say I'm out.

Next day's headline is "Lesbian love twist in missing girl saga," citing rumours that Christine Carlisle was the missing girl's lover as well as her friend. Christine Carlisle was unavailable for comment.

The phone keeps ringing. Mum unplugs it.

"But what if it's Tara, trying to get in touch? What if it's someone with information?"

"Chrissie you need to just step back from this, you're too involved," says Mum.

"Not you as well. You're starting to sound like Grace."

"If anything happens people will contact the police, or the paper," she adds. "You have to trust the authorities to handle it."

"They don't give a shit!", I scream. "What if something terrible's happened to her?"

Mum puts her hands on my shoulders to calm me, then pushes me gently down onto a chair in the kitchen.

"Tara's eighteen now. She's an adult. She can look after herself. She's a seasoned traveller. She's got a passport and money. Leave it, Chris. You've done your bit. It's for her mother and the police to decide on the best course of action."

Chapter Thirty-One

I've kept a copy of the paper where they ran the first story. I open it out, brittle and yellowed, and read the article, Tara's face looks out at me like some ghost from the past.

These days, in our post-millennial digital age, it's much easier to track someone's movements. Tara would have walked past multiple cameras just to get out of the city. If she'd got on a train, hired a car, boarded a plane, there'd have been an electronic record. Her image would have been shared within seconds across multiple social media platforms. Back then, in the eighties, all we could do was wait.

Then again, these days, she may not have felt the need to disappear.

April 1982

NOTHING COULD HAVE prepared me for the way I now feel. Tara has simply vanished. It's left a void in me that grows daily, bigger and more terrifying. I feel it in my solar plexus, slowly and insidiously taking over my body, eating into my brain.

When Grace delivered those words "She's gone," I felt as though somebody had punched me in the stomach. Like I did when my dad died. But in that case, we knew it was coming. And we were carried along in the arms of aunts, friends, family. David and I had time off school. We were allowed to howl and scream and fight and strop. It was expected. My social worker mother and her social worker friends knew how to handle it.

When Claire's dad left, it was tough for her, but the teachers all knew, and made allowances, and there followed resolution and healing. A realisation that it was for the best. There was hope for the future as they kept in touch. New avenues opened up as she had another place to go. A new town to explore. A new bedroom with her own TV in it. Fun things to do with her freed-up father, things she would never have been allowed to do at home.

This is different. The hole Tara left doesn't heal. It grows.

And I'm expected to just carry on as normal.

For a few days, I reel from shock, which gives me an energy to do things. There is much to do in the search for Tara. Avenues to explore. But each one leads to a dead end.

Tara's mother exasperates me. If we worked together, we could locate at least one or two of the missing jigsaw pieces. Instead, she refuses to speak to me. I suspect she blames me and I certainly blame her.

College takes second place. My work suffers. Essays get handed in late. I miss classes. My social life has all but disappeared. My brother tells me I've become obsessed.

There is nothing left to do but wait. And the waiting kills. And the sickness in me spreads. It's like, without Tara, I don't know who I am any more. What have I become? I think back with amazement to the Saturday night when I last saw her, how I'd craved freedom from her. Now, I'd give anything to have her back.

It's like there's a parasite gnawing away at me, burrowing into my brain, stealing my personality. Sometimes I try, for an hour, or half an hour, to be my old self, but it's just a façade, an act. I'm not that person any more. My confidence is shot. And people avoid me, or look at me with pity. I stop going to the common room and venture to the library instead, where I stare at the bottom of a coffee cup and pretend to read. Sometimes I'm conscious of Jason working alongside, somewhere in my orbit. He doesn't say much, but I sense in him a kindred spirit.

"Chrissie's thrown herself into her work," my mother says. She probably sees it as a good thing.

Except I haven't. I sit in the library staring at a book, the words jumping around on the page, meaningless. Nothing penetrates my fog.

ON THE SURFACE, I may seem calm. Inside I rage. At Tara's mother, for her coldness. At my own mother, for her bustling cheerfulness and patent lack of understanding. At my one-time friends, for daring to carry on with their lives like nothing has happened, while mine has been smashed apart.

And I rage against Tara. When I think about the strange land we inhabited together, it scares me. Sometimes I see her as a malevolent being who sought to entrap me. Who lifted me up, flew high with me, dropped me into an impenetrable pit, then left me there. My feelings for Tara are the hardest to fathom because they are the most confused.

My dreams are full of Tara, and the river. Tara jumping in. Tara's outstretched arm, waving. Or drowning? Or trying to pull me in?

I drift around on a wave of sadness. Places we've been, things we've done, ordinary things like the bus to town hold an extra intensity for me. But as I pass these places without her, they become dead.

It's a cold spring, with a deceptive, lazy wind. There's another flu bug going around, and I wonder if I've caught it. I take a couple of days off with non-specific symptoms. I've not been eating properly, my sleep's disturbed, and I have a general feeling of disconnection with the world.

On the day I go back to college, I eat a half bowl of Cornflakes and walk to the bus stop. I feel light-headed, but put that down to whatever lurgy I've contracted. The bus is delayed by roadworks, making me late. I have to rush to get to college on time. There's an address from the head and we've had a three-line whip to attend. When I arrive, it's already started. My pulse is pounding from the brisk walk. The Theatre is packed, so I squeeze into an empty seat in the middle of a row.

As I sit there, my heart rate doesn't return to normal. It continues to race, louder and faster. I'm gripped by a feeling that something is very, very wrong. Is this what a heart attack feels like? The headteacher's voice on the stage sounds distant and unreal. The people around me seem suddenly hostile. Fear grips me, along with a sudden desire to scream the place down. The only thing I'm aware of is the absolute necessity of getting out as fast as possible. So I push past those same people I disturbed just minutes earlier, sensing their irritation. Heart still pounding, I make it to the door, stumble outside, then slump to the ground, leaning against the wall of the building, head in my hands. It's only then that the panic subsides.

First lesson is Maths. People ask if I'm better. Again their voices sound remote, like they're talking to me through an echo chamber. I say I'm still feeling a bit off and they leave me to my solitude. As we wait for the teacher to arrive, I stare at the quadratic equations in my text-book, the numbers jumbled and meaningless. I can hear the voices of the others all around me, chatting, sharing gossip. And out in the corridor, someone laughs. One harsh laugh. Aimed at me? I feel my chest tighten as the voices around me grow louder and become scrambled, incoherent. The guttural sounds of a hostile crowd. I grip the desk in front of me, prickly sweat breaking out on my forehead, arms and shoulders tense. Again, I feel the desire to scream.

The teacher arrives, like a saviour. Quiet is restored. My pulse rate returns to normal.

But not for long. The silence and order I've craved is now my enemy, as the panic inside surfaces again. My heartbeat fills my head, drowning out the teacher's voice, growing faster, accelerating out of control. The room swims out of focus as the terror mounts. I cannot stay in this room a moment longer. I have to get out.

I push back my chair and run from the room.

The teacher sends one of the girls after me. She finds me in the toilets where I stand, leaning on the basin, staring at myself in the mirror. The image looking back is not me. It's a pale, frightened ghost of myself.

"You look terrible," she says. "You should go home." She collects my stuff from the classroom and I walk out of the college gates. The bus is diverted because of roadworks. It goes via Melcombe town centre and it takes almost an hour. Again, I feel the panic rise, but manage to contain it, stop by stop, until we reach West Melcombe. Once home, I lie face down on my bed and cry. I'm still crying when Mum arrives home from work hours later.

I've never known tears like this. A flow that will not stop. Tears dry up, don't they? Not these. For several days, crying displaces everything that I do. I hardly eat, because a vice grips my stomach. I barely set foot outside the door. When I do, the panic comes. Once I make it half-way to the corner shop, but the desire to scream sends me once more running for home and the sanctuary of my bedroom. My record collection fails to comfort me. Even the words of the song that bears my name seem to mock me now. *Christine... disintegrating...*

I've heard of claustrophobia. I've heard of agoraphobia. I appear to have both.

Mum bundles me up and takes me to see Griffiths, our spectacularly useless family doctor. She comes in with me to the consulting room.

"How are your stools?" he asks.

It takes a second or two to register what he's asking. I almost laugh. Then he tells me to take zinc and eat walnuts. As we leave, the weight I'm carrying feels a ton heavier.

I don't sleep for days. When I doze, my sleep is plagued by weird and frightening images, monsters of the night, grotesque faces, leering at me on the bridge, and Tara's outstretched arm, the bear tattoo now a grinning gargoyle. Night and day roll into one interminable half-light, punctuated by bouts of sobbing.

After three more days of this, mum takes me back to the doctors. This time, it isn't Griffiths, it's a locum, who asks my mother to wait outside.

He fires questions at me, brisk and business-like. I describe what's been happening.

"D'you feel like you're going mad?" he asks.

"Yes."

"If you think you're going mad, you're not."

Even through my despair, this strikes me as a strangely arbitrary analysis, but somehow comforting.

He has a name for what I've been experiencing. Panic attacks. He explains the fight or flight mechanism in a simple, scientific sentence. He tells me these attacks are common and can't kill me.

I want to hug him. I am not the only person in the world who has ever felt like this. This thing even has a name.

He prescribes some medication called Imipramine and signs me off college for two weeks. He writes 'Anxiety and depression,' on my sick note.

The pills are meant to lift my mood so that I can take an objective view of my situation and work out what went wrong.

"You may feel worse before you start to feel better," he says.

Is it possible to feel any worse?

He doesn't tell me about the side effects, the weird electric sensations pulsing through my body, the dry mouth, the inability to wee, the blurred vision. Somehow, I get through those two weeks.

Claire comes round, persuades me to eat spaghetti hoops on toast, like we did when we were kids. David makes me play chess. I lose. Aunts come and go, bearing baking I don't want to eat.

"What's the matter, my darling?" Nan descends in her wheelchair, wanting to sweep around and make everything all right.

"Chrissie's not feeling very well," says Mum, one foot out the door on her way to some committee.

"Here. Have an apple from my tree." Nan produces a big, shiny red apple from the village greengrocer. Her tree hasn't borne fruit for years. She inspects it, wipes it on the tea towel hanging in the kitchen, like that would make it any cleaner, and presents it to me.

"Thanks, Nan, I'll have it later."

She shakes her head. "You know what they say. An apple a day."

I don't eat the apple, but it draws my eye to its rich colour and lustre. I run my finger over the smooth surface. It's even, and perfect, there's just one blemish by the stalk. I place it on the table near the vase. It looks like a still-life painting.

Nan examines me through her bifocals. "You're getting very thin and pale."

David appears, yawning, and her face breaks into smiles. "How's my favourite grandson?" She holds out her arms for a hug. He plants an awkward kiss on her head.

"Have you been looking after your sister? She's not herself."

"I know."

"Is it a broken heart?" Nan asks the room.

David looks at me and shrugs.

"Her best friend went missing. She's been worried."

"Now that is bad," says Nan. "A young girl going missing in this day and age. Anything could have happened. You read such awful things in the papers."

Thanks, Nan.

Chapter Thirty-Two

A bunch of greetings cards, held together by an elastic band. Some of them say "seventeen" on them. Some of them say "Get Well".

May 1982

W AKING UP ON my seventeenth birthday, Mum brings me a cup of tea.

"Happy birthday, Chrissie," she sits at the end of my bed, David hovering in the doorway while I open my presents. I got what I asked for. Mostly music. New albums from The Cure, Talking Heads and The Clash, plus vouchers for Topshop and Chelsea Girl.

Mum looks at her watch. "I'm sorry, I have to go to work." She kisses the top of my head. "But we'll have a nice tea later. Unless you've got plans?"

I have no plans except to pull the covers up over my head and shut out the world.

"And don't forget your appointment later."

"What? Oh, that guy. Is that today?"

"What guy?" says David. "You got a date?"

I laugh. "It's some shrink Mum's fixed me up with."

"He's not a shrink, he's a counsellor," Mum corrects me. "Appointment's at eleven, and Aunty Meg will drive you there."

The counsellor works from an office at the back end of some industrial estate on the edge of Bristol. When we eventually find the place, Meg says: "You don't have to go in, you know."

"Thanks," I say, "but I'll never hear the end of it if I don't."

"Ok, but if you can't stand it, I'll be waiting out here in the car."

She makes it sound like I'm going to the dentist.

I press a buzzer which releases a door and I follow signs which take me down a long corridor to a room marked "Therapy".

The door is slightly open. I tap on it. Inside I can see the back of a man's head. Bald, with folds of skin on the neck and a huge ear to ear crease that greets me like a grin.

"Come in," he says, without looking round.

I'm seriously tempted to walk straight back out again and take Meg up on her offer.

I don't. I walk in and face the guy. He has a deadpan face, and an upside-down triangle of hair on his chin.

He asks me a few cursory questions. I give him a potted history while he nods, his face expressionless. I tell him I had a relationship with someone who left. I omit to tell him that person was a girl. Or that nobody knows where she is.

"You have abandonment issues," he tells me.

I thought counsellors weren't supposed to give you a diagnosis. I thought they were supposed to just listen and let you come up with the answers.

According to him, my fear of being abandoned dates

back to Dad dying. Tara leaving has brought all that back, and Mum reinforces this all the time by buggering off to sort out other people's problems. He didn't actually say "buggering off," though.

"Anything else you want to tell me?"

I shrug. "Today's my birthday."

"Happy birthday," he says, with the teeniest hint of a smile, like he's suppressing a giggle. I'm struck by a surreal desire to laugh. I wonder if he is, in fact, an alternative comedian looking for material and not a real counsellor at all.

"Oh, and I can fly."

He leans forward as I tell him about my flying thing.

"Someone said it was a personality disorder. Dissociation, or something."

He shakes his head. "It could actually be a coping mechanism. Remove yourself from the situation and observe how you react. It could be a healthy response. Therapists actively encourage you to take an objective view of yourself."

There's a pause while I digest this. So, I've actually hit on the right thing. But the irony is, I've lost my ability to fly since Tara left. I try, but I can't take off.

He looks at the clock on the wall that says ten to twelve. "We're out of time I'm afraid, but I think we can work with this if you want to make another appointment to see me."

He doesn't get up. As I leave the room, I turn round to see the back of his head grinning at me, like a gargoyle. I know I won't be back.

Aunty Meg is in the car outside, reading a magazine.

"How was it?"

"Awful."

She laughs. "God knows where my sister drags up these

quack counsellors from. You're better off going for a brisk walk with the dog. One day you'll just snap out of it." She clicks her fingers as she says it.

Claire comes round later. She's bought me a rainbow-coloured headband and she's made me a compilation tape. She opens a tin of spaghetti hoops and serves it on toast. Our favourite meal when we were little.

We play my new Cure album.

"No wonder you're depressed if you listen to this," she says, putting on her tape of new romantic dance tracks instead. She gets me up to dance in the living room, but I'm too weak. I collapse onto the sofa.

She puts her arms round me. "I want you to get better, Chris. I want my old friend back."

She's brought a bottle of cider. "Are you allowed to drink on your tablets?"

"A little," I say. "That reminds me."

I pop a pill out of the dispenser, labelled up in days to make sure I don't miss one. I swallow my anti-depressant with a gulp of cider.

Happy birthday, Chrissie.

Chapter Thirty-Three

Diary entry.

Word of the week: discombobulate

May 1982

M UM, BUSY AS ever, has instructed David, of all people, to keep an eye on me and "try to take my mind off it." This means he's doing his homework at the kitchen table, instead of in his room.

David's method of distracting me is to read out dubious facts from his physics notes for my edification. Some of them sound bizarre and not like anything I ever learnt at school.

He's apparently been inspired by some new science teacher at school. How can anyone get excited by physics?

"Did you know, Chris," he says, looking up, "that you're just a collection of atoms. Billions of them. But there's no reason for those atoms to actually stay together. It's completely random that they do."

"What?"

"You're a collection of atoms that stay together for no apparent reason."

"What are *you* then?"

"I'm the same. We all are. Even Arnold. And that dishcloth. And the kettle."

"You've blown my mind." I say. I mean it ironically but it's partly true. I'm now worrying about my atoms.

"Quantum physics," he says.

I look at my hand, and wonder how many billions of atoms it contains.

"So what if," David adds, "all those atoms that make up you decide not to stay together but to disperse. There's nothing stopping them."

Great. So not only have I lost the plot. I'm also in danger of losing my atoms, and actually, physically disintegrating.

I remember what the counsellor said about abandonment. I've got a thing about people leaving me. Dad left, well – died, but the counsellor said that counts as leaving. Andy left – because of Tara. Claire left – because of Simon, and maybe because of Tara too. Tara left, big time – or died, we don't know which. Possibly both. If you believe my brother and Schrödinger. Now even my atoms might get up and leave.

"But they probably won't," David adds. "It'd be weird if they did. Kinda cool though."

Why is it that when you're already feeling peculiar people say strange things to you. David is supposed to be distracting me, not freaking me out.

LITTLE THINGS STAND out in a fortnight of strangeness. Thanks to the pills, I'm no longer experiencing such acute despair. Now I feel almost detached, like I'm watching myself, quietly discombobulating. Sometimes I even feel a peculiar kind of high. For odd moments I almost forget. Then some fleeting memory, some object or road-sign or piece of music, drags me right back down again.

I spend a lot of time in or on my bed, staring at the ceiling, listening to the radio.

David opens the door. "Someone to see you."

Arnold sits on the threshold to my room, paws outstretched just beyond the door frame.

"He's not allowed in bedrooms," I say.

"Who's to know?" says David.

I pat the duvet next to me. Arnold is across the room in two bounds, and up on the bed, sniffing, licking, wagging, filling the space with his doggie presence. I'll push him off in a minute, but for now, this canine affection is healing.

LATER, IN THE kitchen, David asks what we've got for tea. Mum's at some tribunal thing for work, and I can't motivate myself to eat.

"Dunno."

I can almost see the cogs in his brain turning.

"I'm starving!"

"Cook something then. I'm not hungry."

He turns his back on me. I watch him root around. He goes to the freezer.

"We've got chicken."

"It has to defrost or it'll poison you."

He shuts the freezer door and opens the fridge.

"Sausages. There's only three."

"Have them," I say. "I don't want any."

He takes out the packet and stares at it.

"You know how to cook sausages. Just fry or grill them. It tells you how long on the packet."

He reads out loud. "Grill for ten to twelve minutes, turning once." He frowns, like he doesn't know what turning means.

"What shall I have with it?" This is more a rhetorical question. He's seen oven chips in the freezer. He reads the instructions on these too.

"You need to heat the oven up before you put them in," I say. "You put the chips in before you fry the sausages."

"I can work out the timings," he grunts.

In my suspended state, I watch my brother cook. Despite myself, the smell as the sausages start to sizzle awakens my saliva glands. I feel a rush of sensation to my brain. He's in the swing of it now, almost taking pride in what he's doing, turning the sausages with panache. He opens a tin of beans too, and boils them on full heat.

When the meal is ready, he reaches into the cupboard and brings out two plates, a dinner plate and a little side plate. I wonder what the small plate's for. Is he having bread on top of all that stodge? But instead, he puts one sausage on it, and slices it into little pieces.

"Is that for the dog?"

He doesn't answer. He spoons a tiny dollop of beans onto the small plate too, and a handful of chips.

It reminds me of when I was little when Mum used to give me a separate plate for my imaginary friend Marcia. David brings both plates to the table and puts the smaller one in front of me, handing me a fork.

"David!"

"Just have one bit of sausage. Go on. Just one. They're microscopic."

I obey, and the juices race around my mouth. I chew and swallow, and my stomach screams for more. I spoon in another, dipped in beans. Then a chip. Slowly, I consume the lot.

"You want more?" he looks worried now, in case I encroach on his near demolished plateful.

"No, that's enough." I'm not sure I'll keep it down.

I look at him in wonder as he leaves the table.

"What made you do that?"

"We have to take in energy to avoid entropy."

"What?"

"We have to eat," he says. "Both of us."

It reminds me of when we were younger. After Dad died. When Mum was working late and I used to make tea for the two of us. I took it very seriously, making sure we ate.

He turns round to face me, eyes not quite meeting mine.

"There's a girl in my year. Marie Beckenham. She's got anorexia. She's like a skeleton. Her bones jut out. At lunchtime she eats in a separate room. They break her dinner up into little pieces. I don't want my sister to get like her."

A swell of something overcomes me. Sheer, raw emotion. Salt tears sting my eyes.

"Oh David," I say, and jump down from my chair.

"Don't hug me," he says, and walks away.

Chapter Thirty-Four

May 1982

O NE DAY – I've lost count of the days – I wake up feeling different. I ask Mum if she needs anything from the shop and she hands me a list.

I walk outside the front door. The sun is shining. I'm conscious of flowers in the gardens, their colours vivid. I'm fixated by the colour everywhere. I walk and I carry on walking. I make it to the village shop. I articulate the items on the list. I carry the shopping back home. I feel a sense of triumph. Maybe, just maybe, something resembling normality is coming back.

I make it on the bus into Bath the next day. I go mid-morning to minimise the risk of seeing anyone from college. I fulfil mum's challenge of staying in Sainsbury's long enough to find all the items on her list, without running out of the shop, silently screaming, as I feared I would.

I feel a little surge of pride, mixed with relief, as I stand in the line for the checkout.

Then I spot Karl Powell in a parallel queue. I feel heat rising in me. I want to become invisible, to slink out unseen. I pointedly look the other way as the cashier rings through my items, but sense Karl's seen me and is coming over.

"Christine?" Odd to hear someone use my full name. "How are you doing?" he searches my face.

I feel dull, freakish, and unwashed in days-old clothes.

"Oh, not too bad. Getting there." I wonder how much he knows about the state I'm in.

"It's good news about Tara." It's a statement framed like a question.

My pulse pounds so hard it shakes my body. He swims out of focus.

"Is it?" I say weakly.

"Oh, didn't you know? She got in touch with Grace. She's in Canada. She's safe."

I feel acid tears smarting at the back of my eye-sockets. I force myself to focus.

"Is she at her dad's?"

"With friends, I think, at the moment. The important thing is she's safe."

"How long has Grace known?"

He looks over my shoulder and shifts slightly, like I'm keeping him from something important or he's spotted someone more interesting to talk to.

"Er, not sure. So Tara's not contacted you?"

I shake my head.

"I'm sure she'll be in touch soon.". He presses his hand on my shoulder and moves off.

Body shaking, I stop by a phone box and dial the familiar number. After about six rings, Grace's husky voice comes on the phone.

"Yes?"

"It's Chrissie."

"Oh!"

"Any news from Tara?"

I wait for her to tell me, but there's silence on the line.

"Don't bother answering. I saw Karl Powell. I know she's turned up in Canada."

"Yes, that's right."

Once more, the tears, never far away, well up, choking me. I can't speak.

"Are you there?" she says.

I give Grace a taste of her own medicine and put the phone down.

I sling my bag over my shoulder, grab my shopping, and head off in the direction of Grace's flat, overtaken by a new emotion. Anger. I don't care that my clothes are scruffy. That my hair's unwashed. That my make-up's smudged. I have to confront Tara's mother.

"It's Chrissie," I say to the intercom.

"This isn't a convenient time," she says, but as I stand there the couple from the flat above emerge through the front door with their baby, holding the door open long enough to get the pushchair out. I enter with a smile.

"Why didn't you tell me?" I say, now face to face with Grace.

She shrugs. That is one expression Tara inherited, or learnt, from her mother.

"People have been out of their minds worrying about her. How long have you known?"

"Woah!" she holds her palm out as though to repel me. "First you barge in here uninvited, now you interrogate me in my own home. The truth is, Tara asked me not to say anything. She said she'd write to you and to Jason."

"Well, she hasn't. So can I have her address and phone number?"

She places her hands on her hips, like she's bracing for a fight. "No, you cannot. If she wants to be contacted, she'll be in touch. And if you want the truth, even I don't have an address for her. All I had was a brief phone call and a promise she'll write when she's settled."

"So we don't even know where she is? We *still* don't know if she's safe?"

Grace shakes her head. "She'll be safe all right. The thing you have to understand about Tara is that she can look after herself. She's got plenty of friends over there; all over the world in fact. If she wants to get in touch with any of us, she will do. And that, I'm afraid, is that. Now if you don't mind."

The tears come now. They fall on barren ground. Grace may be uncomfortable, but otherwise unmoved.

She turns away and sighs, then moves towards the hallway where she inspects herself in the long mirror. "Whatever went on between you two…"

"What d'you mean?"

"Well, if you hadn't filled her head with this notion she's a lesbian."

"*What?*" I yell the word, but Grace picks up a jacket from a hanger in the hallway and throws it over her shoulders. "You must leave, Chrissie, I'm going out."

THE BUS JOURNEY back is blurred through tears. I hate myself for falling in love with someone capable of hurting me so ferociously. For becoming, without even realising it, so utterly dependent.

I hate Grace. I hate the world. And now, finally, I hate Tara.

The worst thing of all is hating Tara.

David's up in his room playing metal. I don't even have the energy to ask him to turn it down. I collapse on the sofa, my mind a weird kind of nothingness.

I've been there about twenty minutes when the doorbell rings. I nearly don't bother to answer it, then I spot Jason's Triumph outside.

I open the door, and the second I see his face, I know he understands.

"Powell told me," he says. Then he hugs me. And in that hug is a thousand craved emotions.

"Let's go for a drive."

We go to Little Solsbury Hill, where we went for the picnic with Tara. It takes all my energy to tackle the gradient and I have to stop several times on the ascent. Jason waits for me to regain my breath. At the top, we stop and look at the view.

"I loved her too, you know," he says gently.

I look at him, study those perfect features for a few seconds, then say "But I thought…"

"I'm gay, yes. But I loved Tara. It was more… I can't describe it. It was almost spiritual. I adored her."

I know that feeling.

"When I was fifteen I was pretty mixed up. A lost boy. And Tara walked into my life. She'd just moved over from Canada. She singled me out. She saw potential in me and gave me validation. I was confused about my sexuality. And when I met Tara, I thought, maybe I'm not gay. Life would be so much simpler if I just wasn't gay. We gave it a go. But we both knew it was no good. It was a convenient cover for both of us."

I remember how we used that same cover to diffuse the rumours about Tara being gay. How everyone thought they were a couple when they first showed up at college last September. Now I feel a deep pang. I want to be back there in that hopeful beginning. I was looking for something then. But I wasn't sure what. I was open to possibilities.

"She liked you, Chrissie, because you were your own person. She was also jealous," he adds

"Jealous of what?"

"Of all the people around you. She wanted you all to herself."

She got what she wanted.

We look out over the city. The tears that had clouded my vision now spent.

"I need a new friend now," he says, linking arms with me. "And I think you do too."

I nod. I melt into him. His arm encases me. I feel safe.

"I need a friend who won't abandon me."

"Me too," I say, leaning into him. "Me too."

Chapter Thirty-Five

An A5 sketch book. Line drawings. Landscapes. Portraits. A sketch of Jason painting. Images of Tara, grotesque, distorted. Pages covered in thick, dark charcoal strokes.

June 1982

T HE REST OF the summer term is hazy, not vivid like what went before. Jason is a constant presence, an unlikely lifesaver, a soft edge to all the sorrow. Thrown together by loss, we lean on each other. I soak up his wisdom, his calm, his detachment. His friendship is somehow unconditional.

One day, Grace turns up unannounced at my house. "Yours, I believe." She hands me a plastic bag full of letters. My letters to Tara, still in their opened envelopes, bundled together with elastic bands. I take the bag from her without speaking and shut the door. Zombie-like, I carry them up to my room and empty the contents into the pink suitcase Nan gave me at Christmas. At last I've found a use for it.

Fuelled by Imipramine, I drift in and out of college, some days making it through my classes, others barely lasting five minutes. Nobody questions me. I've acquired the licence of craziness. The art room has become my safe space, where I'm frequently to be found, hanging out with Jason, soothed by watching him work.

I miss art. I used to be good at it but when it was time to choose subjects at school, it didn't fit in with my other choices, so I dropped it.

One day, Jason turns up with a sketch pad for me and a set of pencils of varying thickness. "I'm going somewhere to paint. Want to come?"

We drive out into the countryside to an ancient water mill. He has fold-up chairs and an easel in the back of his car. We sit a few yards apart, him painting, me drawing.

It's a bright day, warm with a gentle breeze, the sky unbroken blue. A perfect English summer's day. He's brought a flask of coffee and he pours me some. We stay for a good two hours, hardly speaking. There's no awkwardness, just peace and companionship.

Jason admires my art. "You have a talent."

This is the day I start drawing again. Either out with Jason, up in the art room, or at home. Sometimes I cover the paper with angry charcoal. Sometimes I scrawl something, rip out the page, and throw it away. Other times I draw Tara, witch-like, her chiselled features extenuated.

At the end of term, I phone Karl Powell.

"This is not about Tara," I say. "I've made a decision. When we go back to college in the autumn, I want to give up maths and switch to art."

THAT SWITCH LED me to where I am now. A skilled, qualified, graphic designer, and not a bad artist, if I say so myself.

PART TWO

What Lies Within

I'm done with 1981/2. Reconnecting with all that angst. It's time to tackle the last remaining box: 2005.

A smaller box. By 2005 I'd gone mostly digital. There are memory sticks, a few CDs and some other items. How funny to be reunited with my old Motorola phone. And my pass to the building where we used to work. On the photo I'm smiling, I have long hair and I'm wearing a red work shirt. Underneath the photo it says Christine Carlisle, Graphic Designer LIMITLESS DESIGNS. I have Alex's pass too, for some unfathomable reason – perhaps to prove we worked there, in case our exodus got challenged. He's unsmiling, of course. His eyes burning into the lens. His skin is smoother, he's a fresher, more youthful version of his current self.

Limitless Designs – I chuckle at the company name. Oh the irony.

Chapter Thirty-Six

TWO MOMENTOUS THINGS happen on 28 April 2005.

The first is a call on my landline at one minute past midnight.

"Chris!"

"Alex?"

Alex is my colleague at Limitless Designs. I didn't know he even had my number.

"Your mobile's off."

"I switch it off at night."

"Have you been paid?"

"Um. I don't know."

"Can you check?"

I reach for my laptop on the table by the bed and log onto my online banking.

Nothing. Apart from a big fat looming overdraft as all the pending bills show red. No salary payment.

"Shit!"

"They've done it, Chris. Our bastard employers have fucking screwed us over."

I sigh, trying to quiet the thumping of my pulse.

"Could it be just a mistake?" But we both already know

the answer.

It's been building for weeks. Strange behaviour from Phil and Suki, our two directors. Long meetings behind closed doors. Raised voices, hushed whenever anyone walked past. A palpable tension in the air. And for the last three days, neither of them contactable. Calls going straight to voicemail. Their office locked.

Alex had seen this before. Some place else. But for him I would've blithely carried on.

"So what do we do?" I ask.

"What we planned."

"When?"

"No time to lose. We need to go now, before they shutter the place up. We need to get there before the bailiffs. Oh, and Chris, we'd better take your van."

Which means waking Paul up as it's *his* van, not mine, and only he can drive it. So far, Paul's slept through the phone conversation. On the one hand, he doesn't appreciate being roused from slumber. On the other, Paul likes to be needed.

I leave a note on the kitchen worktop for Charlotte, my daughter, *need to nip to work, won't be long xxx*

"Where are we going?" Paul asks as we set off.

"Work. Via Sneinton to pick up Alex."

"Mercy mission on the midnight express," he says, and chuckles to himself.

Alex joins us and we sit up front in the Sprinter like the three stooges, but I'm starting to get the jitters.

"Shouldn't we wait a day or two? They might have gone on holiday and forgotten to pay."

"Gone away and not told anyone?" says Alex. "I don't think so. Anyway, payroll comes out automatically at one minute past midnight. The only reason we haven't been paid is because there's no money to pay us."

I'm showing my age. Harping back to a decade or so earlier when a boss did exactly that, went overseas and forgot to tell his staff, or pay them. In that instance, payment came through a few days later, with a little extra bonus to make up for the inconvenience. This, of course, is different.

On the way out to the industrial estate which houses Limitless Designs, we list our current jobs. What files we need. What clients we'll try and keep.

I wave my pass at the gate and we get through security with no problem. Alex and I often keep odd hours. It's been known for us to work through the night to finish a job.

Paul pulls into the nearest bay to our unit and stays in the van, keeping watch.

Both of us have keys for the outer door. We're used to locking up. For a second, I think they've changed the inner door key code, then realise, in my excitement, I'm using the old number. "Phew," I say as the door yields.

Everything looks as it does any evening, really. So there's been no mad dash to rescue the hardware from creditors.

We both log into our computers and start transferring files across onto memory devices.

Alex finishes before me, and stands.

"I'm taking my Mac," he says, starting to rip out wires.

"You can't, that's stealing!"

"Tell you what's stealing. Taking my labour and not pissin' paying me." He looks around for a box.

"Alex no. You'll be on CCTV carrying a package to the van at midnight. It doesn't look good."

I forget, momentarily, that I'm talking to an eco-activist whose only regret is that he has never yet been arrested.

"Alex, please! We've already got our laptops."

He puts the computer back on the desk, looking around him at the other gleaming machines. "We could use a lot of this kit," he says, pacing around the office in the dim light.

"We can't, Alex. We have to abide by the law."

Actually, I have no idea how we stand legally. I don't know whether it's even legal to take the files or the contacts database.

Alex spots a roll of bin-liners in the corner, tears one off, shakes it open and stuffs his Mac and keyboard inside.

"Fuck it, I'm taking it. And if they object, they can see me in court." He shoves the bin-liner under his arm. "Okay, let's get the hell out."

"That all you got?" asks Paul when we get back to the van. "Didn't really need the van after all."

"Alex wanted to take all the computers, printers, desks, the lot, but that'd put us in jail." I say. Paul laughs.

"Shit," says Alex as we drive out through the barrier. "The charity banners. They're in the basement. They need them for next weekend."

"What?"

"I got them delivered to work so I could check them over. It's their event on Friday. We need to go back."

"Sorry, forgot something," I say, waving my pass again. This time the guard looks more alert.

The code to the basement hasn't changed either. Evidently, Phil and Suki haven't banked on us being this organised. On the way out, Alex stops by the big Fuck Off printer. "We need this," he announces, disconnecting cables.

"It's too obvious. We can't be on camera carrying this."

"Get Paul to park round the side and we'll take it out the fire exit." Against my better judgement, I relay the message, and help Alex carry it out.

"Should we warn the others?" I say on the way back. "If the company's gone under they'll need to know. Shel's only three months into her first mortgage."

"Tell them in the morning. But don't tell them what we've done. We don't want them getting the same idea and setting up in competition," says Alex.

Why am I letting a man fifteen years my junior dictate my behaviour to me?

It's two am by the time I get home. Charlotte has slept through the whole thing, apparently. Paul goes back to bed. I stay up, brain buzzing.

By five am I've set up Phoenix Designs.

THE OTHER MOMENTOUS thing that happens is that I receive a request to connect on businessconnect.com from someone called Dr Tara Dean. Not realising how significant it is, I choose to ignore it for another day.

Chapter Thirty-Seven

A photo of Charlotte and her best friend Hannah as teenagers. Hair glossy and straight, nails painted to match their outfits, perfect skin, pouting at the camera. Wearing tiny shorts over black tights, the uniform of the young back in 2005.

Saturday 7th May 2005.

M Y LITTLE GIRL is sixteen today and we're in the midst of party prep. I sit at the dining room table surrounded by balloons, each inflated to exactly the same level, secured with identical belly-button knots and strips of purple ribbon. There's bunting waiting to be hung, and a giant banner – designed by Alex in cool graffiti art – ready to be fixed on the gate.

Paul's at the computer compiling a CD from Charlotte's list. "Spice Girls? Do I have to?"

Charlotte pouts. "It's songs from my youth. That's the theme."

Paul laughs. "You mean from your childhood. *This* is your youth!"

She rolls her eyes. "Whatever. Anyway, it's *my* party and

215

I can have what music I want. Isn't that right, Mum? Mum?"

I look up from my laptop where I'm dealing with work emails.

"Don't tell me you're working on my birthday?"

"Sorry Charlie, just finishing something off, then I'm all yours."

One of my clients is on holiday in Spain but still making demands. This client keeps coming back with picky amendments they should have spotted earlier. Just to rub it in, she Skypes me from the poolside bar. She's gone well over the 'small amends' clause we put in the contract. I ought to charge extra for all the changes. Alex would. But these are early days for Phoenix Designs and I don't want to lose a client. Plus, this is a substantial piece of work. A redesign of a whole suite of publications.

I want them to sign off the job so I can send it for print. While I'm searching through my emails a reminder pops up from businessconnect.com about Dr Tara Dean's request to connect. I never used to bother with messages like this as they're usually recruitment agencies or people wanting to sell me stuff, but since setting up the company I've upped my online presence. Any new connection could be a potential client. I click on her profile. Professor of Psychology at The University of British Columbia (UBC). Leader in research and scholarship.

Bizarre how people in far flung places across the globe want to connect with little old me. Recently I've had requests from people in Japan, Barcelona and Connecticut. It all seems totally random.

Then I notice something. Something that makes me stop in my tracks. Makes my pulse accelerate. Makes the blood gush to my head.

Vancouver.

I click on the photo, enlarge it on the screen. "Oh my God," I say.

Charlotte looks over. "You okay, Mum? You look like you've seen a ghost."

"I think perhaps I have."

Is it her? It's hard to tell, after all these years. Hair cropped short and corporate. Still blonde. She'd be forty-two now, but she always did have an ageless sophistication. She's wearing a white work shirt and turquoise business jacket. The photo is taken from some way off. She's standing against a window with blinds drawn across and a pot plant on the sill. I zoom in further but Tara Dean's profile picture pixelates out of focus.

Charlotte's behind me now. "Who's that?"

"If it's who I think it is, I knew her at school."

She's changed her name. Dean, was that her dad's name? I can't remember. Or did she marry?

I say 'Yes' to connect, then look through my own profile. To see what she will see. I've put one of the photos up that Alex took for our new website, black and white and shot at an arty angle. I'm now 'owner' of the business, which sounds good.

Charlotte shrugs, her interest in Tara Dean waning. She'd be interested, of course, if she knew.

businessconnect.com is frustratingly short on detail. No other photos. Nothing personal. Just a string of jobs in Canada. I scroll through the section on education. Hong Kong, Canada, University of Toronto and in the middle, Kingswood School, Bath. No mention of Stoke College. That little interlude erased from history.

I looked for her on Friends Reunited, back when that was

a thing. Most of the old crowd signed up to that. Our names listed alphabetically like the college register. Tara conspicuous by her absence.

I'd given up looking for her, deciding she was lost for ever.

"CONGRATULATIONS – you are now connected to Tara Dean. Let's start a conversation with your new connection."

Steady on businessconnect.com – not sure I'm ready for that. This is someone I've not spoken to since 1982, remember?

"Reach out to Tara!"

The helpful bot even composes a message for me. *"Tara, thanks for connecting. Hope you're doing well."*

Not now. Maybe never. I'll bide my time, thank you very much. And anyway. I'm too busy! I've got a party to plan.

Charlotte's best friend Hannah arrives early so the two of them can get ready together. They're inseparable. They remind me of myself and Claire at their age.

I take a photo of them sitting on the wall outside, underneath the big banner. They're dressed identically in tiny shorts and tights. Charlotte's wearing the ruby ring I've given her which used to be Nan's. It got passed down from Mum to me, but I never wear rings. My daughter's sixteenth birthday seemed an appropriate occasion to pass it on again. For the party they dress as Spice Girls to fit the nineties theme. Hannah's Ginger, Charlotte's Scary. I dig out my (authentic, original) rave t-shirt with the trippy rainbow smiley face as a nod to the decade.

"Mum you're not wearing *that*?"

To me the nineties seems like yesterday. To Charlotte and her mates, it's ancient history.

Paul and I make ourselves scarce upstairs as a bunch of teenagers dressed as characters from Toy Story and other nineties movies and bands take over my house. But I can't help sneaking a look at my laptop at intervals throughout the evening. To see if Tara's responded.

Chapter Thirty-Eight

Hey Siri, play 'Walk Away' by Franz Ferdinand

"HOW LONG ARE you away for?"

We've spent the morning clearing up after Charlotte's party. Amazing how much debris teenagers generate. Plus Buzz Lightyear drank too many alcopops and threw up on the kitchen floor.

Now Paul's packing. He's an electrical engineer who travels around a lot to set up systems and fix things. He goes to hospitals and oil rigs and stadiums and cruise ships. Sometimes he rigs up the electronics for festivals and gets free tickets.

"Week. Possibly longer. Depends how long the job takes."

I watch him fold each shirt meticulously, doing up the buttons first and placing them on top of each other in the case, a thin sheet of tissue between each one. He rolls T-shirts into compact cylinders and places them around the shirts. Shoes – work shoes and trainers – are wrapped in plastic and arranged around the edges. All neat and regimented. I guess it stems from his days in the army.

I've watched him pack before. I find it soothing. Like

watching someone make something on TV.

"Phone when you get there?"

He doesn't' answer. He's focused on the act of packing. His technique is an art form.

"Where is it this time?"

He looks up then, his eyes dark.

"You asked me that yesterday."

He seems to be in a grumpy mood. Grumpy doesn't suit him.

"Sorry!", I say. "I was a bit distracted."

"You're always distracted," he says. "You don't listen to a word I say. Nothing about what I'm doing or where I'm going is of any importance to you."

"Paul!", I say. "Don't talk rubbish."

He returns to his suitcase, presses gently on the contents, lowers the lid and zips it up.

"I love watching you pack." It's probably the wrong thing to say.

"And I bet you love watching me walk out the door even better."

"Paul! What's up?"

He stands the suitcase vertically and extends the handle. His face is set.

"Come on – you can't leave like this. Talk to me. Tell me what this is about."

He stands back, one hand on the handle of the case.

"I just don't know where this is going, Chris. Us I mean. I often get the feeling I'm just a convenience. Someone handy to have around but you could take or leave me."

"Is this because you helped out with the party?"

"Well, there is that. Most of my weekend's been spent either helping set up or clear up afterwards, when you're too busy on your laptop. Even when we came upstairs to leave them to it you kept looking at the bloody thing all evening."

"Sorry. I was working! It's not easy being self-employed, you know."

Actually, I kept checking to see if there was a response from Tara.

"Sure. Well, I work too you know and I'm gonna be gone at least a week. So how about while I'm gone you have a think about whether you really want me in your life or not."

He leaves me reeling, not quite sure where this has come from. I watch from the window as he wheels the case to his van. I admire the contours of his body. He's wearing nice-fitting jeans and a t-shirt that shows off his upper body tone. He walks like an athlete.

I first met Paul in the pub on quiz night. He was on an opposing team sitting at an adjacent table. Our team won by a whisper in a disputed point. There was lots of friendly, competitive banter. Paul and I got talking and stayed in the pub after our teammates had gone. We were still there when the landlord told everyone to "head off home or wherever you're sleeping tonight."

Paul gave me a lift home, and I was tempted to invite him in, but didn't on account of Charlotte. I was attracted to his neat face, smooth, slightly olive skin, thick, dark hair and deep blue eyes that, in certain light, look black. I liked his clothes and the way he smelt. On our first date, he impressed me by telling me he's a seeded real tennis star. Not that impressive as it turns out hardly anybody plays it. The nearest court's in Hendon, but hey.

He slotted neatly into my life. Our lives. Helping Charlotte with her science homework. Fixing anything in the house that needed fixing. Giving the place a technological makeover. He's handy around the house, up to speed with the latest tech, and generous with his van. Oh and he's good in bed, too.

He also shares my taste in indie-rock music. He recorded CDs for me, downloading albums from bands like Gorillaz and Franz Ferdinand, the White Stripes and the Arctic Monkeys. I don't buy music so much these days as funds are tight and my credit cards are maxed. We took out loans to buy our kit for Phoenix Designs – the bits we hadn't lifted from our old company. Luckily we're in an age of easy credit. But Paul's help has saved us cash.

When Alex and I created the company, Paul helped us make the website. Did the techie bits and set up analytics so we can track traffic to the site and did some clever stuff to make it show up on searches. He's been very supportive.

He has his own place on the other side of town. A new build full of neat lines, dust-free surfaces and no visible clutter. I don't very often go there as I feel I make the place look untidy. Instead, he stays at mine, slumming it amid the chaos. He goes around after us, tidying and putting things away. He can't help it.

We have an open house policy here by default. There are always people in and out. Charlotte's friends, my friends, neighbours, Alex. Paul says, "Your life is a cast of thousands." And when it all gets too much, he returns to the privacy and order of his own place.

He also has no baggage. Unless you count an eighteen-year-old old son he's recently reconnected with, and an ex-wife from decades ago he never talks about. We don't talk about politics either – I suspect he may even vote Tory – but otherwise we get on well. Or did.

As I contemplate the possible end of our relationship, I feel more than a twinge of regret.

Chapter Thirty-Nine

A black and white printout of a webpage. Tara Dean's profile page on businessconnect.com, in the corner, an unclear photo of a woman in a business suit.

May 2005

A LEX AND I pulled an all-nighter last night. Strange to have him here, in my house, through the night. It was gone four when he left. I sent him a text just now to make sure he got home okay. Like I'm his mother or something. Didn't like the thought of him cycling home alone in the dark. Even though he's got flashing LED lights and a helmet cam.

We finished the job and I should be going to sleep really, but I'm too wired.

Plus Charlotte has just surfaced and she's late for school. She's not dressed yet, still in her PJs, eating Coco Pops, eyes down at her phone, texting, two-thumbed, at lightning speed.

I open my laptop and start attending to emails.

"Mum, the telly's still not working. Can you get Paul to fix it?" she asks without looking up.

"He's away for at least a week."

"Oh piss," says Charlotte. "I can't get MTV."

"Well, you'll just have to wait. You might have to wait a long time actually because I think we might have split up."

"Oh Mum!" She drags out the word 'mum' to at least three syllables and looks up from her phone.

"My relationships aren't purely for your convenience, you know."

"It's not that. Can't you stay with anyone more than five minutes? I actually like Paul. If you want my opinion, he's the best yet."

I overheard her telling her best friend that Paul was "actually quite hot – for his age."

"Well, it may not be completely dead in the water. We're taking the time while he's away to think about things."

But Charlotte's now lost in conversation with someone not in the room.

"God, you look tired," she says when she eventually looks up. "You work too hard. You'll get burnout."

Touching to think my daughter cares so much. She'd be the first to complain if there was a sudden slump in finances.

"I bet you've been working all night," she says, pointing at the open laptop.

But it's my turn to be distracted, as a message has just pinged in via businessconnect.com – new message from Tara Dean.

<< Hey Chrissie, thanks for connecting.

That sounds suspiciously like a businessconnect.com standard message – but it can't be because she calls me Chrissie. No-one calls me that now.

<< Wow Tara is it really you? How are you? Must be 20 years at least! I'm good thanks. Living in Nottingham and I've set up my own graphic design business. I'm working now although my daughter keeps interrupting me lol.

<< Jeez you have a daughter? How old?

<< Charlotte's 16 going on 20 going on 8, depending what time of day it is.

<< Haha she's the age you were when we first met. You don't look much older than that now! You look the same.

<< I'm a dab hand with the airbrush – I'm a graphic artist lol

<< Haha you always make me laugh Chrissie. Actually I need a graphic artist. I want someone to design a poster for my Dad. Just something with a few pictures and a nice design. He's 70 next month.

<< Sounds straightforward enough. Send me a spec over and I'll give you a quote. I might even do it for free if you leave me a good review.

<< I'll definitely do that but I'm happy to pay. And I'll check out your website. I had a little look earlier. You're very talented.

<< Thanks.

<< So how are your folks? You had a brother, I recall? How come you moved away from beautiful Bath? What's it like in Nottingham?

I can hear her say it. She'd stretch out the word and emphasise the third syllable. Notting *Ham.*

So we continue our conversation from opposite sides of the Atlantic by virtue of the virtual world. She tells me she's lived in Vancouver for years and works at the University.

Her mum, Grace, is still in Bath. She had cancer but recovered. She finally got together with Karl Powell and moved in with him. But Tara doesn't visit.

As we message back and forth, I feel a surge of adrenaline. It's almost like when we first met. Even after twenty-three years. That same buzz. Even four thousand miles apart and via a computer. And just like then, I'm reluctant to sign off.

But we do, because it's one am over there and we're both shattered. And Charlotte wants a lift to school. So we say we'll keep in touch.

And I come away with warning shots firing through my being.

Be careful.

Chapter Forty

A first generation iPod Shuffle – white, oblong and shiny. Long discontinued, but in 2005 it was state of the art, and my constant companion.

May, 2005

"WHO'S THAT IN your house?"

I'm Skyping Mum from the kitchen and Alex has just arrived, clad in lycra and perspiring sweetly. We're Skyping because it's my birthday. My fortieth. But I've barely had time to think about it.

"It's Alex, my colleague and business partner. Alex, meet my mum," I hold the laptop up so she can see him. He doesn't wave, instead he looms in close to the screen with his usual intense expression which makes him seem slightly crazed.

"Morning," he says, then, to me. "I'm off to have a shower." Weird to have my colleague and business partner taking a shower in my en-suite.

"Did I tell you me and Alex have set up on our own? We've got our own graphic design business."

"Oh, my goodness!" she says. She's sat by the pool in a

large sunhat and shades with a red drink in a tall glass next to her. It's hard to gauge her expression.

"The company we worked for went bankrupt."

"Oh, my goodness," she says again. "It never rains but it pours!"

It certainly never rains where Mum is. After Nan died, her own health deteriorated and she made the decision to move to Oz. Faced with the choice of coming to live with me in Nottingham or seeing out her days down under with David, my brother, and his young family, she chose the latter. Can't say I blame her. The warm climate seems to have given her a whole new lease of life. Gone is the breathlessness, her diabetes has reversed, and her blood pressure's now apparently under control.

It does mean I'm somewhat starved of family around here. For a girl brought up by a village of aunties, that's a strange thing. At least Charlotte has lots of friends in the locality, and her friend Hannah spends a lot of time here and is almost like a sister.

"How's Charlotte?"

"She's good, Mum. She's gone to her Saturday job."

"Tell her I miss her. I'm looking forward to seeing her in the holidays."

The plan is for Charlotte to go out to Australia for the summer when she's finished her GCSEs.

There's a crash from upstairs followed closely by "Fuck's sake!" at volume.

"What's that?" says Mum.

"Oh it's Alex. Sounds like he's dropped something. We're working from my back bedroom till we get some office space somewhere."

"What's he doing there on a Saturday? It *is* Saturday over there?"

"Yes, it's Saturday and we work flexible hours, Mum, it's

the nature of the game. We often work evenings and weekends to get a job finished. That's the peril of working for yourself."

My brother appears behind her in shot, tanned and bare-chested in shorts. He built a granny flat extension on their house for Mum, and they share the pool.

"Did you like your present, your Walkman thingy?"

They clubbed together, Mum, David and Charlotte, to get me an iPod Shuffle for my birthday.

"Fantastic, Mum, thanks! Hi, David," I wave.

"Hi, Chris. Happy birthday. Just cooling off after a hard day at the marina." I hear a splash as he dives in.

"He's been fixing up his boat," Mum explains. "Which reminds me. You'll never guess who's bought a place just down the road from here," Her face is frozen on the screen but I can still hear her.

"Your old pal Andy from West Melcombe."

"Andy Collins? There's a turn-up."

I don't mention the other blast from the past that has recently resurfaced in my life.

"Yes, he's got a gorgeous Australian wife and three beautiful children."

I digest this information as she comes back into focus.

"And what about your fella, what's his name again?"

"Paul? I think we might have gone our separate ways, Mum."

She shakes her head and takes a sip of her red drink.

Like Charlotte, she approved of Paul. I even sent her a photograph. "What's not to like?" she said.

I sign off and walk upstairs to find Alex's lycra hung over the banisters, silently steaming. I resolve to get us some proper office space somewhere soon.

Chapter Forty-One

A memory stick shaped like a pen. I plug it in. Bizarrely it still works. I wait for it to load. To reveal its secrets to me. There's a folder called My Chat Files. I open it, and all our conversations are here. Did I keep these for evidence? Conversations between Parksville Bear (aka Tara) and the special account I set up just for her. I called it Strawberry Girl as a nod to our past.

Transcript of MSN chat with Tara

➤ **Parksville Bear:** Show me a photo of your daughter.

➤ **Strawberry Girl:** I'll whizz one over to you. Here you go. I took this on her birthday. She's the girl on the left.

➤ **Parksville Bear:** Oh wow she's beautiful. She has your cheekbones and your sense of style.

➤ **Strawberry Girl:** I thought you'd say what most people say.

➤ **Parksville Bear:** Which is?

➤ **Strawberry Girl:** She doesn't look much like me! Even if they don't say it, they think it.

➤ **Parksville Bear:** She's darker skinned, for sure.

➤ **Strawberry Girl:** Her daddy was dark.

> **Parksville Bear:** You must be so proud of bringing her up on your own.

> **Strawberry Girl:** I had help. Lots of honorary aunties and uncles lol. But she's very independent for 16. She's going to Australia this summer to stay with my brother and work at his marina.

> **Parksville Bear:** She flying out there on her own?

> **Strawberry Girl:** She's 16 not 6 lol. Seem to remember you used to travel the world from the age of 7 with a label round your neck.

> **Parksville Bear:** Don't remind me. Think that traumatised me for life. I'm so much more anxious about flying these days. I have to take a Valium before I board a plane.

> **Strawberry Girl:** I was supposed to go with her but since setting up the business there's no time. Plus I'm broke. David and Mum are clubbing together for her fare. She's flying to Singapore on her own and David's meeting her there.

June 2005

WE'VE GOT AN exciting order in from a local charity who want an entire rebrand. We have a blank canvas. Their existing branding looks like someone's six-year-old designed it. Nothing wrong with that, if it's a kids' charity, but it's for young adults who are long-term unemployed. Alex favours a superhero theme. I think they may need to rein him in on this one.

I'm supposed to be working, but I'm distracted. Tickets have just gone on sale for Live 8 – a concert to mark the twenty-fifth anniversary of Live Aid. It's supposed to highlight world poverty ahead of the G8 summit and there's a line-up of big names. Tickets are free, and it's a text lottery, so I'm trying my luck, texting the magic number. Everyone I know is trying to get tickets.

We have an office now. Charlotte couldn't cope with all the lycra. Plus we needed the spare room for her friend Hannah, who is staying with us on and off while her mum is in hospital.

Office is a grand word for it, since it's just a couple of desks in a space above the café round the corner from my house. We get to it by climbing up a rickety metal fire escape. Alex lugs his bike up the metal steps and hangs his cycling gear over the railings. Nobody minds. Much.

Being over the café has its advantages, although when it's hot, like now, and we have the door open, we can hear people's conversations from the outdoor seating area below. The café's much smarter than our office space, so we use it to meet clients.

In our old company, Alex didn't deal directly with clients. I was the buffer. Now I can see why. He's arranged a meeting with a potential customer in the café and they're sitting outside. From where I sit near the open door, I can witness their exchange. The customer is a young man in a shiny suit and pointed leather shoes. He looks like someone out of the sixties.

"I want the sky to fall in so it looks like Armageddon," says the client. "Like a battle zone. Then in the next one I want a beautiful beach scene with, like, palm trees and pina coladas with dolphins sunning themselves on the sand."

Now I'd have listened, said something like, "That sounds interesting. I'm not quite sure how that'll work, but we'll give it a go." Or I might get them to try and draw it. But Alex stares at the client for a few seconds as if he's an alien, then tips his head back and roars with laughter, and says, "That's the stupidest idea I've heard all year."

The guy bristles. "I know it's a bit out there."

I'm willing Alex to rescue it. Flatter the guy – tell him you admire his vivid, visual imagination. That way we might just keep this client.

But Alex simply says. "It won't work. It'll look *shit.*"

Maybe I shouldn't let him loose on customers.

I don't hear how the meeting concludes, because an email pings in from Tara with the title **Trip to the UK.** My pulse rate accelerates as I read.

> ➢ *Hi Chrissie, Grace is ill. You know I told you she had cancer? Well, it's come back. It's in her bones. This time they say it's incurable. I'm arranging a trip to the UK in July. Fancy meeting up when I'm there? We can discuss nearer the time. Maybe even Skype?*

She suggested Skyping the other day, but it never quite worked out. The time I thought we'd arranged it for turned out not to be the time she was available, so I sat there getting nervous, looking at myself on screen and feeling like a fool. We chat on MSN Messenger, but she now says her webcam's stopped functioning and she doesn't know how to fix it. She describes herself as a 'digital dinosaur,' and says her ex – who worked for a big tech firm – did all the techy stuff around the place. I have a Mac of course, with its in-built camera.

But I wonder if she's purposely avoiding face to face contact. From the photos she's sent, she still looks good. She sent me an uncropped version of her profile pic. She's wearing a short skirt with the turquoise jacket and her legs still look amazing. I scour the photos, scrutinising her face for signs of work – or Botox. She asked me for photos too. Most of the self-portraits that the Mac takes are hideous, so I delete them, but there's one that manages to make me look younger. Might be the light, or the make-up I wore that day. I send her that, and one that Paul took on Whitby beach. I'm wearing sunglasses and I'm wrapped up in a coat and scarf. I'm laughing at the dog, and I don't look bad.

But now we are talking about actually meeting up in person. As early as next month. It's suddenly got real.

I toy with how to respond. Should I invite her up to Nottingham? Meet her in London? Maybe even make a weekend of it down in Bath, for old time's sake?

Now when I consider my environment, I visualise Tara here. I love the place I live and work in, even though I'm in the city. It's a green sort of suburb. My neighbours keep bees, rescue chickens and grow vegetables. There's a strong sense of community. Everyone knows each other. I call it my urban village. But what would Tara's discerning eye make of it?

She certainly approves of my artwork. I whizzed up the poster she wanted for her dad's seventieth, and she raved about it. Shortly afterwards she posted a review on the Phoenix Designs website. It read 'Christine Carlisle is an excellent designer with true creative flair. She took my concept and made it reality. Very happy with the service provided. Highly recommend.' It's signed off Tara D, Vancouver. I puffed up with pride as I read it. A positive review from across the globe is a big boost for a fledgling business like ours. Plus it's from Tara. Not someone who gives away praise lightly.

Chapter Forty-Two

I DON'T RESPOND immediately. It's lunchtime and the beauty of our workspace being so close to home is I can nip back to get a bite to eat, let the dog out, and check on Charlotte and Hannah – at home revising for their exams. As I'm heading back to the office I spot a removal van outside one of the old cottages towards the end of Teal Street. The one I always liked the look of, with the overgrown garden and the stable doors. It's had a sold notice up for weeks now but no sign of the mysterious owner.

The van is taking up more than half of the pavement, so I step into the road to walk round it, allowing a woman with a buggy to pass by on the pavement. As I do so, I get a look inside the van. There are boxes piled high marked BOOKS. There's a butcher's bike with a wicker basket wedged in beside some furniture, there's a grandfather clock wrapped entirely in bubble wrap apart from its face. It appears to be still working. It's telling the right time, anyway – half past one. I look at my watch to check. There's a large canvas with a garish painting of what looks like Armageddon. But what catches my eye the most is a life-size statue of Aphrodite, one arm strategically folded across a breast. One nipple clearly visible. It looks like it's made of real marble.

Stepping back onto the pavement, I spot a set of keys lying in the gutter. I pick them up. Although it rained earlier, the keys are dry, suggesting they've only just been dropped, so I look around for the owner. I run after the woman in the buggy. "Are these yours?" but she shakes her head.

I examine the keys for clues. There's a battered leather keyring with a symbol of a dragon underneath the word "Wales" in faded gold lettering. There's a magnetic key fob like the sort you'd have to get into a workplace. A Yale, a mortice, and a couple of other keys. It's an unremarkable set that could be anybody's, but as I hold them, something happens. My hand tingles. I feel a lightness, a kind of bubbling up of joy, like being carried along by a butterfly. An indescribable sense of homecoming.

There are two men with the van now, about to shift the sofa.

"I just found these. Wondered if you'd dropped them?"

"They could belong to the gentleman we're moving."

One of the men disappears inside the cottage with the keys and returns without them.

"They're his. He says thank you."

I smile, the feeling of lightness still with me. I feel like skipping along the street back to the office.

"You look happy," Alex says as I arrive. He says it almost accusingly.

"I think I might have inherited my aunty's psychic gift," I say.

It's the first time I've thought about my Aunt Nessa for a very long time.

When I walk back down the street at the end of the working day, the removal van has gone, but I see the tail end of a creature walking up the alleyway that leads to the back of the cottage. At first I think it's a tall, shaggy dog, but as I draw level I catch a look at it and see it is in fact a goat, being led around the corner to the garden. Interesting.

THAT EVENING, BACK at home, I get a phone call.

"You won't know me but my name's Kate. I grew up in a foster home in West Melcombe with your aunt Nessa."

Nessa fostered children in her later years, after I'd moved away. Mum tried to intervene with her social worker muscle, saying Nessa was unfit. It deepened the rift between them.

"It's sad news I'm afraid. Your aunt passed away earlier today."

She'd had a fast-growing cancer but didn't want anyone to know. She died at home with her now grown-up foster children around her and a visiting nurse.

"It was peaceful. It was how she'd want to go," says Kate.

I ask what time she died, but I already know the answer. Time of death one-thirty pm. The time when I was heading back to the office and I picked up the keys.

"Bad news?" says Paul, back in my life after our little misunderstanding.

"One of my aunties has died."

It'll mean awkward liaison and a lot of family angst. I'm not looking forward to the funeral and I have an intangible sense of guilt. I wonder if Mum will come back from Australia.

Yes, Paul is back. He just turned up one day on his way to the pub on Thursday and said "You coming to the quiz?"

"But ..."

"We need you for the music questions." And that was that. Afterwards he came back to mine and acted like that little blip never happened. When I tried to talk, he just said, "Let's just see how it goes. I was stressed the other day. You'd done nothing wrong. I just got triggered by some stuff you did. I'm sorry."

He doesn't talk about his ex-wife much, but I sense she may be the source of his insecurity.

I know he married young. He married his teenage girlfriend, Georgie. He 'did the decent thing' and got hitched when she got pregnant. He was on a three-year tour in the army at the time.

Now, in the wake of the news about Nessa, I pour us a beer and bring up the subject of family. I tell him things about my past and ask about his. He starts to open up.

Hot on the heels of his son came child number two, a girl. Someone he'd not, until now, mentioned to me. I've only ever heard him talk about his son.

After his daughter was born, he left the army and joined Civvy Street as a welder, went to night school to get A levels, then did an Open University degree in engineering.

"I wanted to get a good job and provide for my family. I thought things would be perfect now I was living at home full time. But Georgie was having an affair."

"Oh no!"

"With my mate. He was the best man at our wedding."

"Oh my God – a double betrayal?"

"I found out in the worst way possible."

"You caught them?"

"No. I hired a private investigator."

He looks almost smug when he tells me this and it's not what I expected.

"You had her followed?"

"I had suspicions. She'd be on the phone when I walked in and she'd quickly end the conversation. She'd go out all dolled up – with the excuse that she was seeing workmates who I'd never met. She invented friends who didn't exist."

His knuckles are clenched white as he talks.

"Then I saw the photos from the snoop. And it was him. My so-called best mate. We'd even been on holiday together as a foursome, him and his girlfriend and me and Georgie."

"Blimey," I say. "That must've hurt."

"I confronted her. She denied it all, but then I showed her the photos. She broke down, begged me to forgive her. And I was ready to, Chris, for the kids' sake. And it went on for a few weeks but I just couldn't trust her. So I followed her myself one day and saw them in a pub together. I waited for him to go to the bog then I walked in and threw her drink over her."

I look at Paul in a new light, trying to picture the scene.

"It was then she told me my daughter wasn't mine."

"Oh my God."

"I had never been so angry in my life. I went home and I seriously felt like smashing up the house. I waited for her to return but she never came home that night. The kids were at their gran's. Next day, I packed my stuff. I took everything that was mine out of that house. I even cut myself out of the wedding photos, so there was just her, and him as best man of course, and everyone else. Then I put them back in the frame and smashed the glass. I did that with every single one of our wedding pictures."

He's animated as he tells me this. He's standing up and walking around, recounting details as though the events he's describing happened yesterday.

"I loaded up in the car and I just left. Oh, and I posted my wedding ring back through the letter box along with the keys."

I watch him pace around the room and wonder at the passion that lies dormant in this usually quiet man.

I don't ask about his son. I know it was a lengthy court battle to gain access. I think Georgie made allegations about Paul's mental health. He's told me previously that she poisoned his son against him.

Now Daniel – his son – is nineteen, and free to do as he chooses. Occasionally they meet up.

Aren't families complicated? Mine is in turmoil now. Aunt Nessa had fallen out with most people over the years and she'd somehow managed to divide the rest of the family. Now we're going to have to find a way to come together for the funeral.

Chapter Forty-Three

I DON'T BELIEVE in love at first sight, but I do think it's possible to spot a kindred spirit across a crowded space. I'm leaning out over the balcony from our office, idly scanning the punters on the café terrace below and watching out for Alex, when I clock a guy I feel I know entering the yard. He walks with a relaxed lope, face upturned, savouring the sunshine. He wears linen trousers, a loose-fitting shirt and a Panama hat. He has a leather man-bag over his shoulder. He reminds me of people you'd see in Paris. He stops to read the blackboard menu then saunters over to a seat in the shade and opens a tin of tobacco.

I'm still an occasional smoker, and today the sight of this man rolling a cigarette makes me want one. So I walk down the metal steps and sit down at the table nearest to him, a companionable distance between us. He's reading a copy of *The Times*. Although I thought he looked familiar I realise I don't actually know him, but something in me wants to know him. So I ask him for a light.

He studies me as he holds out the flame and lights the tip of my roll-up. Then he says, "I saw you descend that implausible looking staircase and I'm intrigued as to what goes on up there."

He has a considered, precise way of speaking, slightly nasal.

"Oh. It's where I work. We're renting office space up there."

He draws on his cigarette. "And what do you do in your office? Sorry, I don't know your name."

"Chris, short for Christine. I'm a graphic designer."

He holds out his hand to shake mine. He has long, lean fingers and a signet ring on his thumb.

"Stevie, short for Stephen."

"Don't think I've seen you here before?"

"That's because I've just moved in. But the coffee's good so I think I'll make it my local. My cottage is just around the corner from here on Teal Street."

"The one with the stable doors? I found your keys on the day you moved in!" I start to tingle at the memory.

"It was you, was it? I came out to thank you, but you'd gone. So I owe you. I'd have been lost without them."

"How's your goat?"

He pauses a moment, like he doesn't know what I'm talking about. Then recognition dawns.

"Oh the goat! She isn't mine, I just borrowed her for a couple of days to eat the excess foliage in my garden."

"And did it work?"

"Yes, but she started eating everything else too, so I gave her back. Now it's just me and the cat."

I laugh. "I live on Teal Street too, in one of the newer houses round the corner."

"So we're neighbours! You must pop in for a cup of tea when you're passing."

We chat like we've known each other for years. But it's

better, because we haven't, and there's so much to discover.

Stevie admires my boots. Hand-painted from Glastonbury, I tell him. "They suit you," he says. He pauses to draw breath before he speaks. In his presence, I somehow feel we have all the time in the world.

Alex arrives, lycra-clad, sweating and intense, straight from a meeting with the charity rebrand people. He wheels his bike across the yard and carries it up the stairs, securing it to the railing at the top.

I wave as he looks out towards the café.

"Who is that *beautiful* boy?" says Stevie.

Alex spots me and comes straight down, making a beeline for the table, barely noticing Stevie.

"Need caffeine," he says.

"Alex, how was your meeting?"

He glares at me, his eyes dark and huge.

"A fucking omnishambles. They've pulled superheroes. For fuck's sake."

And before I have time to introduce Stevie, he's off to the counter, grabs a takeaway coffee and heads back up the metal staircase.

"I MADE A new friend today, at the café," I tell Paul later.

"Oh yeah? Who's that then?"

"Stevie. He's coming round later to borrow our hedge-cutter."

"*He?*"

"Yeah. Don't worry though. I'm pretty sure he's gay."

From this day Stevie and I are friends. It's as though we've always known each other. His keys were right. There is a sense of homecoming with Stevie.

Charlotte likes him too. He somehow fills the gap left when Jason moved abroad. She misses Uncle Jason, and now she has an Uncle Stevie.

She's also intrigued by his profession.

"What's his actual job?"

"Something in the Civil Service. He says it's too boring to talk about."

She thinks for a moment then says, "I bet he's a spy."

I'm pretty sure they don't employ spies at the government building where he works in Nottingham.

Whatever it is he does, they regularly pay for him to travel first class down to London and put him up in swanky hotels. And when he's away, I am commissioned to feed his cat. If it's nice weather I stay a while, sitting on a stone bench in the sunshine next to the statue of Aphrodite.

Chapter Forty-Four

A ticket for a gig. "One day. One concert. One world".
Live 8 General Admission, Hyde Park. The logo is a
guitar shaped like the continent of Africa. In 2005,
this was a much-coveted thing.

PAUL'S BEEN SUCCESSFUL in the Live 8 ballot and got two tickets.

"Woohoo!" I say. "We're going to Wembley! Isn't that great, Charlie?"

She sits at the computer. She should be revising, but she's engrossed in a virtual conversation with somebody.

"Did you hear that, Charlotte? Paul's got tickets."

She looks up, her sense of irritation visible. "I heard you the first time. That's great Mum. Happy for you. I'll be in Australia. Oh, and it's at Hyde Park you numpty, not Wembley."

She rolls her eyes and returns to her screen, typing with renewed vigour.

"Who you talking to?" I ask.

"Nobody."

She spends hours talking to nobody. When I walk past behind her, she blanks the screen.

She's set herself up on a thing called Myspace which she tells me is for "social networking". She even showed me her site. She has the photo I took of her and Hannah on her birthday as her profile pic, and a picture of our dog Finlay in the park behind it. She borrows my digital camera to take photos to put on it. It seems to me to be like a digital version of a scrapbook, or a journal, only one that's open to lots of other people to read. She already has two hundred people in her "friend space". Who on earth has that many friends? More to the point, who's she making friends *with*?

"Mum," she says, looking up from the computer. "Since when did *you* have a Myspace account?"

"I don't."

"So what's this? It's your name. Look!"

I look.

"It says Christine Carlisle. Nottingham. And it says you're an artist. It has to be you."

There's no photo. And no information other than what she's read out.

"It's not me, Charlie."

"You seriously have not set this up?"

"I wouldn't know how. It must be a different Christine Carlisle."

"There can't be two. In Nottingham. Both artists."

"Is it Nottingham, England?"

"Is there another one?"

"Maybe. There's lots of places in America called after English places." But I've never heard of another Nottingham.

We google, but we can't find another one. Unless it's some one-horse town in the back of beyond.

I think of Alex. I know he's trying to connect Phoenix Designs to various new networks, to increase our profile, but when I ask him, he says Myspace is for bands plugging their music and fifteen-year-olds posting videos of themselves. Also, according to him, it's controlled by the American state so he wouldn't go near the thing. Okay then.

For a while, I wonder idly about this other Christine Carlisle. What her life's like, and whether it's less chaotic than mine.

It feels manic at the moment, juggling work, getting Charlotte through her GCSEs, all the prep for her trip to Australia straight after they're over, supporting her friend Hannah who is going through a rough time, plus the looming, terrifying prospect of a meet-up with Tara.

But hey, at least I have the gig at Hyde Park to look forward to.

Chapter Forty-Five

MSN messenger chat with Tara June 2005

> **Parksville Bear:** So how come you're a lone parent? Did Charlotte have a father?

> **Strawberry Girl:** Well yeah. She's not an immaculate conception!

> **Parksville Bear:** Haha. I thought about getting a sperm donor you know.

> **Strawberry Girl:** What stopped you? Having a kid is the most rewarding thing I've ever done. But the hardest.

> **Parksville Bear:** That's probably what stopped me. The hard work. Plus my ex was so high maintenance I didn't have time for a real child.

> **Strawberry Girl:** Really?

> **Parksville Bear:** Poor thing had a dependent personality disorder. It took me two years to realise. If she'd have been here now she'd be looking over my shoulder giving it 'Tara who you talking to?'. If I went to see an old friend, say, she'd phone after half an hour wanting to know when I was coming home.

She. Still gay then.

- ➢ **Parksville Bear:** I was a classic co-dependent. Spent the next four years trying to fix her. Then I realised it couldn't be done, and it took another two years to get her out of my life.

- ➢ **Strawberry Girl:** How long were you together?

- ➢ **Parksville Bear:** Eight years as a couple. But we'd known each other decades. I actually knew Izzy from school can you believe. Our paths crossed every few years then she moved up here for work and that's when we got together. You might have met her actually, years back. I think I brought her to Bath.

- ➢ **Strawberry Girl:** Did you say her name was Izzy? Was she one of the people we went to Glastonbury with?

- ➢ **Parksville Bear:** That's right, we did! It's all coming back now. It was kind of a weird scene, wasn't it?

- ➢ **Strawberry Girl:** I think there was some heavy duty weed involved lol. Where's she now?

- ➢ **Parksville Bear:** She moved back to the States. We have no contact. Thank God we never got that civil partnership we talked about and the house was in my name. It all got very toxic. I moved out of my own house because I couldn't stand it. I had to get a lawsuit to get her to leave.

- ➢ **Strawberry Girl:** Sounds mega stressful.

- ➢ **Parksville Bear:** It was. But enough about my ex. Tell me about you, Chrissie. What happened with the father of your child?

Hey Siri – play 'My Jamaican Guy' by Grace Jones.

IT WAS THE summer of '89 and I was sharing a house in Carrington, on the edge of town, with Cara, Rachel and Gemma, three post-grad students. We called it the Girly Gaff. I'd moved to Nottingham to do my degree. After leaving college and taking a couple of years out temping, I decided I wanted to be a graphic designer, so here I was, about to start my final year.

It was a Thursday night, which meant it was student night down the Garage club in town. We were in the upstairs room, dancing to indie stuff. It was dark, and I became conscious of someone on the edge of our orbit. I was admiring his moves, then as he drew closer I noticed his face. Gorgeous. Dark skin. Big eyes. He locked me with those eyes as he danced into my life. Then we locked lips and, later, back at the Girly Gaff, we locked bodies.

In the darkness and the noise of the club, I asked his name. He said it several times before I heard him. Guy. So that's what I called him for the five days and nights he stayed at ours. Five days and nights where we barely got out of bed. My housemates sniggered as I appeared in the kitchen, lusted up, to make coffee and toast which I took to him in bed while he rolled a spliff. On day five he left me in the morning. I found a phone number scrawled on a folded-out cigarette paper.

Cara played the track over and over just to tease me. It was a yellow picture disc with Grace Jones' severe angular face rotating on the turntable.

'My Jamaican Guy.'

Except he wasn't called Guy at all. He was called Kai – which rhymes with Guy. Easy mistake to make. And he wasn't Jamaican, either, he told me when I finally got through to him on the phone. He was from Hawaii. The line was crackly and he said he had to go. "I'll come and see you soon," he promised.

He appeared a few times after that, always without warning, always staying several days, with weeks between visits. Where he went in between remained a mystery. I never asked, and he never told me.

We spent most of our time together dancing. In 1989, Nottingham was at the cutting edge of the emerging rave scene. And Kai knew all the places to go, and where to get hold of pastel-coloured pills that looked like love hearts, which made us want to dance all night. Against all my musical instincts, I got into house music. We'd rock up at parties in fields and stay there all weekend. We'd hit the clubs in town and dance till chucking-out time. We'd dance back to Carrington in the early hours, breathing in the smell of fresh bread from the bakery. And when we weren't dancing we were having sex. And sex on Ecstasy is something else. It was the long summer vacation, and I was working in a bar. I'd phone in sick when Kai showed up. They sacked me for being unreliable.

Then a few months after our first meeting, he arrived for more sex and to tell me it was over. He was going back to Hawaii.

But that last time, he left something of himself behind.

Enter Charlotte.

I TOOK AN awkward trip back to West Melcombe, carrying my news.

My baby already had a name – two in case she turned out to be a he – but even at that early stage I had a sense of

Charlotte, as I stood in Mum's kitchen, watching her face contort.

"No Chrissie! Not *this*. Not now. It's not the right time." She did that thing where her breathing quickens and she's almost tearful. That thing designed to make everyone around her feel guilty.

"Mum, there's never a right time. I'm pregnant *now*! You're going to be a grandma. I thought you'd be pleased."

Actually, I knew she'd react like this.

Mum huffed and shrugged her shoulders.

"Think very carefully about this. Do you really want to throw away your life and your career and be a single mum on benefits? Because that's what you'll be and believe me it isn't easy. And *I* should know."

"You were a single mum most of my childhood and we were okay, you, me and David."

She does indignation well, my mum. She shows it by puffing out her chest and dropping her shoulders then exhaling through her mouth with a low whistle.

"That was completely different. Your father was there in the early years and we had lots of support. And *I* had no option. *You* have a choice, but you need to act now. It'll be a lot more complicated further down the line."

I stared at her and it suddenly dawned on me what she was suggesting.

"I'm not killing it, Mum. It's a life." My hands instinctively moved to my stomach.

"Oh Chrissie, it won't feel anything. At the moment it's just a dot. The size of a pinhead."

I'd been to a doctor in Nottingham, but that wasn't good enough for Mum. She bundled me up, me and my dot, to see our old family doctor Griffiths in Melcombe.

Griffiths said it was a mass of non-sentient tissue and he could book me in for a procedure the next day if I wanted.

But the dot, or pinhead, or mass of tissue, already had a beating heart. And I knew I was keeping it.

Once Charlotte arrived, of course, everybody loved her. Especially Mum.

Chapter Forty-Six

June 2005

MSN messenger chat with Tara

> **Strawberry Girl:** So there we have it, the story of Charlotte.

> **Parksville Bear:** Ever hear from the dad again?

> **Strawberry Girl:** Nope. He vanished. But, to be honest, I never tried to find him.

> **Parksville Bear:** Does your daughter ask about him?

> **Strawberry Girl:** She's all or nothing, Charlotte. After I told her that her dad left, she didn't want to know. We don't talk about him.

> **Parksville Bear:** It must've been hard, raising a child on your own?

> **Strawberry Girl:** It was. But so worth it. You could say Charlotte saved me. I was on a road to ruin in the rave culture, and all the exciting new designer drugs that came with it. Having Charlotte made me knuckle down and get my degree.

> **Parksville Bear:** You never needed drugs. You had a vivid enough imagination as it was. D'you still have

magic powers? Do you still fly above the world and predict the future?

> **Strawberry Girl:** Haven't done that for years. Think it was a childhood/teenage thing. I've lost the knack. How about you? Do you still wish you could fly?

> **Parksville Bear:** I've developed a fear of flying. My analyst says it links to flying as a kid. I get the jitters now when I get on an airplane.

> **Strawberry Girl:** Bit unfortunate? Don't you have to fly to conferences and things?

> **Parksville Bear:** It is unfortunate, living out here. I take a Valium before I fly. Makes me like a Zombie when I arrive. And it gets worse with time, not better. There goes your CBT myth.

> **Strawberry Girl:** Remember our debate?

> **Parksville Bear:** Yeah. You won, even though I was right.

> **Strawberry Girl:** It was a draw.

> **Parksville Bear:** You won the popular vote. You always did.

> **Strawberry Girl:** What d'you think about that stuff now?

> **Parksville Bear:** Same. I have to. Too invested in therapy to think anything else. Spent a small fortune on it over the years. Enough to buy several houses.

I'M AT MY desk, trying to squeeze an inordinate amount of text into a too-small gap for a client who knows best, when I hear the sound of footsteps on the metal staircase. Alex is out, and nobody else climbs the steps to our office except by appointment.

There's a tap on the door, which is open anyway. I look up to see a small, rounded woman in uniform. At first I think she's a traffic warden, then I realise she's one of the new community police officers or whatever they're called.

"Can I help you?"

The woman steps inside.

"I'm looking for a Mr Roper."

"Alex? That's my business partner. He's out visiting clients."

She's standing in front of Alex's desk, staring at his 'acquired' Mac. Like she knows it's stolen.

"How long will he be?"

"Oh. Could be an hour. At least. He only recently left." I don't know why I'm lying. But anyone resembling law enforcement puts me on the defensive, especially in a room full of equipment that isn't strictly ours.

"Anything I can help with?"

"I don't think so." She looks around at our messy office. "How long have you been here?"

"Just since June."

"And where were you before?"

"Oh, I worked from home. I'm a graphic designer you see."

She nods, glancing at the sheets of A3 bearing the charity branding designs piled up on top of the printer. Shit – the printer's stolen too.

"You're welcome to wait if you like," I indicate our tiny visitors' sofa. "And I'd make you a coffee but we've got no milk."

"That's kind," she says. "What's your name, please?"

"Chris. What's yours?"

She doesn't answer. Instead she moves to the door and looks down at the café.

"D'you get much noise from that place?"

"Not really. It's convenient for us. Their coffee's a lot better than ours so we use it for our business meetings."

My phone starts ringing. Alex. "Chris. Pretend it's a client. Is there is copper there?"

"Good afternoon. Yes indeed! We should have the designs ready for you in about an hour."

"Can you get rid of them. I'm round the corner."

"Yes indeed. I'll crack on with it now. I know you're on a tight deadline."

I look up. "Really sorry, but I need to get on with some work. Can I get Alex – Mr Roper – to call you?"

She leaves me her card. I watch until she's gone, then give Alex the all clear.

"What was all that about?" I ask him when he shows. "They're not going to impound all our stolen kit are they?"

He looks at me with an intense stare, computes, then explodes into laughter. "God I'd forgotten that. No Chris. Nowt to do with you or the business. I think it's about an action I went on at the weekend. You say she was a CPSO?"

"Yes."

"Obviously not serious then. Policing on the cheap. What a joke!"

Although the Police are his arch enemies, Alex is very dismissive of what he calls "plastic plods".

Chapter Forty-Seven

MSN messenger chat with Tara

➤ **Strawberry Girl:** Do you have other relatives out in Canada? Or just your dad?

➤ **Parksville Bear:** I have half-sisters now. My dad's girlfriend Aisee had two girls. I love them. There's a bunch of second cousins who I've never met. Grace says they're all dust-buckling hillbillies. My grandfather was on the run, heading north. He ended up in Fort Nelson which is real frontier land. A lot of people there were running away from something.

➤ **Strawberry Girl:** Like you were, running away from me. LOL

➤ **Parksville Bear:** It wasn't just you. I had a huge fight with Grace that night before I packed my bag for Canada.

➤ **Strawberry Girl:** The night before you left me.

➤ **Parksville Bear:** You dumped me.

➤ **Strawberry Girl:** Not really. I just wanted some space. I was young and confused. I needed air.

➤ **Parksville Bear:** Chrissie, you dumped me.

➤ **Strawberry Girl:** You left me.

➤ **Parksville Bear:** Yeah. Because you dumped me.

> **Strawberry Girl:** Selective memory, LOL. We remember things differently. What did you row with Grace about?

> **Parksville Bear:** She came back and found me in tears after you dumped me. I told her what happened, wanting some sympathy. But this was Grace, so instead she ranted at me for being gay. She said she wished we'd never come to Bath. She wanted to move us back to London. She thought I'd caught being gay off Jason, or you. I remember her saying, "first Jason, then Christine, now you. It must be something in the water."

> **Strawberry Girl:** The healing spa water?

> **Parksville Bear:** It's poisoned. Obviously.

June 2005

I'VE ACQUIRED A habit, and I'm not sure it's a good one. After Paul's crashed out for the night and Charlotte's gone to her room, I stay up, pour myself a red wine and message Tara. Vancouver is eight hours behind so she's just leaving work when it's midnight over here. From opposite sides of the Atlantic, we're reconnecting. Making up the lost years. Filling in the gaps. Spilling our souls. There's something compulsive about it. But it's remote. It doesn't feel completely real. Even when we plan to meet up in Bath later in the summer.

I message Tara from my work laptop and tell Paul I'm working. It's easier that way. He's insecure enough without knowing I'm messaging a former lover. He's even suspicious of my friendship with Stevie.

> **Parksville Bear:** So d'you love this guy you're with now?

> **Strawberry Girl:** I'm not really with him. Except as friends. Friends with benefits.

> **Parksville Bear:** You mean fuck-buddies?

> **Strawberry Girl:** I guess so. Did you love Izzy?

> **Parksville Bear:** At first.

(Parksville Bear is typing)

> **Parksville Bear:** It was a one way street. She was a leech that sucked the life blood out of me. I'd been obsessed with her as a young teenager and it took me a long time for the scales to fall from my eyes. Did you love Charlotte's dad?

> **Strawberry Girl:** I thought so, at the time. Although I hardly knew him. I loved his physical presence. There was something spiritual in our connection too.

> **Parksville Bear:** What was it that made you choose him to father your child?

> **Strawberry Girl:** I didn't choose him – it was a happy accident.

> **Parksville Bear:** I don't believe in accidents. We make choices subconsciously.

> **Strawberry Girl:** Oh here we go. Psychology. Maybe it was because he was different, exciting, from another part of the world.

> **Parksville Bear:** Like I was?

> **Strawberry Girl:** I've seriously never thought of that. It was mostly sheer animal attraction LOL

> **Parksville Bear:** How many men have you fucked?

> **Strawberry Girl:** OMG! Now there's a question. I'll have to think about that. How about you?

- ➤ **Parksville Bear:** That's easy. One. At High School.
- ➤ **Strawberry Girl:** On Vancouver Beach?
- ➤ **Parksville Bear:** Wow! You remember. Yeah, that's the one. I've been in same-sex relationships since the age of 18.
- ➤ **Strawberry Girl:** Since me?
- ➤ **Parksville Bear:** Yeah. Although there was someone before you.
- ➤ **Strawberry Girl:** The girl at the Lakes?
- ➤ **Parksville Bear:** Jeez you've got a good memory. Yeah. Although you were what I'd call my first love.

(Parksville Bear is typing)

- ➤ **Parksville Bear:** How about girls? Was there anyone else? After me?

Chapter Forty-Eight

C HARLOTTE WAS EIGHT. She'd gone to stay with Mum for half-term. I was stressed and needed a break. I tagged along with a friend from work who wanted to walk along the north Yorkshire coastal path. We headed up to Whitby and stayed in the youth hostel there. I was in my early thirties by then.

We went to a pub at the bottom of the Abbey steps where we met some other people staying at the hostel. Among them was a woman called Tina, who had long red hair and a pierced tongue. She was younger than me, probably late twenties, and I felt a powerful pull. A magnetism. She was hitching to Turkey that summer for Amnesty International. She was going to petition the Turkish government about human rights abuses. I signed her sponsor form.

That night my friend, sleeping in the bunk above me, was violently ill. She had to keep disturbing me to get to the bathroom. "Sorry, Chris, I've got to go again."

Next day she stayed in bed as people swept up around her. "I'm heading home," she said. "You carry on, Chris. I don't want to ruin your week. You'll be fine. Those guys we met in the pub yesterday are heading in the same direction today so you can walk with them."

So I set off along the coastal path with some of the men from the pub. They were faster than me and I wanted to admire the view, so I let them go on ahead.

Once alone, I drew a deep breath and took in the rugged beauty of the coastline. The air was crisp and blue and the sun glinted off the sea. I was glad I was alone. The walking was tough, for me, with lots of up and down and the weight of the rucksack carrying my week's possessions on my back. I could feel it doing me good, stretching my muscles, but I was tired. So I was relieved when Robin Hood's Bay came into view. I stopped to catch my breath, looking down on the village, when I saw her. The girl from the night before. Sitting on a bench, rucksack open, spilling out its contents.

"Hi," she said as I approached, shifting along so I could sit down. Tina was fun, and flirty, with an infectious, musical laugh and a quick Scouse wit.

"Don't it look inviting?" she said, looking at the sea. "I'm tempted to go in for a dip when we get down there." She pronounced it 'thur.'

"Don't let me stop you."

We walked through the village and stopped at a pub by the harbour for fish and chips and cider. The tide was far enough out for us to walk the last stretch along the beach to Boggle Hole Youth Hostel where we were both booked in that night.

"Right," she said. "I'm going in." she threw her rucksack down on the sand. "Join me?"

"It's the North Sea. We'll freeze to death. And anyway, I forgot my swimsuit."

"T-shirt and pants. All you need."

She rolled her leggings up and stepped into the water. I

took off my boots and paddled. The water was freeze-your-bollocks-off cold.

"Sorry," she said. "I've got to do it." She pulled her leggings off, extracted her bra from under her t-shirt, threw them to me, then ran into the water, screeching as it reached up to her chest.

"She's brave," said a man with a dog walking nearby. "You'll not get me in there." All I could see of Tina now was her head, a splash of red bobbing on the water out to sea. I began to wonder about her sanity. Sure, it was May, but this was the North Sea, cooled by currents from Siberia.

A few minutes later Tina emerged, swimming in a fast crawl back to shore, squealing as she ran out of the water. The t-shirt clung to her breasts and she looked like a slightly crazed entrant for a wet t-shirt competition.

"Can you get my towel? It's at the top of my rucksack."

I held it round her as she stripped off.

"Wow, that was unreal," she said, wringing out her wet hair. "Wherever I travel I always have to go in the sea."

"Well you'll get a few opportunities on your trip to Turkey," I said.

"English Channel, French Riviera, the Med, the Adriatic and the Bosphorous. Or is that a river?" She shrugged.

We walked faster then, and checked in at the youth hostel, where I dived into the shower.

We ate there, with some of the blokes we'd met the night before. Then she said, "Wanna come for a walk?" She said it pointedly, just to me.

I was exhausted from walking all day. In fact, walking was the last thing I wanted to do. But I was curious. We yomped back up a set of steep steps to the cliff top, and sat down on a bench looking out to sea. There was no-one around. That's when it happened. I gave in to the pull I'd been feeling ever since I'd met her. We melted into each other.

"Let's go back and get in the shower," she said.

"I already had one."

"So did I, but a girl can never be too clean." Then she leaned in closer and whispered. "I wanna fuck you."

She had a vibrator in her wash bag which we played with in the shower. The whole encounter had this delicious, forbidden thrill. Then we went our separate ways, to our separate dormitory beds. And in the night, from the other side of the room, I kept hearing a giggle.

When I looked for her in the morning she'd gone.

A few months later I received an envelope in the post. It contained a cutting from a Turkish newspaper, with a picture of Tina in a long tie-dyed skirt, and an Amnesty International T-shirt handing in a petition to a slightly bemused looking Turkish official. There was a note with it saying "You owe me £20." With an address of her mum's place in Liverpool. Then a p.s: "The Bosphorous was warm!"

> **Parksville Bear:** So did you keep in touch?

> **Strawberry Girl:** No. I went back to my life. Back to Charlotte. I sent her the £20. As far as I know she carried on travelling after Turkey. She was that kind of gal.

> **Parksville Bear:** Great story!

> **Strawberry Girl:** I've had no other sexual encounters with women in my life.

Chapter Forty-Nine

June 2005

"I HAVE AN addictive personality," says Stevie as he arrives at mine, extracting his tin of tobacco from his man-bag and offering me a smoke. "I've been addicted to many things over the years, now I'm addicted to hanging out around here with you. What you need to know. Chris, is once you've got me, you don't get rid of me very easily."

"Suits me fine because I have a phobia of people leaving me. Or so say successive shrinks."

I see no reason why I'd ever want to get rid of Stevie. He fits my lifestyle like a glove, although there's a slight disconnect with Paul. I usually invite Stevie around when Paul's away, like now.

"What have you been addicted to?"

"Dope in the seventiess, Sex and booze in the eighties and nineties, religion in the noughties."

"And have you given all those things up?"

"All except this old weed," he points to his tin of tobacco.

"And religion?"

"It was less of an addiction, more of a home-coming."

Stevie converted to Catholicism on Millennium Eve.

"I went to a gig in a bar in town, near the Playhouse, opposite the Catholic Cathedral. At midnight everyone piled out to go down to Market Square to watch the fireworks. I took a detour because the Cathedral door was open and it looked inviting. It's Pugin, and ever since moving to Nottingham I'd been meaning to get a look inside. There were people in there chanting. It was peaceful. I stayed for about an hour. Something about the place drew me in."

"I used to go to church sometimes with my Nan," I said. "But mum was very anti-Catholic 'cos she'd been brought up with it."

"I like the ritual. The incense. The holy water. And saints. I love saints. Did you know there's a saint for pretty much everything?"

I remember Nan praying to Saint Anthony whenever she lost things.

"When did you give up sex? Was it when you took up religion?"

"Hmm. Same time I gave up drinking. The two went hand in hand with me."

He tells me he'd go out, head down the Lord Roberts then on to Gatsby's or NG1 – Nottingham's gay haunts – and pick people up.

"There were a lot of one-night-stands and a few disastrous short-term relationships. It's much better now I'm celibate," he says, taking a drag from his roll-up. "There's no arguments at bedtime."

"Have you ever been in a long-term relationship?" I ask him.

He doesn't respond for a long time. He draws slowly on his cigarette, inhaling deeply. I wonder if he's even heard me, or if I've crossed a line. Stevie doesn't normally talk much about himself.

"I lived in London through the eighties and early nineties. I joined the Civil Service when I was eighteen and lived in a hostel with other civil servants. We had a wild time, always out clubbing. I met the love of my life there. Moved into his flat in Tooting Bec. Loved and lost."

I look at him, wanting more.

"It was the eighties, Chris. We were gay men. Think about it."

I think about it. And I leave him to tell me in his own time.

"I knew he was HIV positive. He told me early on. They had drugs by then, but it was still a death sentence. I watched the love of my life die. Slowly. He was my first and only love. Since then, Chris, it's been just me, the odd encounter with unsuitable men, and now celibacy."

Stevie never told his parents he was gay. They went to their graves not knowing.

I go inside to prepare dinner. Stevie pulls a book out of his bag and reads while I cook. He usually has an old, yellowed paperback with him. His cottage is full of books, the shelves buckle under their weight.

When I rejoin him on the terrace with food, he asks about my own past. He says it's clear I'm ambivalent about Paul. He's interested in the way successive men have failed to do it for me.

"I've had a blast from the past."

I tell him about Tara. How I loved her. How she left. How she cut me out for decades. How she's chosen this time in our lives to get in touch again. How she wants to meet up when she comes over.

"What would you do, Stevie, if you could see this guy you

loved one more time, decades later? What should I do?"

He draws slowly on his cigarette.

"If you want my opinion, go. Even after all this time, there might still be a spark. Or you may find, when you see her, there's nothing there. But there's only one way of finding out. Love is rare."

> **Parksville Bear:** I often think that what we had was the purest, most beautiful love I've ever known.

> **Strawberry Girl:** It was the first time I'd been in love.

> **Parksville Bear:** Did we ever tell each other how we really felt?

> **Strawberry Girl:** I was scared to tell you, I think. You were older, more cosmopolitan. You had friends all over the world. I was out of my depth. Deep down I always knew you'd leave.

> **Parksville Bear:** You dumped me.

> **Strawberry Girl:** You left me!

> **Parksville Bear:** Let's not go there again. I left because you wouldn't commit. We were going round in circles.

> **Strawberry Girl:** You left for revenge. Admit it. You left because you could. To make me miss you. You left to hurt me.

> **Parksville Bear:** Maybe partly. But I needed a fresh start. Not just from you. Don't forget there was Grace. My own mother hated me. I had to get out. I needed a complete, clean break.

> **Strawberry Girl:** I had a nervous breakdown after

you left.

- > **Parksville Bear:** Did you, Chrissie? Did you really?
- > **Strawberry Girl:** Yep. I fell apart. Lost the plot. Totally cracked up. It took a long time to put myself back together again.
- > **Parksville Bear:** Oh Chrissie! I never knew!
- > **Strawberry Girl:** How could you? I couldn't exactly tell you. I had no forwarding address.
- > **Parksville Bear:** I'm sorry.
- > **Strawberry Girl:** Jason saved me.
- > **Parksville Bear:** Ah Jason. He was beautiful, wasn't he?
- > **Strawberry Girl:** Still is. We kept in touch. He's Charlotte's Godfather you know.
- > **Parksville Bear:** That's awesome!

Chapter Fifty

*A postcard with a picture of woodland set in rolling
fields and the heading OAKLANDS GREEN BURIAL
GROUND A scrawled note on the back "Nessa is near
the orchard."*

June 2005

C HARLOTTE LEFT FOR Australia yesterday, and there's a
gaping absence around the house. She's away for four
whole weeks.

It nearly didn't happen, because of Nessa's funeral. While
Mum and various aunts were agonising over it, we learnt
Nessa had opted for a Woodland burial and didn't want
family there. Just her foster kids. Kate sent me the address of
the place where she's buried in case we ever want to visit. It's
near Bath. Apparently there's no gravestone, just an
unmarked tree planted in her memory. I felt relieved,
actually. Too busy to go to funerals, but Mum's furious.
Keeps Skyping me to rant. Even after her death, Nessa's
causing family angst.

To distract me, Jason, my old friend from my college
days in Bath, is in town on what he calls his "grand tour of

England."

Jason is famous now. Not so you'd recognise him on the street, but famous enough that when you search his name he's the first person who comes up, with a string of articles about him and listings of his exhibitions. He's even got a Wikipedia page.

In the years since we left college, he's lived in a series of glamorous locations. London, Barcelona, New York (briefly) Paris, and now Besançon, near the Swiss border, where he lives in a rustic farmhouse with his long-term partner Jean-Luc.

Usually Jason and Jean-Luc come over in August, taking in visits to Brighton and Bath, then up north to Manchester, stopping en route at Nottingham to see me and Charlotte. This year Jason's on his own and he's come earlier. He's gutted to miss Charlotte. She's his goddaughter.

I opted for a Catholic baptism to please Nan and to annoy Mum. Although as we stood in the church for the Christening, Nan said in a loud voice, "How can you be a godfather if you don't believe in God?"

But Jason was the obvious choice. A calm, stable mentor. He's been a brilliant godfather to Charlotte. Visiting, taking her out, making educational things fun. We see less of him since he moved abroad, but each summer he does his grand tour. And last year we went to stay with them in their farmhouse in France.

Jason didn't come out to his family till the late eighties. I worried about him during the AIDS crisis, but Jason being Jason, he avoided the scene, even though he lived in London throughout that period. "The scene's not my scene," he said.

I meet Jason in town after I finish work. We meet in the Broadway bar and work our way along the street, taking in the Lord Roberts and Wax Bar and a new place that only serves tea. Then we go for a meal at a little bijou bistro with trendy mis-matched furniture.

We do a review of our year that was, something we do annually, ranking the year from one to ten. "This year it's an eight for me," says Jason.

I muse for a while. "It's been a funny old year, with Limitless Designs going under and me setting up the business. But some good stuff's happened. The business is still afloat. Paul's still in my life and it's kind of a good fit. Charlotte's finished her GCSEs and I've made a new friend called Stevie. So on balance I'd say it's a seven. Oh, and you'll never guess who got in touch. After decades."

"Tara?"

"You don't seem surprised."

"She tracked me down a few years ago in Paris. She contacted me through my website. She must've googled me and found out where I was. She said she was in town and could we meet up. I arranged to meet her in Montmartre, but she never showed."

"Why not?"

"No idea. She sent a text about an hour before we were supposed to meet. Then nothing. Then I got a bit of a garbled voice message that night. Something about an impromptu visit to A and E. No apology."

"Ah, maybe something to do with her ex. I gather she had issues."

Jason shrugs. "Maybe. I didn't waste any sleep over it. I've lived successfully without her in my life for twenty years."

"You never mentioned she'd been in touch."

"I thought about it, but the moment passed. I didn't

know if you wanted reminding of all that. We were only in touch very briefly, and beyond discussing logistics of where to meet, we didn't have any contact. I never even asked what she was doing in Paris."

"She's been messaging me since May," I say. "And now she's coming to Bath, and she wants to meet. Grace is dying."

"Grace?"

"Tara's mum. You remember her?"

"God, yes."

"She's with Karl Powell now. I don't know what happened to Eva."

Jason laughs. "Grace was always with Karl. It was the worst kept secret in town."

"Any messages for Tara if we do meet up?"

"Ask her why she stood me up," he says, then pauses for a moment. "Actually, don't bother."

Chapter Fifty-One

June 2005

H ANNAH, CHARLOTTE'S BEST friend, is staying at mine again for a couple of nights. Her mum is in Highbury Hospital – a place where they treat adults with mental health diagnoses. Her dad's not coping, so I'm helping out by having Hannah here. Actually. I like having her being around the place.

Tonight I'm giving her a lift to visit her mum.

"Shall I wait in the car park?"

"No. Can you come in with me, please? I'm scared to go in there by myself."

We're led into a room with tables, a games console in the corner, and a hatch leading through to a kitchen. It could be a youth club or community centre, if it wasn't for the nurse keeping watch from the hatch and a guy, whom I assume also to be a nurse, sitting at a table in the corner. We announce ourselves, and someone goes to get Hannah's mum. She appears, shuffling, even though as far as I know there's nothing physically wrong with her.

"Visitors for you, Maria," says the nurse.

Maria looks at me a few times—there's a flicker of

recognition—then she turns her gaze on Hannah.

"Hello. Mum."

Her eyes narrow. "Who's this?" she says to the nurse, who's next to her, standing ready.

"It's me, Mum. Hannah."

She stands straighter, hands on hips, and points at Hannah. "This is not my daughter," she says. "It looks like her, but it's not her." Then she starts to wail. The male nurse in the corner stands up.

"Don't you want to sit down and have a cup of tea with your visitors, Maria?" the female nurse is coaxing, kind.

"These aren't my people." Maria turns and paces, wailing as she goes. She turns again, her eyes fierce. "This is not my daughter. This is someone pretending to be her."

She lunges towards Hannah. The male nurse is across the room in a flash, restraining her. She calms, and turns towards the door.

"Do not let these people in again."

The nurse who showed us in shrugs and looks at Hannah, whose eyes are brimming with tears. "I'm sorry, love. It's not her, it's the illness. She has good and bad days."

Once we're in the car, Hannah breaks down. "My own mum doesn't recognise me."

I reach for her hand. "It's not her, it's the illness." I repeat the nurse's words.

At home, I make her a hot chocolate and give her a doughnut.

"Will she get better?"

"I'm sure she will." I say. Even though I'm not at all sure. "They have drugs. They just need to get the levels right."

"My dad says I mustn't talk about it. He doesn't want people to know."

I look at Hannah, and for a second I see my own sixteen-year-old self. Struggling with new emotions and secrets I couldn't share. Shamed by taboo, first by my relationship with Tara, later by my own mental health collapse.

"You *need* to talk about it. It's not good to bottle it up. You can always talk to me, Hannah."

Hannah sobs now. I sit next to her at the kitchen table and rub her shoulders.

"Thank you," she says. "You're like my second mum."

I don't tell her how proud that makes me feel.

"You can stay here whenever you like, whether Charlotte's here or not." Having Hannah here makes up in some small way for missing my own daughter.

"Is it normal?," she asks. "To not recognise someone. Like my Mum didn't recognise me?'

"Probably," I say. "I'm not an expert, but I know someone who is."

Later, I recount the incident to Tara in our chat. She says it's called Capgras Syndrome, and yes, although not common, it's a recognised symptom of psychosis. I relate this to Hannah, and it seems to comfort her that this thing has a name. She's not alone. I take her home the next day, but tell her she can pick up the phone whenever she needs to talk, even if it's in the middle of the night. I remember Jason saying that to me all those years ago and I remember how much it helped, just knowing.

Chapter Fifty-Two

A Motorola flip phone, small and compact, with a short, stubby aerial and a battered silver cover. It's a sturdy thing. I must have dropped it countless times, but there was no such thing as a smashed screen then. I flip it open, look at the tiny keyboard, each number key representing two or three letters of the alphabet. You had to press each one two or three times to get the letter you wanted. How the hell did we get our heads around that? I look at the keys, still clearly legible. I thought they'd be worn through all that texting. I hold the thing in my hand and remember.

June 2005

I HAVE A new phone. Silver. Shiny. Tiny. It flips open and it's small enough to fit in my pocket. I take it everywhere I go. It replaces my clunky old Nokia with the annoying ubiquitous ring-tone. This one rings like a bell. Motorola. State of the art.

Tara and I have exchanged mobile numbers. It's mainly for when she comes to the UK in a week's time. We say we'll use it sparingly, because of the cost of transatlantic phone communication, but we've started texting. And texting is addictive. It began with a test message, and it went from there.

These days, after we've finished our messenger chat, she sends me a good night text before I go to bed. And I send her one in the morning, to find when she surfaces later. It feels special.

Texting has taken over from phone conversations in recent years. Kids caught onto it first, developing their own unique txt msg shorthand. Now my generation are hooked on it too.

I have my phone in my hand as we head down to London for Live 8. Paul's decided to drive there and back. If we're tired after it's over we can always find somewhere to park up and sleep in the van.

Tara's going to watch the gig on TV in Canada. Some of the channels are showing it. She texts me on the journey to tell me.

"Who you texting?" asks Paul.

"Alex has got this work query," I say. It's half true. Alex has. But he's sorting it without my input.

It's a fabulous day and the atmosphere at Hyde Park is sublime. The place is packed, the weather warm, and in among the One World banners and the peaceful fans there's a sense of solidarity, of being with like-minded people. There's even a feeling that simply by being here and watching this fantastic line-up of bands, taking part in this truly global event, we can somehow sweep away world poverty in a single day.

Tara says the coverage over there is annoying as they keep cutting to ads or inane commentary and they can't watch the whole set.

Try MTV I reply.

"Who you texting this time?" Paul again.

"Charlotte, she's watching it in Oz."

Again, not a complete lie. She probably is. And I did text her earlier.

I wonder at the web I'm weaving. Why I'm doing it. Whether it matters. I can talk to who I want, can't I? What business is it of his? But still I feel more than a twinge of guilt. Is it the guilt that makes it exciting?

I keep in text contact with Tara throughout. Each time my phone buzzes it vibrates against my nipple. I get a tingle of excitement.

This is weird. My body is here with Paul, his arm around me. My mind is with someone five thousand miles away across the Atlantic. And I'm living this day with both of them.

I'm floating on air when we leave the gig. But Paul doesn't want to hang around. He seems strangely tense as we weave our way back to where the van is parked. We drive back to Nottingham, barely speaking.

I allow myself one goodnight text to Tara then switch the phone off to avoid suspicion. In less than a week I'll be heading back down to London to meet her.

Chapter Fifty-Three

MSN messenger chat with Tara, 1 July 2005

> **Parksville Bear:** D'you ever wonder what it'd be like if we got together now? I mean, if we were the age we were then, but met each other now, in today's setting?

> **Strawberry Girl:** You mean without the stigma?

> **Parksville Bear:** Exactly. If we could be open about our relationship.

> **Strawberry Girl:** Dunno. Prejudice still exists.

> **Parksville Bear:** True, but nothing like it was back then. And it got worse later on in the 80s with AIDS. But seriously, Chrissie, d'you think if we'd met in today's climate we would've made it?

> **Strawberry Girl:** I don't know. We were very young, especially me. It's pure speculation to think about what might've happened.

> **Parksville Bear:** D'you remember our first kiss?

> **Strawberry Girl:** It was after we'd drunk your mum's drinks cabinet dry I seem to remember. You'd just forgiven me.

> **Parksville Bear:** What'd you done?

> **Strawberry Girl:** You don't remember?

> **Parksville Bear:** I can't imagine what you could have

CLARE STEVENS

done to apologise for, you sweet girl!

> **Strawberry Girl:** The outing incident in the common room. Andy and Mike and the Tom Robinson record.

> **Parksville Bear:** Nope. No recollection. Funny how we remember different things in our selective memories. Remind me what happened!

> **Strawberry Girl:** My mate Claire told everyone you were gay and they played the record at full volume when you walked in. You walked out again and wouldn't speak to me.

> **Parksville Bear:** Must've blanked it from my mind. Too traumatic.

> **Strawberry Girl:** You had to pretend to be with Jason so the rumour wouldn't spread.

> **Parksville Bear:** God yeah, Chrissie, I do remember. It's starting to come back. What was that song called?

> **Strawberry Girl:** Glad to be Gay. Funny thing is though, Tom Robinson turned out to be straight.

> **Parksville Bear:** What is it you say in England? Nothing so queer.

> **Strawberry Girl:** Nowt as queer as folk

"WHO ARE YOU meeting again?"

This time, it's me packing. Paul is watching me as I cram tops and socks and toiletries into my backpack.

"Told you. An old school friend."

"Male or female?"

"Female. Name of Tara."

"Where are you staying?"

"At Pratt's Hotel in Bath. It's near where we went to school."

"When d'you last see her?"

"In 1982."

"So how come you're suddenly meeting her now?"

"She lives in Canada. She's back visiting her mum who's ill."

He frowns.

"Sounds a bit strange."

"Why?"

"That this person would suddenly get in touch."

Paul's been on edge for days. I know something about my trip to Bath is triggering him, but an interrogation is not what I need right now.

"What's the matter, Paul, don't you believe me?"

He starts to pace. Like a caged animal. Caged inside his own brain.

I make him sit down. Make him talk to me. Reassure him there's nothing to worry about. His jealousy is unfounded.

"Listen Paul, I know what happened with Georgie. But it was a long time ago and it's time you moved on and started trusting people again."

"It's just. Your behaviour. Always on your phone. On your laptop. You seem distracted. But when I…"

"When you what?"

"Nothing."

"What, Paul?"

"It'd be easier if I could see a message from her. To prove she exists. It'd put my mind at rest."

I've suspected for some time that Paul monitors the home computer. For all I know he could even have hacked into my account. So I keep my chats with Tara on my work laptop. I show him an email from her now. The one where she says "Grace is ill. I'm coming down to Bath." I then show him her profile on businessconnect.com. Her CV, which clearly shows she went to school in Bath, her photos, which prove she is most definitely female.

I wave the digital camera at him before pushing it into my rucksack.

"I'll take photos. Of me and Tara in Bath. As proof. If that'll help you to believe me."

"I'm sorry, Chris." He reaches out to hug me. "I've been a total dick and I admit it. You go down to Bath and have a nice time with your friend."

> **Parksville Bear:** Just a quickie. I've started packing. What shall I take? What's the weather like there?

> **Strawberry Girl:** Fair to middling.

> **Parksville Bear:** What's that mean, you crazy girl?

> **Strawberry Girl:** This is England, so you never know. Could be torrential rain, could be a scorcher.

> **Parksville Bear:** I'm nervous about meeting. Are you?

> **Strawberry Girl:** Yes, It's been a while.

> **Parksville Bear:** What if we still fancy each other?

> **Strawberry Girl:** Who knows? We'll just have to wait and see.

Chapter Fifty-Four

A train ticket from Nottingham to London marked 'First Premier'. Why did I keep this? To prove I was there on that day?

July 2005

"I T'S NICE OF Stevie to give me a ticket, but I'll have to get up at some godforsaken hour to get to the station this early."

I'm fingering my train ticket for tomorrow, courtesy of Stevie, who was meant to be at a meeting in Whitehall but decided last minute that he didn't want to go. Handy, as it saves me paying out for a peak-time ticket, but Stevie always books trains at some ungodly hour to give him time to walk across London. He doesn't like the Underground.

Alex looks up. "If you're in London at the weekend. why don't you come on our action?"

He and his anti-capitalist friends are planning some sort of demo in the capital on Saturday. It involves attaching themselves to railings with bicycle D-locks.

"Can't. I'm meeting my old friend Tara," He's half listening.

"Bring your mate. More the merrier."

"We're not stopping in London, we're heading down to Bath where we were at school together."

"When d'you last see her?"

"1982." I'm conscious that Alex was barely born then.

"You'll have a lot to talk about."

I guess we will.

"So why are you nervous?"

Who said I was? He's not supposed to pick up on things.

"Not seen her for twenty-three years."

"Well, if it's a disaster, you won't have to see her for another twenty-three years, if ever!"

"We had a very intense relationship back then," I say.

He laughs. "Girls do. I remember when Cori fell out with her best friend. She was devastated. She said 'it's like she's my boyfriend' I said 'What does that make me then?'"

"It was *very* intense," I repeat.

He looks at me now. His interest caught.

"You mean sexual?"

I nod. "Sexual. Emotional. Spiritual."

"Well," he says, his eyes now playful. To my surprise he looks intrigued. Even faintly amused. "I never knew *that* about you. What made you revert to men?"

"Men are more simple creatures. Easier to handle."

He laughs.

"We had to keep it secret. It was taboo back then," I say.

"Still is, in some circles. People my age are cool about it though. You know Lucy, my little sister? She has boyfriends one week, girlfriends the next. And if she gets bored she'll sleep with her best friend."

I nod.

"So what happened to her, this girl? How come you've not been in touch since 1982?"

"She disappeared."

Chapter Fifty-Five

July 2005

A copy of the Guardian Front page with the headline, "London wins 2012 Olympics

- *Blair hails 'momentous day'*
- *UK bid beats France by four votes*
- *Lord Coe transformed 'joke' bid"*

There's a picture of a young David Beckham hugging then London Mayor, Ken Livingstone.

S HE DISAPPEARED, AND I fell into a hole. And it's the memory of that hole that comes to me now, as I sit, stomach churning, on the five-thirty train from Nottingham to St Pancras. First train of the day. In first premiere there's plenty of room to stretch out, plus free food and coffee. Alex says it's obscene that taxpayers' money goes to fund such luxury. I don't mind, as standard class looks cramped. I'm surrounded by business people, tucking into their complementary breakfasts. I was offered one, but I wasn't hungry. I had to get up in the middle of the night to get this train, but it's July. It's light by four. And anyway, I couldn't sleep. My racing thoughts and the butterflies in my stomach made sleep impossible.

They offer me a free newspaper but the choices are limited. Most people around me are reading the *FT* or *The Times*. The coverage is all about the Olympic bid yesterday. After four rounds of voting it came down to a two-horse race between London and Paris and we actually won! Apparently, this has lifted the mood of the nation. As I read, I try to tap into the collective mood of optimism, but I don't feel it. I'm too nervous.

I'm meeting Tara at Paddington so we can travel down on the train to Bath together. We're booked into Pratts Hotel. We used to walk past there on the way from Tara's flat to the bus station and we once saw the actor Dustin Hoffman having breakfast through the window. Tara's booked two adjoining single rooms for us. I wonder if the fact that they're adjoining is significant.

I look at the text she sent yesterday. *At airport. Boarding soon. Can't wait! xxxx*

No text to say she'd landed. She'd booked into a hotel at Heathrow for last night as her flight was due to land in the early hours. I keep looking at my phone, to see if there's a message.

Whenever I fly anywhere, which isn't very often, the first thing I do on landing is contact someone to let them know I've arrived. Maybe Tara's not like that though. All I can do is assume she'll show up at Paddington.

My train gets in at the ridiculous hour of seven twenty-four am, leaving me two and a half hours before meeting Tara. Stevie says you can walk along the Regent's canal to get to Paddington. It takes about an hour and a half apparently.

A good way of killing time and a chance to grab some breakfast at Little Venice before heading to the station. It seems a more attractive prospect than facing the tube at rush hour.

I set off in the direction of Camden Lock. Stevie says the walk is peaceful – a reprieve from the grime of the city. But so far it feels industrial and full of noise. The area around Kings Cross is a building site, the skyline dotted with cranes. A man in a cherry picker shouts inaudible instructions to a team of workers in high vis jackets and hard hats below.

On the canal bank an old man with one trouser leg cut off at the ankle reaches into a tartan shopping bag for bread to feed a solitary duck. It's some exotic, colourful breed. It seems out of place amid the urban grit.

I follow the path under a graffiti-strewn bridge. A bird flutters above my head, startling me. I look up to see a line of roosting pigeons. Their droppings all around. Their cooing sinister in the dank tunnel. A cyclist approaches in stealth mode, nearly knocking me off balance into the murky water.

As I see more tunnels ahead, I feel a sense of growing unease, but I carry on walking until Camden Lock comes into view.

The boating community seems still to be asleep. Drapes drawn cosily across. A black cat peers at me through a gap in the curtains of one of the boats. Some of the barges are beautiful, their paintwork gleaming, thriving floral displays and wood piles on their rooftops. Others seem abandoned, dilapidated. One boat is semi-submerged, its cruising days long over.

The landscape becomes more scenic as the route enters leafy neighbourhoods lined with mansions which probably cost millions. I'm at the part where the path loops around

Regent's Park and passes London Zoo. I take my time. Although I'm travelling light, my rucksack weighs heavier as I walk. I've brought a spare pair of shoes and a couple of changes of clothes for going out. Wonder where we'll go? With each step, I feel less sure this was a good idea.

I have my phone in my jacket pocket. It dings when there's a text, and I'm still waiting for a message from Tara. I jump as I hear an identical ding coming from the bell on a bike speeding up the path behind me. My heart thumps and I feel weirdly detached from everything.

Come on Tara, text to say you're here, to tell me you're on your way. To say you're having breakfast at the hotel. Just text to say your plane landed ok.

But there's nothing.

The towpath is busy now, with runners, cyclists, people walking to work, and someone running a noisy generator outside his boat. Houseboats are lined up two – sometimes three – abreast around here. I guess mooring space is at a premium in London. I look at my watch. Eight-thirty am. Still plenty of time. I stop by a café boat that looks inviting, and I climb on board. I'll have a coffee at least, even if I can't manage breakfast.

I sit looking out over the canal from a booth in the corner, watching a family of swans approach the boat. Two parent swans, majestic and white, their four cygnets as big as they are, with grey down. One pecks at the side of the boat, hoping for crumbs. I remember Nan telling me, "Swans, they'll break your arm."

It all feels surreal. I put that down to lack of sleep, but I'm jumpy, starting at the slightest sound, like the waitress appearing at my arm with my coffee. I wonder whether to smoke. I still do, at times like this, when I'm stressed. It's more of an occasional habit now. I know that Tara wouldn't approve but I start to roll one, partly to keep my hands occupied. Something about it connects me with my sixteen-year-old self.

I take a deep drag on the roll-up and blow the smoke out of the window. I feel that familiar nicotine high that comes with the first smoke of the day. It doesn't last. If anything, it makes the jitters worse. I look at my watch. Almost nine am. I finish my coffee and go.

As I continue walking towards Paddington Basin I'm struck by the noise of the capital. Traffic. Some large vehicle beeping and announcing to the world it's reversing. And sirens. There's always sirens in the city. I'm used to them in Nottingham. Here they seem even more insistent.

A continuous buzzing signals an incoming call. Number withheld. My pulse races as I flip open the phone. I'm expecting Tara, but it's Stevie.

Sharp intake of breath. Then, "Sweetie, are you in London?"

He knows I am.

"Yeah. I'm on the canal. Walking to Paddington."

"Good. Avoid the underground. I just heard there's a power outage on the tube and they're closing the network. That's the official line, although it could be something else."

"Like what?"

"There's unconfirmed reports of an explosion." His voice tails off. I try to phone back. But I can't get through.

Now I notice the sirens more than ever and my pulse-rate accelerates. I hasten my step. An explosion on the tube network will cause massive disruption. Plus, where's Tara? *Shit*. She'd travel by tube from Heathrow. I reach for my phone again. I try to call her. Her number's still unavailable.

As I emerge onto the street the calm of the canal path is abruptly gone. Sirens screech. Car horns beep. But people around me seem unfazed. Nobody's panicking. Perhaps this is just a normal day in the life of a London commuter.

Somewhere in the vicinity, a woman screams. It's an agonising sound. I'm in a mass of people, moving forward, when a police car races up the street, mounts the pavement, cuts its sirens and four armed coppers get out. They block the road. Someone, possibly the woman who screamed, shouts, "there's a bomb!", and the line of people I'm in surges. I go with them, blind, carried along by the crowd. We run straight into a police line, blocking another street.

I can see Paddington Station now, but I can't get to it. There's too many people and pulsing blue lights in the way. My heart is pounding. I'm sweating. My vision's blurred. From somewhere in me a calm voice takes over, and I squeeze my way through the massing throng towards the entrance to the station.

There's a heavy police presence at Paddington. Armed officers with dogs bar the entrance to the Underground. An ancient man carrying a sandwich board which reads "The wages of sin are death; Romans: 6:23" walks up to the line. He's shouting something incomprehensible. A policeman pushes him back. He stumbles.

They're stopping people at the entrance to the main station, but they wave me through.

I look at the big screens. There's no information, just a fuzz of blinking, illegible lines. A beleaguered rail official is being harangued by passengers. What's going on? Are trains still operating? How do I get to…? A young Japanese woman is trying to ask him a question, but can't make herself understood. I wave my ticket at him. Are trains to Bath running? Yes. For now. He points me in the right direction.

On the platform, a woman in a South West Trains uniform is checking tickets and ushering people onto a train. It says Bristol Temple Meads on the front.

I stand on the platform, staring at the open doors of the train as people brush past me. No sign of Tara. I can't move. Or think. It's like my feet are rooted to the ground.

What to do? Wait for Tara here or get on this train and meet her at the other end?

I try to phone Stevie to ask him what to do, but I can't get through.

On the platform next to me two women are talking. "They're saying it's a power outage."

"That's a lie. It's a bomb. I'm telling you it was a bomb. They sent us towards Russell Square but there were people coming the other way covered in blood."

I shudder. I have to get out of London. If Tara's travelled on the Underground she'll be held up for hours. Better to wait for her in Bath.

The whistle blows. I jump on the train with seconds to spare. Then we're off.

It's standing room only. They've crammed people on because they don't know how many other trains will run.

I lean on a wall in the corridor, opposite a man in a suit with a Blackberry smartphone. It buzzes every few minutes with a news alert.

"It's more than one bomb," he says, and frantically starts trying to dial round his contacts, but not getting through.

There's voices all around. Snippets of disconnected information meet my ears. Names of stations. Tube lines. Circle Line. Piccadilly. Edgware Road.

"It's fucking Armageddon," someone says.

I think of Stevie's painting. I feel faint. I slump to the floor in the train and hug my rucksack, fighting back tears.

I reach for my phone to text Tara. Tell her I'm on the train and that I'll meet her in Bath. Assuming she's okay. I keep trying to phone. Her mobile is still switched off. I try to phone Paul, then Stevie, but there's no signal.

Someone says the networks are jammed. Everyone's trying to contact loved ones.

I text Charlotte and Paul, to tell them I'm all right, even though I know the texts won't go. My thoughts race, my stomach lurches, my body drips with sweat. The collective unease on the train is palpable and the hour and a half journey to Bath Spa feels interminable. The train empties out at Reading and I get a seat. I shut my eyes, and try to calm my racing pulse.

Chapter Fifty-Six

Hey Siri, play 'Somewhere Only We Know' by Keane

BATH IS THRONGING with tourists. People are going about their business, like what's happened in London hasn't touched them. I head straight for the hotel where I can at least get to a TV and get the lowdown on the news.

Pratts Hotel is smaller than I remember, and less grand. Back in the day we never went in, just ogled rich American tourists eating their breakfast.

I ask at reception if Tara has turned up. She hasn't, and there's been no message.

Up in my room, I switch on the TV. It's wall-to-wall coverage of the events in London. They're now reporting four bombs including one on a bus. The city is a scene of carnage, with who knows how many dead or injured.

I get out my A-Z and squint at the map, comparing it to the map they're showing on the telly of where the bombs went off. There's one scarily close to Paddington.

Phones are back on and I speak to Paul and Charlotte, to reassure them I'm okay. Charlotte's in Australia, of course, and it's gone midnight over there, but the whole household is still up, glued to CNN.

I tell them I'm okay, but I don't feel it. I'm shaking. Thinking of how close I came, and the fact that Tara's still missing.

There's a helpline you can ring for information. I dial the number. I wait in a queue for what seems eternity, pacing up and down in the hotel room. I give up. I try Tara's number again. Still nothing.

I go downstairs and walk out into the street. I feel myriad emotions, being back in this city that I haven't returned to in years. There's no reason to come. None of my relatives are in Melcombe now. After Nan died and we scattered her ashes her daughters themselves scattered. Nessa was the only one who stayed and now she's gone, too. Although her body rests somewhere nearby in its woodland grave.

The city is the same, but different. The buildings, ancient and protected by heritage status, remain the same. But the businesses that occupy them are different. And the place seems altogether more moneyed than it used to be.

Perhaps it's because I haven't eaten. I feel spacy, unreal, strangely remote from the buzz and bustle of the city all around. I take a walk towards the river, stand on the bridge at South Parade and look across the water at the weir.

Voices from the past surface from the recesses of memory.

"A girl's gone missing."

"They tried the river?"

I shudder and turn back to the hotel, ask reception again if she's arrived. Still no sign. No message. I try her door, next to mine, in case she's somehow snuck in. Nothing.

I sit in the bar, where all the talk is of what's happening in London. A TV is on in the corner, on mute, showing rolling news. I scour the faces on the screen for Tara.

I ask what food they're doing. Not because I'm hungry, but I feel I ought to eat. They rustle up an eggs benedict. My starved stomach is grateful.

I venture out again into the fray. I blend with the tourists, pretending to browse, to stand and stare, to admire the views. But my vision is blurred. I feel largely absent. My legs lead me through the crowds towards the Royal Crescent, where Karl still lives with Grace. Tara was due to visit around now. The plan was she'd go alone, assess the lie of the land, meet me for a late lunch, and then, if Grace seemed receptive, we'd both call round later.

I wonder if I can remember which of the front doors is Karl's. But it's easy. It still has the door-knocker in the shape of a treble clef. I'm about to knock when the door opens and a woman in a nurse's uniform steps out.

"Can I help you?" Her voice is brisk and solid, in that way that nurses have, with a hint of concern. I wonder if I look as freaky as I feel.

"I've come to see Karl and Grace."

"Are you the daughter?" She sounds brighter now.

"No. Tara's not here yet. I'm her friend."

It feels strange to describe myself as Tara's friend after all these years. Karl meets me in the hall. He's aged, of course. Thin and a little hunched. He must be in his mid-60s. His face looks more earnest than ever, his eyes as intense. You can still see traces of the looks that once were. He still has hair, now white. Somehow, he's retained that distinguished air.

"Hi Karl. Remember me? Chrissie. Christine Carlisle."

He looks blank. I wonder if Tara told them about our planned reunion.

"Tara's friend from school."

He looks a little dazed, then recognition dawns.

"Of course! I'm very sorry, I've had hardly any sleep."

He kisses me on both cheeks like a Frenchman, leads me along the hall to the kitchen, and makes me a coffee with a state-of-the-art coffee machine. He too has a television on in the corner.

"We were going to come together, but Tara's not shown up yet."

He creases his forehead. "Is Tara here, in Bath?"

I'm beginning to wonder if she's even told them she was coming.

"No. We were supposed to meet up in London this morning then come down here together. But she's not shown up yet."

"She's in London?"

"Yes, she should be but I can't get hold of her. I'm guessing she's caught up in it all, but for the moment she remains missing."

"Missing." He shakes his head. "Again."

How ironic that I should be the one to break this news.

I don't know who is going to look for her this time.

"I haven't told Grace the full extent of what's happened in London," he says, then leads me to what used to be the front room. The one with the piano where he used to host his soirees.

It's been converted to a sick-bay, with a hospital style bed positioned in the centre. The curtains are closed and a standing lamp throws a dim light around the room.

Tara's mother sits in an upright armchair next to the bed. She was always older than we thought. She now looks ancient, her cheeks and eyelids sunken in a hairless head.

I notice the piano is still there, covered in a dust sheet. I wonder if Karl still plays to her sometimes.

"Karl, who is this person come to visit?"

Grace's voice is still posh, but slower than I remember it, and cracked. The voice of a thousand Marlboros. Her breathing is loud and laboured. Every so often she reaches for an oxygen mask attached to a machine by the bed to take a breath or two. A lifetime of smoking laying heavy on her lungs.

Tara never smoked. Said it was bad for you. Said it made you ugly.

"Remember me? Chrissie? I was Tara's friend."

Grace looks at me with glassy, sad eyes.

"I remember. She abandoned you. She abandoned both of us."

"Sure, she went to Canada. But we hooked up again through the Internet, twenty-three years on."

"Jesus."

"She was coming to Bath today to see you."

Grace's eyes dart around the room.

"Where is she?"

I look at Karl. He nods imperceptibly.

"Her flight would have got here yesterday but there's been a power outage causing delays in London."

Grace shrugs, an expression I remember of old, but with it comes a harrumph, followed by a fit of coughing.

She reaches for the respirator, regains her breath, and says, "There have been so many times when I've waited for her. *So* many times. And there's always some excuse."

"There really is a lot of serious disruption in London," I say again, looking at Karl. He raises his eyebrows.

"If you say so," says Grace. "I'll believe it when I see it. I doubt she even boarded the plane."

The effort of emotion seems to tire her and she reaches once more for her oxygen, takes several deep breaths and waves, as though batting me away.

It occurs to me that this woman has nothing to do with me. She was always cold towards me. I don't really know why I'm here, other than to deliver the news. Or lack of it.

The atmosphere is stifling. I decide to leave.

Grace is not my responsibility. Neither, for that matter, is Tara. A strong voice inside my head is telling me to walk away.

Karl sees me to the door.

"She has a nurse coming from the local hospice at six. I could meet you somewhere for a drink and a bite to eat if you like?"

We arrange where to meet.

"Can I take your number, Karl, just in case?"

He can't remember his mobile number, but it's pinned on a noticeboard in the hall, along with a list of other numbers. I take a photo of it on my digital camera.

I get the feeling he's desperate for a break.

WE MEET ON the city side of Pulteney Bridge.

"There's a pub somewhere around here where Tara and I used to go," I say. "It might be this one."

It's now called The Sam Wellers. I can't remember what it was called back then.

Karl heads for the bar while I choose a seat. The place is full of people in Bath Rugby Club shirts – blue and black and white stripes. They say "Thatchers" on the back.

I look around. The room has dark beams and low ceilings and a snug with an arched entrance. There was a snug in the pub I remember. We made it our sanctuary.

Is this the place?

There's no music, but it's loud with the rich r's of West Country voices. Karl sitting opposite me strains to hear, cupping one ear in his hand. "I'm almost completely deaf in the other one," he says. I wonder if it's all those years of music.

The blokes in here are broad-shouldered, rugby-player build. They probably think Karl is my dad.

I drink a couple of glasses of Stowford Press cider and refuse a third. It's strong and I don't want to become tiddly with Karl. Then we head to an Italian restaurant near the Bridge. I don't remember it from before. This place is spacious and high-ceilinged with a barn-like appearance. It looks out over the weir. It's expensive, but Karl pays. I have an aubergine dish, rich in garlic.

"Tara and Grace didn't see eye to eye for years," he said. "But in recent years she's been over a bit more. They're trying to put stuff behind them. Especially now Grace is…"

I feel a pang. Tara's been over but has only now got in touch. What took her so long?

"So Tara *has* been here?"

"Not here. They met up in London. But not since Grace's recent bout of illness. She had cancer before. you know. They treated it. But it came back."

"How long has Grace got?"

"We don't know. Consultant said it could be six months, six weeks, or six days. I was getting worn out, trying to care for her, until we started having the nurses coming in to help."

"And do they help?"

His eyes mist up.

"Oh Chrissie, they are angels that appear in the night. I couldn't cope without them. They sit with her for a whole twelve hours. It allows me to sleep."

He doesn't look like he gets much sleep.

"She didn't want to die in hospital. I promised her I wouldn't let that happen. I intend to keep that promise."

I wonder at his dedication to this woman. At the hold she's apparently had over him through the years.

"I don't like to be too far away, but they'll call me if anything happens," he says.

He means they'll call him if she's dying. So he can get there in time to say goodbye.

"But the urgency now is Tara," he adds, searching my face. "What's to be done?"

There are words unsaid. He wants to know if I will do anything. If I'll make phone calls. If I'll take it upon myself to search for her. One thing is clear. Karl himself doesn't have the energy.

"There's nothing anyone can do," I say. "Except wait for news." And the person to get such news, as next of kin, must surely be Grace, or Karl. It certainly won't be me.

After the meal, I stroll back along the river to Pratts. I look out over the weir trying to conjure up memories of moonlight and secrets. But the night is cloudy with a touch of moisture in the air. And there are so many lights. Were there always this many lights? I remember the moon glinting off the water. Would you even be able to see that now?

An idea is taking shape in my mind, for now half-formed. A hint of something I know, deep down, that doesn't yet have a name. A niggling sensation, buried deep. I go back to the hotel and decide to sleep on it.

Chapter Fifty-Seven

I'VE JUST TURNED in when my phone dings. Hopes raise that it's Tara at last then, plummet when I see a text from Alex.

Phone ASAP

I told him not to contact me unless it was urgent. Resentfully, I phone back. Maybe he just wants to check that I'm okay.

He sounds cross. "Tried to get you. Couldn't get through."

"Phone lines were down, but I'm fine, I got out of London okay," I'm almost touched that he cares. If he does.

"Never mind that. They're onto us."

"Who are? What are you talking about?"

"Those bastards we used to work for. I've had the Insolvency Service on the phone. And the police. They've tracked down our equipment."

"Shit."

On top of everything else, I really don't need this right now.

"And a lawyer acting for creditors or something.

Threatening us with legal action. But I'm not fucking caving in."

"Alex, slow down. Tell me exactly what happened."

"They looked through the CCTV. They saw me leaving with stuff and getting in Paul's van. Oh, and I never told you this, but I went back the following night on my bike and picked up a few more things."

"Alex!"

"They're on about bailiffs. They'll have to fucking fight me for it. They can see me in court."

I try to control my breathing. To quiet the pounding of my heart.

"I'm not fucking having this. They owe us. We took that stuff in lieu of salary. Chris, we're hanging onto it till they pay us."

I see my business sinking as he speaks.

"No Alex. We absolutely can't do that. We do not want bailiffs turning up at the office. Or the Police. The last thing I need is a criminal record. You may want one but I most certainly don't. Get all your files transferred onto a memory stick. Wipe the Mac clean and give it back to them along with anything else we took from there."

"But Chris."

"Plus Paul's implicated as it's his van. We can't drag him into it. It's not fair."

There's a pause on the line as this sinks in.

"It's not legal what we did, and you know it. Listen. I'm not gonna argue about it. You do as I say or I fold the business. We've done so well setting up Phoenix Designs. We've both worked so hard. We've already got a great customer base. I'm not throwing all that away for some phoney principle."

He's quiet on the line. So quiet I think he's gone.

"Alex. You still there?"

"Yep."

"You gonna do what I say?"

"Okay, but if I see them, I'm giving them a piece of my mind."

"You do that, Alex. And can you do the same with my laptop?"

"It's not here. It's at yours."

Of course it is. I'll have to ask Paul.

I make another phone call. This time to Paul. I explain what's happened, thinking he'll be livid. He isn't. He offers to save the files and wipe the laptop clean. He's good at things like that. I know he'll do it thoroughly.

"I just need the password," he says.

Chapter Fifty-Eight

I PHONE CHARLOTTE in Australia again. It'll cost an absolute fortune in roaming charges but I need to hear her voice. She puts me on speaker phone so David and Mum can chip in too. They've been watching the news from London all day.

"My friend hasn't showed up yet," I say.

"Probably caught up in it all," says Mum.

I tell them about my escape from the capital. My lucky escape. It occurs to me that if it hadn't been for Stevie's first-class ticket that got me in at such an ungodly hour, and his advice to walk to Paddington rather than get the underground, I could easily have been on one of those tube trains.

"I bet he *knew* it was going to happen." says Charlotte.

She's convinced Stevie is a spy.

"He'll have had inside intelligence, Mum."

Just hearing my daughter's voice lifts my spirits.

"Are you having a nice time, Charlie?"

I'm half hoping she'll say she's homesick like she was when she first got there.

But she says, "I love it here, Mum. I'm thinking I might

stay after the summer."

"But what about college?" We've got her into Bilborough College for her A levels. The most desirable sixth form college in Nottingham. Hannah's going too.

"They have colleges here, Mum. Or I could take a year out. Like an early gap year. Carry on working at the marina. Save up some money."

We don't talk for long. We're conscious of the cost.

When I sign off, I feel like someone's hit me in the ribs. I feel a huge pang of separation. I hug the pillow and long for Charlotte. Especially, as I realise, I'll never get her back. She's entering that narcissistic age where she's no longer child, not quite adult. We're facing two years of painful pushing at the last remaining boundaries, then she'll be off.

I'm ready for all that. But I'm not ready for her being the other side of the world. I feel a sudden resentment at Mum and David for inviting her, enticing my little girl away. Keeping her there with promises of warm pools, boats, and maybe boys. Does she have a love interest down there?

My thoughts spiral downwards. What if she's met someone, throws away her prospects, marries young? Or gets pregnant?

I'm being paranoid, of course. I know my Charlotte. How streetwise, single-minded, and ultimately head-screwed-on she is.

I think of myself at her age. Sixteen. How little I knew. How vulnerable I really was. I still feel vulnerable now.

I TRY TO relax. I put the TV on but it's wall-to-wall London bombings on every available channel. I sigh, switch everything off, and eventually sink into a sort of slumber.

My sleep is shallow, plagued by busy city scenes. The

sound of sirens and someone screaming. The sound of laughter. Dream layers on dream. Bath morphs into London then a city I don't recognise. Somewhere abroad. I start to rise above this city, like in the old days when I used to fly.

I'm woken by an insistent buzzing next to me. I sit bolt upright, scrabble around for the bedside light, then try to locate my phone. Missed call. Paul.

What does he want at this time of night? I check the time. It's three am.

He rings straight back.

"Paul? Everything ok?"

There's a momentary silence on the phone then a snarl.

"Hope you're having a nice time?"

"What?"

"Is he there with you now? Whoever you're seeing down there?"

I wonder for a second if this conversation is actually happening, or if I'm dreaming.

"What are you on about?"

Another pause on the line, then, "Who the FUCK is Parksville Bear?"

"It's another name for Tara, you numpty."

"Yeah right. Don't lie to me. I've seen your message files. D'you remember when we first kissed? What happens if we still fancy each other? We'll have to wait and see? What's going on Chris? Just tell me the fucking truth. You've been chatting to this guy for MONTHS!"

So that's what this is about. I gave him my password and he's trawled my laptop for evidence of infidelity.

"Paul, hang on a minute. It's Tara. It's what she calls herself. And she's not here. She hasn't shown up. She's probably dead or horrifically injured in the tube bombings but you don't care about that. All you care about is your stupid jealous obsessions."

"Parksville Bear? What woman calls herself Bear?"

"She's from Canada, you idiot. Vancouver. It's their state symbol."

He's quiet on the other end of the phone.

"You've no right to look at my private messages anyway."

"Why should I believe you? What's all this about kissing and fancying each other."

"It was all a long time ago. We had a… a lesbian fling."

"So it's a *girl* you're seeing. I can't even trust you around girls now?"

"It was twenty-three years ago Paul! I was at school!"

"Forget it, Chris. I don't know who you are any more. I've emptied the laptop like you asked, and saved it all on a memory stick which is on your desk. I'll drop the laptop off with Alex in the morning. Then I'm out of here."

He ends the call. I try to phone back. His number's unavailable.

An hour or so later he sends a text. *Too many people in this relationship. It's over.*

I lie in bed, shaking.

Chapter Fifty-Nine

NEXT DAY, FRIDAY, I wake, amazed that despite everything, I must have slept eventually. There's no word from Tara. Nothing further from Alex. Or Paul.

I feel numb. Acting on automatic, I go down to breakfast, but the fried egg and sausages stick like rubble in my gullet as my throat constricts with tension. The stereo in the lounge is playing "Yesterday".

Yesterday I had a business, a boyfriend, a daughter who was missing me, and a liaison with a former lover to look forward to. Now, I don't know if I have any of those things.

I push the plate away, go back up to the room.

I collapse on my bed, sobbing. I forgot to plug my phone in last night, and it's almost out of charge. But the faint buzzing indicates a call.

Stevie. Thank God.

"Are you okay? Any news?"

I sob down the phone. Tell him about Tara. About Alex and the business. About Paul. About Charlotte.

"I don't know what to do and I feel so alone here," I say.

"Oh, poor darling," he says. "You don't have to stay there another night, you know. You can come home. I can make you a cup of tea, give you a hug, and it'll all look very different."

"But what about Tara?"

"Maybe give it an hour or two, see if she shows up. Try and relax, do something nice. It's a beautiful day and you're in a gorgeous city."

Feeling calmer, I leave the hotel and retrace my steps along the river. The only vessel is a tourist boat. I head into town over Pulteney Bridge. I come across a square I don't remember, where there's a girl playing a viola. You get a better class of busker in this city. Funny that Tara's mum used to call it a rural backwater.

I climb the steps to Upper Borough Walls and see that Moles is still there. There are posters for bands that I've never heard of in the windows. I feel a sense of relief, and hope, that it is apparently unchanged, still showcasing new alternative talent.

I pass Gay Street, remembering the photo Tara and I posed for by the sign. I walk up through the Circus. Is it my imagination or are there fewer of the Chestnut trees than there used to be? There are two groups of tourists being led around by tour guides. I skirt around them.

At the Royal Crescent I hesitate outside Karl's house, but don't lift the treble clef doorknocker.

It's warm. There are girls in crop tops and shorts sunbathing on the Crescent green. I'm wearing a light cotton top and jeans and I'm too hot.

I head for Victoria Park, past the monument, along the main path. I peel off left, looking for the secluded path where Tara and I kissed, but I'm not sure now which one it is.

It feels strange to be in a place like this without the dog. I miss him. I have a sudden desire to phone Paul, get him to come down in the van, bring Finlay. We could walk here and wallow in normality.

Then I remember. Paul and I are over.

I have a sensation of being lost somewhere in time and space, trapped between a poignant past and an indifferent present. I have a strong desire for peace. The place is rammed. Its busyness jars.

I think of Nessa. I have the name of the place where she's buried written down on the card Kate sent in case Tara and I felt like visiting. Peace must surely be found in such a place. I stop by a taxi rank.

"Can you take me to Oakwood Green burial site?"

The grave's not marked. Apparently, they plant trees either side of the bodies but there's nothing to indicate which mound of freshly dug earth relates to which corpse. I only know she's somewhere near the heritage orchard. The place, mercifully, is quiet. Apart from two people in the distance with a dog, there's nobody else here. I stroll among the buttercups and wildflowers and look out at rolling hills, trying to get a sense of Nessa. Trying to feel something.

I lie on the grass, looking up through a clump of trees at a patch of sky, as white fluffy clouds chase each other across the blue expanse. I am conscious of my senses. The smell of hay, the sound of sheep bleating in the surrounding fields, birdsong in the trees. As I lie here, shifting to avoid a hummock under my left shoulder-blade, and something buzzing near my right ear, I realise how exhausted I am. Two nights with hardly any sleep. So many turbulent emotions.

The ground beneath me seems to draw me. I want to fuse my atoms with the earth and stay here forever. Here at last I may find peace.

And now it happens.

I start to drift. Slowly at first, above the green, then over the city and out beyond. I see the Bristol channel. I fly high across the ocean. Now I see the busy scene I saw last night. People like ants heading off in orderly processions in different directions. And here she is, at last. Walking like a Stepford Wife automaton. Wheeling a case to a waiting bus – a big banner on the side which says Whistler Airport Shuttle. I hover, then swoop low as she waits in line. She lifts her face, all too briefly. It's pale and expressionless. She alights. I see the driver take her ticket, and then the bus departs, heading out onto a six-lane highway, driving on the right. Now I know what this means. What I failed to see last night.

She's still in Canada.

I come to with a jolt, the scene dissolved, the calm gone. I rise from the ground with a sudden urgency to get out of this place. The jitters now back with a vengeance. What *is* this? Nessa messing with my head from her woodland grave?

I reach the gate and hail a passing taxi. Back at the hotel, I feel suddenly, terribly weary. I want to be home, in familiar surroundings, with Stevie and the dog and what's left of my life. Instead, I'm alone in the city I once called home, quietly discombobulating, with the weekend stretching ahead of me. And it's only Friday.

I could use the time to call in on Grace again. Or to make some phone calls to find out what's happened to Tara. To try the helpline again and hang on the phone for as long as it takes. To go back to London and search for her. To rock up at some police station and add Tara's name to lists of the missing.

Like I did twenty-three years ago.

I go down to the hotel basement, where there's a computer with Internet connection. I log into MSN and trawl back through her messages. When I asked where she was staying, she responded "Near Heathrow. Think it's a Hilton."

There are three possible hotels. I phone each. Did a Tara Dean stay here last night? Nobody by that name. Or Tara Clinton? Nobody. I find a fourth one, two miles away from the airport. Could it be this one? Still no joy.

I look up flights from Vancouver. I phone the airlines. Was Tara Dean booked onto the flight? They either say no or refuse to give me any information.

I go back to my room, where the atmosphere is still and muggy. Dust particles dance in a shaft of light between the curtains. I have a strong desire to lie on the bed, which has been made up since I left it this morning, and sleep. But I fight it. I switch on the TV to more news about London. I watch the same clips over and over again. I can't stop.

The weirdness of the last twenty-four hours has unsettled me. Floaty feelings from years ago stretch out across the decades with fierce intensity. The thumping pulse. The swimming head. The desire to scream the place down.

My mind is fuddled with what ifs.

What if Tara's in hospital unconscious?

What if she's dead, with no-one to identify her?

What if she's alive, with both her legs blown off?

What if she's stood me up, like she did Jason in Paris?

What if she never boarded that plane?

I recall my brother David's words, from all those years ago. Until we know. She is both alive and dead. She is all these things.

She's back in Schrodinger's box. With the dead cat.

I'm starting to lose it. I need to talk to someone. A voice of reason.

I phone Stevie. "Tara never showed up here. And there's

still no word. What shall I do? I tried phoning the airlines and the hotels. They won't give me any information."

I can hear Stevie's characteristic slow intake of breath on the phone. Then he says, "Want me to run a check on her at work?"

I know, because Stevie's occasionally hinted at it, that he has access to systems not accessible to the general public.

"I don't want you to get into trouble."

"I think someone due to arrive in the UK who cancels plans at the last minute on the day four bombs go off on the London Underground could reasonably be classified as a person of interest," he says. "Leave it with me. But look at it this way, if she was okay she'd have turned up by now or at least got in touch. If she's not there's not much point in you hanging around down there because she'll either be in hospital or…"

He leaves the sentence hanging. The memory of yesterday and the thought of Tara caught up in all the carnage makes me shudder.

"But what about Grace?"

"Grace isn't your responsibility, is she?"

He's right, and I feel calmer now as I decide to pack my bag and make my way back to Nottingham on the next available train.

I linger in the room, taking one last look at the four walls that have defined my nightmare, then the phone by the bed rings.

"It's reception. Your friend is here."

Chapter Sixty

SOMETHING IN ME leaps. I stop by the mirror, dab at my tear-stained face with a touch of makeup, run a comb through my hair and race down the stairs.

I burst through the door, my heart thumping through my ribcage, my body floating, and I look around.

She's not there.

"Chris."

The male voice behind me takes a second to sink in. I swing round.

The face that greets me looks a thousand years older than when I last saw it only yesterday.

"You?" I say.

"I'm so, so sorry."

MY FIRST FEELING is anger. What right does he have to come down here and intrude on my moment with Tara. My magical reunion. I look around frantically. "Where is she?" I ask the receptionist. But she's frowning. And it dawns. By "your friend" she means Paul.

I turn towards him, salt tears stinging, clouding my

vision. My disappointment palpable.

I notice he looks smaller. His athletic body shaking, his pallor white. All the anger from last night gone. He looks dishevelled, his shirt unironed, his jeans ill-fitting.

"Please, Chris. Please. Can we talk?"

I lead him to the lounge, where we are the only people. We sit in armchairs, me slumped and deflated. The rush of adrenaline I had when I thought Tara had arrived has now subsided and I feel utterly exhausted. I let Paul talk.

"After I sent that text, I read through all the messages. And I saw that what you said stacked up. But I still felt insanely jealous because you hadn't told me about Tara. I still thought this weekend was all one big deliberate deceit. I was ready to leave. Then this morning on my way to drop your laptop off I saw Stevie. I was in a kind of red mist when I saw him. He took me round to his garden and sat me down by that ridiculous statue of his and he made me take deep breaths. He told me you were in a state. I asked him if he knew about Tara. He said you'd confided in him. I asked him why you didn't feel you could tell *me* and he just shrugged.

"He said he'd never heard you so upset. That you wanted to come home. So I've driven down to get you, Chris. I'll take you home. I am really, really sorry for what I said last night. I know it's none of my business. I know it was a massive overreaction on my part. I know I've got issues from my past and I promise I'll work on them. I'll get help."

I notice his hands are shaking.

"I realised something last night. When I thought you'd betrayed me. I realised how strong my feelings are for you. I actually love you, Chris, and I want to understand you. I just want you to trust me enough to tell me everything."

I stare at him, incredulous.

"I'll take you home now. And if you want, I'll just leave you at yours, I don't even have to come in. In my imagination, you were down here, with her, or him, or whoever my love rival was or is, wallowing in lies. But I get here, and I see Stevie's right. You're a wreck. Come home with me, Chris, we can start again."

"But what about Tara?"

He looks around him.

"She's not here, is she? And if she shows up, even if we're half-way back to Nottingham, I promise I'll drive you straight back."

"Can you give me a minute?"

"Take as long as you want. I'll be right here."

I go back up to the room, pick up my already packed bag, and head back downstairs where Paul is waiting, leaning forward on the chair, chin cupped in his hands.

He brings the van round to the front of the hotel.

WE DRIVE WITHOUT talking. Later, I will tell him everything. But for now, my thoughts fill the silence.

The theory, which began to take shape yesterday, when Grace said the words, "I doubt if she even boarded the plane," is almost complete.

Years ago I tried to find someone who didn't want to be found. I put all my energy into it and ended up falling into an abyss. An abyss I had to dig myself out of, with a little help from my friends.

Years ago I spent weeks not knowing if she was alive or dead. She *allowed* me to think that.

I am once again in a position where I don't know if she's

alive or dead.

She wants me in this position. She's playing me. I doubt if she even boarded that plane.

Last time, I let her win. I existed in agony until someone opened the box.

This time, whether or not I open the box is within my own control. I can keep it locked, and throw away the key.

Just as I'm thinking this, my phone starts to ring. It's a Bath number. "It might be the hotel."

"Don't answer it," says Paul.

"What?"

"You can call them back, but there's something I need to tell you first."

I look at him, his face set, hands gripping the steering wheel.

"I wasn't going to tell you this till we got home, and I'm not even sure I'm right."

"What, Paul? Right about what?"

"I'm not sure your friend Tara's entirely on the level."

"What d'you mean?"

He pauses a minute while a motorbike roars past us.

"She told you she's in Canada, right?"

"That's where she lives, yes."

"And she's the person who wrote a review on the Phoenix Designs website. After you'd done some work for her?"

"I did a birthday card for her dad. She wrote a really positive review."

"Whoever wrote that review posted it from Cambridge, Massachusetts."

"What?"

"I ran an analytics check on it."

"You *what*?"

"Last night, when I was mad. I was searching through everything I could think of. To prove something. I don't know what. That you were cheating, I suppose. So I looked up everything I could find relating to Tara. To see if she really was who you said she was, or if she was in fact some bloke you were seeing. And I remembered this review."

"So… what if she posted it from somewhere else? She travels a lot with her job."

"Then I looked at all the analytics on views on your site since it was set up. You can get really accurate information these days about where people are based. And I found out that someone with that same IP address, the one listed to Cambridge, Massachusetts, has looked at your website just over twelve hundred times since we set it up in May."

"Bloody hell!"

As I watch, the traffic on the M5 suddenly seems hypnotic. I have a sense there's something momentous I'm not seeing.

"D'you get what I'm saying here?"

"No!"

"Do I have to spell it out to you, Chris? Your friend Tara, you say she's in Vancouver, or that's what she told you, anyway?"

"She is in Vancouver. That's where her job is. I've checked her out. She's listed on the University website. It's all kosher."

"Ok," says Paul. "The other alternative is, the person you've been connecting to isn't Tara."

I stare at him, unable to speak.

"In all the weeks months you've been messaging, did you ever once talk to her on the phone, hear her voice, or see her face on video call?"

"We were going to. We made plans to Skype, but…"

I remember sitting at my keyboard, waiting, but Tara never showed.

"People do it you know, Chris. Set up false profiles to impersonate someone.

I've heard of that happening. But isn't that usually to con money out of people?

"Who would do this? And why? They've never once asked me for money."

I'm not sure I believe him. I know Paul is streets ahead of me in IT but there must be some other reason why an IP address is shown as being somewhere where it isn't.

But more than 1,200 views? That's verging on obsessive.

My phone rings. Stevie. I answer it.

"I ran a check on your friend. Nobody of that name checked into any of the flights to the UK. I tried both names."

"So she didn't board a plane to the UK?"

"Not unless she's got a third name."

"Stevie?"

"Yes."

"Do your systems show you where someone lives?"

There's a pause.

"There's quite a lot of information you can find about a person."

"It's just something very odd's going on and I just need to clarify her address."

"I'll see what I can do."

I don't hear back from Stevie till I'm home. He calls round on his way back from work.

"Ok this is what I've found out," he says. "Don't say where you heard it. Although all of this is in the public domain if you know where to look."

"Go on."

"Doctor Tara Dean who works at the University of British Columbia, Vancouver campus, as a senior professor in Psychology, lives at number eighty-three Hermon Drive, Vancouver."

I breathe a huge sigh of relief. She's told me the truth. I look at Paul.

"She bought the property in nineteen ninety-five and lived there until January this year with a woman called Isabella Flyte."

"Izzy. This all adds up," I say.

"In February of this year Tara Dean took out a lawsuit to evict Isabella from the property."

"This is all true! What she told me is all true. She's not an imposter."

Paul frowns.

"It doesn't explain the other stuff. The fact this stuff is posted from Massachusetts. I still think the person you've been talking to isn't Tara."

"Oh bloody hell, Paul. There must be some other explanation for that, surely? Can't you have an IP address registered to somewhere else?"

We both look at Stevie.

"It would explain the no-show in London, I suppose, if whoever you arranged to meet isn't the person you thought they were. Just stringing you along."

"But they had details, photos, they could never have got. They knew stuff. Grace and Karl knew Tara was coming!"

"Did they though?" said Paul. "What if the imposter's in touch with them too?"

"This is madness," I say, rounding on Paul. "You're

letting your paranoid imagination get the better of you."

Stevie opens his tin of tobacco and starts to roll a cigarette. He does so with precision, taking his time, as he does with all his actions. Precise, thoughtful.

"It's not beyond the realms of possibility," he says. "People do it all the time. Set up fake profiles. It's easy to lift someone's photos, steal their biographical details and get a handle on their speech patterns."

That triggers something in my memory.

"Oh my God!" I say. "Charlotte said there was a Myspace page in my name. Ages ago. What if someone's set up a fake profile for me too?"

There were no photos, and very little information, I recall, so we assumed it was a different Christine Carlisle and promptly forgot about it.

None of us are on Myspace. It's for teenagers and bands and a few parents who want to spy on their kids. And the platform won't let us look unless we join.

So Paul says: "Ok, I'll set up an account. Let's see just how easy it is to set up a fake profile."

Very easy, it turns out. He uses his real email address and a false name. Daniel Slater. He uses a photo of a guy with a guitar lifted off the internet, and adds a bit of invented biographical history, just for fun. But he didn't even really need to do that.

"Great, we're in! Let's look for the fake Christine Carlisle."

There's a few Christine Carlisles, but when we add the word "Nottingham" to the search, only one comes up. And, unlike when Charlotte discovered the account, when there were no images, there's a photo. It's a photo of me. The real me. And there's a picture in the background of Bath –

Pulteney Bridge by moonlight.

Now I'm really freaked out.

Most of the settings are private. And Paul says the only way to see what's on there is to send them a friend request. "Want to be friends with Daniel Slater, Chris?"

"Go on then."

He sends the request.

"What do we do now?"

"We wait."

"What if the fake me ignores the request?"

We look at Stevie.

"I think they'll go for it out of curiosity. People who do this sort of thing like to live dangerously behind their keyboards."

"But *why* do they do it Stevie? If there's nothing in it for them. They're not trying to get money out of you or anything."

He pauses. "I think it's a kind of power game. They get a kick out of deceiving people. They do it to lure people into online intimacy."

"You seem to know a lot about this sort of thing," says Paul. "What exactly is your job?"

"Oh it's really very tedious. Much too boring to talk about." Stevie stands up to leave. "But in the meantime I'll do a bit more digging."

Chapter Sixty-One

NONE OF IT makes sense. Has Tara done this? Set up a fake profile for me? And why? Or is it the imposter, if there *is* an imposter?

My brain is dull from lack of sleep. From dodging bombs. And from too much emotional overload.

I move like an automaton through the house. Paul makes me a meal. Pours me a glass of wine. Massages my shoulders to try to relax me. It doesn't work. Finlay nudges me, wanting attention. I push him away.

Every so often, I have a paranoid thought that shocks me out of my stupor and puts me back on red alert.

Who is impersonating me? What do they want? I log into my online banking and check nobody's cleaned out my account. All good. For now. I go through my accounts and change my passwords. But what if the imposter *knows*. What if they've hacked into my account and they're somehow watching?

Is the person I've been talking to, who I believed to be Tara, *really* an imposter? The person I'd arranged to meet? But the hotel knew Tara was booked in. They had her name. They were expecting someone called Tara Dean to turn up.

This leads me to think, who would have turned up to meet me? The imposter? What if they were on that train, watching me. Maybe they were one of the other guests in the hotel. Watching. But why?

I'm going round in circles. I remember Karl. And Grace. They were expecting Tara, weren't they? But then I remember Karl's vagueness when I turned up. Like he wasn't expecting her that day. I decide to phone him, to see if I can clarify things. I took a photo of his number pinned to the noticeboard in his flat. I refer to my digital camera. There's a few numbers in the shot, one for the district nurse, the local hospice, Karl's number, and, lower down, a number for Tara – the second half of it chopped off.

I whip out my phone and compare the number Karl had for Tara with the one I have stored in my phone.

"It's a different number!" I say.

"What is?"

"The number that Karl has for Tara is different to the one she gave me – the one I've been messaging and trying to phone. The one I had the text from to say she was boarding the plane."

"Right," says Paul. "That fits the imposter theory. So the person you've been messaging isn't the real Tara."

"This is seriously fucked up." I say.

I manage to eat. On the surface, it's a calm, domestic scene. Earlier today, I thought Paul and I were over. Now, somehow, I'm not quite sure how, we seem to be together again.

As I watch him clear away the dishes and wipe the table clean another thought pings into my brain, unwanted.

What if *Paul*'s the imposter? What if he's set this whole thing up?

I shudder as he returns from the kitchen and refills my wine.

"Okay if I stay tonight?" he says. "I've had too much alcohol to drive."

So that's that then.

Later, I skype Charlotte in Australia. I tell her about the fake Myspace profile. She finds it hilarious. "Why would anyone want to impersonate *you,* Mum?"

David appears in shot. He finds it funny too, and so does Mum. They all have a jolly good laugh at my expense. But it does me good just to see their faces.

The wine has lulled me and lowered my resistance. Things feel almost normal. Paul runs me a bath to relax me, and by tacit agreement joins me in bed.

But sleep, once more, eludes me, and the thought I had earlier returns.

I think of Hannah's mother in the hospital saying, "You're not my daughter, you're an imposter." I look at Paul's sleeping face on the pillow and a voice in my head says on repeat. "You're the imposter. You're the imposter."

And that way, madness lies.

Chapter Sixty-Two

MORNING COMES AND with it sunshine. I seem to have slept, in the end. And it feels good to be in my own bed, not in a hotel room. Paul's up and about. He brings me tea. He also brings news that Christine Carlisle the artist from Nottingham has accepted Daniel Slater's friendship request.

I come downstairs in my dressing gown and look at the computer screen as he shows me my own fake profile.

There's a post from Thursday with the picture of Bath and the caption: "Back in my home city."

So whoever this imposter is knew I was in Bath, although the photo looks like something lifted off the Internet.

There are updates every week or so, going back to May when the page was set up. And some of them have photos. Mostly ones we've used on the Phoenix Designs website. There's also one of me on the beach at Whitby.

"I took that," says Paul. "Whoever this creep is, they've stolen my photo. That's a breach of copyright."

There's one of me at a Christmas party with our old company. How have they got *that?*

We scroll on down.

"Oh my God! There's one of Charlotte."

Now an icy chill runs through me.

It's the photo of Charlotte and Hannah from her sixteenth birthday. The one I sent to Tara when she asked to see a photo of my daughter. Except the person I sent it to wasn't Tara.

"They've crossed a line now. I'm not having anyone messing with my daughter. I think I'm going to tell the Police."

"Don't do it yet. I want to send them a message. See if they respond."

He types out a message to the person pretending to be me.

Hey, Chris, how ya doin?

There's a pause and then.

Good thanks. How's you?

I start to shiver. I really don't want to engage in any way with this person who's stolen my identity.

"Don't reply, Paul. I'm going to the Police."

Paul doesn't respond straight away. Instead, he goes through the profile, capturing screenshots. He then finds an option to report the profile to Myspace, which he does, then goes back on the page and types in big, capital letters.

GAME'S UP, IMPOSTER.

The screen goes blank.

We try and get back in, but Daniel Slater is blocked. Later we try again, but the profile of Christine Carlisle has mysteriously disappeared.

I now log onto businessconnect.com, to look at Tara's profile, and it's gone too.

I get a phone call from Stevie. Number withheld. Sharp intake of breath.

"I've done a bit more digging," he says. "And found out

something rather interesting."

"What?"

"Dr Tara Dean has just filed a complaint against her former partner, Isabella Flyte, for theft of intellectual property."

"Really?"

"So I looked into Isabella Flyte. And eventually tracked down where she lives. And guess where that is, Chris?"

I know before he tells me.

"It wouldn't be Cambridge, Massachusetts by any chance?"

Chapter Sixty-Three

Hey Siri, play "You're Beautiful" by James Blunt

September 2005

T HE ENVELOPE COMES to my work address. The one that's listed on our company website. There's an airmail sticker and a postmark from Vancouver.

There's a letter inside along with a photo. Of Tara. She's on some kind of rope bridge, high above a narrow valley, surrounded on either side by giant evergreen trees. Her hair hangs loose. She's wearing stylish capri style trousers and a light jacket. She's holding the handrail with one hand, and the other stretched out across the vista, her long limbs lean and elegant. She's laughing, and she's beautiful. On the back of the photo, in sloping handwriting, it says "On Capilano Suspension Bridge Summer 2004."

The letter is on headed paper from the University of British Columbia. It's from Dr Tara Dean.

It's handwritten.

Dear Chrissie.

Please accept my profound and heartfelt apologies as I know you've been the victim of a sophisticated hoax carried out by my ex-partner Izzy. The Police and lawyers are involved at this end. My lawyer obtained the messages she exchanged with you, from various fake profiles posing as me.

Izzy also, I know, set up fake profiles for various people from my past, including you, for the purpose of connecting with me, and I fell for it too. Seems she played us both. She even lifted your real messages and used them to pose as you, and vice versa, which is what made it all seem so authentic. She has proved herself a scheming, dangerous, highly plausible manipulator. And although most of what she's done isn't actually against the law—can you believe that?— I'm pursuing a claim for damages against her.

I also wanted to thank you for visiting my Mum and Karl. I heard that you dodged the London bombs to get there! They appreciated your visit, albeit on false pretences. In fact your visit was what set off alarm bells in my mind, and led me to discover the fraud. That and the fact that your Myspace profile – which I believed to be real – mysteriously disappeared.

I was due to fly out to the UK that day, on 7/7, but changed my plans last minute and switched my flight to the week after. And in so doing, managed to inadvertently foil whatever scheme Izzy had in store for us. I wanted to get there in time to make my peace with Grace, but it was too late. So you got there where I didn't, and for that I am eternally grateful.

My lawyer showed me the messages you exchanged with my ex – believing her to be me. And I can tell by what I read that you remain the warm, *witty, wonderful human being you always were. The girl I fell in love with all those years ago. I am sorry I left the way I did back then, and for all the heartache and anxiety that caused you.*

I wish you well in your life, Chrissie, you deserve to be happy. And I am truly sorry you got dragged into all this mess. I don't suppose you'll want anything further to do with me, but just in case, here's my real email address below. Or you can contact me via the University email on the letterhead.

Your friend, now and always.
Tara xxx

I've struggled these past few months. Once the identity of the imposter was known, after the mystery was all cleared up. I felt numb.

Tara hadn't sought me out, after all these years. The sense of connection I felt, reading her messages, was all based on lies. The feeling of grief, knowing that she has once more eluded me, as she did twenty-three years ago, has been deep.

I study the photo, and a wave of mixed emotions washes over me. Sadness, longing, and desire. Even at forty-two, she is still utterly beautiful.

I read the letter several times, and let the tears flow. It looks like her handwriting, from what I remember. Sloping, elegant, with a bit of a flourish. Written with a fountain pen. Classy.

I feel a sense of hope resurge as I read it.

But it's easy to fake handwriting, isn't it?

I place the letter in the box with all the other evidence, and shut the lid.

PART THREE

Unboxed

Chapter Sixty-Four

March 2020

"YOU MUST STAY at home."

There's a man who thinks he's Churchill on the screen, flanked by Union Jacks.

There's Charlotte, for once, fully in the room. No makeup makes her look vulnerable, like this crisis has turned her into a little girl again, and there's Paul, sitting back, brow furrowed.

The briefing is brief. We watch without speaking, then as it cuts to questions, Charlotte turns to me.

"This is like living in a history book."

This address to the nation comes after weeks of build-up. When the shops ran out of food. When the hospitals filled up. When grim news from across the water warned what was coming our way. And in the last two weeks, they stopped us gathering. They shut the pubs. They told us to stand six feet apart. They banned hugs. And the hashtag #wfh started trending as people posted photos of their home office setups.

Now we know, even as we saw in the new decade, the unseen monster was reaching out its tentacles across the globe.

I know I'm not alone in experiencing a tsunami of conflicting emotions. Each time measures have ramped up, I've hit a spike of anxiety.

Now that we finally have it, the announcement we've been waiting for, my world erupts with questions.

"How in God's name am I supposed to earn a living?" says Paul.

WTF? (shrug emoji) via WhatsApp from Alex.

"How long am I gonna be stuck here?" Charlotte, wide-eyed, forgetting it was her idea to move back in.

"Charlotte, how long is a piece of string? Better to be locked down here with us than with that waster of an ex-boyfriend of yours."

My millennial daughter moved back in with me when she split with her ex so she could save up to buy a house.

"Your work'll continue. You're a key worker. And with not going out you'll save more money."

She gives me her famous eyeroll.

"I can work from home," I say. "And Alex can work from his place. So we'll carry on with the jobs we've got in the pipeline. Then when that dries up, we'll see what happens."

"And what about me?" says Paul.

Hmm. That's a tricky one. Paul's still an electrical engineer who goes into other people's workplaces. Now forbidden.

"I guess you'll just have to put your work on hold for now. But there'll be some government help. Even *he* can't leave the nation to starve."

Paul sniffs. I can almost see the machinery of his brain working. I know what he's thinking without him saying it.

"I've got to the grand old age of fifty-three without having to resort to government handouts." He says it anyway.

"Now someone in China gets the flu and the whole world has to come to a standstill. This is madness!"

He glowers at the TV, stands up, and paces round the room like a caged animal, toned muscles fit to burst.

"How long is this going to go on for? Weeks, months? What are people going to do with themselves?" He glares at me, like Covid-19 is my own personal invention.

Lockdown hasn't even begun, but already there's tension on Teal Street.

"Also, Paul, you need to decide where home is. Cos wherever it is, that's where you're holed up for the foreseeable."

Paul and I have an arrangement. Although to all intents and purposes he lives at mine, he's got his own house. And when the chaos gets too much, he'll retreat to his own space. Only problem is he's recently gutted the place and is in the slow process of doing it up. Last time I saw it, it was a shell with no glass in the windows and no electricity.

He looks around the room, like I've seen him do when he's quoting for jobs. Now he seems to be sizing up my house to assess its limits, its suitability as a place to hunker down. He turns tail and walks into the kitchen.

He's there a while and I hear him put the radio on. Charlotte returns to her phone and I watch a re-run of what just happened on the TV news.

When Paul returns, beer in hand, he says.

"I'll go back to mine in the morning. At least I've got something useful to do there."

I breathe a little easier.

Meanwhile my phone is being deluged with messages.

There's an email from The Yard, the co-working space that Alex and I run the business from, advising us to pick up what we need in the morning as they're shutting up shop till lockdown is over.

There's a Facebook message from Mum, who's managed to watch the UK briefing even though she's nine thousand miles away and it's three am in Canberra.

There's a string of follow-up WhatsApps from Alex, expressed mostly in emojis.

Then a phone call from Stevie. I know it's Stevie because it says 'number withheld' and there's the habitual slow intake of breath before he speaks. "For the purposes of this governmental edict, can we be part of the same household? I'll die if I have to stare at the same four walls for three months."

I look at Paul, and wonder if I can get away with shipping him out and letting Stevie in.

"I don't mean *live* at yours. I mean you letting me onto your terrace once in a while so I can sit two metres away and have a latte in the presence of another humanoid."

I lower my voice. "We'll work something out."

"Thank you, darling! Oh and is it okay if I come round now? It being the last day we can openly socialise in each other's houses?"

"Yeah, why not."

A last night with the four of us together seems a good enough reason to crack open a bottle of red – even though Stevie doesn't drink. I end up having most of the bottle because Paul's on beer, Charlotte's on gin.

"This is going to be one of those moments when you always remember where you were when you heard the news," says Paul.

"Like nine-eleven."

"And seven-seven."

"I was in Australia," says Charlotte.

"And I was in London on that day, in the thick of it," I say and shudder.

"What about the day John Lennon got shot?"

Charlotte rolls her eyes. "I wasn't *born* then!"

"D'you remember the day Princess Diana died though, Charlie? You went downstairs to watch TV, then came back to tell me there were no cartoons because a princess had died."

We sit in silence for a bit, each immersed in our own memories.

"Let's play the jukebox game."

We turn to the space-age, spherical speaker that is Siri. We take it in turns to request songs, treating Siri like a jukebox in the pub. A jukebox that has every song ever written by any artist in the world.

Paul chooses Lithium by Nirvana. Charlotte goes for Disney, her go-to comfort tunes. Stevie requests "Too drunk to Fuck" by the Dead Kennedys. Siri bleeps out the word "fuck" but plays it anyway. Now it's my turn and I can't think of a single thing to choose.

"This feels like the end times," says Stevie. "Play something apocalyptical." I pick "Dance me to the End of Love" by Leonard Cohen. This sets the theme for the evening as Siri churns out "Ghost Town" by the Specials (Stevie), "Back to Black" by Amy Winehouse (Charlotte), "Eve of Destruction" by Barry McGuire (Paul) "The End" by the Doors (me) – all eleven minutes of it. Charlotte stops playing and reverts to her phone.

It's midnight when Stevie leaves. There's a finality about

him walking out of the front door. And in the morning, Paul will be gone too. It'll be just me and Charlotte. As I drain the last half-glass from the bottle, I feel jittery.

Chapter Sixty-Five

April 2020

I OPEN THE front door. It's warm. An early spring. The sort of weather I usually love. But now it's different. Because of the thing that lurks. I shut the door on it.

Stevie says I should go out, that I'm allowed to for daily exercise. "Its gorgeous out there, Chris. There's absolutely no traffic. You can walk in the middle of the road."

You have to, to avoid people. And I am minimising risk. It's bad enough that Charlotte's still going out on visits – the work of a child protection social worker doesn't stop for Coronavirus. I try not to think about the fact she's in and out of youth detention centres and custody suites during the working day. I make her disinfect her hands, drop her work clothes straight into the washing machine, and shower when she comes home.

Stevie's safe. He's not seeing anyone. He's vulnerable with his emphysema so he's being ultra cautious. I smuggle him in through the back gate every few days and we play table tennis in the garage – standing 2.7 metres apart. He brings his own mug which I fill up from the coffee machine.

Paul stays in his shell of a house. The builders he'd hired

aren't working so he's doing bits himself, where he can. I talk to him daily on WhatsApp, Alex on Zoom, and Mum on Facetime. So many ways of communicating.

I go in the garden and listen to the birds, in their innocence, enjoying this break from the destruction of humankind. They sing louder than ever. As the humans hide away, the animals can play.

I tried walking to the shop the other day but some youth in a tracksuit ran past me, breathing everywhere, and the jitters came and I turned back. What if I collapsed in the street? They'd send an ambulance. They'd take me to the place nobody wants to go. I must stay home. I must stay safe.

I know what this reminds me of. And it's so, so long since I've felt like this. Since I've had anything approaching a panic attack. But this is different. This is a collective angst, not singular to me. The whole world feels it.

I'm addicted to rolling news. Infection rates. Death stats. First-hand accounts from inside the hospitals. Videos from doctors showing us how to breathe, how to cough, what to do if you get this thing.

Charlotte's old schoolfriend Hannah is a nurse now. They've transferred her to a Covid ward where it's all hands on deck. She brings us news from the front line in her video chats with Charlotte. Tells us how relentless it is. Shows us the lines on her face from wearing a mask for twelve hours.

Tonight, we see her on the East Midlands news, being interviewed coming off shift. Her face, pale and beautiful, with her long red hair and edgy fringe, fills the screen.

"What's your message to the people out there who say the rules don't matter?" the reporter asks her.

"Imagine if it was your loved one in there," she points to the hospital behind her. "Every day I'm at the bedside of people fighting for their lives. *I'm* the one with them when they take their last breath. I'm there because their own families *can't* be. So if you think the rules don't apply to you, think again."

Charlotte and I whoop at the TV. Hannah is a star. The face of heroism in the NHS. Charlotte takes a photo of Hannah's face on the screen and shares it among all her friends. I swell with pride, almost like Hannah's my own daughter. She used to call me her second mum.

As a teenager, she stayed with us during her mother's bouts of illness. Now her mother lives in Scotland and is apparently quite well. Hannah, meanwhile, has become a born-again Christian. She goes to one of the big evangelical churches that have sprung up on the outskirts of the city. Now that services have stopped, she attends online. She invited me to watch one day, but it was all "Hallelujah, praise the Lord" and it freaked me out.

The Internet is awash with information and misinformation. And I must read it all. One minute, I'm calm. Reassured. The next I'm terrified. Who to believe? We're told to stay home. We're told to get outside for exercise.

There's a person on a Facebook group who has no food. They're stuck in a flat on the seventh floor of a tower block in town and they can't go out. Powerless to help, I cry on the phone to Paul.

"I'm worried about you, Chris. Want me to come over?"

Part of me wants to say yes. To melt into him. Let him make it all right. But part of me wants to let nobody over the threshold. He's been out running in a busy city park. He's been in the supermarket. It's all right for him if he catches it, Paul's super-fit. But me? All those years of smoking, and asthma, make me vulnerable.

"Mum, you're cracking up." Even Charlotte's noticed, as I disinfect the door handles for the umpteenth time. "I think you're developing OCD."

Night time is the worst. I put the radio on, and the news rolls in from across the globe. This thing is everywhere.

I wake up tearful. I wake up terrified. I wake up joyful— for a few minutes—until I remember. I sometimes wake up wildly optimistic – almost euphoric. But mostly I don't wake up at all because I haven't slept.

It's now three weeks into lockdown. Some people are starting to relax into it, even feeling better than before. But if anything, I'm getting worse.

Our work's dried up. Clients, themselves strapped for cash, cancel or postpone their jobs. I got a brochure out in the first week of lockdown before the mailing house shut down. The money from that will keep me going for a bit. Otherwise, it's just bits and bobs. A logo here, a poster there. The Yard – good socialists that they are – have suspended our rent. And there's some sort of help for the self-employed heading our way, but it doesn't stop me worrying. What if we lose the business? Lose the house? Or worse, lose someone close? People are dying. Daily.

Charlotte's still bringing in a regular income.

"I might end up relying on your earnings," I say. Oh, the irony.

In the absence of gainful employment, I've started going through my boxed-up former life. But it makes me feel worse. Too many memories of anxieties past. Am I really any better than my frightened sixteen-year-old self? Is the confidence and independence I've built up just a façade that is crumbling away?

I could so easily lose it all. I can't see any way out of this.
My daughter finds me crying. "You need help," she says.

Chapter Sixty-Six

HELP COMES IN canine form. I wasn't going to have another dog after we lost Finlay, but Sasha finds *us*. She arrives at night. Someone on the lost and found dogs network has put a message out and the word's gone around, culminating with a phone call from Alex at midnight. "Chris. Can you rehome a dog?"

"What, now?"

"Yes. We've got her here but Cori's allergic."

"Alex, I'm in bed."

"I'll bring her round."

"How?" Alex has seven bicycles but no car.

"She's a dog. Dog's walk. We'll walk."

I don't see why it can't wait till morning, but I'm not awake enough to argue.

In the end, Sasha arrives by van. Alex has persuaded some long-suffering mate to bring her. A mate I've never met before. I mask up and open the door.

"I'm Jed. I've got a dog in the van."

"Oh. Is Alex with you?"

"No. Just me and the dog. It's whining a lot. It growls when I get anywhere near it. Can you come and get it?"

Jed obviously isn't used to dogs. Doesn't attribute them with human qualities.

The dog is indeed whining. Jed has pushed her into a small space in the back next to the wheel arch, wedged in between giant speakers and an amp.

"Is there a collar or a lead?"

"No. It's a stray. It came like this."

"I'll see what I can find."

I dig around in the cupboard where we still keep a box of Finlay's things. The dog snarls as I put the collar on and attach the lead. At least it almost fits.

By now Charlotte's awake. She appears, bleary eyed at the top of the stairs. "What's going on?"

"We're rescuing a dog."

"In the middle of the night?"

"Dogs don't choose when to become homeless."

Charlotte comes down for a closer look. Now we can see the dog in proper light, she's a most peculiar looking thing. She has little Shrek ears and a wide jaw like a Staffie, but she's tall, thin and scrawny with matted hair and a muddy looking face. She lies down in the hallway as Charlotte approaches.

"Be careful, she's been a bit defensive."

But the dog rolls over, exposing a speckled tummy and teats. Charlotte rubs her and she whimpers.

"What's her name?"

"I don't know. There was no collar. That's Finlay's old one."

"Can I name her then?"

"I don't know if we can keep her. She might belong to someone. In the morning we can take her to the vet to check for a chip."

Next day, I phone the vet. They're still open for urgent

cases and this counts as one.

"Fancy taking her?" I ask Charlotte. Going to the vet means emerging from the house, something I'm currently not doing.

"Mum, it's spitting distance. You can get there. You really can. I'll even come with you."

The vet is a three-minute walk round the corner. We used to joke that it was so close Finlay could walk there by himself. I take a deep breath, and step outside. And it's like, with the dog on the other end of the lead and Charlotte by my side, I somehow feel protected.

They make us wait outside while they check the dog over. She has a chip registered to an owner who moved house long ago. She's a bit underweight but otherwise healthy. And she has a name, Sasha.

We get her home and put her in the bath. She struggles, but once in the warm water with Charlotte scrubbing her back she relaxes a little.

"Sasha," says Charlotte. "That's a beautiful name. You're going to be my dog, Sasha."

"If she's your dog, you can walk her."

Charlotte rolls her eyes.

"No Mum, we'll both walk her."

And so it is that we step out, the two of us and our new canine friend. We walk the back route into the park, seeing nobody on the way. We tentatively let her off the lead, hoping she'll come back. We throw a ball for her. She brings it back, which is more than Finlay ever did.

"I have to get back to work, Mum, but why don't you take her round the rest of the park, to see how you get on? You can call me if you need me."

I put the dog back on the lead, and head up to the main

section of the park. Somehow, with Sasha attached to me, I feel safe. We walk slowly. Past the pitch and putt area, now unused, through the ornamental gardens, where someone has thoughtfully placed the wicker art animals that used to be out on the streets in town, and back along the main path.

As Sasha and I explore the park together, she stops to sniff, and I begin to notice things. The warmth of the sun on my back. The smiles of strangers as we step aside to give each other space. The deep colours of the blossom. The fresh, green growth. We walk back through an estate with beautiful gardens. I stop to smell the lilac. We wend our way home through the back streets and I notice something else. In the three weeks since I last ventured out, rainbows have appeared in windows, and children's drawings are chalked on the pavements. There's even hopscotch markings – a throwback to a bygone era. Amid all this angst and isolation, things of beauty and community have sprung up.

I return refreshed, like you would after a holiday. And with a sense that, as long as I have this dog by my side, I'm going to be okay.

My crazy aunty Nessa used to say animals were angels, sent to save us from ourselves. Sasha becomes my reason to keep going and my passport to the outdoors. Walking her, I find new routes in our locality. I walk down streets I never knew existed and find new paths across the park. I even break the rules and go out twice a day.

We rescued a dog. But there's no doubt in my mind that Sasha rescued me.

Chapter Sixty-Seven

C HARLOTTE IS WORKING from home at the dining room table. She's on a work call that sounds tense, so I take her a coffee. I can't decide if I'm happy or not to be waiting on her again.

Social work skipped a generation. But unlike Mum, who sat in on every committee going, got pulled into all sorts of extra-curricular work, let her work take over and was rarely at home, Charlotte maintains clear boundaries. At the end of the working day, she'll shut her laptop, switch her work phone off, take a shower, and – if it's been a bad day – pour herself a gin.

And judging from the little I overhear from her work calls, she needs one. It sounds like the most harrowing job on earth. She deals with kids who've experienced horrific abuse. Kids caught up in gangs – county lines they call it. Children groomed online. Families who have no money to feed their kids. And now that the schools are shut, there's nobody to look out for them.

She deals with it all with calm professionalism and a detachment that is enviable.

I marvel at the mature, level-headed woman she's

become. Somehow, against the odds, I've brought her up okay and she's turned into this smart, independent, beautiful human being.

So on Thursdays, when we go outside to applaud the key workers, I clap for Charlotte – and Hannah.

"Wish I was furloughed," Charlotte sighs as she comes off the call.

"You don't really. It shows they think of you as essential. Plus if you were furloughed you'd have less money to save up to buy a house."

Eyeroll.

"We both know I'll *never* be able to buy a house. Ever."

"Charlotte you're only thirty. I didn't buy my first home till I was thirty-five."

She glares at me and I feel a mother-daughter spat coming on. It's a well-rehearsed routine. She bemoans her millennial lot and gets at me for what she sees as the unfair privilege of my generation. The reason they can't buy houses is because we, selfishly, live in ours.

I tell her she needs to cut her cloth. Stop going abroad for friends' expensive weddings. Four in the last year alone.

"Like we're gonna be doing that any time soon," she says, "I don't even know if I'll be able to go to Australia to see Lucy in September at the rate we're doing with this lockdown."

"First world problems," I mutter. "When I was your age we were lucky if we went to France."

"Your generation didn't have all this debt," she says. "Thirty grand by the time I'd finished my MA."

True. But some of that is credit card debt.

She sighs.

"How about when Paul's house is done up you move in with him and I can have this place?" She looks covetously around the room as though already refurbishing it in her head.

"Not gonna happen Charlie. We tried living together, remember. He can't cope with my mess. We'd drive each other nuts. Plus he watches golf on TV."

I'm not sure our relationship, such as it is, will even survive lockdown.

"Ok, if not Paul, then someone else. How many years have you been seeing him? It's time you stopped messing about with this semi-detached relationship and found someone you actually wanna be with."

Do other people's daughters say things like that?

Throughout Charlotte's childhood, I was a mostly single mum. And we were all right, just the two of us. I didn't start dating again till she was at secondary school. And although there've been a series of blokes in my life, none of them actually lived here. Charlotte says each one left a legacy. She lists them now.

There was Patrick from Belfast, who emigrated to California and left us with Finlay – our previous canine housemate. There was Neil the joiner, who built us a summer house and replaced the fencing. He was great when he wasn't drinking. There was Michael – now Michaela – who introduced new tech, and for a while I didn't know how anything worked. I thought I was being gaslit but in fact I was just stupid.

But since 2005, on and off, there's been Paul. Although we're more companions now than lovers. We tried, after that ill-fated trip to Bath in 2005, to get together properly. Paul rented out his house and moved into mine. But it didn't work out. Our lifestyles were too incompatible. Paul tried hard to deal with the unresolved issues of his past. He even had counselling. I supported him through it. Just as he helped me through the aftermath of what happened on the 7th of July. So we carry on, together but not together. And now there's too much history to ignore.

Of course, the greatest legacy from my former liaisons is Charlotte herself, but we don't mention that.

"Seriously Mum, of all the men you've dated has there ever been anyone you wanted to commit to? You always keep them at arms' length."

I pause a while before answering. And when I do, my voice comes out thoughtful.

"You mean have I ever been in love? Yes, but it was a very long time ago."

Charlotte shoots a look at me that's part scared, part accusing. And I know what she's thinking. She thinks I'm referring to her father. Which means the conversation is over.

Except, this time, it isn't.

"What was his name?"

"You mean your father? Kai."

"What was his second name?"

"I don't know."

"Where was he from?"

"Hawaii. I think. Or some island near there."

She googles. Kai. Hawaii. Nottingham. 1980s.

"Kai's a Hawaiian name," she says. "What was he doing over here?"

"I don't know."

"Oh *Mum!*"

Admonished by my own daughter for my lack of responsibility when I was younger than she is now.

"Were there any mutual connections, even?"

I shake my head. Kai was a one-off. All I had of him at the time was the phone number of a house in Basford where he was sleeping on the sofa of a mate. And I didn't even know the mate. That's how it was back then.

"Didn't you even *try* to find him?"

"He left the country. It was harder to find people then. There was no Internet."

Can young people today even imagine a pre-Internet world?

"So he just upped and left when you told him you were pregnant. He never got in touch to find out if you'd had the baby?"

"He didn't know."

"Didn't know what?"

"He didn't know I was pregnant. I found out after he left."

Her eyes widen as my words sink in.

"You mean you never even *told* him?"

"I couldn't. He'd gone."

She stands up, hands on hips, and glares at me.

"Doesn't sound like you even tried. He might have wanted to know, Mum. He might have stuck around. I don't *believe* this. This changes everything."

She marches out of the room, slamming the door behind her.

I leave her to cool down, and knock on her door.

She's sat, eyes down, looking at her phone, frantically typing.

"Why are you asking all this now? I'd have told you if you asked before. You never wanted to know."

She looks up. Eyes dark and furious.

"Because, Mum, if you catch Coronavirus and die, I want

to have a cat in hell's chance of finding my only other blood relative."

Now doesn't seem the time to point out that she has cousins in Australia, and a wide extended family of second cousins and people twice removed all over the UK.

Chapter Sixty-Eight

C HARLOTTE AND I have made a pact. We are limiting our screentime and spending time together. I've stopped doom-scrolling pandemic news. I've turned off Facebook notifications and told my friends I'm taking a break from social media. "Message me if anything important happens," I say.

I'm cooking a proper meal each day which we sit down at the table to eat. And it's doing us both good. I feel lucky to spend lockdown with my daughter as so many people are separated. She opens up about the relationship with the boyfriend she lived with for three years. And I start to tell her snippets from my past.

"My first love was a girl," I tell her. And she doesn't judge, or comment, or express surprise. She actually listens. These are precious moments with my daughter. Made possible through lockdown.

In the mornings I walk Sasha. I find new routes in the neighbourhood. I've linked up with a local charity that provides food for families in need. I've started making meals for them in my kitchen, which they collect and distribute. It's a small thing but it makes me feel less helpless.

And I spend time each day sorting through my boxes.

I've kept journals, old photos – prints from a non-digital age – and letters going back years. Stevie says I should turn them into a memoir. So I scan in images, transcribe diary extracts, and summon Siri to play songs that bring it all back.

Sasha sits and watches as I go through things, look at the photos, immerse myself in diaries and letters from my past. If I cry, she looks at me with big, concerned doggy-eyes. If I call her, she joins me on the sofa. As the cost of lockdown puppies soars, I feel so lucky that we found her.

The only person I've kept in touch since college days is Jason. He messages from his home in France where they, too, are locked down. His ageing parents are still in Bath. They sometimes send him cuttings from the *Bath Chronicle*.

He sends me a photo of an article with the warning. "So sad. He was one of the good guys."

It's an obituary of my old muso mate Ben who we knew at Stoke College. He's someone I rarely think about these days. Like Jason, Ben went on to be semi-famous. He achieved his dream of writing for the NME and later set up his own indie record label. There's a quote in the article from the owner of Moles, the club where we used to go to see new bands. It doesn't say how he died, other than it was "a short illness".

I google Ben. There's stuff about him online. A photo of him and his wife. And the words "died with Covid".

I allow myself tears. Among all the narcissism, immaturity and petty squabbles of our crowd back then, Ben stood out. He transcended college politics and never fell out with anyone. Judging by the comments I read about him, he remained like that. As Jason says, one of the good guys.

A tribute site has been set up for him where bands he

produced in the nineties and noughties have shared their music. I play it now and think of Ben.

"You ok, Mum?"

"Someone I used to know has died of Covid."

She hugs me. She's used to her mum being flaky these days. It takes little to set me off. These are strange times. Introspective. Retrospective. And as I journey back into my past, I often wonder about life, and death.

This illness is picking people off, seemingly at random. Ben was my age. Did he have an underlying condition? There's no mention of it. Alex phoned me the other day to tell me someone we worked with back at Limitless Designs had died of the disease. This guy was younger than me, in his forties, and super fit. Used to run marathons and things. If even he can catch Covid and die, what hope is there for the rest of us?

I think of Ben. I knew him only briefly and I feel a twinge of regret that after college, we never kept in touch. But we moved in different circles. And I had Charlotte. So how can I be feeling anything like grief now? I haven't seen him for decades, so why does it matter if he's dead? But I like to think of people, good people anyway, living on in a parallel reality, even if I never see them.

When my Dad died, in my childlike imagination I had a theory that he didn't really die. I didn't see it happen. So he must be still alive.

I think of all the names I've recently rediscovered in my boxes from the past. Rob from the dusty bookshop where I did my Saturday job. Mum's friend, Mo. Andy's mate, Mike. Imogen, who taught us Psychology at college. Bit part players in my formative years. Are these people alive, or dead? My thoughts move onto the more major players. Claire, Andy

Collins, and of course, Tara. People very important to me then, but I don't see them now. What about them?

I think of my brother David and his Schrodinger's Cat obsession. Maybe now, in Covid times, we are all in a collective box. Alive? Dead? Or both?

When I went through the 2005 box, I found a cutting Jason sent me through the post, from the *Bath Chronicle*. It's an article about Karl Powell and Grace, getting married on her deathbed. There are photos of them both when they were younger, looking glamorous. One is the picture I remember from the cover of *Vogue*. And there's one from the wedding day. Someone had put a wedding dress on Grace – gaunt, and half dead, sitting up on the hospital bed in Karl's front room where I saw her on my visit, and a wig with flowers in on her hairless head. Karl's wearing a tux. There's a comment from Tara in the article, thanking the local hospice who arranged the ceremony.

"I couldn't get there, sadly, but I'm so glad Mum got her dying wish," said Grace's only daughter Tara Dean, 42, who lives in Canada.

I found Tara's letter again when I looked through the box. The one she sent me after all that business with the fake profiles. I never emailed her at the University of British Columbia, even though I'm pretty sure that final letter on the University letterhead was genuine. Back in 2005 I was too bruised. Everything too raw. I let the past stay where it belonged. Inside the box.

I spoke to the Police back then, about the online deception. They said no law had actually been broken, so there was nothing left to do. But I still hung onto all the evidence. There's a name now for what Tara's ex did. It's called Catfishing. There's even a film about it.

Recently, I looked Tara up on the University of British Columbia website, to see if she still works there. There's a note by her name which says: "Professor Dean is currently on Sabbatical in Bath, England." It's dated January 2020. Presumably she got locked down in Bath. Perhaps she went back there to reconnect with Karl.

Tara, the unfinished story. The one that perennially eludes me.

I'm woken from my reverie by the thumping beat of music and a woman's strident voice coming from the TV. Charlotte is doing her Zumba class on Zoom. My daughter, jumping around the living room, is very much alive. Maybe one of these days I'll join in.

Chapter Sixty-Nine

SOMETHING'S GOING WRONG with the weather. It's hot. Like step-off-a-plane-in-a-hot-country, hot, where a wall of heat greets you. I'm out on the patio, looking at the dandelions poking out through the cracks, waiting for Stevie.

Today is my birthday. Fifty-five today. How did I ever get this old? I think back to birthdays past and I don't remember it ever being this hot.

Hot air from Africa, say the weather men and women. We're not equipped for such heat.

I had a shower an hour ago. An almost cold shower. But in minutes I was once again hot. And it's not my age. Everyone is hot. Even the dog. She lies in the sun till she pants, then finds a shady spot and flops down.

There's a car in the neighbourhood – I'm told it's an old VW – that when driven sounds like a woman having a squealing orgasm. All through lockdown when the edict is "Stay home", whoever drives this car sees fit to drive around. All day. When I hear it, I'm irrationally wound up. Filled with petty outrage. Maybe jealousy too – of the non-existent woman having the non-existent orgasm. *Get a grip.*

I love my urban village, and my place within it. Before

lockdown I loved being able to walk to the pub on a Friday, sit in the garden with its terracotta walls and gorgeous planting, and catch up with people. I loved going to the little street market on a Saturday and buying samosas for lunch, and local honey to have with my porridge. Since lockdown we've all improvised. I walk by people's houses and leave cash outside for jars of honey or a box of home-laid eggs. We've taken to bartering goods for produce.

Stevie arrives, discreetly, through the back entrance, as we're still not allowed visitors. He's bearing a bottle of bubbly. 'Happy lockdown, birthday darling,' he says, less discreetly, blowing me a kiss.

He hovers by the gate. "Will you step outside a moment, Chris?"

I'm reluctant, but I follow, and as I walk out onto the street, I notice. People are outside their front doors. And it isn't even a Thursday, when we go outside to clap for the NHS.

Paul's here, somehow, illegally. He's placed the folding chairs from his van on our front drive. He's also brought bottles of bubbly which he's lined up on the wall.

Charlotte pulls up in her car. She's just come back from a particularly harrowing domestic abuse case and she needs gin.

Neighbours start to walk past, with glasses, and Paul fills them up. Some leave bottles of wine for me on the wall.

"Who organised all this?" I ask. "I didn't expect a party."

"It's not a party. That would be illegal. It's a walk past," says Charlotte. "Me, Paul and Stevie cooked it up together. Are you impressed?"

The students from the house opposite emerge, one of them carrying a guitar. He breaks into a chorus of "Happy birthday". The little girl from two doors down puts her hands over her ears.

"I hate this song," she says with passion. "We have to sing it at school every single time we wash our hands. Twice!"

"Let's have a different version then."

We run through as many different versions of Happy Birthday as we know, the guitarist doing his best to accompany. We do Stevie Wonder then the Chipmunks.

"Can you play the Altered Images one?" I shout across the street.

"The what?"

He looks up the chords. And it takes me back to a sweaty Bath nightclub and a boxed-up memory recently released. Leaving the club early and Tara telling me her secret. A moment immortalised in memory.

It's warm till late, and we sit out front, chatting, long into the evening.

"Are you enjoying your birthday, Mum?"

"I can honestly say, I think it's the best birthday ever."

In these Covid times, I'm starting to realise, everything I need is close to home.

Paul's had too much alcohol to drive home. He offers to sleep in the van. "Don't be silly." I invite him inside.

I stopped doing all the Zoom stuff that was happening early in lockdown. All the video socials with people I don't even see much in real life. It all got too much. Tonight, I'm buzzing from actual face-to-face human contact. And when I get to bed it's good to feel Paul's warm body next to mine.

"I've missed this," he says.

Chapter Seventy

I'M WATCHING SOMETHING on BBC4 in which Professor Brian Cox is walking through an Oxfordshire wood talking about space and time.

While Paul snores.

Professor Brian Cox says that if you move on from a place, that place doesn't cease to exist. In the same way, as you move on from an event in time, that event doesn't cease to exist.

Yesterday, I had a flashback. A fleeting memory of standing on the river path in Bath at midnight, watching the moon glinting off the water, as Tara told me her secret. According to Brian Cox, that moment still exists. All my unboxed memories are still there. Preserved somewhere in the universe of space and time.

I wonder how long it will be before the clever Brian Coxs' of the world devise a way to get back there.

I always thought when I got to the gates to Heaven or Purgatory or Hell or wherever I'm going that God or Saint Peter or Buddha or whoever would sit me down and show me a video of my life—or selected highlights—and say, "You did good here," or "You messed up there," or even, "What was going on here? Explain your thinking." Then it would be like a trial or a select committee and I'd have a chance to reflect on my actions and defend myself. And I'd watch myself in the video from a detached viewpoint. Well maybe this is a little bit like that.

I've been going through the boxes from my past. Immersing myself in the moments. Emerging dazed, like you do when you've watched a great film or had your head stuck in a book.

According to Professor Brian Cox, it's all still there. Somewhere in the great mystery of the universe.

"That's amazing!" I say, and Paul twitches in sleep then jolts wide awake. "What is?"

"What Brian Cox just said. You missed it."

I don't think Paul will understand the nuances of what I've just learnt about time and space. I'll save it for Stevie or for my brother next time I Facetime them. It's the sort of thing David loves.

Paul is a semi-permanent resident at my house again. After my birthday he just kind of stayed. It's against the rules, probably. But we flex them to fit our circumstances. Plus, his place is still a building site. And he's taken a shine to Sasha.

Chapter Seventy-One

I FIND A random box, undated. A shoe box with an elastic band round it. I open it. It contains a few prints in a Kodak folder. The sort you used to get back from the developers in the good old days of film. A few photos from my university days, taken mostly in the Girly Gaff. I flick through them. Then I see it.

There's five of us in the shot. We're in some bar or club, crammed into a semi-circular seat with assorted pint glasses on the table in front of us and a sign on the wall that says "Cocktail of the day – Frozen Cactus." There's Rachel and her boyfriend, Gemma and me. Sat behind me on the arm of the chair is Kai. He's wearing a fluorescent green t-shirt and a brown suede jacket and a woolly hat with a slight peak. He has both arms around me. It's one of just five prints in the folder, and the only one of him, but there are a bunch of negatives too. I have no recollection of this being taken or of where we were.

I am transported back to another moment preserved in space and time. A voice to go with the face. A mood. A feeling.

"Never change." He was looking into my eyes when he

said it. My crystal blue meeting his darkness. We were playful. Floaty and high on that intangible connection they call love, and all the weed we smoked back then.

"Promise me you'll never change."

In that moment, I wanted that meeting of hearts, minds, bodies to last forever. I had only ever felt this way once before. But life and time marches on, and Monday morning with it, and the looming of lectures and umbrellas and autumn. Clouds obscured that little taste of paradise.

"I love you, Chrissie, never change."

I knew love was an illusion, but I'd settle for that.

Life came in the shape of Charlotte, and looking at the photo of her father, I see her in his eyes. Can it be coincidence that now, in lockdown, she actually wants to know about him?

I take the photo downstairs to where she's working on her laptop at the dining room table. I place it in front of her.

"Charlotte, I have this."

She takes a moment to register.

"That's him behind me," I say. "Your father." Although it's obvious.

"How long have you had this?" she screams. "I can't *believe* you kept it from me."

"I genuinely didn't know I had it until today."

She holds the photo. Transfixed by Kai's face.

"Was he a student?"

"No."

"What did he do then?"

"I don't know."

She puts her head in her hands and leans over the computer keyboard. I wonder for a moment if she's crying. She looks up. She's just exasperated.

"You must remember something. What did you *talk* about?"

We didn't. We mostly danced. And made love. And smoked. He carried with him at all times a high-grade cannabis resin. I'd watch him unfurl the lump from its tin foil wrap, heat it with a lighter and crumble it in a metal spoon before mixing it with leaf tobacco. Then we'd smoke. First thing we'd do in the morning was smoke a spliff. Gemma said she got high on the fumes emerging from my room when he was over. Rachel said the smell made her retch.

We must have talked, too, in the language of love. But I can hardly remember a single thing we said.

"He told me loved me and he told me not to change. Ever. And then he left me. That's all I remember."

Charlotte pouts and rolls her eyes. "Mother!"

Have I changed? I take the photo, to scrutinise my own image. She grabs it back.

"I'm keeping this."

"Why?"

"It's all I have of my dad. Is it the only one?"

"Yep. There might have been more, but they're negatives."

I give her the envelope containing the strips of transparent plastic film. She holds them one by one up to the light.

"This is him again! Mum, look at this."

I squint at the reversed image, his hair, eyes and eyebrows glowing white. It's taken in the same venue from a different angle. There are guys either side of him. Kai's leaning in on one of them, making a peace sign at the camera.

"Who are the people with him?"

"They could have been his housemates."

She puts the images back in their envelope and takes them up to her room.

I don't like to bring the subject up again. It only serves to confirm my woeful inadequacy as a mother.

At least I kept you. Brought you into the world. Nurtured you and brought you up, I think but do not say.

I had the photos all too briefly. Now they're in her custody.

Chapter Seventy-Two

I'M FEELING PECULIAR today. Slightly sick and my brain's fogged up. But it's not Covid, I don't have the symptoms. I don't have a persistent dry cough. I can still smell the coffee and my temperature's normal. Phew, that means I don't have to get myself to a test place. How anyone manages it when they're ill is beyond me.

Paul's gone back to his place, and Charlotte's working, as the visits that stopped at the beginning of lockdown are all now happening with a vengeance. She says there's been a pandemic of domestic abuse during lockdown and this is just the tip of the iceberg. She has a huge backlog of cases.

I lie down on the bed and drift off, but my phone pings as a WhatsApp comes in from one of my friends. I told them to contact me if anything important happened.

"Look what your daughter's been up to," it reads. And there's screenshots from a post on the Sherwood in Nottingham Facebook Page created by Charlotte Claire Carlisle.

There's a photo of Kai, the one from the pub with his flatmates. Where he's making a peace sign at the camera and there's the 'cocktail of the day' notice behind him. She's obviously found some way of turning the negative into a digital image. The post reads.

> *Long shot, but does anyone who was around Nottm in the late 80s recognise anyone on this photo? I'm trying to trace the guy with the orange t-shirt. He was a friend of my Mum's. All I know is his name's Kai, he lived in Basford and he went back to Hawaii where he came from. The other people could have been his housemates.*
>
> *10 Shares*
> *25 Comments:*

I try to go on Facebook to find the post, but I've taken the app off my phone and I can't remember any of my passwords. I message my friend back. Get her to send me screenshots of the comments. Helpful comments from the good burghers of Sherwood.

> ➢ *Hope you find him hun. Shared Basford*
> ➢ *The one on the left looks like Ned. Is this Ned from when you was living in Forest Road? tagged* **Mark Walker**
> ➢ *Shared Mansfield*
> ➢ *Where's this pub? Looks like the old Angel?*
> ➢ *Never the Angel mate. They didn't know wot a cocktail was!*
> ➢ *Shared to Mapperley People.*

There are several screenshots containing more of the same, then in the last one, a comment from somebody called Angus White which reads: *'I've sent you a DM.'*

I resolve to get back on my social media to keep a track on this, when I'm feeling better. In the meantime I sink into slumber.

Chapter Seventy-Three

T HE PAST COMES, not as a blast, but as a whimper. A flicker on a screen, vanished in seconds. A name. A hint of a message. A ghost on a device. A flash of memory. An apparition.

And in my fevered head, I wonder if it's real. Or another attempt to deceive me.

My hands are clammy. My thumb-print unreadable. This piece of the past lies locked.

IT'S HOT. EVEN hotter than before.

Standing two metres apart in the queue outside the pharmacy, I see the colours come. Like when I was a child, in church with Nan. And when I was in France, sunburnt, on my French exchange. "Elle tombe," I heard the words before I blacked out.

This time, the heat exacerbated by the cloth mask, I pre-empt the faint and slump to the pavement, head between my knees.

"Are you okay?"

"Feel dizzy," I mumble through the fabric.

"It's the heat, duck."

Someone brings me water. They help me to the front of the queue where I collect my meds. Then a woman from our street, one of the flower ladies who tends the community garden, accompanies me home.

I sit, sipping water, then go to lie down. I'm out for the count when Charlotte gets back.

"You ok, Mum?"

"Just had a funny turn in the pharmacy. It's the heat."

Now it's dark, and I have my windows wide open. The sound of dance music emanates from somewhere. A party in a garden, contravening Coronavirus rules, or an illicit rave up on the park.

I get up, woozy on my legs, steady myself on the window ledge, and try to locate the source of the sound. The music ebbs and flows. It sounds more like an outdoor gig with a proper sound system than a party in somebody's back garden.

I fall back into bed as the beat invades my head.

I'm back in the nineties, dancing. The time when the rave scene first hit. When the new designer drugs swept the nation. Drugs that made you dance all night. I didn't do it often. I had Charlotte to think about by then.

I shut my eyes and I'm in a field in an unknown location, dancing. And Charlotte's father is there, moving with his whole body, his eyes dancing with mine.

"Kai!" I say.

"It's me, Mum, Charlotte."

"You have your father's eyes."

"Mum, are you okay?" She touches my brow with a purple-nailed finger. "You're boiling." She puts the fan on.

"Turn it off!" I say. "I want to hear the music."

Charlotte turns the fan off, shrugging.

"Mum, you're weird. Call me if you need me. And I think in the morning we should get you to a test centre." She leaves the door ajar.

The thump of the sound system and the voices of the revellers draw me. Wherever this party is, I want to be there. I stand, and fumble around for my clothes, pulling on my jeans and my rainbow top. I may be fifty-five, but I still know how to party.

My head spins and I collapse with a thump on the floor next to the bed. Charlotte appears. "What are you doing? Why are you dressed?"

"There's a party going on and I'm going to find it."

"It's not even eleven o clock,' she says. "But if it's bothering you, I'll ring one-oh-one."

I laugh. "I'm not going to call the police on them. I'm going to join them. I wanna dance! You can come too!"

She stands, hands on hips, that look of defiance on her face I know so well.

"Absolutely not, Mum. Get back in bed. You're not going out. You're in no fit state. You been smoking something?"

I do as I'm told and I giggle.

"It's not funny, Mum."

But it is. It's role reversal.

Now I'm in the club in Ljubljana and Tara draws me near. We kiss, right there on the dance floor.

Then all the lights go on.

"Mum!" It's Charlotte again. She's switched the big light on. "You were shouting."

"I was dreaming," I say.

"Who's Tara?"

I CAN'T SLEEP. And I reach for my mobile, trying to find the message I saw earlier. That name. Surfacing again. That little piece of unresolved history.

Did I see it? Or did I dream it? I scroll through my phone. There's a video doing the rounds. A man in America with a policeman kneeling on his neck. He's saying, "I can't breathe."

I can't breathe. But there's nobody kneeling on my neck.

Now I'm looking up at the ceiling and someone's asking Charlotte if I have an underlying condition.

"She's asthmatic."

At the hospital, they give me a machine to help me breathe.

Chapter Seventy-Four

THEY SAY WE'RE brave, but all we are doing is continuing to breathe. A basic human response. Without this oxygen they're channelling into me, my organs would fail, my body would shut down.

The brave ones are those who come in day and night, risking their own health, putting their own lives and wellbeing on hold for ours. I can't see their faces, but they tell me their names. This one's Verity. It means truth. I can tell she's pretty, under the mask.

Today, I feel lucid. I can string a sentence together.

I ask her how she is.

"I got married on Saturday," she says.

"Congratulations! But shouldn't you be on your honeymoon?"

"We've postponed it. Too much to do here. Nowhere to go at the minute, anyway."

"How does your husband feel about it?"

"Wife," she says quickly. I can't see her expression under the mask, only her eyes. I detect a hint of anxiety, mixed with defiance and resolve, like this is a test of my reaction.

"What's her name?" I ask.

"Jane," she says. "Plain Jane."

"I bet she isn't plain."

"No, she's beautiful."

I smile. "Well Verity, I hope you and Jane are very happy together. You deserve to be."

I'd hug her if I could.

Chapter Seventy-Five

"**B**E CAREFUL WITH this one. She's like my second mum." I recognise her voice. I feel her hand as she holds mine.

I open my eyes. She's head to toe in plastic, but it's most definitely Hannah.

The light hurts my eyes, so I close them again, but she leaves her hand in mine. I can feel her warmth, even through the latex. This human contact, craved for I don't know how long, is a moment that stands out in a day of despair.

"I've gone back to my normal ward, but they let me in to see you," she says. "Charlotte sends her love. She wishes she could be here. Everyone sends their love. We're all rooting for you. My church are all praying for you. You're in the best place. And these nurses are the absolute best. You're going to be okay. And I'll come back and see you soon."

Hannah's voice, comforting and reminding me of home, is the last thing I hear before a male voice tells me they are "taking over my breathing".

I'm in a hinterland. A twilight world. I come and go. I hear voices, some sharp, some anxious, some kind and soothing. I hear angels singing on the wind, and the sound of a dog barking.

I float above the bed, like I used to, and I see myself, immobile, as white-clad figures flit about.

Am I dead, or alive?

Now I'm in a tunnel. Faces loom out of the walls. Are these people dead or alive? Nan. Nessa. Both dead. Tara. Who knows? What about Stevie? Paul? Alive? Or did they all die? Did the plague kill us all off? Dead or alive. Maybe both. I see my brother. He's in a box. Or is it me in the box? Charlotte. Very much alive. I hear her voice. But it can't be her. They won't allow her in. It must be an illusion. A hand holds mine. "It's me, Mum. Charlotte. I don't know if you can hear me."

It sounds like her. But I can't be sure. Who knows what's real in here?

"They said I can play you a song. But I knew one song would never be enough, not for you, so I've done you a mix." I feel the soft pads of the headphones as she places them on my ears. Then the music plays. She is clever, my daughter. She's put snatches of the songs I've got Siri to play all through lockdown. The soundtrack to my past. Martha and the Muffins, Human League, Grace Jones. And finally, Siouxie and the Banshees and the song that bears my name.

She holds my hand as I listen, then removes the headphones, gently. Now it's her voice I hear again, soft and a little shaky. "Mum, they said this could be goodbye. But we're all praying for a miracle. Hannah's praying at her happy clappy Vineyard place and they're bloody loud so someone's got to listen. Stevie's put you on some prayer list at the Catholic Cathedral. Even I'm praying and I'm an atheist. So you can't go, Mum. You've got too much to live for. Too many people love you. And I've got a surprise for you when you come out. Someone who wants to see you. Someone you've not seen for a very, very long time."

She's found her father then.

She loosens her grip on my hand, but I don't want her to go. I will my fingers to move. I reach round the latex glove and feel for her ring. I feel the chunky, smooth band, central stone surrounded by delicate little jewels. I remember them, tiny, glinting diamonds twelve of them – around the deep red ruby.

The ring that passed from Nan to mum to me and now to Charlotte.

"Nurse! Nurse!" she calls out. "Can someone come please? She just gripped my hand."

Chapter Seventy-Six

I HAVE WALKED through fog, but it is lifting. My horizontal world now shifts. My view of the ceiling tiles exchanged for a different landscape.

Each day, they tell me, is a triumph. They congratulate me for continuing to breathe.

The day they give me back my phone is another milestone. I can't look for long, But when I do look there are myriad messages of love and hope. My daughter has been busy going through my contacts, updating everyone on my progress.

The day I Facetime Charlotte, I cry. She's there, alive and well. She brings Sasha up to the screen to greet me.

"You're coming home, Mum. Soon. Just keep on getting better." I praise whoever invented modern means of keeping in touch. My phone is now my lifeline. Peppered with daily messages of support. Each one a reason to get stronger.

BEFORE, I SAW a tunnel. But this is a corridor. And faces line the walls. All masked, but not grotesque, like those of the dead which loomed out of the shadows in the dark days.

These are faces of the living from the very real present. The nurses, the doctors, the consultants who've worked together to give me back my life. And they're all clapping. Like *I'm* the hero here.

Hannah is behind me, steering me down the line. She wheels me past the entrance, and as we move towards the daylight, I see her. My Charlotte, my life blood. My radiant, resilient daughter.

"Mum!" she cries in disbelief and runs towards me.

She's masked too, and not allowed to hug me.

The outside air is cool, and feels fresh on my face. I've no idea what day it is, or even what month. It was hot when I entered this place, but now, beneath the blanket they've wrapped round me, I shiver.

A masked man with a large camera approaches. "Are you up to doing a quick interview, Christine?"

Hannah tries to send them away, but I say. "I've come back from the dead, I'm up for anything." I like that line.

The man extends his super long microphone, stands some distance away and asks.

"How does it feel coming out of hospital after ninety-eight days?"

No way can it have been that long? Apparently, I spent a fair amount of it out for the count in an induced coma.

Although it's still an effort to talk, I gush about the NHS and how absolutely amazing they've been. I thank Hannah, and Verity, and all the others whose names I can't remember. He even gets me to repeat my "I'm back from the dead" line. I've given him what he wanted. His miracle story. He interviews Charlotte too, and Hannah. Hannah's a pro at this media stuff now.

They bundle me into the car, and we head off.

I guess it must be evening time as it's getting dark, and the street lights are coming on.

"Now, Mum," says Charlotte. "Are you up to seeing people? They won't come in the house. It's just, I think a few people might quite like to see you?"

"Told you, Charlie, I'm up for anything."

"Even someone who you've not seen for ages, the person from your past I told you about? They might be there."

"Of course! I'm excited to find out who it is."

I don't tell her I already know. I won't spoil the surprise.

My eyes are dazzled by the car lights, so I shut them as we travel.

"We're here, Mum." Charlotte says as we round the last corner. The car stops, I open my eyes, and Charlotte helps me out. I lean on her for support.

As we walk towards the house, a roar goes out. A roar of recognition.

People line the street. Distanced at intervals. This is like the hospital corridor, only better. These are faces from my life, my neighbourhood. I see Stevie, and Paul, Alex and his girlfriend Cori, my neighbours up and down the street. Everyone, it seems, is outside their houses.

It's like what happened on my birthday.

There's a giant banner strung across the house which says, "Welcome home!"

I lean on the wall, and survey the gathering.

The student from the house opposite, the one with the guitar, strikes up with "Homeward Bound".

I turn to the people.

"I didn't expect a party."

My voice is weak, and hoarse, but they hear me. And they cheer.

"It's not a party, Mum, it's a welcoming committee. And anyway, we're allowed gatherings of up to thirty people now."

"Since when?"

"Where've you *been*, Mum?"

Laughter.

I nudge Charlotte. "Where's this person you want me to meet? Are they here?"

I scour the line of people for the face I'm looking for. He'll be older, but I'm sure I'll recognise him. Those dancing eyes I've not seen for so long.

She nods at someone further down the line, and beckons. I prepare to act surprised. Like I didn't know all along she'd traced him.

I'm searching so hard I barely notice the woman striding towards us, even though she's head and shoulders above the rest, a halo of blonde hair crowning her stylish mask.

I don't look at her until she stops in front of us. And even then, it doesn't register. Until she speaks. And I hear that soft Canadian accent.

"Chrissie, it's been a long time. And yes. This time, it really is me."

The past no longer shrouded.

I am home.

Dear Reader

Thank you for reading *Heartsound*. If you enjoyed this book (or even if you didn't) please consider leaving a star rating or review online.

Your feedback is important, and will help other readers to find the book and decide whether to read it, too.

Acknowledgements

An extensive cast of characters have contributed to this novel. This is a long list.

Thank you to Sara-Jayne Slack at Inspired Quill, for once again believing in my writing enough to bring this novel to fruition.

To Rebekah Parrott for the excellent cover design.

To Kate Fletcher, Anne Goodwin, John Perkins, Scotty Clark, Marie Peach, Rob Edwards and Judy Malek who read drafts at various stages as the novel evolved.

To Dave Smith and Peter Smith for your proofreading prowess.

To members of the SherWords writing group for offering encouragement and a sounding board to bounce ideas around.

To members of the Bath Born & Bred or Live in the City of Facebook page who responded so enthusiastically to requests for information about the city I grew up in, helping to fill in the blanks in my sometimes hazy memory. Special thanks to Phil Andrews, Martyn Stevens, Tim Carter, Diane Starling, Jill Kelly and William Lidstone.

To Damjan Zorc from Ljubljana City of Literature, plus Brane Mozetic, Esad Babacic, Monika Skaberne, and Tone, who helped shape the Ljubljana scenes.

To Maggie Lucas, for insights into the world of a graphic designer.

And countless others who've helped with random pieces of research – including Maura Launchbury, Debbie Parish, Jo Weston, Monica and Rebecca.

About the Author

Clare Stevens grew up in the wilds of Somerset where she was fed a daily diet of ghost stories cooked up in her older sister's imagination. This fostered an early love of storytelling long before she could read or write.

Her favourite writing time is first thing in the morning when she's still half in dreamland. She also writes in cafes and other public spaces, drawing inspiration from the unlimited supply of human interest.

When not writing or working, Clare can be found walking Max, her inexhaustible springer/pointer cross, heading off for weekends in Whitby (her spiritual home), or trying to learn ukelele. She runs a half-marathon once a decade.

Find the author via her website: clarestevens.com

Or follow her: @ClareWynStevens

More From This Author

Blue Tide Rising

"Somewhere in me a scream is rising, but I contain it. Just."

Diazepam-fogged Amy isn't the best person to investigate an unexplained death, but she's the only one Jay can get through to.

On the run from her troubled past and controlling older (ex) lover, she winds up on a Welsh eco farm where she starts to rebuild her life, grounded by the earth and healed by the salt air.

But it isn't just her inner self that she manages to uncover. There are living ghosts at Môr Tawel, and they're as loud as the waters crashing over the shingle on the beach.

Amy's new life has just started, and she's already running out of time.

Get It Here (Multiple Options!)

books2read.com/u/mZpvWp

Also available from all major online and offline outlets.